*"No one's going to believe you're human
if you let your eyes go red
and hellish like that."*

Becca recovered in less than a second, blinking twice to clear her eyes. Without the red glow, they were green and lovely. Far more feminine than he would have expected from a woman who tortured innocents for pleasure and emasculated grown men just to hear them scream. Her light green eyes made a striking contrast to her short dark hair, tousled on top of her head as if she'd just rolled out of bed after a night a lovemaking.

"Stop looking at me like that," she ordered.

Nick dragged his gaze off her hair and back down to her face. *Get it together, Nick. You're here to work.* "How am I looking at you?"

"Like you want to eat me."

*Please turn this page for raves
for the books of Stephanie Rowe...*

Also by Stephanie Rowe

Must Love Dragons
Date Me, Baby, One More Time

HE
LOVES ME,
HE LOVES
ME HOT

STEPHANIE ROWE

WARNER
FOREVER

NEW YORK   BOSTON

Copyright © 2007 by Stephanie Rowe
Excerpt from *Sex & The Immortal Bad Boy*
copyright © 2007 by Stephanie Rowe

Warner Forever is an imprint of Warner Books, Inc.

Warner Forever is a trademark of Time Warner Inc. or an affiliated company. Used under license by Hachette Book Group USA, which is not affiliated with Time Warner Inc.

Cover art and design by Michael Storrings

Warner Forever
Hachette Book Group USA
237 Park Avenue
New York, NY 10169
Visit our Web site at www.HachetteBookGroupUSA.com.

Printed in the United States of America

First Printing: May 2007

10 9 8 7 6 5 4 3 2 1

For Kara Goucher,
a brilliant runner and dear friend,
whose determination to follow her dreams
is a constant inspiration to me.
You are a goddess, Kara!

Acknowledgments

I would never be where I am today without the support of my family, who doesn't question my burning need to be at a keyboard in order to stay sane. And to my great friend, Guinevere Jones, for coming up with the title to the book. And, as always, to my fantastic agent, Michelle Grajkowski, for her guidance, enthusiasm, and overall support. And to Melanie Murray, an amazing editor, who continues to bring my writing to new levels with her brilliant insight, editing, and wonderful sense of humor. And to Beth deGuzman, Marcy Haggag, Tanisha Christie, Laura Adams, the art department, and everyone else at Warner who does so much for my books. To J&A, you are my world.

One

Nick Rawlings hoped he got attacked today. He was bored, itchy for action, and fast coming to the conclusion that even the undying gratitude of his best pal, Jerome Doumani (and the large stack of gold bullion that Jerome was forking over), wasn't worth three weeks of sitting in a small room with nothing but a frozen sociopath to keep him company.

Nick peered hopefully at the platinum deadbolt on the inside of the steel door to see if someone was trying to jimmy it off from the other side. No luck.

He sighed and wandered across the polished oak floor, his heavy steel-toed boots thudding on the perfect varnish. He glanced back over his shoulder, taking mild satisfaction in the fact that the floors were getting scuffed from his pacing. The Council (the morally questionable, self-appointed governing body of all beings nonhuman) would have to pry open their wallets to ante up for refinishing by the time Nick was sprung from guard duty. Not exactly a fair trade for the Council getting Nick's pa and grandpa offed and for wiping out Nick's race, but hey, a guy who'd promised his dying pa that he wouldn't take revenge had to accept the small paybacks life offered him.

Nick's friend Jerome was one-third of the Council triad, an ex-pirate who still lived by the code of the high seas, and Nick's best friend since they were kids. Nothing bonds a couple of boys like practicing swordplay with real blades and no safety masks. Jerome had been recruited to join the Council because of his moral flexibility and consequent willingness to do the tough-guy enforcing that the Council pretended not to support. In reality, the Council was way more bloodthirsty than any pirate, and they were a little too hung up on their power for the good of those they ruled. Their punishments were so brutal that some beings didn't survive them, especially the Chamber of Unspeakable Horrors.

Nick surveyed the stacks of food and beverages in the corner, which were supposed to sustain him for the next few weeks while he was on guard duty. No beer. No pizza. He was a man's man, and he liked beer and pizza.

He pulled a plate of crudités out of the fridge and started munching on a carrot. Or not.

He sauntered over to the white horizontal SubZero freezer (nothing but the best for the Council), stuck the carrot between his teeth, then grabbed the industrial-size padlock with both hands. Two tugs, and it broke off with a loud crack. He leveraged the heavy lid up, letting it slam against the wall with a crash that left a nice dent.

More maintenance costs for the Council.

Such a pity.

He peered into the cooler, and a three-by-five-foot block of ice stared back up at him. The ice chunk was swirled with a mixture of blurred colors—pink, blue, and a large amount of gold—as if someone had tie-dyed it. He took a bite of carrot while he surveyed his charge.

"So, you're the oh-so-evil disinherited son of the leader of hell, huh?"

The ice cube trembled, and Nick smiled. "Jerome tells me you were stupid enough to get yourself melted and then frozen before you could re-form. Bested by an ex-pirate, a no-carb–eating dragon, and a mathematician. True?"

The frozen block vibrated even more fiercely, and Nick heard the faint whisper of a particularly creative epithet he hadn't heard since he'd lived in hell. "Yeah, I hear you. Life can be a bitch sometimes."

The cube had no response, and Nick let the lid drop shut. So much for entertainment.

Jerome was sure the other members of the Council were corrupt, and he didn't enjoy being set up as a scape-goat for all the Council's crimes against the Otherworld, a classification which included all beings nonhuman. Mor-tal world was the physical place where humans hung out on earth, totally clueless that beings from the Otherworld rode the trains with them, babysat their kids, and laughed at their ignorance.

So, when Jerome heard rumors in the Council men's room that someone was going to try to spring Satan Jr., he did what any smart guy would do: hired the baddest badass in the Otherworld to keep Satan Jr. safe, which was Nick, of course.

Helping out his best friend had seemed like a good plan at the time, but now that Nick had been there for a week and no one had come through the ceiling with laser guns or Uzis, he was beginning to think his buddy needed counseling for paranoia.

Then Nick heard the key turn in the deadbolt, and his

adrenaline spiked. He spun around to face the door, knowing Jerome wasn't due for poker for another two hours. *Playtime.*

He leaned against the freezer and rested his palms on the lid, on either side of his hips. He drummed his fingers on the metal, waiting.

The deadbolt turned and the steel door flew open like it was made of paper.

Ah, a challenge. Nice.

A man stepped inside, and Nick immediately rose to his feet as an intense sensation of belonging swept over him. There was no mistaking the wavering air around the man's body, like the heat rising off a sidewalk on a hot summer day. Was he Markku? Impossible. Markku were extinct.

Well, except Nick, but he was only half Markku, so he didn't count.

The man stopped suddenly and stared at the air above Nick's head, his eyes widening in surprise, which made Nick frown even deeper, since his mixed blood had pretty much spared him from the hot-air blur that was typical of the Markku. But this dude was inspecting Nick as if he could see it. And if he were Markku, he probably could. Damn. Was Nick really not one of a kind, after all?

The man was just over six feet and solid, but not nearly as big as Nick. His black pants, black turtleneck sweater, and black boots were overkill and made him look like he was trying too hard, as did the military buzz cut. The man's gaze flicked down to Nick's face. "Who are you?"

"Nick Rawlings. You?"

The man cocked his head. "You're not with us."

"Us being...?" Were there *more* Markku?

But instead of answering, the man dropped his shoulder and charged.

Nick barely jumped out of the way in time, nearly paying for his failure to expect another being to be almost as fast as he was. The man slammed into the side of the cooler, his head smashing all the way through the metal. He roared and reared back, dragging the cooler as he tried to get his head free. The freezer screeched across the floor, and Nick grabbed his gun, leveling it at the base of the man's skull, where it was protruding from the freezer.

No. You must protect your men.

Nick hesitated at the command in his head. His men? He had no men.

This is your man. All the men are your men to protect.

He shook his head to clear it. His damned healer gene was always interfering with his ability to kick some ass. Trying to make him soft and mushy when he was all about violence and enjoying a good fight.

The visiting Markku bellowed and tried to yank himself free.

"Yeah, not so fast." Nick ground his boot into the back of the man's neck, pinning him to the side of the cooler. "So, let's chat. I've got loads of questions for you. Are you after Satan Jr.? Who sent you? Who's 'us?' Are you really Markku, or do you just do the hot-air thing to attract women?"

"I'm better than Markku," the man announced, his voice echoing inside the SubZero.

"Better? Given that the Markku are descended from Satan and are pretty much indestructible except for gold, that's some kind of claim. So, better in what way, exactly?" Nick dug the heel of his boot in as the man started to struggle more fiercely. "Better fashion sense? Maybe don't have to shave as often? Do tell."

"No battle weakness."

Nick's foot nearly slipped off the man's skull. Post-battle weakness was a terrible nuisance that required him to conk out for a day or so after every decent fight, not that he had gotten in many lately. But seeing as how that weakness had been the key to Satan's Rivka army wiping out the Markku race, it was something to note. "You're kidding."

"Nope." The man paused in his struggling. "Want in? I could hook you up. It's a sweet deal."

"Tempting." Nick cocked his head. "But no thanks. Sounds like one of those 'deals' where I end up chained to a wall, being tortured."

"You're sure?" the Markku asked.

"Yeah."

"Then I'll have to kill you and steal the kid."

Nick grinned. "Be my guest."

He felt the Markku gathering strength, so he put his gun to the back of the man's head.

Don't shoot your man.

Great. His alter ego again. *I'll shoot whoever I want.* He gritted his teeth against the almost overwhelming urge not to fire, covered his right eye with his left hand to protect against ricochets, and forced himself to pull the trigger.

The bullets bounced off the man's skull, ricocheting all over the room, embedding themselves in the wall, the ceiling, shattering the water cooler that was supposed to keep Nick hydrated for the next three weeks, whizzing through the weapons closet in the corner, and setting off a cascade of fireworks. One bullet even bounced off Nick's shin. The man shouted in protest and twisted so his feet and palms were flat against the cooler. He shoved hard, trying to yank his head free as his body shuddered with the impact of so much repeated force.

"You sure you don't want to chat instead?" Nick yelled over the gunfire. "Just tell me who wants Satan Jr., admit you can't beat me, and then we can kick back and play some poker when Jerome gets here. It'll be fun. What do you say?"

The Markku used the same epithet that Satan Jr. had used. An old-school swear descended straight from hell's origins. Coincidence? Probably not so much. The rescuer likely had late-night sleepovers with Junior when the kid wasn't frozen. Apparently, Satan Jr. was hooking up with his dad's former servants. Interesting.

"Okay, then. Don't say I didn't offer." Nick emptied his clip, grabbed his second gun, and kept firing, slamming bullet after bullet against the Markku's skull as the Poland Spring water sloshed around his feet, ruining the floor.

The Markku yanked his head free and pieces of the steel cooler went flying. Nick ducked as one piece whizzed past his shoulder and sliced through the wall, disappearing from sight with the power of the Markku's thrust.

The Markku whirled around and slammed his foot into the side of Nick's knee with enough force to split a redwood in half.

"Son of a *bitch*." Nick's knee gave out and he fell to the floor, gritting his teeth against the pain. He rolled to his left, dodging the Markku as he tried to jump on Nick. "You say you're *better* than a Markku, huh? Slower, maybe."

"Better." The Markku pulled out a knife with a golden blade, and Nick swore under his breath. What the hell was he doing with *that* kind of weapon?

The Markku drove the blade down toward Nick's right eye, and Nick jerked his head hard to the side. The blade scraped Nick's cheek and slammed into the wooden floor, barely missing its target.

Hot pain flashed through Nick at the touch of gold. *Holy mother of pearl.* He'd felt pain before, but this was something *else*.

The Markku yanked the blade out of the floor as Nick grabbed him and flung him into the wall, denting the plaster with a satisfying thud.

Nick was on his feet before the man had stopped sliding down the wall.

The man hurled the knife, and the blade plunged into the front of Nick's right shoulder. Nick cursed as the poisonous fire raked through his body, and he dropped to his knees, clutching his shoulder.

Then he heard his pa's voice, whispering the instructions he'd repeated to Nick so many times when training him as a kid. *Use the heat, Nick. Channel it.*

Nick gritted his teeth, then pulled the golden fire into his body, recharging himself with the flames, using the pain to fuel his body even as that same heat drained him, sucked away his life force.

The Markku jumped to his feet and lunged for the knife, but Nick grabbed it first. He whipped it out of his shoulder with a roar of anguish, then slammed it in the Markku's right eye. The man exploded in a cascade of gold dust, his death scream his only legacy as it bounced off the steel door and echoed in Nick's ears.

Nick clutched the blade and shook the gold dust off his eyelashes, watching it float down, mixing with the Poland Spring water to create a river of sparkling mud. "Better, my ass."

The door flew open, and Nick reared back to throw the knife, diverting his aim at the last second when he realized who it was.

Jerome yelped and ducked as the blade sung past his ear and embedded itself in the wall behind him. "It's me!"

"No kidding." Nick pressed his left hand to his stab wound, trying to stem the flow of blood. The more he could mitigate the damage now, the less trouble he'd be in later.

"Right. Because you'd have killed me if I'd been anyone else." Jerome straightened up, his scabbard swinging by his side. In honor of his mortal life pillaging on the high seas, he was sporting full pirate regalia today, including an eye patch, even though both his eyes were fine.

Nick kicked a piece of the water cooler out of his way, then stumbled with sudden weakness. *Shit.* He had to get out of there. He had less than a half hour before he was dead to the world for at least a couple of days. Jerome was the only one besides Nick's ma who knew Nick was half Markku, so they'd have a hell of a time explaining it away if Nick went unconscious in the middle of Council headquarters.

"You look like hell," Jerome said. "What happened?"

"Markku."

Jerome paled, and he tugged the eye patch up so he could look at Nick with both light blue eyes. "No kidding?"

Nick waved at the gold dust, and Jerome scanned the room, his gaze coming to a stop on the ice chest. A big hole gaped in the side, and the sound of dripping water was coming from the inside of the SubZero. "You couldn't keep him from breaking the freezer while you killed him? Getting soft in your old age, are you?"

"Shut up." Nick turned his back on Jerome to hide a shudder of fatigue. Then he grabbed his stash of weapons and turned to head out, only to find Jerome blocking his exit. "What now?"

"You can't leave. What if they send another Markku?"

Nick shrugged his injured shoulder. "Gold blade. Gotta run."

Jerome frowned, his forehead furrowing with concern as he took in Nick's bloodstained shoulder. "Shit, man. Have you ever been hit with gold before? Are you going to be okay?"

"I'll be fine, but I'm going to crash. I need to—" He stopped talking as an old, bearded man in a white robe strode into the room, followed by a businessman in an Armani suit. Paul and Otis, the other two members of the Council.

Paul and Otis were the Council members who'd worked with Satan to wipe out the Markku, and they'd killed Nick's dad, all before Jerome came on board. The Markku had gotten tired of being Satan's slaves, so when Nick's grandpa had figured out how to escape hell, he'd made a deal with the Council: if they'd help him lead the rest of the Markku to safety, he'd make the Markku available to help the Council any time they needed some muscle.

But once the Markku had gotten free and the Council

realized how powerful they really were, they decided it was bad to have the Markku be a free people, and they made another deal, this time with Satan. The Council traded an entire race of beings in exchange for Satan's Chamber of Unspeakable Horrors.

Satan had been irate that his whole Markku army had bailed on him, and he'd ordered his Rivkas to destroy all Markku they found. With the help of the Council, who were happy to point out the safe houses they'd created for the Markku to recover after battle, the Rivka had decimated the race with their gold fireballs while they'd slept, except for one or two Markku who'd crashed elsewhere.

Like Nick's grandpa, which is why Nick's pa and Nick himself existed.

But they were all who had survived, and the Council had killed Nick's pa when they'd found him. It was damned annoying Nick had promised his pa he wouldn't stalk, torture, and maim the Council in retribution. Paul and Otis had no idea who Nick was, and Nick had to keep it that way, or else they'd be so threatened by his existence that they'd find a way to kill him, leaving Nick's ma and sister alone.

He'd promised his pa, and he'd stand by it, which meant walking away, no matter how hard it was. But that didn't mean he wasn't going to try to find out what was up with that Markku who'd tried to kill him. Were there really others out there, hiding like he was?

"Jerome! What's going on here?" Paul, the old guy, asked, his hands hiding inside the flowing folds of his white robe.

The businessman, Otis, whipped out a Blackberry and started typing on it, his manicured fingers flying over the keys as he typed out an e-mail. "I'm going to have to file a report for destruction of property."

Jerome raised his brows. "Satan Jr.'s melting. Shouldn't we order backup refrigeration immediately?"

Otis looked up, peered at the battered ice chest, then cleared his throat. "Yes, well, I suppose we do need to make sure he doesn't thaw and re-form, don't we?"

Nick and Jerome exchanged glances at the lack of urgency in Otis's voice, and Nick suddenly wished he didn't have to go pass out for a day or two. Satan Jr. would be serious trouble if he got unfrozen.

Jerome opened his own cell phone and ordered emergency freezer backup himself, while Otis walked around the room, tallying up the damage.

Paul moved in front of Nick. "Who are you, and what are you doing here?"

Nick tensed at Paul's probing gaze. As a half Markku, he blended into human society better than a full-blood Markku, but Otis and Paul had spent a lot of time with the Markku during the rebellion, and Nick wasn't sure exactly how sensitive they were. Time to vacate. "I was just delivering Jerome's dry cleaning. Gotta take care of those puffy silk things he calls shirts." Nick hoisted his machine gun over his shoulder, shoved his guns into his shoulder holsters, and walked out, ignoring the protests of Paul and the curious stare of Otis.

"Wait!" Jerome grabbed his arm. "Who am I going get to protect Satan Jr.?"

"From what? Explain what's going on, Jerome. I insist—" Paul stopped suddenly and held out his hand, letting the glittering remains of the dead Markku settle on his palm. "Is this what I think it is?"

The trembling in Nick's legs told him he didn't have time to hang around. He and Jerome looked at each other, then Nick walked over to the block of ice, pulled out his gun, and peppered the corner of the block until a twelve-inch piece fell off. He ignored the shouted protests of Otis and Paul, who didn't dare approach him while the bullets were flying.

Too bad. Death by friendly fire would have worked for Nick.

He holstered his gun, and Paul lunged for the small block of ice. Nick swept it out of his reach and walked over to the portable fridge that Jerome had set up for him.

He dumped out the contents, grinned at the beer that had been hidden in the back, then shoved the chunk of Satan Jr. inside and tucked the fridge under his arm. "If anyone tries to re-form Satan Jr. without this piece, he'll be missing something important. Probably not worth the risk."

"You can't take that!" Paul threw himself in front of the door. "Otis. Call for backup."

As Otis fumbled with his headset, Nick rolled his eyes at Jerome, then grabbed Paul and tossed him aside. The Council member landed with a splash, spluttering, and Jerome had to turn away coughing.

Nick shuddered with weakness again and broke into an uneven jog, forcing his failing body to hurry and willing his way through the pain in his damaged knee. No way did he have the thirty minutes he'd initially thought. The gold blade had taken more out of him than he'd anticipated. Twenty feet to Jerome's office, where he'd anchored his black-market portal. He preferred using his motorcycle, but he'd figured he might not have time to get back to his safe house by ordinary means, and now he was glad he'd had the foresight.

He shoved open the door, kicked it shut, then strode to the middle of the room, to the faint circle outlined on the floor. The portal kicked on automatically as soon as it sensed him, and he closed his eyes against the faint humming in his body. A couple more minutes. That's all he had to hang on.

The humming stopped, and he opened his eyes to find himself surrounded by four walls of steel, deep underground. It held only a bed, a fridge, his armoire, and a bathroom. His body trembled, and he dropped the icebox.

He grabbed the chunk of Satan Jr., his muscles aching with the effort, staggered over to the freezer, and threw it inside. Then he made it the three feet to the bed and collapsed, letting the weakness overtake him like a black cloud.

He had a minute, maybe two, left of consciousness, and he relaxed. He was safe now.

Then his phone rang. He smiled at the sound of Toby Keith, the ring his little sister had programmed into his phone for her calls. He hadn't heard from her in over a week, and he'd been starting to worry.

Groaning, he yanked his phone out of his pocket and flipped it open, letting it rest against the side of his head. "Where've you been, squirt?" He closed his eyes and let his hand flop to the mattress.

"Nick! You have to help me!"

The franticness in his sister's voice caught him, and he battled against the wave of pending unconsciousness. "What's wrong?" His tongue felt thick and heavy.

"They're going to kill me if you don't do what they want!"

Her voice became distant and fuzzy, and he cursed, struggling to stay conscious. *Not now.* "Who?"

Another voice came on the phone. "Kill the leader of hell by Sunday or your sister dies."

Sunday? It was already Tuesday. That was kind of a short deadline for killing the leader of hell, wasn't it? "Dani—" And then the world went black.

Two

"I can't believe you want your life force to be a goldfish."

"It's better than having my life force be Satan." Her heart thudding, Becca Gibbs, Satan's favorite Rivka and personal slave, carefully set the Tupperware container holding Ellie the fish in the middle of the spot she'd cleared in New York's Central Park. Three large flashlights were set up around them, illuminating the isolated clearing. It was just before midnight on Wednesday, and the park was relatively quiet. "A hundred years is my limit for being forced to obey his every command, torture and harvest souls, genuflect to his greatness, kill my own friends, and have my personality be nothing but an extension of his warped one." She set her hands on her hips. "I can't take it anymore."

"But how do you know Ellie isn't some evil life force just waiting for a chance to force her soggy will on the world?" Theresa Nichols-Siccardi swished her tail in typical aggravated-dragon fashion, upending a small tree and crushing a drinking fountain. "Maybe she's Satan's worst nightmare and once you give her your body to act through, the world as we know it will be destroyed."

Becca slanted a glance at the testy dragon as she wiped her sweaty hands on her jeans. "She's a *goldfish*. There's no way she's harboring some evil soul."

"And everyone thinks Mona is only an espresso machine, but she's actually the Goblet of Eternal Youth, chock full of enough power to disrupt the natural order of hell and the mortal world. Looks can be deceiving." Theresa blew a puff of ash out of her nose.

Becca tensed at a crackle in the dark woods, staring into the black night for a long moment.

"Yo', Rivka, what if you turn into a fish, huh?" Theresa wrinkled her scaled blue-green nose. "You want me to eat you and put you out of your misery? I'm generally not into eating friends, but if it's that important to you, I suppose I could be persuaded."

There was no other noise in the woods, so Becca turned back to the circle she was creating, trying not to wince at each gust of wind. She knew Satan would figure out what she was doing. Her only hope was to get it done before he showed up. "First of all, we're not friends. Second, if you even think about eating me, I'll turn you into a pile of ash." She hadn't spent an entire century thwarting Satan only to have a primadonna dragon have her for a late-night snack. "Third, I'm not going to turn into a fish. I'm only going to connect to her life force."

The dragon snorted. "But you're nothing but a figment of Satan's imagination, kept alive by his life force and his personality, so if you switch your life-support machine over to Ellie's, won't you have the personality of the fish? Is a goldfish really better than Satan?" She flashed an apologetic smile at the fish. "No offense intended."

"If I link to a weaker spirit, then my personality will trump and I'll be able to be myself, in theory anyway." *And then I'll truly be free.* She eyed the dragon, who was just crazy enough to understand. "I mean, seriously, my life was bad enough already, but this morning Satan ordered me to quit my job at Vic's so I could concentrate on hell stuff." She was vice president at Vic's, the only place where she had control over her life, where people respected her for who she was. She felt like *someone* there, and it was her oasis.

"What?" Theresa yelped. "Who would run Vic's if you left? I live for those pretzels."

"That's why I'm quitting Satan instead." She frowned. "But even worse than that, someone tried to kill me last week! What if he'd succeeded and I'd spent a hundred years suffering and then died before I could get free?" She shuddered. "I can't wait any longer. I have to get out now before I lose everything."

"I hear you, girlfriend. Premature death would suck. Especially for you, because if you died, then you'd really be dead and not sent to the Afterlife, where everyone else gets to go for round number two."

"Yeah, the benefits of being a resident of hell. Yet another reason to get out now." Becca paused again to listen to the night. Crickets chirped, an owl hooted off to her left, and frogs croaked down at the nearby pond. Normal night sounds that indicated that the leader of hell wasn't out in the darkness, sipping wine and waiting for her to cross that line.

She took a deep breath, then walked a circle around herself and Ellie, pouring the purified water in an unbroken line.

The dragon burned a mosquito out of the air. "Are you worried that it's wishful thinking that you actually have your own scintillating personality buried under there somewhere?"

"No." Sweat dripped down her back, even though it was a cool night for summer. What if she didn't have her own personality? What if everything she was *was* Satan, and when she linked her life force to a goldfish, she no longer existed? She faltered in her steps and had to clamp her hand over the top of the gold vase to keep the purified water from spilling. No. She'd done her research. She was certain this would work.

"I mean, do you wonder whether he bothered to give you an identity when he created you?"

"Would you please *shut up?* You're driving me *insane!*" She clamped her fingers around the vase of purified water so she didn't drop it by accident.

"Sorry." Theresa sat back on her haunches and folded her wings. "So, who did you say found this spell?"

"It's not a spell. It's a process. And I came up with it myself after a century of research." She finished pouring the circle, set the vase in the middle of the circle, and took off her black boots and set them aside, wiggling her toes in the grass and the earth. Dirt was pure. Elemental. Real. Everything Satan wasn't.

The dragon snapped a stick as she shifted position, making Becca jump. "Why don't you find a spell that allows you to generate your own life force instead of merely transferring your lifeline from one being to another?"

She shot the dragon a disbelieving look. "You seriously think I'd be out here with a goldfish if there was a way for me to generate my own life force? I'm not hardwired that way."

"Well, that sucks."

"Gee, you think?"

Theresa was thankfully silent while Becca set up eight shot glasses at evenly spaced intervals around the inside of the circle, dropped a twenty-four-karat gold ball inside each one, then filled each of them to the top with purified water.

"So, if you succeed and then some owl swoops down here and eats that fish, you're dead, right? It dies, you die?"

"I can protect a goldfish long enough to get her back to the Goblet of Eternal Youth to make her immortal."

Theresa sucked in her breath. "She can't drink from Mona! That's so illegal! The Council would kick all our asses from here to hell! Have you *met* the Council? They are scary shit, girlfriend. No way am I crossing them!" She clutched her claws to her chest. "They'll put me in the Chamber of Unspeakable Horrors! Have you heard about it? It's an eternity of the worst tortures imaginable. I can imagine really, really bad tortures, and it's worse than that!"

Becca looked up and met the dragon's gaze across the eerie shadows from the flashlights. "They won't put you in there. You don't work for them anymore. They have no authority over you." But she knew all about the Chamber. Satan had created it as a joke to threaten Rivkas into submission, then traded it to the Council, who actually used it whenever they wanted to make a point. It was brutal, horrible, and no one had ever emerged sane enough to even explain what happened when you were inside. Three minutes in there was enough to fry you for eternity. "How many favors do you owe me, dragon?"

Theresa whistled softly. "Damn, girl, you drive a harder bargain than Satan."

Becca managed a grim smile as she laid one of Satan's custom dress shirts in the center of the circle, and then poured a spoonful of Ellie's water in the center of it. "So, you'll help?"

Theresa held her claw over her heart. "I love you, girl-friend. I'll do anything you need."

Becca tensed and shot the dragon a red-eyed glare. "How many times have I told you that we're not friends? It's too dangerous for you."

The dragon snorted and flicked her tail in irritation. "Shut up already. You can't scare me. I'm an immortal dragon who survived making a deal with Satan. Do your spell and let's get you and Ellie to Mona already, okay?"

Becca piled a stash of cedar sticks on top of the shirt, then sat back on her heels. "We are *not* friends."

Theresa put her claws over her ears and started humming the theme from *The Brady Bunch*.

"Oh, for God's sake." Becca gave up on the dragon, took a deep breath, and closed her eyes. She hugged herself and whispered a prayer to the heavens that she wasn't allowed to acknowledge. *It was time.*

For a brief moment, she hesitated. As much of an egotistic tyrant as Satan was, she'd miss him. He was such fun to annoy, and it was more than a little scary to think about going off on her own... No, it was time to move

on. A girl had to have standards, and between the near as-
sassination and being ordered to give up the one thing she
valued in her life, well, the line had been crossed.

Game on.

Becca held out both hands and a fireball popped up on
each hand, heat and flame whirling in the dark night. She
blew a kiss to Ellie, who swam happily in her little bowl.
"Don't let me down, girl," she whispered.

She fixed her gaze on Satan's shirt and then whispered
the words she'd spent so long working out. As soon as
they left her mouth, she crossed her wrists and shot the
pile of sticks with both fireballs. The shirt exploded in an
array of golden sparks, and her voice rose above the din
as she shouted the next words.

"Shit!" Theresa shouted. "You melted the Tupperware
container! Save Ellie!"

Becca felt her concentration slip, but she yanked it
back. *I have to finish.*

She grabbed the northernmost shot glass and threw the
contents down her throat.

The pain was instant, blinding, and it knocked her to
the ground. *Jesus.* She felt like her insides were being
bled with acid.

"Becca? Are you all right?"

Bitterness sliced through her throat, blades ripped
through her gut, searing agony tore her chest. This was
wrong. Something was terribly wrong. Couldn't breathe.
Couldn't think. It hurt like a mother-f—

"Rivka! You betray me! I am much chagrined!"

She flinched at the sound of a familiar male voice, in
too much pain to lift her head and look up. Satan had

found her too soon. Dammit! "You are *such* a pain in my ass."

"As you are in mine," Satan crooned. "I adore you, Rivka! You make my life so interesting while you try to thwart me at every moment. You are my greatest pride."

"I know." She hunched over as thousands of invisible knives stabbed at her flesh, tasting blood as she bit her lip to keep herself from screaming. She was *not* going to give him the satisfaction. *Never.* "I rock," she managed, her voice raspy.

"Hey, asshole," Theresa said.

No, Theresa. Don't get involved. Becca struggled to find her voice, but the pain was too extreme. If she opened her mouth again, she'd start screaming or sobbing or something equally unworthy of Satan's best Rivka. "Um...boss..."

"Theresa!" Satan exclaimed. "It is so lovely to see the comrade of the fruit of my loins. You are wonderful with fire. Would you care to replace my best Rivka after I kill her? The benefits of working for me are extensive. I can send you copy of my employee handbook, if you like."

"Let her go," Theresa said.

"Go where? She is dying, cannot you see that?"

Becca dropped to her knees, clutching her throat, trying to yank out the unseen daggers slicing at her skin. It *really* hurt. She couldn't...think...

"Why is she dying?" Theresa's voice was blurry and distant, nearly obliterated by the pain shredding Becca's body.

"Because she tried to cut my lifeline to her. So I poison the lifeline and threw it back at her, and now she dies. It is delightfully ironic, is it not? She gets what she wants and then she dies for it? I love irony."

"Let her go, or I'll kill you."

Oh, no. Take it back, Theresa. Don't take on Satan for me.

Satan was silent for a moment, and Becca forced her eyes to open a slit and squinted up at her boss. Satan was dressed in an impeccable Italian suit, and he was wearing a boutonniere. His luscious dark hair was styled in a new coif, he was freshly shaven, and he looked debonair enough to be welcomed into any palace. He was inspecting Theresa with an interested gleam in his eye that made Becca's stomach curl. "You care very much for the Rivka?" he asked.

"Of course I do," Theresa snapped. "She rocks, not that you'd ever be man enough to realize it."

Shut up, you stupid dragon!

"Does she care for you, as well? She would be upset if something happened to you, no?" He turned his head toward Becca, and she felt him ease up slightly on her pain, momentarily distracted. "Answer me, Rivka. Do you care what happens to the dragon?"

Once again, Satan had forgotten who he was dealing with. Hello? When he ordered her to answer his question, he'd neglected to specify that she give him the truth. She met his gaze, taking a deep breath to try to fight off the thrum of pain so she could speak. "Satan, you know I think you're the man." She almost grinned as he preened under her words. "The dragon means nothing to me. Chop her up. You're it for me, big guy."

Theresa squawked in protest, but Becca didn't dare look at the dragon.

Satan narrowed his eyes. "I think I will take you up on that. I have never tortured dragon before. Would it hurt very much to pluck each scale off, one by one? Perhaps if I made you do it? That would be much fun, no?"

There was a thud and a whoosh of air, and she knew Theresa had decided to vacate. She relaxed slightly. Whatever Satan did to her she could handle, now that Theresa was gone.

"You're such a great torturer. I'd be honored to watch you in action," she gushed, hoping his insecurities would fade in the face of such devotion from his loyal Rivka. Given that he ruled all of hell, one would think he wouldn't be threatened by his favorite Rivka having friends, but hey, even Satan had insecurities. It wasn't his fault, but until he started going to therapy, Becca wasn't about to endanger anyone by getting close and snuggly with them. Been there, done that, no room for any more guilt.

The leader of hell and his right hand stared at each other, and she gave him the wide-eyed look of utter adoration that she'd perfected over the decades. "Is that a new suit? It's gorgeous."

Satan blinked, then smiled and patted his breast. "Yes, yes, I hope to woo the fair Iris with it. Do you know she is not easy to dominate and manipulate in relationship? I am feeling quite lost."

Iris Bennett was the former Guardian of the Goblet of Eternal Youth. After getting her killed and demoted two hundred years ago in his quest to steal the Goblet from her Guardianship, Satan had been trying to woo her ever since, and he'd finally gotten her in his bed a few weeks ago, but it sounded like things weren't going so well.

"You'll figure it out. Dating's tough. Want me to talk to her?"

"Yes..." Satan's face suddenly darkened, and Becca's pain level shot back up. "How can you help me? You try to leave me! How is Satan supposed to terrorize the entire world without his best Rivka? Why do you not like me anymore? Why do you reject me?"

Becca hunched over, gritting her teeth. "I don't reject you," she managed. "I just need a little space—" She gasped as something sharp pierced her spine. "Or not."

Satan harrumphed and straightened up, and a fresh surge of violent pain stabbed every inch of her. Her body spasmed and she screamed, unable to stop herself. "Satan...stop..."

"It will take you several thousand years to die. The pain will increase exponentially every six hours, and your body will eat itself from the inside out. Does it not sound delightful? One of my new scientist souls just figured out how to do that to my Rivkas, and this is my first chance to try it." He peered more closely at her. "Does it hurt very much, Rivka?"

Several thousand years of this? Impossible. She gazed up into his beautiful blue eyes and knew he'd won. But she'd won, too, because he hadn't hurt Theresa. "Re-establish the link." Her voice was harsh with agony, but she knew he understood.

His smile became broader. "Hmm..."

Her stomach lurched, and she turned her head toward his feet. If she lost it, the least she could do was ruin his polished shoes.

"You are my best Rivka. I gain much benefit from having your services. Perhaps I should spare you despite your ultimate betrayal." Satan rubbed his chin and studied her thoughtfully. "So, what shall I demand in return for permitting you to continue to wreak havoc upon the world in my name? Hmm...so many choices."

A groan leaked out of her, and she crumbled the rest of the way to the ground, no longer able to will herself to stay on her knees. Satan chuckled. *God help me.*

How could she owe him anything? Was there really something that he had to negotiate for, that she didn't have to give automatically? She gave a raspy hack as she rolled to her side in the grass, crunched in a ball.

"I shall have to consult my experts on how best to use this situation to benefit me and torture you," Satan said. "But I will collect. We agree to agree. Agreed?"

She knew it would be a mistake, but she had no choice. She managed a nod. She grimaced when Satan clapped his hands together with glee. "This is a monumental event. I have outsmarted my best Rivka for the first time. This is quite fun. No wonder you do this to me all the time. I shall have to develop this skill more completely so I can torture you more often."

Lucky me. "And you wonder why I need space," she mumbled.

"What?"

"I can't wait. It'll be good bonding."

"Yes, it will, my favorite Rivka." He leaned down and patted her head. "I release you from the pain. You will live, and I will be back to tell you what you owe me. Have a lovely evening. And tell dragon I will still hire her as my second-best Rivka. And please, come to dinner on Sunday night. We can converse about how powerful and virile I am, and you shall regale me with stories about all the people you met this week who idolize me." And with that, he vanished in an explosion of gold bubbles, and the pain vanished abruptly from Becca's body.

She sagged against the ground, her face mashed in the cool dirt as she gasped for air.

There was a fluttering sound, a loud crash on the earth, and the ground shuddered as Theresa landed where Satan had been. She scooped up Ellie with the vase and sat next to Becca with a thump. "Wow. Are you okay?"

"Peachy." Becca closed her eyes as tremors began to wrack her body. She was so cold. So weak. Couldn't move. Just wanted to lie there.

"Cold?" Theresa leaned closer, let out a growl, then set Becca on fire.

Yes. Becca arched under the heat, absorbing it into her body, pulling it into all the damaged cells as the tremors began to fade.

"So, he crushed you like a gnat, huh?"

Becca took a shuddering breath. "I'm not a gnat."

"You look sort of like one."

"Feel like one." Was she drooling? Probably. Too much effort to swallow. She'd just lie here for the next decade or so until she got her strength back.

She felt Theresa shift beside her. "Well, Ellie survived though. That's good news."

"I'm so glad to hear that." One less thing to feel guilty about. The night was looking up.

"So, are we going to try your spell again?"

"Not tonight." Such a bummer. A century of planning and anticipation shot to hell. Literally. God, she felt like crying. Like sobbing. Like lying on her stomach and throwing a full-fledged temper tantrum. "Thanks for coming back."

"It's not because we're friends, just so you know."

Becca managed to peel her eyes open, then jerked back to find Theresa's golden eyes less than an inch from her face. "So you understand now why we can't be friends?"

Theresa's scaly face bobbed up and down. "Oh, I *get* it."

"It's about damned time." Becca couldn't keep from grinning, even though it hurt to move her face. She felt like her body was melting into the restoring earth.

"So, you going to stay there all night?" Theresa asked.

"No. Let's go." She mentally ordered herself home.

Nothing happened. She didn't turn into an inky black cloud and melt through the ground and then pop up through the floor of her condo. She was still in human form, and still in the park. Damn. She'd never been too weak to shimmer.

Theresa sighed. "Seeing as how I still owe you for about a zillion favors, I guess that means I'll have to fly you home." She wedged Ellie's vase carefully between her teeth, then slid her claws under Becca's body.

Home. Her bed sounded so good right now.

They took to the air, and she felt Theresa's scales snag on her jacket. She realized Satan would be watching Theresa closely now, looking for any evidence that Becca actually cared about her.

It was time to break off with the dragon completely.

She swallowed hard at the sudden bleakness in her gut,

then forced herself to remember that she'd actually broken the link tonight.

Her process had worked. She was close, she knew it. So damned close.

She closed her eyes and forced herself to concentrate on that small victory, refusing to acknowledge the aching emptiness inside her that never went away.

Three

Becca woke up the next morning to find a fire-breathing dragon trying to set her hair on fire. "Dammit, Theresa. You need to get out of here. Did you learn nothing last night?" Becca tugged the pillow over her head and rolled away from her, almost tempted to wallow in self-pity over last night's failure. She burrowed deeper under the down comforter, snuggling into its warmth, not quite able to make herself get up and force the dragon out the door. "I'm still traumatized."

"You are not. You're a Rivka. You have no emotions." Theresa gave the covers a yank and sent them tumbling to the floor. "Holy cow! What are you sleeping in?"

She cringed as she recalled the sleeping attire she'd put on in the middle of the night after a Satan-induced nightmare had woken her up. "Shut up." She flung her legs over the side of the bed and stalked to her closet, trying to ignore Theresa gawking at her. So what if she slept in a pale pink lace camisole and silk boxers? Didn't mean she was soft.

The dragon whistled softly. "I had no idea you were a sex kitten. Rabid wolverine who sleeps fully armed in leather or chain-link armor, yes. Fluffy little sex kitten? Not so much."

Becca grinned at the analogy. "Usually I do. I was too tired to put it on." She yanked on a pair of black spandex shorts and a sports bra. Her body was still shaky and weak, and her head hurt like a mother. She needed to clear her brain and focus on last night. Figure out what went wrong and how to fix it. She was so close, too close to give up. "What are you doing in my condo? Shouldn't you be trading sexual favors with Zeke or something?"

"Zeke's out of town looking for one of my sisters, so I crashed here last night." The dragon sprawled out on Becca's bed, eliciting groans of protest from the springs. "I figured you wouldn't be in shape to take on Satan if he showed up, so I decided to stay and take care of you. In full dragon form, of course. My human form isn't quite up to hand-to-hand combat with your boss, you know?"

Becca's throat tightened at the thought of Theresa hanging out all night keeping an eye on her, but she quickly shook it off. "I don't need a dragon to keep me safe."

"And you don't need friends, either. I know, you've said it like a million times already."

Becca couldn't help but grin at Theresa's dismissive tone. "You're like a self-destructive stalker." She jerked a brush through her short hair, then grabbed a pair of ankle socks and her running shoes and sat down next to the dragon to pull them on.

Theresa bobbed her blue-scaled head. "Oh, and when you didn't arrive at Vic's central offices at your usual hour of five-thirty in the morning, your admin called in search of you. I told her you'd gotten a minor case of food poisoning and would be in as soon as possible." She flicked her gaze over Becca. "Figured that would explain the pale, wan look you're sporting today."

Great. She must look as crappy as she felt. That wasn't acceptable. Looking good was half the battle to feeling decent. "And she believed you?"

"Yep. She told you to get well as soon as possible, preferably by three o'clock, because the president of Mc-Donald's wants to meet with you to iron out the sticky points of their distribution."

"Okay, that's fine then. I can make it by three." A long hot shower, a couple of rounds with the coffeemaker, her black power suit, some concealer for the dark circles under her eyes, and she'd be all set.

"So, you want to go to the Vic's on the corner for pretzels and coffee, or what?"

Becca smiled as she tugged on a pair of sneakers. "Thanks for the invite, but I don't have time. I'm going for a run to shake the aches out before work."

"Exercise, huh? Maybe I should add that to my regime..." Theresa rubbed her jaw as she considered it. "Or maybe not. There are too many runners in this world already, don't you think? Wouldn't want to overpopulate."

Becca strapped her running watch around her wrist. "Okay, I'm out of here." She hesitated. "Thanks for...um..."

The dragon waved a claw. "No need to torture yourself by thanking me. We're good."

Becca took a deep breath and looked at the dragon. "That whole Markku rebellion really scarred him, you know? Having all his servants turn on him in a major mutiny made him go a little crazy on any of his minions who have friends." She shrugged. "He can't stand his Rivkas having loyalty to anyone but him."

There was a flicker of acknowledgment in the dragon's yellow eyes. "Why do boys have such problems sharing their toys? Girls share. Boys own. So annoying."

Becca smiled at Theresa's irreverent tone. "Satan's in his own class of being a spoiled little boy."

Theresa rolled to her feet, landing with a thud that rattled the mirror over Becca's pine bureau. "If it was up to me, I wouldn't let you cut me out, but I have a dependent now. It would majorly bum Zeke out if Satan abducted me and tortured me for all eternity."

Becca saw the scales on the dragon's face soften at the thought of her husband. "You go take care of Zeke. I'll be fine. I've got things to do."

Theresa nodded, and for a moment they looked at each other. "If you need me, you know where to find me."

"I'll never call," Becca said.

"I know you won't." Theresa sighed, then marched over to the closet and pulled out one of the studded leather jackets Becca used when she was on Rivka duty. "I'm going to steal this to remember you by, okay?"

"It's my favorite coat."

"All the more reason." Theresa dropped some sparks on Becca's maple floors, leaving a series of burn marks. "For you to remember me. Dragon kisses." She carefully wrapped Becca's leather jacket in a blanket, then laid it over her scaly forearm. "There's just one more thing before I go."

"Dare I ask?" Becca put her hand on the doorknob and opened it, suddenly wanting the good-bye over.

Theresa's dragon eyes glittered with anticipation.

"There's a flighty blonde in your kitchen that needs to be whacked upside the head with a frying pan, and I was hoping you'd let me have the honors before I left. Sort of a good-bye present from one badass to another?"

Becca stared at the dragon. "What are you talking about?"

"The girl in your kitchen. She showed up here around four in the morning. I had to gag her and tie her up to shut her up. She was giving me a headache. I don't know why you can't have hot guys visit you instead of ditzy females." Theresa sighed, setting fire to the pale blue quilt. "Then I could have strip-searched him to make sure he was no danger to you."

Like she had time to deal with some intruder. Becca pointed to the flaming comforter. "What'd she want?"

Theresa sat down on the fire and smothered it with a few wiggles of her dragon butt. "She said Satan sent her, which is why I refrained from toasting her. Thought maybe you'd want to do it, but if you don't, then I would *love* to."

"Satan sent her?" Becca frowned as she worked that one through her mind. "Is she an assassin?" Was he really *that* pissed about her trying to break free of him? He'd be lost without her, though. He couldn't afford to kill her. Dammit. Why was everyone trying to kill her now, when she was so close to getting free?

"Could be. If so, she's not a very good one. She tried to knock me out with a kick to the head. Idiot. Everyone knows you can't take down a dragon that way." Theresa sat up. "Let's have a contest. We'll take turns assaulting the blonde and whoever knocks her out first will be declared Badass of the Day."

Becca rolled her eyes as she grabbed a lightweight running jacket and zipped it up. "You're the one who should be a Rivka, not me." She opened the cream-colored wicker armoire by her bed, pulled out her hot pink running hat and shoved it on her head, grabbed her favorite gun in case the assassin was fireball-proof, then headed toward the kitchen while Theresa followed, listing all the ways they could kill Satan's minion.

Becca stopped in the kitchen doorway. Sure enough, there was a blond-haired, fully stacked woman tied to her kitchen chair. She looked to be about twenty-two, but that could simply be the age Satan had decided to give her when he'd created her, assuming she really was Satan's spawn.

The instant the woman saw Becca, she widened her eyes and started making all sorts of wimpy pleading noises.

Either she was the most pathetic assassin Becca had ever seen, or she was a cheerleader who had knocked on the wrong door this morning. Becca relaxed, realizing that her death wasn't going to come at the hands of this particular assassin. Not this morning, at least. She still had time to get free before she lost everything.

Theresa blew a puff of smoke into the kitchen, her hind claws tapping restlessly on the new floor Becca had just installed after spending weeks selecting the perfect tile. Pale blue with white swirls. Girly and sweet. The antithesis of Satan's decorating style, which was why she loved it.

She carefully flicked a blade through the gag, so it dropped around the woman's throat. "Who—"

"Omigosh! I can't believe it's you! You're my hero!

You're the best Rivka in history and I heard you almost got free of Satan last night. I am sooooo lucky to meet you. Will you autograph something for me?" Her eyes were wide, her mouth babbling, and Becca was tempted to re-gag her.

"You have a fan club?" Theresa sighed. "That's so cool. I want a fan club."

Becca flicked the nose of her gun at the cheerleader. "Who are you and what do you want? In ten words or less."

The woman's cheeks blushed a dainty pink. "Omigosh. I'm so rude! I didn't introduce myself. I'm Paige Darlington." She beamed at Becca, waiting for a response.

She flicked a glance at Theresa, who shrugged. "Sorry, but that name doesn't mean anything to me."

Paige's face immediately turned bright red. "He didn't tell you, did he? Is this my first test? Oh, wow. I didn't realize my training would start so soon. You won't kill me, will you? Before I explain? Oh, wow. Are you going to be mad? I mean—"

"Stop talking." Oy. Her head was already hurting. "Just tell me why you're here."

"I'm your apprentice," Paige blurted, tugging on the ropes and sliding her chair across the tile with a squeak.

Becca stuck her toe against the chair leg so it couldn't move and scratch her new floor. "My what?"

"Your apprentice. You're supposed to train me on everything Rivka. Won't that be fun?" Paige tried to move the chair closer to Becca and frowned when it didn't move. "I got the highest test scores, so that's why I got selected. Plus I'm hot. That was Satan's requirement. Oh, and because I showed highest loyalty to Satan."

Becca rolled her eyes at the dragon. "High test scores, hotness, and brownnosing. All the hallmarks of a great warrior."

"Totally," Paige agreed, not quite catching on to the sarcasm. "Everyone is mega jealous that I got picked to be your apprentice. So it's a good thing I'll be under your protection because I think some of them might otherwise try to kill me to get this position. It's so coveted. I swear this is my best day ever. When will we start? Will you teach me how to shoot fireballs? And what about harvesting souls? How long 'til I can do that? I'll work really hard and—"

"Can I cut out her tongue?" Theresa asked, her tail whipping side to side and barely missing Becca's fridge.

"Please do." Becca turned away and flipped on her coffee maker. Caffeine would so be needed to deal with this chick.

"What?" Paige shrieked, scooting the chair backward so fast that it slammed into the wall with a crash that made Becca wince and Theresa snicker.

"Stop ruining my new kitchen." Becca shoved Paige away from the wall, then wet a sponge and carefully scrubbed the wall to get rid of the mark that Paige had just left. "I've never heard of any Rivka having an apprentice. Tell me what you're really doing here."

Theresa sidled up next to Becca and mimicked her stance, glaring at the girl.

Paige's eyes flicked nervously to the dragon, then to Becca. "I swear I'm your apprentice. I mean, I'm also supposed to spy on you and report to Satan about everything you do, like if the dragon's around, but really, it's all about being your apprentice." Paige bounced in her chair, dragging it over the floor again with a squeal that made Becca wince. "I have proof in my purse. I dropped it when the dragon tried to kill me."

"Purse is probably booby-trapped," Theresa said. "Let's burn it."

Becca slammed her foot down on the chair seat between Paige's knees to hold the chair immobile, then noticed a small black handbag on the floor. "Stay." At Paige's nod, she walked over and picked it up. Inside was a paper etched in gold, the sight of which made her shoulders tense. She held it up. "This?"

Paige nodded again, relief evident on her face.

Becca grabbed the paper between her thumb and forefinger to rip it up, and Paige shrieked in protest. "He ordered me to tell you he orders you to read it immediately!"

"Oh, he's getting wise to you," Theresa commented. "That sucks."

"He tries, but he'll never be able to keep up with me." Then she glared at Paige. "Next time, keep your mouth shut."

The cheerleader's perky little lips pursed in a cute pout. "But if he orders me to do it, I have to."

"But he didn't say *when* you had to give me those orders, did he? You could have given me the order after I ripped it up."

"But I knew what he *meant*." Paige drew her shoulders back, pride gleaming in her eyes. "I'll get his orders right every time, I swear, even if he doesn't make them perfect."

Theresa snorted and Becca rolled her eyes. Just what she needed. An apprentice who actually thought Satan rocked. She sighed as she unfolded the paper. "What's with the old-fashioned document?"

"His new lawyer soul suggested that you might have more trouble disobeying his orders if they were written out this way." Paige leaned forward, trying to peer at the paper.

Theresa flattened Paige back in the chair with a well-placed claw to the chest.

Lawyer soul again? She was going to have to stop getting him such helpful souls, and Paige needed to be fire-balled. She gritted her teeth and silently read the letter as Theresa rested her scaly chin on Becca's shoulder and read it, as well.

> *My best Rivka.*
>
> *Bravo for last night. I much enjoyed besting you. An evening most pleasurable. I hereby present Paige Darlington. She is your new apprentice. I Order you to teach her everything you know about being a Rivka and to assist her in her special assignment. You shall notify me when she is ready, unless she is a liability, in which case, kill her.*
>
> *I am taking my true love Iris dancing on Saturday, and I need to learn all the new dance moves of today. I Order you to harvest cool and hip souls who will assist me in this endeavor to become even more irresistible than I already am.*
>
> > *Your lord and creator,*
> > *Satan, the best lover in the Afterlife*

He'd used the "O" word.

She hated when he did that. Made it so much more difficult to thwart him.

"Huh. She really is your apprentice," Theresa mused,

her breath setting Becca's hat on fire. "You think you're training your own replacement?"

Becca patted her hat until the flames went out, waving her other hand through the billow of smoke Theresa had just released. "What do you mean?"

"You think it's a fluke that you piss off Satan royally last night, and then three hours later, the first Rivka apprentice in history shows up at your door? One who apparently worships him and would never stray from her mission to be his personal ego booster and servant?"

Becca frowned. "She does seem a little overly enthusiastic."

Theresa nodded. "He needs you too badly to let you die, unless he can get you to create another you, who is you, but even better. Then he kills you and puts Paige in your place. Paige will render you obsolete." She met Becca's gaze. "I think Satan has just declared war on his favorite Rivka."

Four

Becca and Theresa both eyed Paige, who had turned pale. "I swear I'm not after your job, Becca. I think you're awesome and I just want to learn from you and make Satan happy by reporting on your every move."

Becca rubbed her chin while she considered her options. "He did order me to kill her if I needed to."

"Oh, you need to kill her." Theresa grinned, her lips pulled back to reveal a formidable set of dragon teeth. "She's definitely a liability."

"What?" Paige shrieked. "How can you teach me if I'm dead?" She struggled against the ropes but succeeded only in tipping over the chair and landing on her side with a thump.

"The cheerleader has a point." Theresa stepped over Paige and opened a cabinet. "Coffee for two?"

Becca studied the cheerleader writhing on the tile, her feet all tangled up in the chair legs and her ponytail caught under her shoulder, twisting her head at a painful angle. The girl looked so pathetic...it would be a slaughter if Becca killed her. She grimaced at the realization, because she didn't kill innocents. It was her one way of staying sane.

"Can I have some coffee, too?" Paige called out from the floor, her face contorted in pain.

The coffee *did* smell good. "I'll have some." Becca sighed and tipped Paige back up, ignoring the girl's babbles of appreciation. "Trust me, apprentice, I can figure out a way to kill you without actually violating Satan's orders." *Yeah, yeah, like that. Just kill her, Rivka. You can do it. She's going to be responsible for your demise. It's preemptive self-defense.* She flared up a fireball before she could think about it or look at Paige's sweet face for another second.

"Well, you can't do it today, because when my teacher told me I'd won this assignment, she said Satan specifically said we have to go soul hunting tonight," Paige announced, rotating her neck to try to get the kinks out.

"Tonight?" Becca crushed the fireball in her fist, cursing to herself while Theresa snorted with disgust. "Fine." She'd kill her after soul hunting.

"So, can you untie me, or what?" Paige tugged at her wrists, turning her hands pink from lack of circulation. "I can't wait to get started. Soul hunting tonight! How cool is that?"

Theresa handed Becca a mug of coffee. "She's actually sort of cute, in an annoying little puppy kind of way, don't you think?"

"Cute?" Paige scowled at Theresa. "I'm a badass."

"Yeah, we can tell." Becca winced at the bunny mug that Theresa had selected, wondering how the dragon had found it hidden in the back of her cabinet.

She watched Paige argue with the dragon. Satan might have been trying to take care of his ego when creating

Paige, but the girl would be dead within a minute of trying to take on Rivka duties. She was clueless and too excitable for her own safety. But she wasn't backing down from a dragon, so that meant she was brave. Or stupid.

Probably the latter.

The girl was needy and unpredictable and would cause plenty of trouble for Becca. And she was most likely an innocent... Becca sighed and wrapped her hands around her mug as she walked around the apprentice, thinking. If she did manage to turn Paige into a mirror image of herself, only more obedient and groveling, then maybe Satan would let his favorite Rivka go. She felt a surge of hope.

Or maybe once he didn't need Becca, Satan would finally kill his favorite Rivka in return for all the trouble she'd caused him over the years. Her hope was chased away by a heavy sigh.

More analysis needed before deciding whether to kill the apprentice or train her. If she had to kill her, well, she'd just have to do it, innocent or not.

Paige twisted in her seat, trying to look behind her where Becca was standing. "So, boss? Where are we going tonight? To a dark alley? Or to a bar?"

Becca swallowed the rest of the coffee, then set the mug on the counter with a thud. "We'll go to a bar after I get back from work. It'll be a test."

Paige jutted out her lower jaw in determination. "I'm really good at tests. What happens if I pass?"

"You live until tomorrow."

Paige paled slightly. "And if I fail?"

"You die."

Theresa grinned and put her arm around Becca's shoulder and gave her an affectionate squeeze. "You're such a heartless bitch. No wonder I love you."

Becca smiled back. She was really going to miss that dragon.

Nick groaned as consciousness slammed back into him with a painful thrust. He peeled his eyes open, his mouth fuzzy like he'd gone on a drinking binge, and then saw his cell phone on the pillow in front of him. *Dani.*

He grabbed his phone and sat up. Eleven missed calls from Dani. One from Jerome. *Shit.* Two messages.

His heart thudding, he called Dani as he swung his legs off the bed and tested his knee. Still gimpy, but not too bad. Should hold up long enough to kill Satan.

Dani answered on the first ring, and he dropped his head with relief at her voice. Still alive. "Nick! Where have you been? It's been almost twenty-four hours! They're about to cut off my finger!"

He frowned at the undercurrent in Dani's voice. Something wasn't quite right. A lack of…desperation. What was up? "What else are they going to do to you?"

As she rattled on about a number of torture methods, he closed his eyes to tune in to her, trying to get a read on her emotions. Excitement, adrenaline, and a little bit of nervousness. But no deadly panic or fear, which she should be feeling if she was really in danger of dying.

"Nick! Hello? Are you listening?"

He sighed and flexed his knee, trying to work out the stiffness. "Dani, I know you're not actually in danger of being killed. What's going on?"

There was a scuffle, and then Dani's voice muffled. "I

told you this wouldn't work. He always knows when I'm lying."

He ground his teeth and stood up, walking over to the freezer to make sure Satan Jr.'s unidentified body part was still intact.

It was.

Someone else came on the line. A woman. "Dani's fate is in your hands. We will kill her."

"Put Dani back on." He shut the freezer and opened the fridge to see what he had inside. Moldy cheese, old yogurt, and something he couldn't quite identify. It had been a long time since he'd needed to crash here, but he hadn't realized it had been *that* long.

He really needed to get a life.

"No! She will die! You must kill Satan."

He sighed with impatience and opened a wooden cabinet that hadn't been there last time he'd been here. One he hadn't noticed before he'd crashed. It was fully stocked with nonperishable goods. Obviously, his ma had found his place and decided to do a little restocking. "I don't like being manipulated, so put her on the phone or I'm hanging up."

"She will lose one finger at a time—"

He hung up. His sister was twenty-two years old and still trying to manipulate him, this time by pretending to be kidnapped. No appreciation whatsoever for the fact that he'd been taking care of her since her pa had been driven off by their ma. Nick had taken over dad duty, and Dani had never fully appreciated his efforts. He sensed that a part of her had always resented the fact that her pa had been nothing more than a brief fling by their ma after her true love, Nick's pa, had died.

Nick grabbed an unopened jar of peanut butter and some whole wheat crackers and dug in while he checked his messages. He skipped Dani's without bothering to listen, knowing it would be more lies, then played Jerome's. "Good move on taking a piece of Satan Jr. That was brilliant. I told everyone that was his head, and now the Council's freaking out that if he re-forms he'll be dead because of the whole 'I've got no head' problem. It's hilarious. Of course, Isabella Marcellini, the head of the Council, is now involved, and she ordered me to call you and tell you to and bring it back, so that's what I'm doing. Bring it back or I'll lose my job, yada, yada, yada. Stay tight and give me a ring when you're back on your feet. And…um…let me know if you've heard from Dani lately. I…ah…she borrowed my iPod and I need to get it back."

Nick tossed the phone on his bed. Yeah, he'd be bringing Junior back. Isabella might be somewhat legit, but there was no way the kid's body part was going back until the Council headquarters were secure. As for Jerome's iPod…something was off about that request. He wouldn't be surprised if Dani was trying to manipulate Jerome, as well. He'd have to remind Jerome to keep an eye out.

Munching on the peanut butter, Nick tested his shoulder, surprised to find it was still sore. Obviously, he'd be avoiding gold weapons in the future. He was impressed the Markku had been able to damage his knee, though. Nothing had ever hurt Nick before. Must have been a hell of a blow.

He sighed as he shucked his clothes and headed into

the bathroom. He had a feeling it would be too long before he got in another fun altercation like that.

By the time Dani called back, he'd already taken a shower, inspected the shriveled black skin around where the blade had gone in, and cleaned out the jar of peanut butter.

He let the phone ring three times before he answered. "Willing to talk now, squirt?"

"Oh, thanks, Nick." Dani was truly annoyed now, he could tell. "You had to go and blow it."

"Me? Sure, it's my fault." He walked over to his steel armoire and moved aside some of his weapons to get to the stash of clean clothes that were in there somewhere.

"You couldn't have just gone and killed Satan, could you?"

"Dani, did you really expect you could tell me to murder the leader of hell and I'd just do it? Pick up takeout for you, and maybe I wouldn't have bothered to question it. But murdering Satan's a little different." He picked up a plaid shirt and frowned. Since when did he wear plaid shirts? Ma. He tossed it aside and went hunting for a T-shirt instead.

"You're a jerk."

He sighed as he tugged on a pair of jeans that smelled a little musty from being stored for so long. "Yeah, well, that's life."

"No, it's not life," she snapped. "It's death now. They weren't going to kill me before, but now that you proved I can't lie to you, they're actually going to do it, and it's all your fault."

He hesitated as he caught a hint of actual fear in her voice. "Where are you?"

"Come to my apartment. You'll see." Then she hung up.

Just after ten on Thursday morning, ex-Guardian Iris Bennett came out of her bathroom to find Satan posed seductively on her new satin comforter, a scarf woven with gold leaf draped over his manly regions. He was tanned, ripped, and completely naked, except for a new watch that looked like it cost high six figures. His rich black hair was usually perfectly coiffed and styled, but it was in total disarray, as if someone had been running their fingers through it...she smiled at the memory of their amazing night. He was beautiful and sexy and...looking guilty as sin? Hmm...

She folded her arms over her chest as he wiggled his eyebrows. "My luscious pancake of love, I shall bring you to orgasmic peaks that no mortal could survive. Sounds good, no?"

"Where did you go for three hours in the middle of last night?" she asked.

He blinked once, very slowly, and his face went carefully blank, except for the lust gleaming in his eyes. "I do not know of which you speak."

"Fine." She knew from experience that there was no point in arguing with him, but blackmail was another story. "No sex, then." She walked back into the bathroom and locked the door.

"Oh, my feisty lioness, do not deprive yourself of my lovemaking talents!" The door flew off the hinges, and Iris jumped back as it crashed into the bathtub.

She glared at him as the splintered wood flew up around them. "You broke my door!"

"Yes, I did. I am quite magnificent, am I not?"

"I thought we agreed that you would use none of your hell-talents in my house."

Satan paused in the doorway, a look of chagrin curving his lovely features. "I forget my strength. I do not intend to bring hell's business to your quaint and small house that is like a matchbox compared to my many and expensive mansions. I apologize. Now forgive me and let us continue our exceptional lovemaking."

Iris stepped back, holding out her hand to block him as he approached. He pressed his chest against her hand, and her belly jumped at the feel of his hot skin, as it always did. "Satan, I can't live like this."

"Of course not. You live in a hovel. Move to my island in the Caribbean and—" He paused when she shook her head. "My flat in Paris?" When she shook her head again, he broke into a delighted smile and grabbed her around the waist before she could stop him. "You have decided to move to hell! I am so thrilled, my happiness will explode from my head and shower us with—"

"Stop!" She poked him in the ear. "I'm not moving to hell!"

He stopped and looked at her, his face so disappointed that she almost caved and agreed to pack her bags and move south of the border with him. *Don't be an idiot, Iris. You don't want to live in hell.* So, instead, she laid her hands on either side of his face and forced him to look at her. "What did you do that's making you look so guilty?"

He met her gaze. "I cannot lie to the woman whom

my heart yearns for. Despite your specific request to the contrary, I have ordered my Rivka to harvest more souls and I tortured her last night. But she is most deserving and recovers well. She enjoys it as much as I do, of that I am most certain."

"You're trying to tell me that she enjoys being tortured?" At his vigorous nod, Iris looked into the face of the man she was starting to grow fond of and wondered what she'd been thinking. How could she date the leader of hell? Even her women's support group in purgatory thought she was being too optimistic about the chances for their relationship. "Satan, she doesn't enjoy it."

He waved his hands around his ears, trying to block her words. "Yes, she does! We bond through our shared life force! My Rivka and I are tight like sex addict and his women! There is no misunderstanding! She thinks I am boss most worthy!"

Could he be more deluded? She'd met Becca. The woman practically oozed unhappiness at being Satan's pet. "Satan, I can't take this anymore. You need to change, or I'm out of here." She saw the panic in his eyes and had to dig her fingernails into her palms to continue with her speech, hearing the members of her women's group chanting their mantra: *You must be true to yourself first and the man second.* She had to at least try it their way, because she was miserable trying to live with his morals. "Promise me you'll reform hell. That you won't abuse your Rivkas anymore, that you won't harvest any more souls."

He stared at her. "This is important to you?"

"Very."

He spun around and marched out into the bedroom and

began to pace, fiddling with his new watch and muttering to himself. As she watched, his golden aura slowly became visible, shimmering around his body in a beautiful display. She shaded her eyes, wondering why it was showing now. She'd only seen it once before, when he'd *intentionally* revealed it to her.

He came to a stop in front of her, then dropped to his bare knees, thunking to the tile, a deep rose pink mixing with the gold in his aura. "Iris Bennett, matchless beauty to whom I have devoted all my fantasies, I will be the man you yearn for. I hereby take a leave of absence from hell. I will harvest no souls and order none to be harvested." His eyes were wide, fixated on Iris like she was his reason for living, and pink began to fill his aura.

Iris felt something swell deep in her heart, and she touched his face. "You will do all this for me? Release all the souls in hell, too?" That was what her new friend Rosemarie had told her to ask for at the end of the last women's support group, after hearing how upset Iris was with Satan's nefarious activities. They both had felt that if Iris could use her relationship with Satan to help people, then she might be able to live with the other hellish things he did.

A muddy gray seeped into Satan's aura, dimming the colors. "Release the souls?" he echoed, his voice hollow with disbelief. "But they are my minions. Without my souls to rule, I cease to be the virile and dominating man who makes your body hot and throbbing. It is who I am." His aura grew darker, and some black came into it, and his eyes became bleak. "I cannot do that. Please do not make this a condition of your love. I would beg, but that is unmanly, and I am never unmanly."

Iris bit her lower lip, realizing she'd asked too much. She could not take away the essence of what made Satan who he was. But he seemed to want to change for her. Was there a chance she could reform him and save his soul, little by little? She wanted to try, and she thought of Rosemarie's backup suggestion. "You're right. I can't ask you to do that." She idly flicked his hair with her fingers. "Okay, how about this? For every time we have sex, you have to release one soul. You have billions and billions of souls. I get to pick who you release."

"Done!" Satan leapt to his feet. "It is done! I am your stallion! Ride me along the beach until there is no more sand!"

Iris laughed as he swept her up in his arms, wrapping her arms around his delicious shoulders, filled with hope for their future. "I think I can live with that."

And then he tossed her on the bed, and she opened her arms to welcome him, giggling at the thought of how the world was going to change when the leader of hell became a new man.

"Dani?" It was already noon on Thursday when Nick flung open the door to Dani's condo. She hadn't answered the door, making him glad he'd insisted on keeping a set of keys when he'd bought it for her. He'd tried to call her repeatedly since she hung up on him, but her phone had kept going to voicemail.

And he was getting worried.

The instant he stepped inside the apartment, he felt cold. Bleak. "Dani!"

The apartment was ominously silent and heavy, and he knew Dani wasn't there. The place was devoid of all emotions. Empty. Something else was there, though. Something he didn't like. Something that made him feel like his bones had been plunged into freezing water for days. But what?

He whipped a gun out of his shoulder rig, then strode down the hall toward her bedroom, adrenaline racing as he scanned her condo for any sign of threat. He yanked open her door and stepped into her room, gun up, then froze at the sight of a transparent black dome that nearly filled the space.

His chest clamped when he saw Dani inside it, lying on her back on her bed, motionless. She was wearing jeans and a sweatshirt. Her hair was limp, and for the first time since she'd turned twelve, she wasn't wearing any makeup. She looked young, and her skin was pale.

And she wasn't emanating any emotions.

It was as if she were dead.

Jesus. "Dani!" He roared her name and charged, slamming his shoulder into the bubble. He hit it, and it flung him back, slamming him through her wall and into the hallway. "What the hell?" He shook off the ringing in his head and stood up, ignoring the plaster hanging from his clothes as he crunched over the wall remnants littering the hardwood floor and stepped through the hole and back into the room.

For a long moment, he forced himself to simply stand there and listen. Look. Assess. He reached out with his senses, trying to detect any living force coming from her room.

But all he felt was cold. No emotions of any sort. Simply emptiness.

After a few minutes of coming up with nothing, he nudged the bubble with the muzzle of his gun. The bubble sprang back softly. He pressed harder, and the bubble rebounded with more force. Then he slammed his fist into it, and the bubble flung him back against the desk.

What the hell was it? He jumped to his feet with a scowl and reapproached the bubble. He laid his bare palm against it and once again reached out with his senses.

It was cold, silent, and left him feeling empty and dark.

And it wasn't letting him in to get his sister.

Cursing, he peered at Dani again, this time noticing that her chest was still rising and falling slightly with her breath. "Oh, God, squirt," he whispered. "You're alive. Good girl." He closed his eyes for a moment to tamp down on the sudden tightness in his chest, then opened them, trying to focus. Trying to figure out a plan. "Dani? Can you hear me?"

No response.

He tried again for a few minutes but got nowhere.

Dani was out.

Grinding his teeth restlessly, he walked around the bubble, testing it for weakness, his mind racing. Every time he touched it, the dome tugged at his warmth, at the pulsing light within him that kept him alive. "Dani! Get up!"

He wound up at the doorway again and opened his senses, trying to get a bead on Dani's emotions. But all he could feel was a soul-sucking emptiness that made him want to drop to his knees and bawl like a ninny.

It felt like death.

It felt like evil.

What it felt like was *hell*.

He stood for a minute longer while he contemplated, then he holstered his gun, spun on his heels, and sprinted for the door.

Five

Becca's fake belly button ring was in danger of falling out, and the glitter she'd put on her breasts was itching. She'd worn the sluttiest outfit she could find, and the lascivious stares from some of the skankier occupants of Club Axe told her she'd chosen well. A scum would no doubt be hitting on her before too long.

First lesson for Paige had been that Rivkas only harvested souls who deserved it.

When Becca'd had to pry Paige off a nun outside St. Mary's Cathedral on their way to Club Axe, she'd realized that the lesson hadn't quite sunk in.

She caught one guy eying her chest with a particularly lecherous look. Excellent. She pulled her shoulders back, fluffed her breasts, and ran her hand up her thigh as seductively as she could, trying to make it look like she actually meant it.

He was just setting his drink on the counter to move toward her when a bundle of sunshine danced across her vision. "Okay, so I got your drink, boss," Paige announced, bounding up to Becca, her breasts nearly falling out of her too-small bustier. "Can I take someone's soul *now*? Ooo...you found a victim?" She spun around. "Oh, that guy at the bar, right? The blond guy who looks like he's humping the stool while he stares at you? Wow. So that's what humping looks like, huh?"

Becca frowned at the question in Paige's voice and caught the girl's wrist just as she began heading across the room toward the scum. "Hang on a sec, apprentice."

"What's up, boss?" Paige stared at her expectantly, waiting for orders.

"Are you a virgin?"

Paige threw up her hands. "Well, totally! I mean, I've only been alive for like three weeks and I had to learn all this stuff about humans so I could blend in and stuff and then I had to learn the history of Satan and some basic Rivka stuff, like how to get around hell without falling into an acid pit. It wasn't like we had time for the sex part, you know?"

Satan saddled her with a *virgin*? Becca became suddenly aware of the heavy odor of sex in the air, of the couples in the upstairs rooms grunting, of the gyrating threesome on the dance floor in front of them. She looked at the slut outfit Paige was wearing and felt like an irresponsible mom. She shrugged out of her thigh-length leather jacket and held it up. "Put this on."

"Your leather jacket?" Paige set the drinks on a nearby table, totally oblivious to the snarl from one of the women already parked there, and reverently took the coat, pressing it up to her nose to breathe in the scent. "I can't believe I'm holding Becca Gibbs's soul-harvesting coat."

At the excited gleam in Paige's eyes, Becca didn't have the heart to tell her that it was actually just a regular coat because the dragon had absconded with her soul-harvesting coat. "Yeah, I've brought down entire countries in that thing. Be careful with it. It's loaded."

"Ooo..." Paige carefully put her hand in the pocket as she slid it on. "I can feel all the souls in the leather, screaming for release."

Becca turned away to stifle her grin, then saw the scum from the bar heading toward them. She moved next to Paige and lowered her voice. "Okay, so he's coming over here—"

"Do I get to have sex with him?"

"You don't have to have sex in order to harvest a soul."

"Really?" Paige frowned. "My teacher said Satan says you do. Why would she lie?"

"Okay, fine, the intimacy of sex *can* help you access someone's innermost sanctum, but you won't be harvesting any souls until you're strong enough to do it without sex. Got it?"

Paige folded her arms over her chest. "I want to harvest souls now. I'll have sex. I don't mind."

"You're not old enough to have sex."

"Since when?" Paige gave her a skeptical look. "How old do you have to be?"

"Older than three weeks." She grabbed Paige's chin and pointed her back toward the approaching lecher. "When he gets close, hold your hand out over his torso. If your fingers tingle, he's ripe for harvesting."

"Can I harvest him even if they don't tingle?"

"No. I told you, we only harvest souls that deserve it."

"Bo-ring..." Her voice trailed off as the guy leered at them and let his gaze drift over their bodies as he neared. "Ooo...look at *him*..."

Becca's stomach crawled, but she saw Paige begin to glow with excitement. "Paige—"

"He is so HOT," Paige whispered. "I can practically hear his soul calling my name..."

The man came to a stop in front of them, staring right at Paige's cleavage. "Want to go to a motel?"

"Yes!" Paige flung herself on him and wrapped her legs around his waist, slamming her mouth onto his before Becca could reach out to stop her.

Becca glared at him and let her eyes flash red, letting a low growl roll off her tongue. He immediately paled, dropped Paige with a crash, and bolted for the door. Knocked over two women and a waitress on his way.

Becca grinned, suddenly feeling much better.

"Let's go get him!" Paige jumped to her feet and was already shoving past Becca.

Becca just managed to grab the tail of the coat and hauled the girl to a stop. "Chill out, girl! We're not going to chase him down." No way was she going to have Paige harvest a lecher's soul. She'd have to wait for a drug addict. Or maybe a carjacker. Yeah, that would work. Or an embezzler. Even better. "You're way too excitable. Where's your strategic thinking?"

Paige was instantly contrite. "Don't kill me. I'll get better, I swear. Next time, I'll—"

Becca slapped her hand over Paige's mouth as a chill shot up Becca's spine. *He was here.*

She shoved Paige aside and spun toward the room, keeping the wall at their backs.

"Boss—"

"Quiet." She scanned the room. It was dark. So many bodies. So many scents. But she could definitely sense the man who'd nearly killed her two weeks ago when she'd tried to harvest his black soul. He'd convinced her he was human until the last instant, and her idiocy had almost gotten her killed. She'd been searching for him for the last two weeks, and now he was at the club. Watching her. If she could find him, persuade him to tell her who'd hired him, and then kill them both, she'd feel so much better about the fact she was still tied to Satan and would have no future if this assassin succeeded in taking her out.

She could feel him. But where?

"Omigod." Paige clutched her arm. "You see someone. What? Who?"

"Go to the bar and wait for me there." She had to get the kid away from the danger. Now.

"Right. I'm gone." Paige sprinted away, dodging entwined couples and groping hands as she headed toward the bar and safety.

Becca found him on her second pass.

He was leaning against the other end of the bar, wearing faded jeans, well-worn hiking boots, a dark T-shirt, and a leather jacket that looked like it had been through a few battles. His face was angular and sharp, his whiskers too long to be called a five-clock shadow but too short to be called a beard. His eyes were hooded under the rim of a black baseball cap, but his fingers rested loosely around a martini glass. Tan hands, leading into forearms that were strong and sinewy, arms that had spent time working outdoors at something far more strenuous than golf or sailing.

He gave her a deliberate nod that was so stereotypically manly-man that she wanted to shoot him with a fireball just to make him take her seriously. But if she killed him first, she wouldn't find out who'd hired him.

Patience was sometimes a bitch.

Mr. Rugged He-Man shoved back his bar stool, stood up, and headed toward her, and her belly actually coiled in anticipation of his approach. He wasn't looking at her breasts like all the other lechers in the place were, but he brimmed with sexual potency that made her blood race.

She watched him approach and suddenly realized she'd been wrong. He *wasn't* the man who'd stabbed her in the side two weeks ago. This guy was quite a bit taller than her original assailant. Close to six five, with shoulders that would knock down a brick wall.

But he had the same aura. Same energy. Whatever the first man had been, this guy was the same. But this guy was deadlier. She could tell just by the way the air parted in front of him. He was different. He was *more*.

He stopped in front of her and stared down at her, and she wanted to lean into the wall of energy he carried. Sex, but more than sex. Passion. Heat. Fire. Rage. Joy. Love. Grief. Violence. All of it twisted up into one pulsating web of heated emotion. Every emotion she had to deny about herself in order to stay sane.

I want him.

She blinked in surprise at the thought, then realized it was completely true. But she didn't want him just as a man. She wanted him for all the rumbling emotions brewing inside him. She wanted to wrap herself around his boiling inner core and see what it was like to be alive like that.

Whoa, girl. If she touched him like that and then had to return to her own delightful life of being bitter, cynical, and alone, that would seriously screw her up. Paige might have been born without a shred of self-preservation instincts, but Becca had them.

Which meant this bubbling cauldron of maleness was going home alone tonight.

Or without her, at least.

And she was perfectly okay with that. Really.

Six

"Becca Gibbs?" Nick felt a sense of satisfaction when the Rivka blinked in surprise at hearing her name. He knew enough about her to realize he had to keep her off-balance to have any chance with her. She was tough, smart, and savvy... and drop-dead gorgeous. All the rumors about her focused on how she could wipe out entire populations with the flick of her finger. Obviously, people were too caught up in her destructive side to notice that she was a woman.

He'd noticed.

The instant he'd seen her from across the bar, the force of his attraction to her had hit him so hard that his gut still ached, along with other parts of his body. Maybe it was because he knew what a badass she was. Maybe it was the curve of her bare shoulder. Or the twinkle of the thin gold chain around her neck, so feminine and delicate. Or maybe it was the look of total "I'll kick your ass if you mess with me" that she'd given him.

Didn't matter.

He was here on business.

"Who are you?" She set her hands on her hips and met

his gaze. Her tone commanded a response, just like her reputation. All business, no pleasure.

"I'm Nick Rawlings."

She pursed her lips, no doubt searching her memories for his name. "How do you know me?"

He grinned at the faint flash of red in her eyes. "No one's going to believe you're human if you let your eyes go red and hellish like that."

She recovered in less than a second, blinking twice to clear her eyes. Without the red glow, they were green and lovely. Far more feminine than he would have expected from a woman who tortured innocents for pleasure and demasculated grown men just to hear them scream. Her light eyes made a striking contrast to her short dark hair, tousled on top of her head as if she'd just rolled out of bed after a night of lovemaking.

"Stop looking at me like that," she ordered.

He dragged his gaze off her hair and back down to her face. *Get it together, Nick. You're here to work.* "How am I looking at you?"

"Like you want to eat me."

Oh, like *that*. Crap. She'd killed men for far less, and he needed her on his side, not trying to put a fireball through him. "Sorry. Didn't realize I was."

"What do you want?" she asked.

He fed her the line he'd prepared before he'd met her. "I'm looking for a badass bitch from hell, and I hear you've got the goods."

She broke into a smile that had him reeling. Gone was the hard edge, replaced by a flicker of amusement and appreciation. "That's the best pickup line I've ever heard," she said. "I'm always a sucker for a guy who doesn't mind my day job. Your place or mine?"

Heat plunged into the southern parts of his body. "You want to have *sex*?"

She stared at him, as if she could feel his arousal. "*You* do." It was a statement, not a question. "I was kidding..." Her voice trailed off as she took a step backward, away from the heat he knew he was sending out, even as she lifted her chin and drew her shoulders back in a show of defiance. "What *are* you?"

"I need a favor." He watched her throat bob as she swallowed, and he opened his senses to try to get a read on how she was reacting to his request. Her emotions were so tightly strung that he couldn't sense any of them. He'd never met anyone who could shield her emotions against him. Not to this extent. Damned infuriating. Was it a Rivka trait, or just her?

Her hand went to her neck, obscuring his view of the soft skin, and her jaw tightened. "I don't do favors. Everything comes with a price. Boss's orders." Her eyes flickered with a tinge of regret that he knew had to be entirely her own, not Satan's.

He couldn't help but grin with relief. He'd been hoping the rumors of her independence had been true, that she was capable of acting for herself instead of only on Satan's behalf. "I need you to come check something out and tell me what it is."

Both her eyebrows went up. "Now, see, *that's* a bad pickup line."

He scowled. "It wasn't a line. I need your help."

"Ah." Her eyes narrowed as she assessed him. "Why me?"

Someone bumped into him, and he took a step closer to Becca to get out of the way. "Because I've got a situation and I think it has to do with hell. You're the resident expert, and the rumors are that you also manage to do what you want. I need your expertise, and your independence. This has to be kept separate from Satan."

A faint smile curved her lips. "Ah, yes, those rumors. You're right. I'm completely independent from Satan and he has no control over me whatsoever. It's such a bore to be me, since I rule the world."

He scowled at her cavalier attitude. "I'm serious. You in? I'll make it worthwhile."

She eyed him, and he could see the flare of interest in her gaze, but she shook her head. "No. I'm really busy right now. New apprentice, trying to harvest souls who can dance, keeping up with the day job, et cetera, et cetera. I'm quite the busy girl."

He ground his teeth in frustration at her careless dismissal. "I'm rich. I can pay you."

"I don't want money. I want to know what you are."

"I'm an elf."

She laughed, a charming sound that was out of character with her hard reputation. "Yeah, and I'm an angel. Nice to meet you, Mr. Elf."

He caught Becca's arm, his finger tight around her biceps. The instant he touched her bare skin, he caught a flicker of her emotions. Cold, empty, a void where her emotions should be. But deep inside, he caught the hint of something hotter. A faint flame trying to survive in the vast wasteland she kept wrapped around herself. "You don't understand, Becca." His voice was getting low, strained, as he tried to keep his own emotions under control. "This isn't optional. I need your help. Now."

Something dangerous flickered in her eyes, and he felt her muscles tense under his grip. "Back off. I don't respond well when people try to pressure me."

"Yeah, well, get over it." He let his own anger answer hers, and he felt her absorb his rage. She actually leaned into him, drawing his simmering fury into her own body and channeling it into herself. So he moved into her space, and she didn't back away, until their bodies were almost touching, and he could feel the air between them heating up. Literally.

Her eyes flared a soft red, almost amber. "I like your energy," she said. "Very dark. Heated."

He growled and grabbed her around the waist, releasing all his anger and hitting her hard with it. Let her feel his commitment to doing anything necessary to save his sister.

But her hands wrapped around his biceps, her grip firm and decisive. "There's no way you're going to intimidate me. It's not my style." She met his gaze, and her voice became throaty. "You don't scare me, Nick Rawlings. Not at all."

"That's a mistake, Rivka." Desperation rumbled in his chest, and he pulled her hard against him, palming her around the waist with his hands, skin to skin for maximum conduction. "I fight dirty." He slammed her with his energy, and her eyes widened and she sucked in her breath.

Then a perky young blond with blue eyes and a tiny little nose popped up over Becca's right shoulder, her eyes wide as she peered at him.

She and Nick stared at each other for a second, then he cursed and dropped his hands from Becca, stepping back so he wouldn't scare the girl.

Becca frowned and glanced over her shoulder to see what he was looking at. She made a noise of exasperation when she saw the girl. "Paige! What are you doing here? I told you to go away!" She moved closer to Paige, using her body to shield her from Nick.

"I would never hurt an innocent," he growled.

"Oh, I'm not an innocent." Paige reached around Becca and held out her hand. "I'm Becca's apprentice, Paige Darlington. I'm very evil and bad."

He shook her hand, probing her emotions. Love, passion, fire. And purity. The girl was untouched in all ways, more than anyone he'd met in years, even small children. No shields at all. "Yeah, I can tell you're evil."

"Really? Wow. That's great. How can you tell?"

Becca pulled their hands apart. "Paige, never touch someone if you don't know what he is. Too dangerous."

"Ooo…" Paige lowered her voice and leaned in close to Becca. "Are you going to have sex with him and then bind his soul? Can I help?" She winced and smacked her forehead. "Right. No sex. Just binding. It's hard to remember which rules aren't what I learned originally, but I'll totally get it."

Nick raised his brow. "No sex? Part of the job requirements?"

"Oh, no," Paige said. "It's just Becca. She's—"

Becca clapped her hand over Paige's mouth. "She's new."

"She reminds me of my little sister." Fresh anger and worry rose at the thought of Dani, motionless in her black bubble. He balled his fists against the emotions rolling inside him, but a nearby glass still exploded, sending fragments all over the three of them.

Becca jerked her head toward the glass, then snapped her gaze back to him, her face getting wary when she saw the expression in his eyes. She shoved Paige away from her at the look on his face. "Apprentice, wait for me out front."

"Again? I'm supposed to learn from you, and I haven't seen you bind a single soul yet."

Becca was pleased by Paige's first show of defiance, but now was not the time. Nick Rawlings looked like death and murder, and she had a feeling the glass was only a hint at the power that raged inside of him. "You're still a liability. Get over it, and get out."

Nick's face turned even darker as Paige stomped her foot. "Oh, come on! I'm having the best night of my life. I'm supposed to learn, and you're not teaching me!"

"This is the first time you've been away from hell. Of course it's the best night of your life." She didn't like the way the air around Nick was beginning to vibrate.

"Paige." Nick's voice was deep, barely restrained, and Paige squeaked as she looked at him. "Listen to your mentor. She's trying to keep you safe."

Paige stared at him for a long second, then he narrowed his eyes. She visibly flinched, then bolted across the dance floor. Becca bristled at the way he'd bossed around Paige, the way he'd controlled her, but now was not the time to address that. She needed to find out what he was. Now. Before he blew up the bar with so many innocents in it.

Nick watched Paige until she'd disappeared out the

door, then turned back to Becca. "She's going to get into trouble if you don't start keeping better control over her."

"Is that a threat?"

His eyes grew darker. "It's a helpful suggestion from personal experience."

She opened her palm down by her left hip and summoned up a fireball, and let him see it. "You touch her, you die. She's mine to kill."

"You're going to kill her?"

"If I decide it's prudent."

He narrowed his eyes again. "I can't let you do that."

"Yeah, well, considering how well I take orders from Satan, don't be surprised if I don't take them from you." She lifted the fireball, spinning it between her fingers, charging it until the flames turned from orange to deep blue, realizing suddenly that she was enjoying Nick Rawlings. He wasn't backing down from her, he wasn't afraid of her, but she could tell he respected her. Made her feel all warm and fuzzy inside, actually.

Nick grabbed her upper arms and pulled her so close she could feel the heat from his body against her breasts. "I won't let you kill an innocent girl, and you *will* help me save Dani."

"*Dani?* Who's Dani?" Someone near and dear, if the desperation cascading off him was any indication. The air around his body was starting to vibrate and curve, like the heat off a hot sidewalk on a summer day. She could feel it pushing against her body... *Whoa.* She jerked her head back so she could look at him more carefully. Was it possible? But Markku were extinct. Wiped out. Kaput. But... she passed her hand over his chest, feeling the tightly strung air clinging to him. It felt dense and hot, the way she'd heard Markku described. No *way*. Possibilities whizzed through her mind, and sudden hope flared inside her. *Way.*

Nick's grip tightened, and she realized he could pluck her arms from her body and toss them on the dance floor in a heartbeat. She felt a vibration coming from him, the same kind she'd felt right before the glass had exploded, but this was exponentially stronger. Dangerous. "Get a grip, Nick," she said quietly. "There are innocents here."

He shook his head. "Not until she's safe." His voice was desperate, his eyes so angry and helpless. "Not until I find who did this to her and how to get her free, and you're going to help me—"

A beer stein exploded to her left, and she heard a girl shriek.

"Nick!" A hot wall of energy slammed into her, and the mirror on the wall behind them shattered. Becca ducked as micro-shards of glass flew at her, plunging into her skin like white-hot little needles. "Dammit, Nick! There are innocents here!" She grabbed his arm and yanked him through the floor with her, dissolving them both into an inky black pool.

Seven

Becca and Nick popped up through the ground of an abandoned alley behind the club, and the instant they emerged, a Dumpster exploded, sending the contents cascading through the air. "Nick! Get it together already."

His eyes were black, heat was sizzling into the air around his body, and he grabbed Becca's shoulders. "You have to help me save Dani." His voice was harsh and strained, and a second Dumpster flew up into the air behind him and slammed into the side of the brick building.

"You need to chill out, hell boy." She whipped up an orange fireball, laced it with gold threads, then slammed it into his chest.

Nick groaned and dropped to his knees, clutching his chest, his breath wheezing. *"Jesus."*

Gold had taken him down. Hot damn! She'd been right! He was Markku!

Everyone knew the Markku had once been Satan's personal minions, and then had broken free, but no one knew how because Satan had covered up all the details.

But if Nick was Markku, then he might know...and maybe what the Markku had done to break their ties to

Satan would help her get free. A shiver ran through her, and she had to clasp her hands behind her back to keep from tackling him and demanding he tell all. *Be strategic, Becca.*

The Dumpster dropped to the ground behind him with a thump, and pieces of trash began to drift down around them, littering the alley with rotting food, old newspapers, and some unidentifiable things. Becca flicked a moldy blueberry muffin off her shoulder. "Better?"

He sat up and leaned back against the dumpster. "Yeah. Thanks."

"Any time." She squatted in front him and pulled aside the charred threads of his shirt. His chest was well muscled and broad, and the fireball had left a blistered red circle. She brushed a hand over his dark chest hair, pausing to finger the burnt skin there.

"What'd you hit me with?"

"Fireball."

He let his head fall back against the Dumpster with a clunk and closed his eyes. "No way was that a fireball. Fireballs can't hurt me."

"I put some gold in it. Rivkas can do that."

His eyes snapped open, and he searched her face. "What did you just say?"

She sat back on her heels, unable to keep the satisfaction of her discovery out of her voice. "You're Markku, right?"

"No." He closed his eyes again and changed the subject. "Thanks for getting me out of there. I haven't lost control like that in a long time."

"Scary sight." She pursed her lips, then laid her hand over his chest so she could draw her golden fire back into her own body. His skin was warm, humming with energy. Not that she could heal him, but she could keep further damage from occurring by taking back her fire. Gold was bad news for Markku, and she'd probably put a little too much in there. As she drew the gold out, however, she could feel the thrum of his emotions, his passion, his boiling energies. She hadn't realized Markku were like that. "I thought Markku were extinct."

He winced at her touch, then opened his eyes, and she noticed they were an interesting shade of green. A brilliant jade, with flecks of sea foam, and there was a hardness in them that said he wasn't going to discuss the Markku.

Fine. She'd work back to it. "Who's Dani?"

He studied her for a long moment, and she could practically see him considering how to convince her to help him. She felt an energy pulse where she had her palm on the bare skin of his chest, and a flicker of interest flared in his eyes.

Crud. What had he sensed from her?

"Have you ever loved anyone?" he asked.

Whoa. "Where'd that come from?" She pressed her lips together and concentrated on pulling the gold fire out of his body.

He caught her chin with his thumb and lifted her face so he could look at her. She met his gaze, doing her best to keep her face impassive, but she felt another pulse on her chin where he grasped her. She scowled and slammed up her shields even as he smiled with satisfaction and dropped his hand. "You have."

Yeah, and it was the worst decision I've ever made in my life. She put her hand back on his chest and continued to retrieve her fire, frowning as some of his essence came along with it and started warming her cells. She didn't need his hot emotions pouring into her. She was just fine as she was, and she forced herself to try to block them. "What's your point?"

"My sister got mixed up with some bad people, and now her life's in danger unless I can figure out how to help her." His anger and frustration pulsed at her through her apparently weak shields. "I can't let anything happen to her."

"So don't." She tugged his shirt back over his burned chest, realizing that her best option to keep his emotions away from her was to stop touching him. She was pretty good at suppressing her own emotions, but she'd never been around someone who could project his onto her, and she didn't like it. Made her want more. "You should get some cream for that or something."

He caught her wrist as she tried to pull away. "You know what I'm going through. I know you do. Help me save my sister's life."

She twisted free, and he let her go.

"Help me, Becca." There was a raw edge to his voice that caught her interest. He wasn't simply putting on an act. He really *was* desperate…and in a convenient twist of fate, so was she.

She sat back on her heels and studied him as an idea formed in her mind. "I'll help you if you help me."

He frowned. "You'd charge me for saving an innocent?"

"Many innocents die. It's part of the cycle of life," she intoned automatically. "It's the balance."

"I won't let my sister be part of that balance," he growled.

She looked at him, suddenly filled with sorrow for his pain, for the lessons he hadn't yet learned. He was like an innocent kid hidden inside a big, muscular, hard manshell. "We don't get to choose."

"I always choose."

"Well, Mr. He-man, aren't you the lucky one? Just think. Someone always in control of everything." Just the thought of it made her want to pop him with a fireball. Rubbing it in her face that he was Mr. In-Control-of-His-Life, when the only thing she had control over was… well…come to think of it, there really wasn't anything.

Which is why she needed to cut the apron strings and get a life.

Nick reached out and wrapped his fingers around her wrist, pulsing his anger, his rage through her…and underneath, she sensed such a raw and burning passion and love for his sister that it made her stumble. She yanked her hand free and stepped back, his emotions still whirling through her with an intensity she hadn't realized existed. God, was *this* what she was missing by being Satan's minion? This kind of love and emotional intensity? It was like all her senses had suddenly become aware in a way they never had been. Alive. Real. *I want that.*

"Becca…"

She shook her head and took another step back, trying to regain control, trying to cleanse her body of all that was Nick. Trying to forget what she'd just felt. *You can't have it, so you have to let it go.* But God, she wanted it.

Nick Rawlings might be her key to getting free of Satan, but he was too much for her. His passion and radiating emotions cracked through the walls she'd worked so hard to erect to protect herself. She couldn't afford to feel what he felt, not with her life the way it was, not with the things she had to do every day for Satan.

She took a deep breath. The guy who'd tried to kill her had the same aura as Nick, so he must have been Markku. She hadn't sensed any emotions from him, so he was different from Nick in that way. Safer. She'd find him and torture him into telling her all that he knew. Much better plan.

She drew her shoulders back as Nick pulled himself to his feet, leaning heavily against the Dumpster.

"See you around, Nick Rawlings." Then she started to dissolve.

"The people who took my sister want me to kill Satan to save her."

She re-formed instantly at his words, clenching her fists in aggravation. "Seriously?" That would completely piss her off if Satan died, killing her before she was able to get free of him. "Are you going to accept the assignment? Just a hypothetical question designed to help me decide if I need to kill you."

His eyes glistened with the knowledge that he'd finally hooked her. "If it's my only option, yeah."

She narrowed her eyes at his admission. Either he was a total idiot for telling her that, or he was so arrogant about his ability to kill her that he didn't mind telling her. Or maybe there was something that she was missing. "Do you think I won't kill you? I'm sure a gold fireball in the right eye would take care of business quite nicely, don't you think?"

He shrugged and propped himself up on the Dumpster, still looking a little wobbly. Now that he'd figured out how to get to her, he looked like a man who had all the time in the world to reel her in. Gone was his desperation, replaced by a quiet confidence that was actually quite appealing. "I'm not worried. You're too smart to kill me."

She grinned. "Compliments like that will get you a quick death instead of a long, drawn-out torture, but you'll still end up dead. I'm not quite the pushover I seem, you know."

He shrugged off her threat. "Killing me accomplishes nothing, because if I don't kill Satan, the people manipulating me will keep trying until they get it done. So either way, Satan will end up dead, and then you and all the other Rivkas go 'poof.' And if you kill me, you lose the inside track, since I know details about my sister that you don't. We need each other."

Damn the man for being so logical.

"Killing Satan would seriously screw up the balance of all our worlds, so I'm trying to avoid it, and I need your help to do so. I figure we could team up to find the person who wants Satan dead and kill them first. Then you get to stay alive, and I get my sister back, and the bad guy dies. Everyone wins, we drink champagne, have a party, and then call it a day."

She cocked her head. "So, why do you need *me?* You seem like quite the capable guy."

"I need a Rivka because they know all about hell, but only one who can make decisions without Satan's permission can help me, because I seriously doubt Satan would allow you to waste your time saving an innocent. You're the only Rivka who has the ability to act independently." He watched her. "So... you in?"

She kicked a rusted can out of her way while she contemplated, then turned to face him. "I'm perfectly capable of killing you and then tracking down this annoying little troublemaker on my own, but you have something I want, so I'll make a deal."

His face got serious. "My soul?"

She reached out and laid her hand on his belly... erm...rock-hard washboard stomach...and felt no tingle indicating he was black-hearted scum who needed a good ass-whupping by Satan.

She paused, realizing she hadn't touched a man in a nonviolent way since before electricity was invented. He wasn't throwing his emotions at her through their contact, giving her the chance to simply feel the warmth of his skin.

It felt nice.

She cleared her throat and peeled her hand off his body. "You're too pure to be harvested." She hooked her thumbs on the waistband of her skirt and looked at him. "I want to know all the details about how the Markku got free."

"My grandpa's generation broke free, not me."

"But I'm sure you know the story. Or at the very least, the answer's inside you." She walked up to him and laid her hands on his chest, dropping her shields completely. Hot, passionate energies tumbled out of him and flooded her body, but she forced herself to ignore them, as she searched for what she knew had to be there.

And then she found it: deep inside him she could feel the cold stillness that she carried every day. Satan's life force lived on inside his being. He was truly Markku.

She dropped her hands and sighed with relief as the

emotional bombardment stopped. "You're definitely from hell, but now you're free. I want to know how it all happened. Your family history and your body have stories to tell. Lessons I can learn. I want access to all of it."

Hope gleamed in his eyes. "And you'll help me with my sister?"

"First you give me the information."

He shook his head. "You're a Rivka. Once you get what you want, you'll split before I get any help from you."

She set her hands on her hips and glared at him. "Just because I'm from hell, that automatically means my word can't be trusted?"

"Well, when you say it like that ... yes."

He had a point. Satan tried to make her break her promises as much as possible, and if he found out about this one, it would be the same. "Well, you're also from hell, so how can I trust you not to bail as soon as your sister is free from whatever oh-so-scary thing has her in its scaly tentacles?"

"Because you have Underworld resources at your disposal and you'd have no trouble finding me if I tried to hide from you."

"Um ... yeah, true." It wasn't, actually. Hell wasn't all that up-to-date in its ability to track every single human and Otherworld being on the planet, but it was a rumor Satan liked to foster because it kept people from thinking they could sell their soul and then hide when he came to collect it. Satan did have tracking devices that he saved for high-profile souls that were flight risks, but they were all in use right now. If O. J. Simpson would just hurry up and die ...

"So, it's a deal?" he pressed.

"Sure. Deal."

He grinned, and she felt the relief cascading off him. It was such a fresh, sunny sensation that she wanted to lean into him and let it wash over her body. How cool would it be to embrace her emotions like that?

His hands went around her upper arms, and she suddenly realized she actually *had* been leaning into him and he'd grabbed her to stop her from actually falling onto his chest. She started to jerk back, when she realized that his grip on her arms was doing all sorts of funky things to her body. Heat. Light. Simmering energies. All of it pulsating where he was gripping her. It was such a rush. Felt so good...

"Are you all right?" His voice was low and a little bit husky.

Um, hello? *What are you doing?* She immediately pulled back. "Yeah, I was just checking to see that you had the goods. Markku ones, I mean."

"Yeah, that's what it felt like." He was sporting the smug look that all men wore when they realized a woman had the hots for them, and it instantly made her want to pop him with a fireball.

But she *was* a little woozy from his playing emotional footsie with her. God, what was wrong with her? Men didn't affect her like this.

No, but apparently men like Nick Rawlings did.

She pointed at him. "This deal is business only. Got it?"

"Oh, I *got* it."

And what, exactly, did he mean by *that*? "Nick—"

There was a sudden explosion of gold bubbles, and she snapped her mouth shut as Satan burst out of the

Dumpster, flew into the air, and landed with a graceful swish between her and Nick. He was wearing black satin pants, a white silk shirt, and a thick gold chain with diamonds in it. He threw his hands onto his hips and puffed out his chest. "Rivka! We need to talk."

Oh, shit.

Eight

Nick stepped back when the leader of hell appeared in front of him. When the Markku had broken free of hell with their well-organized mutiny, Satan hadn't exactly been happy with them, and he had used his Rivkas to wipe out any that he discovered over the years. And now, here Nick was, stuck in an alley with Satan.

Which would have been great if he was actually planning to kill Satan to save his sister, but until he was convinced that his sister really would be released upon the death of Satan, he wasn't going to do it. Not only was he averse to being manipulated, but he was well aware that killing Satan would create a power void with major implications for all living and Afterlife beings. Bad implications. Especially since Satan Jr. would probably try to take over hell, and he was pure evil in a way that Satan wasn't. As bad as Satan was, the world was better off with him alive.

And then there was that whole thing that killing Satan would also kill Becca...not that Nick was concerned about the fate of any evil, soul-sucking Rivka.

Really. He wasn't.

Satan didn't turn around, however. He kept his attention focused on Becca. "Rivka. I have big love problem."

Becca let her breath out in apparent relief at the question. "Problem with the ex-Guardian?"

Satan sighed and hopped up to sit on the Dumpster, swinging his Italian-leather-clad feet like an agitated little boy. "Yes, I promise her much and I cannot live with my promise. So I shall break promise and not tell her, no?"

She raised her brows. "Isn't that what you always do?"

"Yes, yes, I am very proud of my ability to break promises." He sighed heavily. "As woman, would you continue to enjoy my airplane rides of love if you know I lie and break promise?"

She shifted and glanced at Nick, as if she were embarrassed to be talking about anything personal. "Um, listen, I don't have a whole lot of experience with the dating thing, but I have to think that Iris will be a little pissed."

How could she not have dating experience? She was gorgeous and spunky, and she had so much attitude that he could spend years trying to figure her out. Then again, having her boss be Satan might be a bit intimidating to some guys, he supposed.

"Yes, yes, but she ask me to not be who I am. Is that love?" Satan frowned and tapped his heels against the Dumpster, making it thud. "You would not ask me to change. You embrace my inner demon, no?"

Becca winced. "Satan, you can't judge any relationship based on you and me. You threaten and torture me, and I tell you what you want to hear in order to keep you somewhat sane."

"Yes, yes, it is lovely what we have, is it not?" He gave her a smile that actually looked genuine.

Wasn't that interesting? Based on what his pa had told him, Nick had always assumed Satan was just an evil, heartless leader of hell, but he was getting some hits of definite affection off Satan, directed toward Becca. He opened his senses and realized Satan was projecting all sorts of emotions, including confusion and fear.

Fear? Satan afraid? Of what?

"Satan," Becca said. "You need her. She needs you. It's just a little bit of work to get past the 'leader of hell/Guardian of all that's good' conflict. You guys can do it."

He frowned at her. "But I torture and pillage, and that is what makes women swoon for me. If I become wussy she-man, then no woman will want me." His scowl deepened, and he jumped off the Dumpster and stomped his foot. "Is that the plan of fair Iris? To de-masculate me so she has no competition?" A spiral of smoke began to float up from the top of his head. "I cannot allow her to nip my manly parts off with a pair of clippers! I must resist!" He stopped suddenly and sniffed the air, then whirled around to face Nick.

Uh-oh.

Satan pointed a glowing red finger at Nick. "You eavesdrop on my therapy session with my personal servant! No one is permitted to hear that Satan has feelings! You die, mortal!" And then a fireball shot out of his finger and slammed Nick in the chest.

Nick took the hit without moving.

Satan raised his brows and peered at him. "How are you not dead?"

Oh, hell. "I'm an elf," he lied.

"Elf? *Elf?*" Satan whirled toward Becca. "Elf do not die from fireball? Did I know this?"

She looked at Nick, and he could see her thinking. Was she going to give him away? She had no reason to protect him...depending on how badly she wanted to be free of Satan. He tensed his body, ready to fight if he had to. Finally, Becca said, "He's a mutant elf."

"Mutant? How interesting." Satan peered at him and flicked his ear. "No pointy ears either. Do you have any elf qualities at all?"

Um...he really had no idea what elf qualities were...

"Hey, he's a guy." Becca was suddenly between them. "Why don't you ask Nick for advice on how to date? I'm sure if you promised to cut out his tongue if he repeats the conversation, he'd be happy to keep it quiet."

Nick shot Becca a look at the tongue suggestion, and she gave him an innocent smile that made him snort.

"Man to man?" Satan rubbed his chin while he considered Nick. "I have never had a man-to-man discussion." He peered into Nick's face. "You are quite masculine and virile. Have you had many women?"

Nick glanced at Becca, who mouthed "a lot" at him. "Hundreds..." Becca jerked upward with her thumb. "...of thousands."

"Eh." Satan sounded unimpressed. "That is it? For a man as virile as you?" Satan flicked his fingers in disgust. "You are not worthy if that is all you have conquered."

Becca rolled her eyes and jerked her thumb upward again.

Nick looked at Satan. "Oh, you meant *ever*? I thought you meant this year. I'm just under a million for the year."

"Oh, this year?" Satan clapped a hand on Nick's shoulder. "All right, then, man to man, you are sexually not my equal, but at least you are manly enough that I do not have to cut off your manly regions for failure to appreciate them. So, what shall I do with fair Iris?"

Nick glanced at Becca, and she made a motion with her hands to answer him. God, talk about pressure. Love advice wasn't his thing, and to have to coach Satan on it? Crap. He shifted, trying to think about how he'd talk about sex and women with Jerome. "Is she good in bed?"

"It is making love!" Satan shouted, and he bopped Nick in the head with a fireball that had a faint tingle of gold, dropping Nick on his ass. "Do not denigrate the love act with my woman!"

Nick shook his head to clear it, his fists clenching with frustration. He was too strung out to be dealing with this kind of shit. He wasn't touchy-feely, he wasn't used to walking away from a potential battle, even to save his sister, and he was sick of this crap.

He pulled himself off the floor of the alley with a growl, dusted himself off, and marched back up to Satan and shoved him right back. "Listen, Satan, when men bond about women, they talk crassly, and they don't fireball each other when receiving advice." He shoved him again, and Satan took a surprised step back. "So, here's the deal. You want to keep Iris around, then give her what she wants. If you don't care, then don't. But don't lie to her. Women find out, and they get mad, and then you won't get laid for centuries. Got it?"

Satan stared back at him, and Nick became aware that he was up in Satan's grill, jammering about Satan's love life. He balled his fists and readied for the battle he knew would come. *Bring it on, big guy. Let's take care of this now.*

Then Satan broke into a delighted smile and yanked Nick into a big hug and thudded on his back with his fists. "You are what I need in my life! A man-friend who is not afraid to stand up to me! You are like my Rivka, but you are more! We will watch porn, drink beer, and be man-friends together." He straightened his shirt and turned to face Becca. "Most excellent work for finding me a man-friend, Rivka. As always, you are indispensable."

She grimaced. "Trust me, I'm not indispensable. There are so many other—"

Satan beamed at her. "The love of my loins says I must be nicer to you. So I gave compliment to satisfy you for next several hundred years until next one. Are you over-whelmed with adoration and awe for me now?"

"Yeah, sure..." She suddenly emanated so much emotional distress that Nick actually raised his hand to touch her shoulder in comfort before he realized what he was doing and dropped his hand.

But just as quickly, she replaced the distress with confidence as she got a sudden gleam in her eye. "Hang on. I want you to meet someone. Man-bond for a minute, okay?" She immediately vanished through the ground.

Becca dragged Paige up through the floor of the alley less than a minute later, and she grinned when Satan's eyes nearly popped out of his head. Then he shrieked with protest and slapped his hand over his eyes. "Take her away, Rivka! Iris will skewer my eyeballs if she learns I gawked at such beautiful breasts."

"Omigod. Satan." Paige's voice was breathless as she dropped to her knees in front of him. "You are my *idol.*"

He parted two fingers to peek at her. "I am quite magnificent, am I not?" Satan's gaze dipped to her breasts, and he made a noise of pain and covered his eyes again. "Rivka! Why are you torturing me when you know Iris does not permit this kind of gawking? Man-friend, this girl is a most bountiful supply of luscious femaleness, is she not?"

Nick scowled, his hands curling into fists. "She's too young for you."

"Young?" Satan peeked through his hands again, to where Paige was bent over, kissing his toes. "You think?"

"Touch her and I'll rip out your throat. She's a *kid.*"

Satan eyed Nick, raising a glowing finger toward him. "Man-friend. Do not overstep your bounds, or I shall be forced to kill you in most painful way."

Becca immediately stepped between them. "Satan, I would like you to meet my new apprentice. Paige Darlington is a Rivka in training, the one you assigned to me last night. The one you ordered to spy on me."

He dropped his hand to stare at Paige. "This is the one?"

"Yes."

"*Oh.*" He grabbed Paige's hair and tugged her to her feet, where she stood swaying as she gazed at him. "I do nice work, do I not?"

"Depends on your goals." Becca smiled innocently when he shot a sharp look at her. "I'm training her to be just like me, as you ordered."

"Excellent." Satan spun her around, inspecting her. "She is feisty? Disobedient?"

"No, she adores everything you do and takes commands like a well-trained dog."

"Ah, well, then you may as well kill her now." He released Paige, immediately dismissing her as Paige gave a squawk of dismay.

Dammit. Becca should have realized Satan wouldn't go for a Rivka who idolized him that much. He liked Becca because she gave him grief. She looked at Paige, who had tears of adoration and sadness streaming down her cheeks. Why the hell had he created an adoring Rivka if he didn't want one? "Paige. Toughen up."

Paige blinked at her. "What?"

"So, I go now to find Iris and apply my man-friend's advice." Satan turned to shake Nick's hand. "I be in touch. You answer my calls, or I skin you and make lampshade from your intestine, no?"

"You try to make a lampshade of my intestine and I'll kill you."

"Excellent. Good man. I like you." Gold bubbles began to float up around Satan, and Becca lunged for his arm.

"Wait! I need a list of people who want you dead."

He snorted. "Everyone wants me dead! I am Satan! Why do you bother me with such piddle?" His eyes flashed black. "Rivka, I order you to harvest me a love therapist soul. Dr. Phil. Yes, that is who I want. He is much expert. But do not tell Iris, or I find your dragon and impale her on a fence post so birds can use her as toilet, yes?"

Damn. "I'll get right on it, but I really need a list of people who'd want you dead. There seems to be a legitimate threat to your life and—"

"No threat to my life is legitimate. I am going to seduce my lady lover. I order you to not bother me until I am ready to be bothered." He brightened. "In fact, I order you never to interrupt me when I am with Iris. Satan must keep personal and business separate." He beamed at Nick. "Good man-plan, no?"

"Yeah, sure." Not worth disagreeing with Satan on that one, though privately, he was beginning to suspect that Becca was all that kept Satan from crashing and burning.

"Excellent." Satan clapped Nick on the shoulder, then shook his leg to dislodge Paige, who was now wrapped around it. The apprentice went flying and landed in a trash heap before Becca had time to catch her. "I bid you all farewell. May you have almost as many and as great orgasms as I am going to have." And then he was gone in a poof of golden bubbles.

The bubbles were still floating when Nick gave her a look. "Man-friend?"

Becca walked over to Paige. "I'm trying to help him build his independence from me. Teaching him that there are others in this world that can give good advice." Paige was blinking and shaking her head, as if to clear it. "You all right?"

Paige staggered to her feet and blew her nose in Becca's leather coat. "He wants me dead. Did you hear him? Why? What did I do wrong? All I wanted to do was make him proud of me." She plopped down on a trash can, in a saggy little lump. "I am so depressed."

Becca patted the kid awkwardly on the head. "You're a little too soft for him. You need to be bitchy and sarcastic."

"But how?" Paige raised her weepy eyes to Becca. "Whenever I see him or think of him, I'm overwhelmed by my love and adoration for him."

"He bred it into you. Now you have to get over it and develop some independence."

"Independence?" Paige pulled her shoulders back, her eyes losing the dazed gleam they'd had when Satan was present. "You mean, like give him attitude?"

"Exactly." She sighed as she eyed a dark stain on her leather jacket. "Think you can manage that?"

"Maybe..." Paige popped the end of lock of hair in her mouth to chew while she thought on it.

Nick grabbed Becca's arm and spun her toward him. "My ancestors gave their lives to get free of Satan, and you just put me back in his life."

She had? Dammit. She had. What a shitty thing to do to someone. "I'm sorry. I didn't think of that. Let's just go get your sister, okay?" She held out her hand. "Come on."

Anger still flowed off him, but he folded his hand around hers without another word. A burr of his heat and his life force slipped down her arm, making her want to... well, never mind. "Apprentice. Coming?"

Paige shook her head as if to clear it, then grabbed her arm. "When do I get to do this inky-black-melty thing myself?"

"When I'm sure I don't need to kill you. I can't have you melting right before I deliver the final blow."

Paige stuck out her lower lip in a pout, then Nick shook his head at Becca and parted his lips, no doubt to chastise her for scaring the apprentice, so she turned them all into mist before he could speak.

Nine

The instant Becca pulled Nick and Paige up through the floor of Dani's front hall, she was slammed with a howling emptiness that had her stumbling. Nick caught her before she pitched into the rack of coats hanging behind the door, his hands firm on her shoulders. "What's wrong?"

"Jet lag." She blinked hard and twisted free of him, trying to shake the dizziness making her head spin. A cold wind tore through her body, ripping into every cranny of her soul. She felt like she was standing in hell, stripped naked of all her defenses while the scorched aridness sucked whatever life she had left out of her body. "What's in this place?"

"It's freezing in here," Paige said, tugging Becca's coat tighter around her body. "Doesn't this place have heat?"

"It's not cold. It's...something else." Becca could tell her body was shutting down.

"Becca!" Nick's voice was distant.

"What's wrong with her?" Paige asked. "Boss, you okay? Want me to get Satan?"

"No." She stumbled again, and Nick grabbed her again. This time, she noticed a faint pulse of warmth where he held her shoulders, an abatement from the howling emptiness inside her. Instinctively, she turned toward him and burrowed into his body, sliding her hands under his shirt against his warm skin, and the barrenness eased ever so slightly. What the hell was going on?

Nick could feel the aching desolation trying to consume Becca, felt her trying to reach out to his heat, so he wrapped his arms around her, pulled her tight, nestling his face in the curve of her bare neck. He released all control of his emotions and sent them cascading into her; his fear for Dani's safety, his frustration at not knowing how to save her, his love for his family, his raging hatred for the Council for taking away his pa. "Do you feel that?"

"Yes," she whispered against his chest, pressing her face harder against him. "It's working."

He pulled her against him so the length of their bodies were crushed together and sent his energy through every inch of his skin, through his clothes and hers. He felt the chasm hesitate and then begin to retreat, and he pressed harder, chasing it with all that was bubbling inside him, all that was who he was. And then the void was contained, held at bay by the fiery hot wall he'd created inside her. And that's when he felt it. An answering heat, somewhere deep inside her, behind the vortex of emptiness that swirled through her. A heat that was hers, fighting to stay alive. "Becca? You doing all right?"

She nodded, and he felt her breasts swell against his chest as she took a deep breath. "Yeah." She lifted her head to look at him, not relinquishing her tight grip on his waist. "What was that about?"

"I think it's because of what's in Dani's room." He looked down at her, watched the strength and determination reassemble in her gaze. "It makes me feel bleak, but it got you even worse."

"I feel bleak, too," Paige announced. "I'm freezing, actually."

Becca turned her head to look at her hovering apprentice, who appeared worried as she hugged her arms around her upper body. "Go find a thermostat and crank up the heat."

"Good call. I'm on it." Paige darted around the corner, leaving them alone.

Becca slowly peeled her arms away from Nick, but the instant she let go of him, he saw her face tighten under the renewed assault, and he grabbed her and hauled her against him again. "Came back?"

"Yeah." She pressed her face into his chest and emoted crankiness and irritation that he found interesting. He'd have thought she was all hardness and was above such human emotions. "I hate being dependent on anyone," she grouched. She kept a tight grip on his waist but eased her body away from him.

He watched her face for signs that the devastating blackness was regaining its hold in her soul. "Okay so far?"

"Yeah." She glanced around the room, still holding tight to him. "So, which way?"

"Down the hall. Second door on the right." He saw her look down the hall and then frown, no doubt trying to figure out how to get there without letting go of him. "I could carry you," he suggested.

She glared at him. "Why don't you just put your hand on the back of my neck and see if that works."

"I can do that." He slipped his hand around the back of

her neck, continuing to send his emotions into her through their touch. The cold void was still there, waiting for his energy to leave, but his touch was enough so far. He wondered what that void was like when it wasn't being fed by whatever was in Dani's room. How pervasive was it for her? And how much did it suck?

She started walking down the hall, and he fell in next to her, keeping a tight grip on her.

They reached the hole in Dani's wall, and he tensed as Becca stuck her head inside and then stepped through, dreading what he was going to find. He ducked in after her, and for an instant he thought the power had gone out.

Then he realized the dome was no longer transparent. It was almost opaque, and he could barely see the outline of his sister, still lying motionless on her bed. "Dani," he whispered, dropping his hand from Becca to press his palms against the bubble. He shoved against it, and it shoved back. "Dani!"

Becca felt Nick's anguish just before she was slammed with the sudden crash of emptiness at the loss of his touch. She immediately shoved her hand under his shirt to touch the bare skin of his back, anchoring her hand under the waistband of his jeans so it couldn't slip off.

Instantly, the barren chasm inside her quieted, chased away by Nick's essence, giving her life. He was heat and he was light and he was passion, and it was the most amazing feeling ever. His muscles flexed under her hand, and she remembered that not only was he alive with life force, but he was also a man. A man who made her feel alive.

"What is this thing?" he whispered, finally drawing her attention away from herself and to the room.

Becca cursed when she saw what was there.

His body tensed at her words and he spun around, nearly breaking her wrist as it twisted in the back of his jeans. She clenched her teeth as her hand fell free, but he remembered to grab her shoulders before the void could consume her again. "I really didn't like your response, did I?" he asked.

"She's not dead right now, Nick. She's just in a trance. That's the good news."

He didn't relax his hold. "And the bad?"

She looked over the dome again, inspecting it for authenticity. "Well, I'd need to check a few things out to be sure…"

"Tell me." His voice was low and rumbling again, and she had a feeling that walls were going to start collapsing from his energy if she didn't get him to ease down.

"It's from hell. That's why it affects me worse than you or Paige, because I'm basically made of hell and you two are more distantly affiliated right now." She eyed it, looking at the faint etchings in the surface that were so telling. "It's called a death blister. It's like a giant sac filled with the invisible pus of hell, and your sister's in the middle of it." When the mirror over the dresser exploded from Nick's vibrating rage, she decided maybe it was best to gloss over the graphic description. "See, it's a…" She decided not to call it a torture device. "…*toy* Satan made. He makes a vesicle, sets a timer, and then links it to someone's life force. Then, the only way to destroy it is to kill whoever's life force is supporting it. It's a handy way of getting someone to kill someone else for him."

The air around Nick continued to hum, and it wasn't a feel-good kind of vibration. "So, what's the timer for?"

He sort of shuddered, and ratcheted down his emotions. "How does it work?"

"Well..." She turned toward the dome, looking for what she knew had to be there. She found it just under the window. "See that little black spot?" She leaned back against him, as she began to get cold and her mind started to get a little blinky.

Nick put his arms around her and rested his chin on her head while he assessed the situation, and the void lessened slightly, though not as much as it had when he was intentionally pouring his emotions into her. "I see it. What is it?"

"It's an acid pit that serves as a conduit to hell." She couldn't believe how good it felt to be in his arms. To have his body wrapped around hers as he tried to protect her. She didn't need protection, adored her independence...but damn. This was some kind of addicting feeling. It was...incredible. She'd had no idea what she'd really been missing, but now...

"The acid pit is small," he said. "That's good, right?"

"It'll keep growing, filling the area around your sister until the spot she's on is an oasis in the middle of it. When the timer goes off, the last bit will be consumed, and she'll be on her way to hell in an acid pit."

He was quiet for a moment, and she nestled into his body, getting warmer by the minute as his worry about his sister continued to escalate.

"And if we kill the life force supporting the... bubble?"

She smiled at his word choice. Calling it a bubble instead of a pus blister from hell wasn't going to save his sister, but it was sort of cute that he'd tried it. "If we kill the life force it's linked to, Dani's home free." She laid her arms over his where they were wrapped around her waist, trying to suck in even more of his light. "Do you know when the timer's set for?"

"Sunday at midnight."

She wiggled her bottom against him, trying to get even closer, drinking the feeling of being alive. She could feel his worry, his love, his determination, and it made her feel almost giddy and light-headed. "So, that gives us almost four days to find out who it's linked to and who set it up."

"Satan didn't set it up?"

"He has a little machine that does this. Anyone with hell in their blood could use it. You or I could do it." She sighed and pushed harder against him, trying to nestle her bum into the curve of his body that seemed to be built for it.

If he felt this good holding her with all their clothes on, how intense would it be if there was full skin-to-skin contact? Or if he was inside her, making love to her, exposing her to her most vulnerable core?

Crap. Where had that thought come from? *Get a grip, Becca.* "I gave you info," she said briskly. "Time for a trade. Why do you have all these emotions if you're Markku? I've never heard of that trait." Where had that question come from? What did that have to do with getting herself free of Satan?

"I'm half healer. The touchy-feely side comes from my mother. It's a pain in the ass."

"Yeah, it seems like it would be." *Yeah, right.* Okay, time to focus on the more important questions, the ones that should actually matter to her. "Were the Markku supported by Satan's life force when they were in hell, or were they independent life forms?"

"Both. They were supported by Satan when they were in hell, but when they left hell, they were on their own. They stored up his life force for their forays out of hell, and had to return to be replenished before they depleted their stores." His hands tightened around her waist, and she caught the faint hint of lust coming from him. "So, can you tell who set it up?"

She reached back and grasped his butt, tugging his hips against her as she closed her eyes and let her head rest against his chest, nearly giggling at the tingling in her body. "If it really is linked to Satan's life force, then he obviously wouldn't have set it up. Even Satan's not that stupid." She sighed and dug her fingers into the hard curves of his butt, willing his energy into her body. "So, you support yourself now, right? You don't need to get a Satan hit every so often?" She giggled. "A Satan hit. He'd love that." Weird. She was having trouble articulating her words. Tongue felt a little clumsy.

"No Satan hits needed." He paused. "Are you getting drunk off my emotions?" There was a hint of masculine satisfaction in his voice, an awareness that a woman was nearly swooning because of his touch.

She tried to straighten up. But all she did was bump his chin and elicit a curse from him. "No, that would be dumb. I'm not dumb. I'm smart. Shut up and let me finish our plan." She relaxed against him again, letting the tingle grow into something else. A thrumming. A humming. No, a sizzling. Yes, she was starting to sizzle with life. And passion. Was this was it was like to be human? God, it was amazing . . . delicious . . . scrumptiously mouthwatering...Damn him for showing her what she was missing.

"Becca?"

"Shh. I'm concentrating."

"On what? Turning me on by rubbing your sexy little bottom against my crotch until I throw you down and rip your clothes off and offer to do anything you want?" His breath was hot against the side her neck. "Forget it, woman. I'm not backing off. I need your help with Dani, and you're not getting info from me until she's taken care of." He inhaled deeply. "You smell like roses. I'd have guessed smoke or ash. But it's flowers."

Becca froze at the husky tone in his voice. Oh, *God*. What was she doing? She shook her head and tried to clear it, yanking her hands off his butt. "You're the one trying to seduce me with all these emotions," she snapped. "Tone it down, big guy." The protest came out as more of a moan than she's intended. *Get yourself together, Becca.*

"You're the one sucking the emotions out of me. I don't know what talent you've got, but this little moment is all you," he growled, his fingers moving slowly along her waist as his lust began to trickle through her body. "Cut it out."

She caught her breath as a jolt of electricity sparked through her while his fingers brushed against her bare skin. She slapped her hands over his wrists, aware of the pounding of his heart against her back where she was still pressed against him. She could feel his lust and could sense that he was responding to her, not pushing her toward it. This *was* her fault. Who the hell knew that emotions were a turn-on for her? A turn-on that she apparently passed right back to Nick.

She peeled herself off him and stepped away, until their only contact was her fingers around his wrist. The buzzing eased off and her mind cleared. The familiar void blanketed her, only now it didn't feel comfortable. It felt not enough, which was exactly what she'd known would happen. "Sorry about that whole thing."

He nodded, his own eyes beginning to clear. "It was a moment. We move on." His voice was a little strained, and she felt his discomfort with the fact that he'd gotten caught up in her when he should have been worrying about his bubbled sister. "So, what next on the bubble?"

She nodded, cleared her throat, and tried to focus. "Okay, so we need to find out who this is linked to."

He adjusted the front of his jeans. "They said it was Satan. How do we confirm it?"

She averted her eyes from his crotch and turned to stare at the bubble. *Must regain cold, detached mindset.* "Find the machine that set it up."

"And then? Is there any way to shut this dome down other than killing the being whose life force is supporting it?"

She stalled for time by scratching her chin.

"Becca."

"I'm sure there's a back door. Isn't there always?"

He grabbed her wrist and turned her toward him, his eyes searching hers with a desperation that had her wanting to wrap herself around him and absorb everything that made his soul thrum with life. "Are you just saying that to protect Satan?" he asked. "If it's between his life and my sister's, I'm picking Dani."

"Gee, thanks. Nothing like coming right out and telling me you'll murder me to make a girl feel good."

He frowned, and she felt his frustration and regret as he realized what he'd said.

"Omigod! Here you guys are!" Paige hopped into the room. "This place is like a maze. Your sister must be loaded." She stopped suddenly and looked at the death blister. "Oh, wow. What is *this?*" She reached for it, and Becca lunged for her just as Paige's hand went through the filmy surface.

"No!" She hauled Paige back and the girl flew into the desk and sent papers flying.

Then the devastating emptiness slammed into Becca, and she gasped and dropped to her knees. Nick was there instantly, grabbing her shoulders and pulling her to her feet, easing the howling wasteland with his touch. He started to pull her against him, but she shook her head, not willing to trust herself with that much life force. "No. Just hold my wrist."

"Will that be enough?"

"It has to be." She swayed slightly from the barrenness inside her, but Nick's touch was enough to keep it from completely consuming her. She'd just have to manage the rest on her own until she could get out of there. She turned toward Paige, who was climbing to her feet. "Don't touch that dome. It was set up to trap Nick's sister, but any innocent who goes into it will be stuck, as well."

Paige threw her hands on her hips. "I'm not an innocent! How many times do I need to say that?"

"Only an innocent can penetrate." Becca backed up and threw herself against it to prove her point. It rebounded twice as hard, flinging her against Nick. His body was hard where she slammed into it, unyielding, and his arms snapped around her to keep her from rebounding into the wall. She quickly untangled herself from him as heat flared inside her. *Do not get hooked on how this man makes you feel, Becca.* "See? I can't get past it. You can."

"No way. You're wrong." Paige marched over to the bubble and thrust her hand right through it. "Damn." She pulled it out, looked at it, then did it again. "Double damn. You're sure that's why I can get through?"

"Yeah," she said. Nick was playing with her hair, the tips of his fingers brushing against her scalp. She eyed him. "Cut it out."

His fingers stilled. "Sorry. Didn't realize I was doing it."

Paige watched them. "So, what now?"

Becca cleared her throat, wanting to melt into Nick at the same time she wanted to rip out of his grasp and reclaim her independence. "We need to get out of here so I can think."

"I agree." His voice was slightly strained, and she could feel his lust pulsing at her, trying to break free of his control. "New location." He paused. "Is Dani going to be okay if we leave her?"

Worry leaked in with the lust, and she felt his struggle. "She's safe for the moment. Nothing's going to happen to her."

"Dani? Did you just say *Dani*?" Paige grabbed Nick's wrist. "What's her last name?"

Nick stilled. "Rawlings."

"No way!" Paige spun toward the bubble. "Dani! It's me! Can you hear me? Dani!" Her voice got more shrill. "Dani! You wake up right now and get out here or I will come in there and drag you out!" She shrugged off Becca's leather jacket and tossed it aside. "I'm coming in after you and—"

"Paige!" Becca lunged for her apprentice as she dove at the bubble, grabbing the girl's waist as the vesicle parted for the innocent, sucking Becca into the bubble right along with her. Becca tried to stop them, but she couldn't fight their momentum.

"Becca!" She heard Nick's outraged roar, and then she felt his fingers dig into the waistband of her jeans. She was sucked into the bubble and the world became black.

Ten

Heavy blackness embraced Nick as he was pulled into the death blister, and he couldn't see anything. It felt like the air was compressing down around them, crushing his body. He tightened his grip on Becca, pulling her toward him as he tried to halt their catapult into the bubble.

"Stop us!" Becca shouted. "Nick! Stop us!"

Her body tensed under his, and his adrenaline shot up at the fierce command in Becca's voice. He dug his heels into the floor and threw all his weight backward, gripping Becca's waist and hauling her back toward him while Paige yelled Dani's name.

Becca leaned back into him, her body straining against his. He felt another body bump hers, and he realized she was still holding on to Paige. He threw his other arm forward, grabbing Paige, as well.

Then the blackness vanished and they were inside the vesicle, being dragged toward the acid pit in the corner, which was now a good two feet in diameter, and bubbling ferociously. *Jesus.*

Adrenaline kicked in again and he hauled them back. The pressure suddenly broke and they all flew backward, landing with a crash against the wall of the blob in a mixture of arms and legs. He grunted as his hand hit a breast. *God help me if that belongs to Paige.* But he heard Becca suck in her breath, and his own body answered as he muttered an apology. "Everyone okay?"

"Let go of me!" Paige twisted out of the mess and ran over to the bed and kneeled on it, huddled over Dani. She patted Dani's cheeks. "Hey, Dani, can you hear me? This is all my fault. I'm so sorry. Dani? Come on, wake up, girlfriend."

Nick climbed to his feet as Becca scrambled up. "Paige? How do you know Dani?"

"Why is this your fault?" Nick asked at the same time.

The apprentice ignored them both as she hovered over Dani, getting louder and louder as she realized Dani wasn't going to wake up.

"What do you know about this?" Nick lunged for Paige, grabbed her shoulders, and whirled her to face him. "Who set up the bubble? Who hurt my sister? What do you know?"

Becca was suddenly between them, her hands on his chest. "Back off, Nick." Her voice was quiet and calm, devoid of emotion. "You're going to bring down the building."

He was suddenly aware of the creaking of the walls and some plaster falling from the ceiling onto the bubble, and he cursed and released Paige, letting Becca's touch on his chest draw out some of the destructive energy. He took a deep breath as Paige turned back to his sister. "Get the information from her," he ordered Becca.

"I will. You back under control?"

He grunted, and she studied him for a moment, set his hand on her shoulder, and then spun the apprentice back around by her ponytail. "What's going on, Paige?"

Paige stared up at them, tear-streaked mascara cascading down her cheeks. "I didn't even look at her when I was outside the blister. Does that make me a bad friend? It does, doesn't it?"

A look of pity crossed Becca's face as she laid her hand on the apprentice's shoulder. "Oh, Paige, you care about her, don't you?" she asked softly.

"Of course I do! She's my only friend…besides you, of course."

Becca pressed her lips together, and Nick thought she looked suddenly exhausted. "Does Satan know you're friends with her?" Becca asked.

"Satan hasn't been around," Paige said. "Why would he care, anyway? She's just a human." Paige leaned forward and patted Dani's cheeks. "Dani? Wake up, please?"

"What does that have to do with who put her in the bubble?" Nick growled.

Becca glanced at Nick, and he was startled by the sadness in her eyes. "Fine. You talk to her. Go ahead and wring her neck. Put her out of her misery before she realizes what she's done to herself by caring about your sister." She turned and looked out the window, keeping one hand on Nick's waist for grounding. "Just kill her already. Please."

Paige stopped babbling to stare at them. "What? He's going to kill me? Why? What did I do?" She scrambled back across the bed as he approached. "Go away or I'll fireball you."

Nick stopped next to the bed and leaned on it with his

fists. "Paige." He managed to keep his voice gentle. "Tell me what you know about what's going on with Dani."

At his soft tone, Paige relaxed and sat back down on the bed. She picked up Dani's hand. "On my first day of Rivka training, she sneaked up to me outside the beheading dungeon and offered me almost a hundred grand to kill Satan."

Nick couldn't keep the look of surprise off his face. "Dani was in hell? Hiring an assassin to kill Satan? Are you sure? How'd she get there?"

"Apparently there's some sort of express-elevator type thing in the Council offices. Did you know that?"

He looked at Becca, who nodded. "It's highly restricted, though," she said. "I can't imagine how she got in there." She gestured at Paige. "Continue."

Paige snuggled next to Dani and stroked the hair off her friend's forehead. "So, I took the money and then didn't kill him. Then a few days later, she came after me to kick my ass and I told her that she was crazy and I'd kill her before I'd let anything happen to the big kahuna and she should know better than to trust a Rivka's word and then she told me that she'd done it to piss off her ex-boyfriend and then we started guy-bashing and we became total best friends, of course." She blinked hard several times. "I had no idea she was in danger, though, or I wouldn't have let her go that last time when she seemed all worried but wouldn't tell me what was wrong. A true best friend would have tortured her to force her to confide, right?" Big, fat tears trickled down her cheeks. "I'm so not a best friend, am I?"

Becca cleared her throat, and Nick felt a weird humming from her. Some emotion that was trying to get out, but she had such a tight grip on it he couldn't even identify it. "Paige, look at me."

The kid ignored him, instead lifting her tearstained face to Becca. "You should kill me, I think."

"A true best friend doesn't torture her friends. You did okay," Becca said, her voice strained.

Nick caught a flash of pain shot from Becca where her hand was still on his waist, and he was shocked by its intensity. He looked at Becca, wondering what in her past had created that kind of emotional devastation.

She didn't seem aware of his perusal. "Paige, we need to know who told Dani to hire you to kill Satan."

"Her boyfriend." Paige sighed. "He convinced her he was going to be the new leader of hell even though I *told* her Satan would always rule. She totally thought that if she helped him take over then he'd propose to her. She was so excited because her brother always made her feel like a total underachiever and he never treated her like an adult and she was finally going to prove to him that she was capable of handling her life on her own..." She faded to a stop and looked at Nick. "Oh. You're *that* Nick." Her eyes got hostile. "Would it have killed you to treat her like an adult?"

Nick stared at the apprentice. "She said that about me?"

Paige cocked her head to study Nick. He knew he was being judged, and he didn't like it. "She told me about her senior prom and you showed up at the after party at two in the morning and tossed her date through the wall."

Nick scowled. "The guy was trying to get her *naked*. What was I supposed to do? Let him? She's my little sister." Dani hadn't spoken to him for weeks after that, but he'd never regretted it. Without a dad around, he'd taken on the role as best he could, even if she didn't appreciate it.

"She said you were overcontrolling because you had no life of your own and so you tried to rule hers," Paige continued. "She said you needed to get lai—"

"Who is her boyfriend?" he interrupted quickly, glancing at Becca.

"I don't know," Paige said. "We never used names, because of the whole being-on-opposite-sides thing. If I knew who her boyfriend was, then I'd have to kill him, and that would have been a major strain on our friendship, you know?" Paige threw her legs off the bed and landed on the floor. "This is all the fault of that loser boyfriend of hers!" Paige stalked toward the bubble. "Frozen, my ass. That son-of-a-bitch put her up to it and screwed with us both—" She walked into the side of the bubble and bounced off it, landing on her butt. "I'm going to go find him and kill him and—"

"Frozen?" Nick echoed in stunned disbelief. "Did you just say her boyfriend was *frozen*?"

"She calls him the ice king ever since he stopped calling her, as if that's an excuse. Cell phones work in sub-freezing temperatures. Everyone knows that, but would she listen to me? No. She just mooned on about him even when I threatened to send her to the Afterlife with a fireball." Paige hopped up and charged the bubble but was flung backward, crashing into the bed. "Dammit." She pounded her fists on the floor. "Get me out of *here*!"

"You can't leave," Becca said. "You're an innocent."

"I'm not innocent!" Paige shouted. "I'm a Rivka! I'm

supported by Satan's life force! How can I *possibly* be an innocent?"

Nick slammed his fist in his palm, fury ripping through him. How dare Satan Jr. seduce his sister and put her in a death blister? "I have that bastard's head in my freezer right now! How do I get out of here?" He *knew* he should have defrosted him at Council headquarters and taken him out right there.

But Becca didn't move, her brow furrowed in thought. "Satan Jr.'s been frozen for three weeks. He didn't put her in this vesicle."

"Who the hell cares? He seduced my sister, and that's enough." He took a moment to try to calm himself. "Can you get us out with that shimmer thing?"

"It won't work through the bubble." She eyed the steaming black cauldron in the corner. "I can get myself out through the acid pit. But I don't know if you'll be okay or not. The bubble will let you go through the pit if you're not an innocent, but your relationship to hell is pretty distant. I think the acid will notice your presence and eat you." She shrugged. "It's a sucky way to go, from what I've heard."

"Only gold can hurt me."

"Stick your finger in there and see."

"It won't hurt me either. I'll come, too." Paige dove over to the pit and jabbed her finger into it, then ripped it out with a screech. "Holy mother of hell!" She stuck it in her mouth and bounced around the room, cursing.

Nick held his hand over the pit and felt the heat from it, then touched it with the tip of his finger. Pain shot through him, but he gritted his teeth and left it in there to see what happened. After a full minute, he took it out, and he and

Becca peered at it. His finger was bright red and burning like a mother, but it was still attached. "I can handle that," he said. "Take me through."

"We'll be in it for about five minutes."

He nodded. "I'm good. Let's go."

She didn't move. "How do you generate your own life force now? How come you don't need Satan? What did your ancestors do? How did you break the link?"

He cursed. "Can we talk about this later?"

There was a flicker of regret in her eyes, then she tightened her jaw and shook her head. "Tell me."

He narrowed his eyes. "That's what you want to know, isn't it? How to get free of Satan? So you can be your own woman." He couldn't keep his voice from softening in empathy.

Her gaze flicked to Paige, who was fluffing Dani's pillow and not listening to them. "My goals are irrelevant. I want the information."

He scowled at her attitude, at the reminder of who she was. Nothing but Satan's minion. "You're bargaining with my sister's life, and that pisses me off." He bent down until his face was level with hers. "If I tell you how the Markku broke free of Satan, then you'll have no reason to stay and help me. I'm stuck in a damned pus blister, and without your help, my sister's going to die. So you get nothing from me until my sister's free."

She ground her teeth. "I won't walk. I made a deal and I'll follow through."

"You want me to risk my sister's life on a promise by Satan's right hand?" He shook his head. "I'm part Satan, remember? I know how it works in his world."

They stared at each other, and he felt the desperation

coming from her. Guilt stabbed at his chest. "Dammit, Becca, I want to help you. But I have to save my sister. I swear on her life I will tell you all I know when this is over." He grabbed her hand and set it over his heart so she could feel that he meant it.

Her eyes widened as her fingers curled into his chest. "How do you do that?"

"I told you, my ma's a healer. Does weird shit to my emotions. You read me?"

She nodded and dropped her hand. "Are there any other Markku left? Besides you?"

He thought of the attack at the Council headquarters. "I didn't think so, but I might be wrong. I met one that could be Markku."

"Dark hair? Violet eyes? Good with a knife?"

He frowned. "Shaved head, dark eyes. Knife skills questionable. Why?"

"Violet-eyed guy tried to kill me." She tapped her fingers against her chin. "So there's three of you?" She shifted, and he knew what she was thinking. She was thinking that maybe she didn't need him, after all.

So he threw out the one tidbit that he knew would snare her, the one tidbit that would sign his death warrant if Satan ever found out. "My grandfather was the leader of the Markku rebellion. He's the one who got everyone out of hell. It's my family who harvested Satan's power so the rest of the Markku could live off it." He met her gaze. "I'm it, Becca. I'm the one you're looking for."

Without waiting for an invite, she pressed her hand to his heart again, and he opened to her. Let her see he was telling the truth. He felt her brush against his soul, cautiously probing as if she were afraid to go too deep. He couldn't resist reaching out to her, and he felt such a stab of desperation that he grabbed her wrist and held her hand to his chest, summoning his healer gene to try to ease her pain...but he couldn't get past her shields. He growled with frustration as she dropped her hand, seemingly unaware of his attempts to soothe her.

"I hate needing anyone," she muttered.

"So, we're good?"

She eyed him with a disgruntled expression. "You keep feeding me tidbits, and I'll hang around."

He felt like closing his eyes in relief, but instead, he kept his face stoic. "Then let's go. Into the acid pit, right?"

"Right." She took his hand. "Don't let go of me. I don't know where you'll end up if we get separated, and I have too much invested in you to get you get sucked off into some black vortex and disintegrated into a pile of acid-ridden flesh, okay?"

"Wouldn't want to inconvenience you. I'll hang on." Her hand was cool in his, as if she was tamping back what little heat existed inside her. He tightened his grip and sent a little pulse into her.

She jumped, and he felt her instinctively reach out and draw it into her, even as she glared at him. "Don't tease me."

"Wait! You're going?" Paige vaulted over the bed. "Take me with you!" She grabbed Becca's other wrist. "I have to save Dani and kill that bastard who blistered her."

Becca raised her brows. "You mean, you need to save Satan from being assassinated? As a Rivka, aren't all your loyalties to Satan?"

Paige's eyes widened. "Oh, crud, I do, don't I? But I also need to save Dani." She pressed her palms to her forehead. "God, I have such a headache. This is such a nightmare. I feel like two parts of my brain are trying to beat the daylights out of each other. How can I feel the call to save both of them?"

Becca's jaw flexed. "You need to get over Dani. Now." Her voice was sharp. "It will only endanger her if you care about her."

"Oh, like she's not already in danger now," Paige snapped, then looked horrified. "Omigod. I didn't mean to talk back to you like that. God, what's wrong with me?"

"You're developing a backbone, which is good, but you need to get over your feelings for Dani."

"How? I don't want to."

Becca shrugged. "I don't know. Try some aversion therapy. Every time you think about how much you like Dani, stab yourself with a pencil."

Paige squeaked, and Nick shot a look at Becca. "Chill out, Becca, she's just a kid."

"She's not a kid. She's Satan's Rivka. Big difference, trust me. She can't afford to care about anyone but him." She clenched her free hand, and Nick saw the tension in her neck, felt pain radiating from where they clasped hands. "It doesn't matter anyway, Paige. You're stuck here until you do something that makes you no longer innocent. Kill Dani and the bubble will let you come out through the acid pit."

"Kill Dani?" Paige echoed, looking so horrified that Nick didn't mind leaving his sister in her care, despite Becca's suggestion.

Becca turned away, and he could feel a war inside her

that surprised him. She wasn't completely empty inside. Far, far from it. But the emotions were stunted, like they were buried deep and couldn't get free. He tightened his grip on her hand, trying to feel what was going on inside her. So much pain, and in so much denial.

"You coming, Nick?"

He reluctantly stopped trying to search out her core and glanced at the bubbling acid pit. "Yeah."

She nodded, then wrapped her hand around his wrist. He did the same to hers, locking their grip tight. "Hang on."

"I'm hanging."

She met his gaze and then stepped over the edge and disappeared into the boiling pit of acid. He had a fraction of a second to prepare, and then he was in it with her.

The pain hit him so hard and so fast it slammed the air out of his lungs. It felt like his skin was being ripped off, like his eyeballs were being clawed out of his face. *Jesus.* He'd never make it. He could tell it was consuming him, devouring him, eating through his essence.

"Come on, hell boy." Becca's voice came at him through the darkness. "Channel your dark side."

He ground his teeth. "How?"

And then she was there, her body against his. "Reverse the flow of emotions between us. Take mine."

He wrapped his body around hers and buried his face in her neck, and started to draw on her emotions. Icy cold hit him, chased away the heat inside him. Emptiness, a void that began to build in his chest and spread throughout his soul.

"Keep it up," she whispered against his chest. "Keep drawing from me."

God, but he didn't want to. It was a horrible feeling.

But he did it anyway, and the emptier he got, the less his body hurt. He stopped worrying about Dani. He stopped hating the Council for killing his pa. He stopped lusting after Becca, even with her body pressed up against his, her breasts crushed against his chest. He just *was*.

And then they were hit with light and they tumbled to a hard marble floor. He protected Becca's body from the impact, instinctively.

He frowned as she looked down at him, stretched across his body. "Nice work, Markku. You did all right."

"Get off me." He couldn't stand that empty feeling anymore. He needed light. He needed to feel whole. "Off."

Hurt flickered in Becca's face, but she rolled off him and hopped to her feet. "You're welcome."

He stood up and thought about Dani, tapped into his love for her, his anger at whoever put her in the bubble, and his life force returned with a roar that had him stumbling. He took a deep breath and flexed his fingers, embracing who he was. He opened his eyes to see Becca watching him with envy, and now he understood why. "That's how you live?"

She shrugged. "It's what it is."

"How do you survive it?"

"It's not a big deal." She rolled her shoulders.

"How can you say that?" He was still shaken by the experience, and she didn't seem bothered?

She looked at him. "Because it's not a big deal. Really."

He moved closer and reached out to clasp her wrist,

needing to know whether that emptiness was a result of the bubble, or whether it was her. "It's really you. That's how you live."

"I'm fine." She wrenched her arm free and glared at him. "Don't go all soft on me, hell boy. We've got things to do."

But in her eyes was such deep pain, such vibrant lone-liness, that he felt his own heart stutter from it. A faint humming filled his body as he slipped his hands to her shoulders, cupping the bare skin, unable to stop himself. "You hate it."

"No, I—"

"I can't let you live like that. My healer side...I can't walk away from your pain..." Before he could think, he yanked her against him and slammed his mouth onto hers, flooding her with his life force. *Take it, Becca. Feel alive.*

Becca folded against him instantly, her body warm and soft against his, her mouth opening to him. He groaned and deepened the kiss, plunging into her depths, search-ing for more, desperate to find the heat he knew she was hiding, to extract it from the void. To heal her. To bring her the light he could sense she so desperately craved.

Her fingers gripped his jacket, and he felt her lust...but that was it. Just empty lust. Nothing else. He was flooding her with his heat and she was giving nothing back. She was a void in the middle of his swirling energies. But he could tell it wasn't the barren emptiness of Dani's condo; it was more like a practiced barrier that was her world. Not as crushing, but equally empty in its own way.

I can still help you. He dropped his mouth to the side of her neck, nibbling at her skin as he cupped her buttocks, pressing her hips against the front of his jeans, grinding into her. He didn't hold back his emotions, saturating her energies with his worry over Dani, his admiration for Becca's resistance to Satan, his anger over someone using his sister, his need to show Becca what her world could be like if she'd let it go. "Come on," he whispered against her skin. "Becca, drop your shields."

She moaned softly and tipped her head back, exposing her throat to him. Her body moved against his, her fingers digging into the back of his hair, but the void was still there. It was actually growing, getting stronger and larger, trying to negate what he was thrusting at her. Now that she wasn't being debilitated by the bubble, she was back in control, keeping him at bay, protecting her core. Maintaining rigid control.

He frowned and released her.

She stumbled back, her face flushed with lust and surprise. "What kind of kiss was that?" She fumbled with her skimpy top, not that he'd touched it.

He narrowed his eyes and studied the Rivka. "That's what I want to know. You always kiss like that?"

"Do *you*?" She shuddered and ran her hand through her short hair, making it stand up.

"Yeah. I do." He caught her wrist again and pulled her close so he could look into her eyes. He searched for the emotion he'd sensed in her when she'd been upset with Paige. The anger, the passion, everything he'd been so certain was there, which is why he'd kissed her, to draw out the emotions rumbling inside her, to center her and ease her pain. But now there was only cool blackness.

No more pain, but it was a facade. Not peace. A wall that held the pain at bay, but didn't take it away.

He leaned forward and kissed her again, soft and promising, and her mouth yielded under his. He slipped his tongue between her lips, a gentle kiss, teasing her, coaxing her, playing with her. After a moment, he felt her sigh and relax into him, and he felt the wall weaken ever so slightly and got the whisper of a deeply painful emotion, and a name. He frowned and pulled back. "Who's Gabriel?"

Becca's eyes widened. "How did you do that?"

"There's a lot of emotion attached to his name. Who is he?" He tugged on her hair, continuing to send heat into her.

A faint smile curved her lips and she didn't pull away. He could feel her basking in his energy. Not absorbing it, but letting it wash over her, like a coating

"Gabriel was one of Satan's executioners," she said. "Sweet kid. Great with an axe."

Something inside him stirred at the obvious affection her voice. "What happened to him?"

"Satan got mad when he found out I'd lost my virginity to him, so he made me kill him." She shrugged and turned away. "It sucked, I got over it, and we move on."

Well, damn. He could feel the guilt when she said Gabriel's name. His cold Rivka had actually loved Gabriel, and she'd shut it down after that. How could he compete with that kind of love?

Wait a sec. Did he want to compete with it?

He watched her walk away to study the heavy gold locks on a set of enormous double doors.

"This is Satan's Goody Room," she said. "The blister machine is in here." She tested the doors. "Locked. As I'd expect."

He knew he couldn't let her live in the emptiness that consumed her. Before he'd met her, he wouldn't have cared what torment raged inside her. A Rivka wasn't innocent. Becca had no doubt harvested billions of souls and tortured many. She didn't matter. Not in comparison to Dani. Becca didn't deserve mercy.

But she did.

Because she'd saved him from taking out a bar of innocents without worrying about her own safety.

Because he'd seen the pain her own eyes, a deep desperation that clung to every inch of her soul.

Because he knew she cared and tried desperately not to. She'd been so upset about Paige's affection toward Dani that her emotions had almost burst free, even while under the influence of the bubble.

Because she'd tried to heal him after she'd fireballed him.

He thought of her warm hand on his skin, drawing the golden flames back out of his body before they could do any more damage. She'd had no reason to help him, and she'd done it anyway.

Becca might be a Rivka, but she was also a woman, who had to fight every minute to retain her own identity and sanity. She was strength and fire, and he wanted to know what other secrets she had buried inside. Oh, yeah. He wanted to know.

She turned back to face him. "Satan has ordered me never to go in there and take anything, but he's never ordered me not to show someone else how to do it. You game?"

He smiled. "Do you ever do anything Satan tells you?"

"I try my best not to."

"Have I told you how impressive that is?"

Her eyes lit up, but she ignored his comment. "I'll describe the machine, you get it, and then I'll get us out of here." She flared up a blue fireball. "Ready to piss off the leader of hell?"

Eleven

Becca was still reeling from Nick's kiss when she blew up the doors to the Goody Room and Nick darted inside to search the rubble. She could still feel the warm hardness of his body against hers. His lips trailing down the side of her neck, drawing heat into parts of her she didn't even know existed...

Get a grip, Becca.

She wiped her wrist across her forehead, where perspiration was beading.

What had been in that kiss? It had taken every defense she had not to be overwhelmed by the intensity of it. Kisses weren't supposed to be like that. They were about lips meeting, bodies doing their thing, and maybe a few hormones getting into the act.

They were not about ripping away at her walls and invading every cell in her soul.

She shuddered as there was a crash and a curse from inside the Goody Room. She should never have let Nick overwhelm her with his life force when they were in Dani's apartment. For God's sake, she'd actually gotten tipsy on him! And she still wanted more. More of his heat. More of his kisses. More of his touch. She wanted to feel alive the way only he could make her feel, and there was just no place for that in her life.

Because the second he let go of her, it was gone again, leaving her feeling worse than before. If she wasn't careful, she could become a Nick junkie, and she'd have to go into rehab when this whole thing was over.

Nick rehab. Hah. That would be productive.

Nick emerged from the rubble, his shirt off and wrapped around a heavy object. "I can't touch gold," he explained.

She stared at his dust-covered chest, at the curves of his muscle, at the ripples on his belly and felt desire flare through her. *Think of where he could take me if I let him.* Just once. God, she wanted to feel that alive just one time.

He cursed and stopped dead, staring at her.

"Nick?" Could he sense what she was feeling? If he made a move again right now, she wouldn't stop him. She couldn't. She wanted him too much. "Nick..."

He said nothing, and his gaze flicked off her, to somewhere behind her.

Okay, so it would be up to her. She lifted her chin and walked up to him. "Kiss me."

He stared down at her, his eyes dark. "No."

She frowned. "Why not?"

"Because if I do, I'll want to rip apart all your shields and possess you on every level of your existence."

Oh. She felt hot, and it was more than lust. It was the anticipation of his life force pouring into her, filling her with light and life and everything she didn't get to have.

"And because some guy just popped out of the floor behind you and he looks really, really pissed."

She spun around, then all the hair on her arms sprung up when she saw who was standing there. He was tall and wiry, and still missing his right ear from the fight in which Becca had harvested him for Satan. He was wearing black leather chaps, silver-toed cowboy boots, and a ten-gallon hat with daggers neatly lined up around the brim. He leered, his gold teeth winking at her, his eyes black with hate. "Rivka."

"What are you doing here, Checkmate?" She churned up a fireball in her hand as sweat trickled down her back.

"You know him?" Nick's lips were next to her ear, his voice low.

"It's Checkmate Max," she whispered. "He used to kidnap innocents and make them play chess. He'd chop off a body part for each chess piece he won from one of his victims. He made them play until they bled to death. Satan put him in charge of one of his early torture chambers. A real prize for hell."

"I can imagine." He shifted, and suddenly there was a gun in his hand.

"No, he's already dead. A gun won't work." She pushed it back out of sight. "This is my world, Nick. Let me handle it."

Nick scowled, but he didn't protest when she shook her head at him.

But he also didn't put away his gun.

Max took a sip of the latte she hadn't noticed in his hand, watching her oh-so-carefully over the rim of his cup. "Well, if it isn't the Rivka who got me taken off torture duty and put in my own little cell of hell. I was a hero in hell before you stuck your nose into my life."

"Your torture methods were archaic. We had to keep

modernizing." And she'd never been able to stomach the fact Satan revered a sociopath who preyed on true innocents. The guy deserved the bowels of hell, not the throne. "What are you doing up here in Satan's chambers?"

"I don't know. I was sitting in my little vat of acid with all my skin melted off and millions of rats chewing on my bones, when suddenly it was all gone. I was standing outside the gates of hell with a couple hundred grand in my pocket, the keys to Satan's personal quarters, and a bevy of willing women at my feet. So, I went uptown, snagged myself a few innocents, and came back down here to play with them. And then you came sliding down the acid pit, and I realized that today really is my lucky day." He jangled a set of keys in his fingers.

Satan must have set him free...oh, *no*. Was that what he'd promised Iris? Releasing souls? This was bad. So very, very bad. It was never a good thing when idealists get involved in politics. "Do you have your soul back, or are you still a member of hell's finest?" She'd never encountered a soul that had been released from hell before. Could she even take it back if he had?

"Oh, I have a soul." Checkmate grinned. "I'm a free man, and I'm enjoying every minute of it."

Nick waited behind her. She could feel his tension, but he wasn't saying anything. Deferring to her leadership in hell. What a guy. She had to like a man who respected a woman's space, even as she could feel the air heating up around them. Nick was ready for Checkmate to come at him, eager for it.

As if she'd need his help. But before she took Checkmate down, she needed to make sure his victims were accounted for. "Where are your opponents, Checkmate?"

He grinned and sloshed the latte. "Where do you think?"

She studied him for a minute as she tried to recall exactly what his modus operandi was; then she looked up. A girl was hanging upside down from the ceiling by her toes, a chessboard by her face, with all the pieces on it. Her arms were free and she was gesticulating wildly, making grunting noises that barely made it through the duct tape on her face.

In her moment of distraction, Checkmate whipped out a gun. Nick slammed her to the side at the same time she heard the crack of a gunshot and felt the shudder of Nick's body as the bullet slammed into it. They both rolled with the impact, and Nick kept his body between hers and the gun as the bullets flew.

There was a sudden yodeling from above, and Becca looked up just in time to see Paige emerge from the acid pit in the ceiling and catapult down to the marble. She landed on top of Checkmate. He grunted as Paige bounced off him, then she leapt to her feet and dove on top of him. "I'll take him out, boss! I got him!"

Becca sat back on her heels and Nick jerked upright, shoving her behind him as he shouted at Paige. "Did you kill Dani to get out of the bubble?"

"No, of course not. I've been watching Becca. I know how to get around the rules," Paige announced as she tried to stab Checkmate in the eye with her index finger, while sitting on his chest. "I burned all Dani's love notes from the guy she lost her virginity to. She had a total crush on him, and she was going to frame them for her daughter someday. Of course, he broke her heart and drove her into the arms of this new loser, so it's not really a loss in my opinion..." Paige choked up as she stuck her thumb in Checkmate's eye. "She's going to be so upset with me, but it had to be done for the greater good, you know? The pus blister wouldn't let me out if I was an innocent, so I had to do something bad."

"My sister's not a virgin?" Nick lunged to his feet, and the walls began to rattle and the ceiling began to shudder.

Becca peered up as cracks began to appear in the marble ceiling. "Nick, she's twenty-two. Get over it before you make the roof fall down on us."

"Who did it?" Nick shouted. "Who was it, Paige? Tell me."

A hunk of marble crashed down next to Becca's head, and she jumped in front of Nick and grabbed his arms, trying to draw his rage into her own body. "Nick. Calm down." The air around him was so hot she felt like it was searing her skin.

"Some guy named Jerome." Paige slammed her finger toward Checkmate's eye.

Nick's jaw dropped. "Jerome? My best friend *Jerome* had sex with my *sister*?"

"Nick." Becca grabbed his ear and forced him to look at her as a huge chunk of the ceiling landed dangerously close to the bubble machine. "Reel it in, big guy. You'll be no good to me if you get yourself squashed. And you almost broke the blister machine."

He shot a wild look at the machine, then cursed and grabbed her shoulders. She felt him suck at her control and her void, the same way he had in the acid pit, and she let him feed on her rigid self-control and draw it in as his own. Almost immediately, the heat emanating from him began to fade.

Checkmate batted Paige's hands away and tried to dump her off him. "Get off me, psycho bitch."

Both Nick and Becca looked over at Paige, but neither of them released the other. "Need help?" Nick asked, just as Becca was warming up a fireball to save her apprentice.

"I'm good. Did you hear what he called me?" Paige shot a delighted smile at Becca. "He called me a psycho *and* a bitch in the same sentence! Too cool—" She was suddenly sent flying by a left hook to the gut, and she crashed into a pile of rubble. "Ow…." She moaned, rolling onto her side. "That hurt."

Checkmate lifted the gun again, and Becca threw two fireballs as Nick fired off a few rounds. Her fireballs knocked Checkmate off his feet, then she anchored him to the floor with a flaming chain of fireballs. She dropped to his chest, set her palm on his forehead, and closed her eyes. A warm little bubble moved under his skin, trying to get through his forehead and into her skin. His soul. Satan must have given it back. How was that possible? Not that she minded. Harvesting souls like Checkmate's was the one true pleasure in her job. He deserved hell, and she was going to enjoy sending him there. "You die again, Checkmate."

He grinned. "Then we'll meet again in hell, Rivka."

She plunged a fireball into his heart and called his soul into her left hand. The pulsating warmth filled her palm, and a sharp pain stung her hand and shuddered all the way up her arm. She gritted her teeth as she let it run through her, trying to find a place to settle. It was like having a hamster under her skin, and she hated the feeling of it every single time.

Finally his soul settled under her right kneecap and curled up to take a nap, and she stood up, trying to shake off the creepy crawlies as numbness began to settle in her left arm. Nick was right there beside her, completely unharmed, aside from some bullet holes in his shirt. "You okay?" He touched her cheek. "Nice moves."

"Yeah, fine." She grinned. "Thanks."

"Oh, *wow*." Paige dropped to her knees next to them, a trickle of blood smeared on her forehead. "That was the most amazing thing I've ever seen." She touched Checkmate's forehead. "You just plucked it right out, huh?" She closed her eyes. "He feels empty. I think I can feel that his soul's gone." Paige opened her eyes. "Where is it? Can I touch it?"

Becca cocked her head, amused at Paige's excitement. Ah, the joys of being young and innocent instead of old, cynical, and bitter. "You tell me where it is."

"Oh..." Paige held out her hands and waved them over Becca's body, then grabbed Becca's knee. "It's right here."

Becca froze when Nick put his hand on her knee next to Paige's. His hand was warm, brimming with life force, and she steeled herself against it. After a moment, he shook his head. "I don't feel it."

"Feel my other knee and compare." He was Markku, after all. He should have some sensitivity to souls.

He put his other hand on her left knee, his hands spanning her leg easily. She caught a whiff of his scent, a clean, musky smell that made her belly curl. He nodded

suddenly. "Your right knee has a pulse. Your left doesn't."
He dropped his hands. "That's a weird feeling."

"Try having a soul in your knee. That's even weirder."

He looked curious. "What happens to it after you take
it?"

"I bind it to hell. At that point, his body will pop up to
be reunited with his soul in a theoretical sort of way. Lots
of tears and hugging and crying. Very emotional."

He raised his brows. "You Rivkas. You're all about the
touchy-feely, aren't you?"

"Totally."

Paige scooted next to her. "Can I carry it? Please?"

"Sure." She put Paige's left hand on her knee and told
her how to pull it out. It took a moment, and then Paige
yelped and doubled over as the soul jumped from Becca
into Paige.

"Oh, God! It's alive. Get it out of me!" Paige screeched
and clawed at her skin. "This is too gross!"

Becca felt a flash of sympathy, recalling what it had
felt like the first time she'd harvested a soul. "Want me to
take it back?"

"No!" Paige continued to jump around, scratching at
her skin. "I'll get used to it, I'm sure." She screeched and
grabbed a rock from the rubble and started pounding it
against her thigh. "Just give me a minute while I kill this
fucker and make it stop running around my body like it
owns me."

Becca smiled as she stood up. Maybe Paige did have
what it took. She certainly had the enthusiasm, an admira-
ble tenacity. A glimmer of pride tickled her throat. "She's
pretty good, huh?"

Instead of answering, Nick fired his gun and Becca jerked her gaze toward him. "What's wrong?"

"Can you get her down? My bullet goes right through the rope like it doesn't exist."

She glanced up and saw that Nick had moved to stand beneath Checkmate's victim, who was still squirming and making muffled noises. She was too high up for Nick to reach her, and he looked completely strung out. Frustrated he couldn't reach her, worried for her safety.

"Catch her." Becca shot a fireball through the rope, and the girl fell with a scream into Nick's waiting arms.

Through Nick's arms.

And disappeared through the floor.

Nick stared at his empty arms. "What the hell was that?"

Becca walked over to the floor and toed it, then looked up. "She must have already been dead when Checkmate found her. He probably plucked her out of purgatory. On the plus side, that'll give her a free pass to heaven. Being tossed by a violent sadist usually gives you a lot of brownie points." She chewed her lower lip. "I think I need to have a little chat with Satan." Not that she wanted to jump in and give Satan advice on ruling hell, but she couldn't sit around while he released souls that would endanger innocents. Or herself, for that matter. What was with all these threats to her life these days? It was as if the universe knew she was trying to break free and had joined together with all of her enemies to stop her before she succeeded.

"We get my sister first." Nick walked over to where he'd dropped the machine, taking a wide berth around

Paige, who was shouting at her body and trying to order the soul into submission. "We have a deal, remember?"

"Yeah, I remember." She watched him step over the rubble, his hips narrow and lithe under his jeans. He moved like a man who was more than a man. "As long as we're holding to the deal, tell me why, when we're both from hell, you're Mr. In-touch-with-your-emotions and I'm..." She paused, not quite able to admit what she was like inside. "I don't buy it's all your healer side."

He shot her a knowing look that was full of empathy. It almost made her want to sit him down and pour out all her miseries, because he *got it*. But what would that accomplish? Nothing.

Nick stepped over the bleeding body of Checkmate. "Rivkas are the new and improved version of Satan's minions. Markku are indestructible, except gold, but that made it too hard for him to control us, especially because we got pissed at him for pushing us around. So he created Rivkas, who are easier to kill and control, and he made you less emotional so you wouldn't have issues about him and his leadership. That's why you guys are fully supported by his life force. No more forays into the world of independent living." He picked up his shirt, with the bubble machine still inside. "Except you, of course." He studied her. "You're different. You do feel something."

"Paige has the same issue, and I feel bad about that. She's a little too human for her own sanity." She glanced over at her apprentice, who was stretched out on her back on the floor, her chest heaving, having apparently won the battle with the soul. She smiled. *You go, girl.* "I can't believe she likes your sister. I'm so going to have to brainwash that girl before she can replace me."

He hoisted the machine up and set it on his hip. "What exactly do you mean by 'replace?'"

She squatted down and peeled Checkmate's fingers off his gun and inspected it. "I figured out how to break Satan's lifeline, but he got pissed because he didn't want to let me go. I'm hoping I can turn Paige into such a great Rivka that he doesn't care if he loses me." She checked the clip, then stood up and wedged the gun in the back of her pants, keeping her voice low enough that Paige couldn't hear over her panting. "So far, it's not going so well, though." She flicked a gaze at the girl again, realizing how really young she was. Too young to be shoved into life as Satan's right hand? Becca bit her lip and tried not to think about it. That was Paige's destiny, and it wasn't Becca's job to interfere.

"How are you going to stay alive without his life force?" Nick asked, drawing her attention back to him. "I mean, if you've already figured out how to break it, then you don't need me, right?"

"Ellie the immortal goldfish will support me. We're a great team, but I need to know how you guys broke free without him killing you instantly. And if there's a way to support myself, like you do." She stepped over some of the rubble from the explosion that opened the Goody Room and reached Nick. "Can I have that?"

He handed the machine to her. "Only Satan will support you. The fish won't work."

She unwrapped the item to reveal a giant gold penis on a mahogany pedestal, and set the entire contraption on the floor. "What do you mean?"

"You have to be supported by *his* life force specifically." He looked at her. "And I don't know that you can support yourself like we do. You're different."

"I'll judge that for myself based on the info, if you ever give it to me." She looked up at him. "Trust me, I've done a lot of research, and I would know if only his life force would support me. Of that, at least, I'm certain. I'd be hosed if it were true."

He paused, trying to recall what Jerome had told him about Rivkas. "No, I'm pretty sure I'm right. The Council tried to recruit some Rivkas a while ago. They tried linking them to all sorts of creatures from hell, but they all died. The Council kept it quiet because they figured it wouldn't be good for public relations with hell if Satan found out they'd been kidnapping his Rivkas and conducting fatal experiments on them."

"They died because Satan killed them." Her tone demanded acquiescence as she set her hand around the base of the golden penis. "I'm going to succeed." She took a piece of jagged brick from the rubble and slammed it into the penis, and he flinched. "Ellie and I will live happily ever after." She hit it again, and he flinched again, then grabbed the rock out of her hand.

"You're killing me here. Can you at least be gentle?"

"What?" She looked up at him, then looked at his crotch. "Oh. Sorry. I forget how sensitive men are about these things. I'm done anyway." She flicked the dented gold plate off the penis and pulled out a small gold ball. She held it in the palm of her hand. "Watch." It started to spin in her hand, then lifted off her palm, whirling around, then burst into an explosion of gold dust that formed the image of Satan in a tuxedo before it drifted away.

Becca sat back on her heels. "Damn."

Nick knew it couldn't be good to see Satan's image. "Did that mean he set it, or that his life force is supporting the bubble?"

"It means it's linked to his life force."

Nick cursed to himself, and they were both silent for a long moment. The only sound was Paige's heavy breathing and soft moans of pain.

Finally, Nick spoke, asking the question that was preying on his mind. "Is there any way to break that bubble besides killing Satan?"

And you.

He didn't say the words, but the implication was out there. She looked at him, her green eyes fixed on his. She was working so hard to remain impassive, but he could see the flicker of tension in them. "No, there isn't," she said quietly. "It's your sister or Satan. Take your pick."

Twelve

W e will kill him so there is no choice," a deep voice announced.

Paige yelped and scrambled to her feet. Becca's heart lurched in stunned shock and she felt the blood drain from her face.

Nick whipped out his gun and aimed it behind Becca, shoving her behind him. "Get your hands out where I can see them," he barked.

Becca shook her head and slowly turned around, unable to believe what she'd heard.

There *he* stood.

Gabriel, her sweet little executioner who'd devirginized her. All six feet eight inches of burly man, dressed in black from head to toe, including his wraparound sunglasses. The only shiny thing on him was the gold chain around his neck. His biceps were bulging under his black T-shirt, his pecs flexed and ready. But how...?

No. It was impossible. She steeled her heart and turned away from the image of the man whose memory had haunted her for decades. "It's a mirage."

Keeping his gun aimed at Gabriel, Nick shot her a questioning glance. "You're sure? He looks real." Then he caught the look on her face, and he frowned. "Are you all right?"

She managed a nod. "Satan can conjure up images to torture his souls. That's all it is. I must have triggered something when I blew up the Goody Room. Let's go find the frozen boyfriend and see what he has to tell us." She picked up the machine and set it on her hip, then held out her hand so she could take Nick through the floor. They both looked at her hand, which was shaking violently.

Ah, well, so much for her image of being a tough badass.

He clasped her trembling hand in one of his steady ones and sent his warmth into it, chasing away some of her angst. "What's up, hell girl?"

She shook her head, biting her lower lip as she tried desperately not to remember what it had been like to hear Gabriel begging for his life, declaring his love for her, while Satan stood next to her and ordered her to kill him. "I can't talk about it—"

"Becca!" Gabriel shouted. "How can you walk away from me? I have pined for you for decades, waiting for you to rescue me!"

Nick dropped her hand and spun to face Gabriel, his gun aimed at the other man's chest. "If he's a mirage, then you won't mind if I shoot his ass, right? I don't like him."

"It's a trap." Becca's heart was racing so hard her chest hurt, and a deep ache in her gut toyed with her. "Trust me. I killed him, and since he was already in the Afterlife, dead is dead, just like I'll be if someone takes Satan out."

"Ah." Nick's face softened in understanding and empathy, and little bit of annoyance, though he didn't lower his gun. Lifted it higher, in fact. "It's Gabriel. Your old lover. Back from the dead."

She shook her head. "No, it can't be Gabriel. I killed him."

He eyed the mirage, the tendons on his forearms bulging. "He looks real."

"He has to be real," Paige said. "No one could fake those muscles." She was standing just behind Nick, peering past his shoulder at Gabriel. "He looks mean. Is he mean? I don't like mean."

"Nick Rawlings is not to be trusted," Gabriel announced in his booming voice. "There is a plot afoot to take out hell and you included, and Nick is part of it. Come to me and we shall defend hell against him and his kind."

"My kind?" Nick narrowed his eyes at Gabriel. "At least I didn't sit back and let my lady suffer with guilt for a hundred years because I wasn't man enough to keep her from killing me when she didn't want to."

Becca almost snorted at Nick's obvious hostility, amused at how good it felt to have someone defend her. *Oh, get over yourself, Becca.* She couldn't let Nick deal with it. It was her issue, not his, and she was certainly strong enough to face it. Ahem.

Paige wiggled closer to Nick. "I think that dude is the one who shouldn't be trusted. Take him out, boss."

Becca took a deep breath, then turned and faced Gabriel. He sounded and looked so real that she had to clench her fists to keep from reaching out to touch him. "How do you know Nick?"

His face broke into a huge smile that made her knees go a little wiggly. *I remember that smile.*

"It's so great to see you again, Becca." He held out his arms. "Kiss?"

Nick made a low growl, and Becca shook her head to clear it, still trying to understand what she was dealing with. *Forget the emotions, Becca. Focus on the facts.* That was her modus operandi. She should be able to do it, right? She willed her pain back into its box and tried to study Gabriel objectively. "I killed you."

"He looks alive to me," Paige whispered. "And scary. Is that axe real?"

"Yes," Becca said. "It's real. If he's real."

Gabriel dropped his arms, scowling as he apparently realized she wasn't going to fall into his embrace. "You didn't kill me. Satan just wanted you to think he did, but I'm so good at executing people that he couldn't actually let me die. So we faked it and let you suffer the guilt." He winked. "And now I'm back, and I'm here to take up where we left off." His head turned toward Nick with a faint lift of his eyebrows. "Unless you object?"

Becca held up her hand before Nick could answer. "Wait a second." Her mind started to whirl. "I really didn't kill you?" All these years of thinking she was the worst kind of being? Gone, just like that?

"Honestly, I thought you'd figure it out and come rescue me, but whatever." He put his hands on his hips. "If I can forgive you for killing me and not rescuing me, then I think you can forgive me for letting you suffer with guilt for a few decades. Call it even and let me buy you dinner?"

She stared at him, and finally it hit her. *Gabriel was*

really alive. "I thought you were *dead!*" She sat down hard on the rubble, stunned. "I can't believe this. Satan kept you *alive?*" She was vaguely aware of Nick squatting beside her, setting his hand on her shoulder, his warmth a soft pulse through her. She could tell he was trying to probe her, to figure out what she was feeling, and she didn't have the strength to block him.

After a minute, he scowled, squeezed her shoulder, and stood up, glaring at Gabriel.

"But I've felt horrible about this for so long!" This made no sense. Satan would never have let Gabriel live once he'd realized that Gabriel was competition for Becca's loyalties.

Gabriel frowned, glancing warily at Nick as the Markku began to circle behind him, his hand still wrapped around his gun, his finger resting on the trigger. "Can we put it behind us already?" Gabriel asked. "I'm back. I still love you. You still love me, and we'll get back on track." He walked over and knelt in front of her, his hands going to her knees. "I will save your heart for you."

Paige sat next to Becca. "Wow. He is so into you," she whispered. "How cool is that?"

Nick walked up behind Gabriel and reached out as if to touch him, but he kept his hand just above the executioner's head, like he was trying to read him. The heat was rising off Nick's body.

She pulled away from Gabriel as he reached for her thighs, not able to trust him, or herself. *I can't go through this again.* "Sorry, but I don't want to be saved. I'm going to save myself."

Nick glanced at her, his eyes dark and unreadable as he tapped his gun against his thigh and worked his jaw.

"Ah, but you cannot," Gabriel said. "There is a team of very pissed-off souls on their way to take you out as we speak. We had to take numbers." He held up a slip of paper with the number two on it. "Checkmate was number one, but I got two. But I'm here to save you, not kill you. I had to lie about that, so if you hear any rumors that I was describing all the ways I'd torture you before actually killing you, don't believe it. I had to play a role, you know? To get the good number. I'm here to save you." He took her hand and held it between his hands. "Come with me. I will—"

"Becca."

She looked at Nick, and he flicked the tip of his gun at Gabriel and gave a slight head shake. His shoulders were tense, and the tendons in his neck were strung tight like cords...like he was ready for a battle. Slowly, she returned her gaze to Gabriel, who was still talking about his love for her and how they would start over. He was real...but...she tried to clear her body of the shock at his reappearance. He looked like Gabriel, for sure. Then he caught her face between his hands and lifted her face, leaning forward to kiss her.

She immediately tensed, and she glanced at Nick, whose face was dark and thundering. He almost looked...jealous? He lifted the gun and pointed it at the back of Gabriel's head, his eyes on hers as if he were asking permission to end it.

Seriously? He was that jealous? Nick cocked one eyebrow in surprise, as if he'd read her mind, and then he tapped his index finger to his temple, telling her to think.

Think? Um...

She realized Gabriel's lips were almost on hers...then

she caught a soft, flowery scent that would never, ever be Gabriel. Stunned, she slammed a fireball upward, catching him in the gut.

Nick jerked his gun out of the way as Gabriel groaned and dropped to his knees, clutching his stomach. "You did it twice, you bitch!"

Becca stared at him, horror swelling inside as she watched the man she had once loved die again in front of her. She lurched to her feet.

"Nice work, Becca." Nick glared down at Gabriel, a sense of satisfaction on his face as he watched the other man suffer. "Good call."

"Holy cow," Paige said. "He gets killed just for trying to get a kiss? You're such a badass!"

"I didn't mean to kill him," she whispered, then stopped as Gabriel began to shimmer and flicker, and then in his place was the form of a five-foot-five woman with a snake tattoo wrapped all the way up her body from her feet to her ears and a giant knife in her hand where the axe had been. *"Roxanne?"* Relief flooded her. She hadn't killed Gabriel again. She'd *known* something was off! She grinned at Nick, who gave her a nod of acknowledgment. "I knew it wasn't him."

Then she realized that meant she really *had* killed Gabriel the first time.

Damn.

She sat down again and pressed her palms to her eyes. "It took me years to accept Gabriel's death, and now I have to start over again." She swore as Nick approached and set his hand on her shoulder, squeezing gently. "I do *not* have time for therapy right now."

"Who's that chick? What happened to the big baddie?" Paige asked. "And how did you know it wasn't him?"

Becca allowed herself to accept the comfort from Nick's touch. Cheaper than therapy, plus it made nice things happen in her lower region that would be a good distraction from the fact she wanted to curl up in a ball and cry. Not that she would. She never cried. Too impractical. She peeled her fists out of her eyes and looked at Paige, who was staring at Becca with an expression of total adoration and awe. She sat up straighter. "I put Roxanne in hell after she kidnapped and killed over two hundred children from neighboring villages in Europe."

She watched Paige nudge the charred woman with her toe.

"She's a Mablevi, which means she can take the form of any person, even if they are a different shape or size. As a human, she used to take on the forms of the parents of the kids. When I took her to hell, she swore she'd kill me someday." She pressed her hand to her forehead. "I can't believe I almost thought she was Gabriel." She groaned and dropped her head to her knees. "I really need a vacation."

Paige passed her hand over Roxanne's forehead. "Ooo . . . she's still got a soul. Can I take it?"

Becca frowned and tested Roxanne. Paige was right. "Sure. It's basically the same process you used to take it out of my knee."

"Sweet." Paige straddled Roxanne and pressed her left hand to her forehead and lifted her face toward the ceiling. "I command thy soul be released into my safekeeping." She grinned at Becca. "Did that sound good? I think I need a stage presence to impress people."

Becca couldn't help but smile back. Maybe she'd keep Paige around. The kid was good for a laugh, and she could really use a little levity in her life sometimes. "It's great. Go for it."

"Cool!" Paige turned back to Roxanne and scrunched her eyes shut, repeating her mantra in increasingly loud tones.

Nick tapped Becca's shoulder, and she glanced up at him. He held out a hand to her. "Come talk."

She sighed and grabbed his hand and let him haul her to her feet.

They walked a short distance from Paige, who was trying out a new soul-harvesting mantra that included threats of damnation and torture.

He kept his voice low. "You okay?"

She nodded. "Thanks for pointing out that something was off. I can't believe I didn't notice. It's not like me."

"I'm sure Roxanne knew the only way to fool you was to come as Gabriel, then make her move while you were still in shock." He held his hand out, poised over her shoulder. "Yes?"

She knew he was offering the kind of comfort only he could give her, and she wanted to accept it so badly, but she shook her head. "No. I'm back in control now, and I need to deal with this by shutting it down." She took a deep breath.

He nodded and dropped his hand. "You must be a popular girl." He looked around the room. "I think we need to get out of here before more of your enemies show up."

She scowled. "Why does everyone make it personal? It really bugs me. If they wouldn't run around and kill people and do other evil things, I wouldn't have shown up to reel them in. People need to take responsibility for themselves, you know?"

He smiled. "I don't blame you for your job. I'm very impressed at how little you actually do for Satan."

She pushed at his chest. "Stop trying to woo me with compliments. It won't work, you know. I'm immune to your charm."

"I have charm?" He looked surprised and pleased at the thought.

Paige shrieked, and they both turned around to see her leap off Roxanne and start clawing at her skin. "Mother fucker! I hate this part!" She started beating at her left breast. "Get out of there, you pervert!"

Becca sighed at the sight of her apprentice trying to subdue the newly harvested soul. "She's a piece of work."

"I like her pluckiness. I think she's got potential. I can see why she and Dani hit it off..." His smile faded, and Becca felt the angst building inside him again.

"So, how'd you know he wasn't right?" Becca asked, not wanting to feel his pain when hers was so close to the surface.

"He wasn't giving off the right emotions. He didn't feel like love or guilt. There was joy to see you, but it was a dark joy, not a happy one that I'd expect from someone who'd loved you." He looked at her. "It wasn't the kind of love you were feeling for him."

She looked away from his dark gaze, watching Paige as she sat up and brushed the rubble off herself. "Just because I slept with him didn't mean there was love."

"I felt it from you."

"No, you didn't. It was guilt."

"Both."

She looked at Nick. "I would be a fool to love anyone except Satan."

He traced his finger over the tip of her nose. "Sometimes we're fools. It happens."

She smacked his hand. "Go away."

He raised his brows, as if there was no chance of that. Which there wasn't, of course. But before he could say anything, Paige interrupted. "Hey, Nick."

He turned toward Paige. "What's up, little one?"

Paige was studying him, her forearms draped over her knees as she caught her breath. "What are you, exactly?"

Becca felt Nick tense beside her. "What do you mean?"

"You're talking about how you can sense all these emotions and stuff. So, you're not human. Plus you survived the acid pit conduit because of your supposed dark side." She hauled herself to her feet, walked up to him, and peered at him curiously. "So, I can't figure out what you are."

He smiled down at her, as if he had nothing to hide. "I'm an elf."

Becca had to turn away at the innocent look on his face.

"Elf?" Paige studied him as she picked some dirt out of her hair. "Elf? An elf can make it through an acid pit?"

"I'm a very sturdy elf."

Becca giggled, and they both turned to look at her. Her giggle faded under their surprised expressions. "What?"

"I've never heard you giggle before," Nick said. "Since when do you giggle?"

Paige beamed at Nick. "You made her laugh." She peeked at Becca. "You're way prettier when you smile. Not nearly as scary and cold-looking."

Becca immediately stopped smiling.

Nick was still staring at her as if he'd never seen her before. "You really giggled."

"So?"

"So, it was cute. I didn't think you did cute."

She snorted, even though a part of her felt like cleaning out her ears to make sure she was hearing correctly. "I'm not cute."

"That was cute." He looked at Paige. "Wasn't it cute?"

Paige nodded. "Definitely cute."

Becca set her hands on her hips and gave them her best glare. "Would you guys cut it out? I'm not cute." But it did feel sort of fun to be *called* cute. It sounded so innocent and pure, two things she so wasn't.

"Well, not now that you're thrusting your breasts out while wearing your soul-harvesting outfit. *Now* you look like a prostitute," Paige said.

Becca rolled her eyes, not quite as annoyed as she wanted them to think. "I'm leaving."

"I'm coming with you." Nick threw a warm, muscular arm around her shoulders while Paige latched her fingers around her wrist.

Nick leaned down near her ear. "Cute *and* deadly is a very good combination."

Becca's belly tightened, and she turned her head to look at Nick. His gaze was intent, and she knew he was completely serious. And her traitorous body hoped he meant it personally. "Nick..."

Then they dissolved into the floor, and she didn't have to finish the sentence that she'd had no idea how to finish.

They popped up in the Council's dungeon floor just in time to see an old man and a businessman throwing a trussed-up pirate into the Chamber of Unspeakable Horrors.

Thirteen

J erome!" Nick lunged across the room and dove into the Chamber just as the pirate slipped out of sight.

"No!" Horror knifed through Becca as Nick disappeared into the Chamber and the old man and the businessman slammed the door shut and locked him inside. "Nick!" Becca yanked herself free of Paige's clinging grip and hurled a fireball at the men. Both men flew up and back from the explosion, and crashed into the wall. "Deal with them, Paige!"

"I'm on it!" Paige shouted as she leapt over a coffee table and landed on the businessman. "You move and I'll fry you!"

Becca rushed over to the Chamber and yanked on the lock while Paige shouted threats and obscenities at the men, naming tortures in hell that Becca didn't even know existed.

The lock didn't give. "Dammit! Nick!" She slammed a fireball into the lock, but nothing happened. She shouted her frustration and slammed another against the door, then another, and another and another, until Paige grabbed her arm and hauled her back.

"Let go of me! I have to get him out!" What if he was

dead already? Or insane? What kind of hell was he going through? She hurled a blue fireball at the door, but it didn't even rattle. "Nick!"

"Boss! It's not working!"

Becca froze and stared at Paige, suddenly realizing what she was doing. Of course her fireballs wouldn't open it. Satan had made that lock strong enough to keep Rivkas inside, before he'd traded it to the Council. Since when had she lost her ability to think strategically? Since Nick had thrown himself in that damned Chamber, apparently. She banged on the door. "Nick! Nick! Can you hear me?"

Nothing, but the sounds of screams, which is all anyone ever heard coming from the Chamber of Unspeakable Horrors. Very few emerged from the Chamber alive, and those who did were so scrambled that they were no good for anything but walking in circles in fenced-in areas, chattering gibberish and being kept away from sharp objects.

It might already be too late.

No! She wouldn't think like that!

Her hands shaking, she whirled away from the door and grabbed the businessman by the shirt and hauled him to his feet. "How do I open that door?"

His face was white, and he was still coughing from the explosion. "Let me go and I'll make you rich."

She leaned her face against his. "I'm from hell. I have all the money I need."

Paige grabbed the old man and pulled him up. "I will pull out all your entrails and eat them for dinner if you don't tell me!" When he turned ashen and passed out, she cursed and started patting the old guy's face, ordering him to wake up.

Becca's hostage's eyes widened. "You're Satan's favorite Rivka! You can't threaten me! We have a peace accord. If you hurt me, then the peace accord is off."

Becca hesitated for a fraction of a second, knowing that Satan would be beyond livid if she broke the peace accord. There was nothing he valued more than his political power, and even Becca wouldn't be spared his wrath if she screwed that up.

Screw it. *Nick was in the Chamber.*

"If you don't help me get my man out of that Chamber now, the peace accord will be the least of your concerns. I assume you have personal fire insurance?" She flared up a fireball and held it under his chin, watching his skin turn red. "Open the door, or I'll kill you." She let him look into her eyes and showed him exactly what she was willing to do.

Paige was suddenly over her shoulder. "Just stick it between his legs."

A bead of sweat dripped down the man's brow. "There are two keys!" he blurted. "I have one, and Paul has the other. They both have to be turned at the same time, by two different people, and you have to chant 'Satan is my hero' three times in a row while you're doing it, and then they'll open."

Becca grabbed the key out his pocket while Paige retrieved the one from the old man. Then they both ran across the room and inserted their keys in the lock. "Ready?"

Paige nodded. "So ready."

They both turned their keys and there was a click.

Paige made a grunt of satisfaction, and then they began to chant the magic words.

The instant they finished, the door popped ajar. Becca yanked it open, and Nick fell out on top of her, holding on to a screaming, convulsing pirate. "Nick!" She grabbed his face, forcing him to look at her so she could see into his eyes. They were clear and green and sane. She nearly collapsed with relief and kissed him hard on the mouth. "Don't ever do that again, or I swear I'll shove a gold fireball down your throat. Got it?"

He grabbed her hair and pulled her close so he could kiss her back, just as hard, with a desperation that had her fists digging into his shirt as his body jerked with the effort of holding the pirate still.

Paige took a flying leap and landed on top of Jerome, trying to catch his flailing limbs. "I'm with you, Nick. I've got your back."

Nick's fingers tightened in Becca's hair, and she could feel him drawing on her self-control, and she let him, realizing he was still fighting the Chamber and needed her inner strength. "Take it, Nick," she whispered, sending him everything she had, her throat tightening when she felt him building his own walls against the Terrors racing around inside him.

He rested his forehead against hers and took a deep breath, even while he and Paige fought to keep the pirate from hurting himself in his seizures. "Take us to my place."

She wrapped her arms around all three of them immediately. "Where is it?"

He muttered an address in upstate New York, and she took them there instantly.

*   *   *

"Ma!" Nick shouted for his mother before they'd even come up through the rich pine floor of the log cabin she had raised him and Dani in. "Are you around?"

"Out back!" Yasmine Rawlings's voice bellowed through the French doors.

Nick turned to Becca. "Take him upstairs. There's a room at the top. I'll be there in one second."

Without hesitation, she grabbed the convulsing Jerome under the arms. "Paige. His feet."

"I'm on it." Paige grabbed his feet, then yelped as he kicked her in the shin. "I'm okay. I got it." Groaning softly, she followed Becca up the stairs, Jerome twisting and flailing between them.

"Wait."

Becca turned to look at him. "What?"

"I . . ." God, where did he start? "Thanks."

She smiled down at him. "It was purely in my own self-interest."

He raised his brows, knowing full well that he'd sensed a lot more than that when he'd fed on her self-control outside the Chamber.

Becca frowned. "I hate that look."

He couldn't help but chuckle; then he turned and bolted out into the backyard. He didn't see his ma anywhere, just a broad expanse of woods and lawn. "Ma?"

"Up here."

He looked up, tensing immediately. His ma was at the top of one of their huge pine trees with a chainsaw, wearing a helmet over her gray hair. She let go with one hand to wave down at him. "I was about to do some trimming before winter hits. Keeps the trees healthy. What are you doing here? I thought you were helping Jerome with guard duty. And what is that godawful screaming?"

At fifty-seven years of age, his mom was too old for tree trimming, not that she'd ever accept that. "I need your help." He tried to keep his voice calm enough to get her down safely before he told her what was going on. "Can you come inside for a minute?"

His mom stared at him for a long moment, then slung the chainsaw over her shoulder and started climbing down the tree as fast as she could. "What's going on? Talk to me, Nicky. It is Dani?" She landed on the grass in front of Nick and shoved the goggles onto her hard hat. "Tell me it's not Dani."

He ignored the question about Dani, for the moment. "It's Jerome. He was in the Chamber of Unspeakable Horrors."

"Are you kidding? Where is he?"

"In Dani's room…"

Yasmine was already running into the house, ripping off her helmet and goggles, and tossing her gloves over her shoulder. "How long was he in?"

Nick sprinted after her. "A minute. Maybe two."

"Then we have a chance." She leapt up the three steps into the house, her gray hair flying as she bolted around the old pine dining room chairs and vaulted up the stairs two steps at time.

She flung open the door to the bedroom, and Nick cringed when he saw Jerome writhing on the bed, Becca sitting on his legs while Paige tried to hold his arms still. Paige's tongue was out to the side and her brow was furrowed with concentration, but it was Becca he really noticed. Her eyes were wide and she looked terrified. Not for her own safety. For Jerome's? He reached out for her emotions, confirming his suspicions. His Rivka was truly worried about Jerome.

His throat tightened and she cocked her head at him, her brows puckered together ever so slightly. What was she reading on his face right now? "Could use a little help here, big guy."

He scooted past his ma to grab Jerome's legs from Becca, and she sat on his chest, using her weight to keep him on the bed.

Yasmine clasped her hand to her heart. "Dear Lord, the poor boy."

"Want me to kill him and put him out of his misery?" Paige asked. "This is a bad way to go."

Yasmine smacked Paige in the forehead with her palm. "Don't say that! He can hear you! I will not allow that kind of attitude in here. Shape up or get out!" Paige's mouth dropped open as the tiny lady palmed her once more.

"Ma, she's a kid. Leave her alone." He grunted as Jerome's foot slipped free and clocked him in the nuts. He gritted his teeth against the pain, then noticed the look of surprise on Becca's face. "Yeah, that's the other way besides gold to get to me."

"Nicky!" Yasmine looked stunned. "You told her what you are?"

"Yeah, a sturdy elf," Paige said. "Who cares? Can you fix this guy already or what? He's really strong."

"I don't know yet." Yasmine gave Nick a long look, then leaned around Becca and set her hands on Jerome's forehead.

"Should I move?" Becca asked. "Can I help?"

"You're a Rivka?"

Becca nodded.

"I am, too," Paige said, her teeth gritted with the effort of trying to keep Jerome's arms from flailing. One wrist got free and he clocked her in the side of the head. She cursed and sat down hard, blinking several times, but not letting go of his left wrist.

Yasmine shot a skeptical glance at Nick, then laid her hand on Becca's belly, testing her for healing skills, as she always did with someone new when she needed help. Almost never found anyone, but she always checked anyway.

But this time her eyebrows went up in surprise. "Apparently, you *can* help me. Put your palms over his heart."

"She can?" Nick looked at Becca in shock. How was that possible? She was a Rivka. Born to destroy. Not heal.

Both the women ignored him as Becca scooted to the side and Paige struggled to her feet again, locking Jerome's left wrist between her thighs while she lunged for the other one.

Nick moved closer to Jerome's head to help hold his upper body still, his shoulder brushing against Becca.

Becca laid her hands over Jerome's heart. "Now what?"

Yasmine laid her fingertips on Jerome's forehead. "Close your eyes."

Becca did as instructed.

"Now go into his heart and find one of the Terrors that has hold of him."

Becca's forehead furrowed in concentration; then she sucked her breath and her body jerked. She cursed under her breath. "Found one."

"No swearing, please," Yasmine instructed, her own eyes closed. "This is a healing process, not a bar in hell."

"Sorry." Becca was pale and trembling, and Nick shifted so his shoulder was against her back. She immediately leaned into him, and he felt her draw on his energy. "Now what?"

"Draw the Terror into your own body. Then find another one and do it again until there aren't any more left. I'm doing the same thing. Now stop talking and concentrate."

Becca nodded, and she scrunched her eyes shut. Beads of perspiration formed on her upper lip, and she flinched suddenly and let out a small noise of pain. "Got one," she whispered.

Yasmine was too absorbed working on Jerome's head to respond, so Nick leaned forward and set his chin on her shoulder, the only contact he could give her with his hands occupied holding down Jerome. "Good work," he said quietly. "Are you all right doing this?"

She nodded once, not opening her eyes. "Keep touching me. It helps."

"You got it." Jerome started struggling more fiercely, and Nick shifted his position to keep him pinned down, but not losing contact with Becca. He reached out and sent her his worry, his admiration for what she was doing, and she drank it in, drawing on it even while she sucked Jerome's darkness out of his heart.

He caught a glimpse at the darkness in Jerome, and a sudden flare inside him answered, and he knew he hadn't gotten out of the Chamber unscathed, though he'd been able to use his Markku indestructibility to protect himself fairly well.

Becca's eyes flipped open and she looked at him. "I felt that. You need help, too."

"Jerome first. I'm fine for now."

She looked at him for a long moment, then closed her eyes and went back to work.

Twenty minutes later, Jerome stopped twitching. Paige sighed with relief when Nick dismissed her, and staggered to the door, muttering something about disability benefits, pressing her palm to her rapidly swelling eye. Nick shifted position to sit behind Becca, wrapping his arms around her and placing his hands over hers while she worked. She pulled on his life force as hard as he gave it to her, and he knew they were a team.

"That's good," she whispered.

Forty-five minutes after that, Becca sat back and Nick caught her. "I can't find any more," she said. "I think they're gone."

Her body was trembling and slick with sweat. She was still wearing her outfit from the bar last night, though it seemed so long ago. She leaned heavily against him. "That's the creepiest thing I've ever done."

Yasmine looked up, her own eyes bleary. "I'll finish up. You go rest." She smiled briefly. "What's your name?"

"Becca."

"Okay, Becca, after you and I rest, we are going to have a little talk. Good work."

Becca stared at Yasmine as if she couldn't believe Yasmine's compliment, and Nick stood up. "Come on. I'll show you where you can crash." He tugged her to her feet and she swayed against him.

"I'm fine." She pushed off him to stand up on her own, tilting only slightly. "We need to get back to the Council offices to find out what happened. The Council has the means and motivation to send someone to kill Satan, so I need to know if they're involved." She sighed and looked at Nick. "And they were around for the Markku rebellion, and I have some questions I want to ask."

Yasmine glared at her. "You will *not*. It is critical you rest after healing. Cleanse and rest."

"I don't have time. Those men will be gone." She started to fade through the floor, though she was so drained that it took longer than usual, which gave Nick time to grab on and Yasmine time to lecture her before they finally faded away.

Becca's head was still hurting from her first ever mom-lecture when they came up slowly through the floor of the Council offices.

The two downed men were gone, and the entire place was on fire.

"*Satan Jr.*" Nick cursed and started sprinting for the door and the roaring flames.

Fourteen

Nick shouldered his way through the fire, ran down the hall, and reached the door to the room Satan Jr. had been kept in, waving aside the black smoke so he could see where he was going. Flames were licking the walls and sparks were flying out of the light fixtures in the ceiling. He slammed his body against the steel door. It flew open and a roar of flames burst through the opening and into the hall.

He charged inside, ignoring his shirt as it caught fire and burned right off him. The freezer was standing in the corner, misshapen from the heat of the flames, with a pool of colored water on the floor around it. "Dammit!"

He grabbed the cooler and looked around for Becca. "Becca!"

After a minute, she appeared in the doorway, holding her T-shirt over her face. "Did he melt?"

"Get us out of here."

"With the cooler?" She ducked as a light fixture exploded over her head, and a burning ceiling panel landed on her bare arm. She flipped it aside and jumped into the room. "Good thing I'm from hell," she said. "Me and fire go way back."

At that moment, there was a crackling from the corner and Nick realized the cabinet where Jerome had set up a stash of weapons for his stay was about to go. "Get down!"

She dropped to the floor as the metal cabinet exploded, and a huge serrated knife flew right toward her. She rolled to the side, and it slammed into her thigh.

Nick cursed and let go of the cooler, dropped to the ground next to her, and yanked the knife out of her thigh. A groan of anguish slipped out of her mouth, and Nick caught her as she started to collapse, his heart racing as he felt her pain.

"Showoff." He pressed his palm over the flow of blood gushing from her leg. "You're immune to fire. You couldn't have left it at that? Had to get yourself impaled?"

"I like a challenge." She winced when he adjusted his hand, then gestured at the floor, where the water had turned rosy from her blood. "What about all the water on the floor? Isn't this Satan Jr.?"

As if he cared about a stupid sociopath right now! She was losing way too much blood, but the smoke was so thick he could barely see her through it. "We have to get you out of here." He swallowed hard, trying not to look at the blood gushing out of her leg. Dammit! Why hadn't he inherited the true healer gift from his ma? He had all the annoying emotions of a healer, but minimal healer skills. He felt her shudder, and he scowled. "Stay with me, gorgeous."

"I'm fine." She coughed, then splashed water onto the T-shirt before pulling it up over her face again. "I have to get out of here. Smoke's a killer. Get the freezer, will you?"

He smiled at her insistence, then reached out to put a hand on the freezer. "I've got it."

She coughed again, then turned a murky gray, almost the color of the smoke that was circling them.

Then re-formed right where she was.

He pressed harder on her leg and she let out a squeal of pain that had his heart twisting. "Sorry."

"Don't let me lose any more blood," she ordered.

Another crash came from somewhere in the building. "I'm not planning on it. Just get us out of here."

She nodded, closed her eyes, and this time shimmered only briefly before taking solid form again. "Dammit! Come on!" She coughed again, a brutal hack that shook her body.

Nick pressed harder on her leg and tried to send her his energy through his palm. "Come on, Becca. You can do it."

She bunched her fist and the muscles in her neck flexed, but nothing happened. She jerked her eyes open. "I can't do it. I'm too exhausted. That healing stuff wiped me out. I feel like hell." She looked around the room, her eyes wild but calculating. "We have to get out another way."

The ceiling crashed down in the hallway and flaming boards blocked the door.

He thought frantically for a second, then nearly sagged with relief. "I never reset my portal. It should still be linked to Jerome's office down the hall. We'll have to go through the fire."

"Fine with me. I like fire."

"Take over." He pressed her hand to her thigh, then yanked off his sweats and cranked them around her leg.

Her face got white and she started to waver.

"Becca. Stay with me." He helped her to her feet and pulled her shirt up over her face as another cough wracked her body. He kept his hands around her waist. "You can manage?"

She looked at the door, then at him. "Of course." She gritted her teeth and took a step.

Her leg gave out instantly and she fell to the floor, cursing the whole way down.

He picked her back up, careful to protect her leg. "Nice language."

"It inspires me." She stood on one leg, gripping his arm. "Turn around and get down on your knees."

He did it as the outer wall exploded inward, sending studs and plaster flying at them. Becca shuddered as she threw herself onto his back, and wrapped her arms around his neck. "Help me with my leg."

He grabbed her injured leg and pulled it gently around to his stomach, wincing at the moan of pain from Becca as he hooked her heels around his waist. "I'm glad you're not one of those women who's too proud to let a guy carry her."

"I can let you carry me because we both know I could kill you in a heartbeat. I have nothing to prove." She rested her head against his back, and he squatted down and grabbed the freezer with both arms. "Just hurry up already."

"You're so demanding. No wonder you're single." The fact she was ordering him around had to mean she was going to be okay. So what if she couldn't shimmer. Didn't mean she was in danger of a total collapse. *Keep it together, Nick.* He got a grip on the freezer and then bolted for the door, slamming through the burning wall of boards.

"What makes you think I'm single?" Her arms tightened around his neck as a beam fell toward them. "Maybe I have hordes of boyfriends."

He bolted past it and it landed with a crash behind them. "I'd be willing to bet that there's been no one since Gabriel." He slammed the freezer into Jerome's office door, shattering the wood. "You need to stop obsessing about killing him."

She flinched as her leg caught the doorframe. "I'm not obsessing." Her voice was strained.

"Yes, you are." There was too much smoke to see if his portal was still there, so he sprinted to where it had been, and he sighed with relief as the humming vibrated through his body. "It's not your fault you killed him. You did nothing wrong."

She tightened her grip around him as the room began to disappear. "You're not just saying that so I won't kill you before you can kill Satan? Trying to get on my good side?"

"I'm already there, aren't I?" He sighed with relief as his safe room came into focus.

She let go of him and slid down his body, until she landed with a moan on the floor. "You're so arrogant."

"Yeah, maybe." He set the freezer on its back so no more water could leak out, then went to scrape Becca off the floor.

She waved him off as she rolled onto her butt. "How much of him is still in the freezer?"

"I don't know." He squatted in front of her, his heart

tightening at how pale her face was. "Let me see your leg."

"We have to see to Satan Jr. first." She batted his hand when he went for her leg anyway. "You can do whatever you want to my leg after we get Satan Jr. secured. That's my priority, Nick. He's involved in this situation with your sister, which means he's involved in trying to get me killed. That's my focus, not my leg."

He scowled at her, and she glared back, and he realized she wasn't going back down. "You're a stubborn wench."

She grinned. "Thank you. Now check on Junior."

He sighed and walked over to the freezer, keeping one eye on her in case she suddenly toppled over in a death spiral. He flipped open the lid and glanced inside, then took a closer look and cursed. "It's empty."

"Really?" She scooted across the floor and pulled herself up on the edge of the freezer and peered inside. "It's not even wet in here." She looked up at him, grimacing with pain. "You think that colored water on the floor was him?"

"No." He grabbed her under her arms and scooped her up, relieved when she didn't protest, but worried when he felt her sag against him. "I think someone took him somewhere else to melt and re-form and left that water to distract us. And it worked." He scowled as he carried her across the room and set her on his bed. "Do you have any idea how dangerous he is?"

"Yes, I do." She groaned and stretched on her back and closed her eyes. "Satan's a lamb compared to him."

"That what I've heard." He checked the bloodstained wrap on her thigh to make sure it was still secure. Blood was still leaking, but its rate had slowed. "You need to get this cleaned out. I don't have any first-aid supplies, since I never need them."

Her brow furrowed. "Yeah, I think it sliced my quad muscles pretty good. Maybe broke my femur, too. Hurts like a mother, actually." She propped herself up on her elbows to look at him. "You do realize that Satan Jr. escaping is a major problem, don't you? I just helped Satan redo his will, and he listed Satan Jr. as his sole heir. If you kill Satan now, Satan Jr. will automatically get hell, and that's *really* bad. I can't control him, he's got no redeeming characteristics, and he certainly wouldn't adhere to his daddy's treaty with the Council. Plus, he's trying to kill your sister and me. Double whammy."

"But I've got part of him in my freezer." Nick frowned as her movement caused the blood to start to flow more quickly. "Lie back down." He gently propped a pillow under her leg. "And if your quad is sliced, you need surgery. Now." He cleared his throat. "Because you won't be any good to me if you're too injured to function."

She eyed him, as if she heard the hesitation in his last comment. "If he's anything like Satan, it doesn't matter if part of him is in your freezer. As long as Satan has more than fifty percent of his body in liquid form, he can re-form entirely. The other part can't re-form into anything. So you'd need to melt him and then divide the water into two separate containers of exactly fifty percent and never let them touch." She shifted slightly and winced. "I don't have time for surgery. We have things to do."

Nick cursed and sat down heavily on the bed, suddenly exhausted. "So he's out there somewhere, re-forming, right now." He set his hand on her thigh and reached inside to see if he could sense the extent of the damage. He frowned at the dark pulsing inside her. "There's something wrong with you."

"I'd say there's a good chance of that, yeah." She raised her brows. "I meant, of Satan Jr. off re-forming somewhere." Then she grinned. "And yeah, there's probably more than one thing wrong with me, too."

"No, something other than the leg."

She gently peeled his hand away. "I'm fine. Just a scratch." Then she negated her words by groaning and collapsing back onto the pillows. "So, we'll have to find Junior and kill him before he can destroy everything about hell that's good." She draped her arm over her face and sighed.

"Is there anything that's good?" *Besides you.* He was startled by his thought, then realized it was true. Too true for his comfort.

She opened one eye. "You'd be surprised. Satan's a big fan of the luxuries of life, and it's pretty easy to creatively reallocate them to the peons." She tried to lift her leg and shuddered. "This isn't going to work. I'm never going to be able to do everything I need to do if I have only one good leg." She dug into her bodice and pulled out a tiny cell phone. "No pockets in my slut outfit," she explained when she realized he was staring at her in surprise.

"I can fix that." He rolled off the bed and headed toward a metal armoire in the corner, needing something to do to take his mind off what he'd felt inside Becca. Something was really wrong, and her leg was a mess, and he knew she wasn't going to admit it. And they still had to figure out how to save Dani, and now Satan Jr. was missing. He cursed and yanked open the door to the armoire, slamming it into the wall. He glared over his shoulder at her. "I forbid you to die."

"It's not your choice."

"Give me a break, Becca."

She hesitated, then managed a small smile. "Okay, Nick. I promise I won't die. Happy?"

"Swear?"

"I swear."

Nick grunted a response and turned back to the armoire, and Becca realized for the first time that he was wearing only his boxers. His body was well muscled and lean, making her recall the hardness of his body when she'd hitched a ride out of the Council offices.

Like she had time to be attracted to him. She scowled and hit the number-two speed dial on her phone.

Theresa answered on the first ring. "You want your coat back, don't you?"

Becca smiled at the sound of the dragon's voice. "Actually, I need to call in one of the favors you owe me."

"Excellent. Zeke's still out of town and I'm bored out of my mind. You want me to kill your apprentice, don't you? She's driving you mad but you're too soft to do it yourself, so you need a badass dragon to take her out? I'm down with that. Tell me where she is, and I'll take care of her."

"Actually, I need some espresso."

Silence.

"Dragon?"

"You know I can't give you a drink from the Goblet

of Eternal Youth! And why do you need it? Aren't you immortal?"

"I'm immortal in that I'll never die of natural causes or grow old, but other than that, I'm no tougher than a human. And I currently have a hole the size of a grape-fruit in my thigh. Also, I have a sociopath to slay, a leader of hell to protect, and a lifeline to break. I can't do it all on one leg, and if I don't do it soon, there will be major problems that will reverberate throughout the mortal world and the Otherworld." She peeked at Nick, who was now dressed in gray sweatpants and was back to digging in the ugly metal armoire. But at least he hadn't put a shirt on yet…Argh. *Focus, Becca.* What was wrong with her?

"Well, that sucks and all, but I'm not even the Guard-ian anymore," Theresa said. "Mona is back at Justine's under house arrest. I actually feel kind of bad, because Justine never lets her go *anywhere*—"

"Perfect. So she's looking for a holiday. Steal her, and bring her to me. I'll take a sip, you can pretend you don't know what I'm doing, and all's good."

Theresa sighed. "Fine. I'm coming. Where are you?"

"Hang on." She moved the phone away from her mouth. "I have a friend bringing me medical supplies. Where is this place?"

He held out his hand for the phone, and she handed it to him.

"Hello?" He frowned almost immediately. "No, we're not naked." He raised his brows at Becca, and she shot him a look of apology. Like she needed Theresa bringing *that* up right now.

Fifteen

Becca closed her eyes and snuggled back down on the bed as Nick gave directions to Theresa. She was completely drained and her leg was seriously hurting, but she was also amazed and exhilarated at the same time. She'd felt the blackness around Jerome's heart, tormenting him, and she'd actually pulled it out. It was almost like taking out a soul, but it was different. It was like peeling away darkness to let the sun shine through, and it had felt unbelievable.

She sighed and let the exhaustion take her, and her muscles began to relax. Why was she so tired? She felt like her body weighed a thousand pounds.

The bed shifted under her, and she cracked her eyes to see Nick stretching out next to her, a look of total exhaustion on his face.

He held out a pair of red sweats and a gray T-shirt. "They'll probably be too big, but I thought you might want out of those clothes while we wait for your friend. She said she'll be here in the morning." The worry in his eyes clearly said that he wasn't sure Becca would last that long. Or maybe he was worried about waiting that long to work on saving his sister.

"Thanks." She rolled to the side of the bed and willed herself to sit up, so tired she could barely hold herself upright. She'd noticed a bathroom, but she was way too beat to make it there for privacy, so she just turned her back on Nick while she unhooked the leather bustier...um...*tried* to unhook it. Her fingers were trembling so badly she couldn't get a grip on it.

She felt Nick's fingers on hers and she dropped her hands to let him unhook it, bracing herself with her hands on the bed so she didn't tip over. His hands brushed against her bare back, and it was all she could do not to suck in her breath at the contact.

The bodice fell free and Nick caught it and pulled it off her upper body. Leaving her naked from the waist up, her back toward him.

For a minute, neither of them moved. Then his fingers traced over her right shoulder blade, light against her skin. "What's this scar from?"

She thought for a minute "What's it shaped like?"

"A circle."

"Oh, yeah. A fifteen-year-old kid shot me on my first soul-hunting mission as a Rivka. I figured anyone under eighteen was safe. Not so much. I was pretty naive back then. Sort of like Paige, actually..."

He rubbed the scar gently. "So, you're pretty mortal?"

"I'm not going to lose my girlish figure, but a bullet in my gut will have the same effect on me that it'd have on any human. Or a knife in my thigh." She swallowed hard, trying to concentrate, but not having much success. All she wanted to do was press herself against his hand and let it go where it wanted. "Satan decided that any Rivka who couldn't stay alive wasn't worth having on the payroll."

"Hmmm…" His fingers trailed down her spine and touched her lower back. "What about this?"

"Fireball. When Satan promoted me to his number-one Rivka, his previous number-one Rivka wasn't so happy."

He spread his palm over the damaged area. "How did that not kill you?"

"Once I became the number-one Rivka, other Rivkas' fireballs became less effective against me. Perk of the job." She tensed as his hand went around her waist, his fingers on her ribs, just below her breasts.

He shifted, and she felt his breath against the bullet wound on her bare shoulder. "So, what do we do about the bubble?"

"Ask Satan if there's a back door."

"And if there isn't?" His lips brushed the curve of her neck.

She caught her breath. "I'll have to kill you," she whispered. "Don't forget, you're merely a pawn in my plan to secure freedom for myself." She couldn't stop the shudder that went through her from his kiss. *Time to redirect this conversation.* "How badly are you bugging from the Chamber?"

He stopped kissing her for a moment while he considered her question. "I'm okay."

She retrieved the T-shirt from her lap and yanked it over her head before he could start kissing her again. He sighed and helped tug it down over her back.

"Okay? Meaning you have a good hour or so before you start to go crazy?" She tried to stand up to slip off her thong, and immediately sat back down when her leg rebelled with a flash of pain.

Something rumbled deep in his chest. "Don't be a martyr. You can ask for help."

"You're just trying to cop a feel."

"I don't take advantage of injured women." He scooted behind her and set his hands on her waist to steady her as she stood up again.

"Good to know." She slipped the thong off under her skirt and felt a thrill rush through her as it dropped to the ground, a sliver of black satin on the wood floor.

He leaned forward to look at it. "So, what would you be wearing if you weren't in your working clothes?"

"Pale pink lace." She felt her cheeks flush as she tugged the sweats up to her thighs, lifting them carefully over her bandage while Nick held her steady.

"Pink." He seemed to roll it over in his mind. "I'd like to see you in pale pink. I bet it's a good look for you."

"No one gets to see me in pale pink." She unhooked the skirt, tugged it over her legs, and dropped it on the floor with the rest of her slut outfit, then eased back to the bed with his help. "It would kill my reputation."

He helped settle her, then moved to her feet to unstrap the slut heels from her feet, his fingers caressing her feet a little more than was necessary. Not that she could quite bring herself to protest. "I already know you're a heartless, cold killing machine," he said. "What harm could a little pink do?"

"It makes me forget myself."

He tossed both shoes onto the floor, then crawled up next to her and propped his head up on his elbow. "From everything you've said, I'd have thought that would be a good thing."

She fiddled with the edge of her T-shirt, noticing that it

smelled like him, curving around her and comforting her. "Not if it makes it too hard to go back to my life."

"Ah." Nick was watching her too intently, and she started to get uncomfortable. He touched her hair. "I like the casual look for you. It softens you." His hand brushed her belly. "Very sexy."

"Yeah, well, a T-shirt and sweats are my best weapon," she muttered. "Men can't resist a little cotton."

He raised his brows. "I can see why."

There was a little too much interest in his gaze, so she looked away, glancing around the room as she snuggled down next to him, letting her body relax among the soft down, feeling much happier in the T-shirt and sweats. So much more her style.

The room was painted a pale gray, and the furniture was old pine, big and homey. There were a few paintings around the room, mostly nature scenes. Dark green curtains, hanging from wooden rods. The room was masculine and cozy. "This your room?"

"It's my safe room. I used to have just gray walls and floor, but then my mom came in and redecorated. Threw out all my girlie magazines and posters."

She smiled. "Girlie magazines? I doubt it. You probably have real girls offering themselves to you constantly." She suddenly became aware of exactly how close they were in his bed and how naked his chest was. "Um...so, anyway...about those Terrors from the Chamber..." She laid a hand on his chest, and he leaned back against the pillows, clasping his hands behind his head and propping one knee up.

His body was relaxed, but his gaze was fixed on her, his eyes flickering with something she didn't want to decipher. So she closed her eyes and listened with her touch. There was discord inside him, circulating and binding to his light. It wasn't nearly as bad as Jerome's, but it was still there, and she could feel it seeking nourishment, like a parasite. She opened her eyes. "You're not okay."

"You're too tired to do me." He put his hand over hers and peeled it off him. "Just sleep. My ma can work on me later."

She snorted and willed her weary body into an upright position. "That stuff is gaining strength the longer it sits in your body. You're going to be useless to me if you go crazy." She sighed and rolled onto her knees, barely suppressing a yelp of pain.

"Because it's all about you, right? You'd never do anything just to help someone else."

"Glad you understand me." She scooted up next to him and slid her good leg over his torso.

He caught her leg and helped her straddle him, settling across his hips to keep the pressure off her bad leg. "Your legs are shaking. You can't do this." He rested his hands on her thighs, supporting her.

"I'm shaking because I'm so in awe of being in this intimate position with such a manly man." She leaned forward and set her palms on her chest. "You thought you could get out of the Chamber intact because you're Markku, right?"

"I hoped. It was worth the risk."

She nodded, reaching into him to find a spot of rot on his heart. "Because you love Jerome."

"Yeah, he's like my brother." He scowled. "Or he was before I found out he slept with my sister. As soon as he wakes up, I'm going to kill him."

"Yeah, I'm sure you will." She latched on to a dark spot and began to pull it out. Nick's fingers tightened around her legs, and she felt his pain and stopped. "Sorry. Jerome was too out of it. I didn't realize it hurt."

He shook his head. "I'm fine. Go ahead. If you're up to it."

"I'm a Rivka. I never stop." She closed her eyes so she wouldn't have to look at the pain in his eyes and concentrated on the spot again. She wrapped her metaphysical hand around it, then yanked it free. Much like a soul, it shot up her arm and whistled through her body, trying to find a place to take hold, but there was none. Instinctively, she knew how to keep it from binding, though it was a little unsettling to have it whirling around her body along with all the tainted stuff she'd taken out of Jerome. "I have to say, though, this is some weird shit I'm doing."

Nick grunted, his fingers tight on her legs, but carefully avoiding her injury. "It's called healing."

She shook her head as she focused on his heart again. "I can't be a healer." She found another small spot and drew it into her left palm, trying to ignore the tightening in Nick's body as she pulled it out of him.

"You can't disobey Satan, either, and you do it."

"This is different. Maybe I can do this because I'm a Rivka and all nasty things like me. It's like pulling a dark soul out of someone's body. Same concept." She swept his heart again and found it clean, so she scooted up to check his forehead, where Yasmine had been working on Jerome. She sat down on his bare chest, and Nick rested his forearms on her thighs, his hands under her shirt, against the bare skin of her waist, his energy pulsing softly against her. His touch wasn't about seducing her. It was about supporting her, and she was chagrined to realize that she needed it. Wanted it. Wouldn't turn it down.

Because she was so tired. That was it. As soon as she got rest, she'd be fine on her own again...because she had to be.

She sighed and let herself succumb to her need, closing her eyes and pulling in his energy.

He was quiet, feeding her with his life force, and she caught the faint scent of his lust for her, buried deep in his concern for her...

His concern was legitimate. She could feel it.

I don't want it. She needed to reject it before she could sigh and snuggle down with it, letting it wrap around her soul.

But, God, she was so exhausted. She'd never been this tired, not even when Satan had cut the lifeline. What was wrong with her?

"You're tired." Nick's voice was soft. "You've done enough already. You don't need to keep pushing yourself."

She opened her eyes. "I'm almost finished." She reached out, searching for anything else to clean, and found one more spot. "Last one." She moved her palm to the front of his shoulder. "There's gold in here." She concentrated on pulling it free.

"You're really not that good at this. Could you hurry up? It doesn't hurt like this when my ma does it." His voice was getting strained.

"Shut up, you ungrateful sod. I'm a rookie." She gave it a final yank and it flew out of his shoulder and slammed up her arm. She shuddered and collapsed on top of him, too tired to move anywhere. Besides, it felt too good to be sprawled on top of him.

He wrapped his arms around her, and she could feel him sending his life force into her. His relief that Jerome was going to be all right, his gratitude for her helping, and all the other emotions flooding through him that made him who he was.

She tucked her head under his chin and snuggled under him, even as she felt his own weariness. "You feel so good. I wish I could crawl inside you and take a nap."

He kissed the top of her head. "I know."

She lifted her head and looked at him, his face mere inches from hers. "How do you know?"

"Because I can feel it inside you."

She frowned. "I didn't give you permission to be inside me." She wasn't sure how she felt about that.

"I can't help it. When I feed you my life force, I get the insider's tour of who you are."

She narrowed her eyes. "I don't like—"

"Thank you."

She smiled at the gratitude she could feel emanating from him. This was a man who'd never be able to lie to her, for sure. "For saving Jerome?"

"Yeah." His hands slid up her back to her hair. "For getting us out of the Chamber. For working with my ma to save Jerome. For helping me out when I know you were beat."

"I told you. It was all for my own benefit."

He lifted his head and kissed her softly. "Yeah, I know. You're cold and heartless."

She stared at him, her heart suddenly going all fluttery. "I am. Don't think I'm not."

He kissed her again, and his lips were warm and soft. Her mouth parted under his gentle touch, and her body curled into his, wanting more of him. His fingers tightened in her hair, and then he pulled away, his gaze tight on hers. "You need to sleep. So do I."

She opened her mouth to protest but yawned instead. He smiled and pressed her head to his chest, and she gave in, nestling up under his chin. "Why are *you* tired?" she asked. "All you did was sit around while the women saved the day."

"Post-battle weakness after the Chamber and the little trip through the Council headquarters. Plus, it took more out of me than I thought to fight off the Terrors. Trust me, without the weakness, I wouldn't have been so willing to hang out here tonight being unproductive." He rested his chin on her head. "I would have tossed you over my shoulder and made you go with me."

"I would have gone. I hate sitting around."

"Yeah, I figured that about you."

She closed her eyes as she thought about his comment, sinking into the scent that was Nick. "So, you've got the post-battle weakness?"

"Yeah. That's what my safe room is for."

"Bummer."

"Mmm..."

She felt the heavy rise of his chest and realized he was already asleep. Deeply asleep. She considered doing something proper like rolling off him and sleeping on her side of the bed, but decided against it. Even in his sleep, when he wasn't sending his emotions into her, he still filled her with a light that she didn't want to give up.

The Terrors she'd pulled out of the men whizzed around

inside her and she snuggled into the curves of his body, letting him help her keep them from taking over. When she recovered from the healing or whatever was making her so tired, she'd let go of him.

Really. She would.

Sixteen

O h, he *is* delicious."

Nick opened his eyes to find an attractive woman with light brown highlights and a form-fitting pair of jeans grinning at him from the foot of the bed. Becca was still sprawled across his chest, deeply asleep, and somehow, his hands had worked his way underneath her sweats to cup her butt.

He immediately yanked his hands out and grabbed his gun off the bedside table, aiming it at the woman's heart.

The woman smiled, totally ignoring the gun. "Oh, don't deprive yourself on account of me. I heartily approve of intimacy."

She walked around to the side of the bed and held out her hand. "I'm Theresa Nichols-Siccardi, immortal dragon and a far badder badass than Becca."

Was it morning already? God, he'd been totally out. He retracted the gun and reached around Becca to shake Theresa's hand. "Nick Rawlings. What time is it?"

"Almost ten in the morning on Saturday. Sorry I'm late, but I ran into some issues." Theresa sat down next to him and smiled at his biceps. "And the pleasure is all mine."

He glanced at the door, which was open. "How'd you get in here? The electronic keypad's unbreakable."

"I brought a magic weapon. Quin, say hello to Becca's love machine."

"I'm not her—" Nick stopped when a tall, dark-haired man peered around the door frame into the room. *So much for the security of his safe house.* His gun went up again, and this time he was rewarded with a slight paling of the man's skin. "Who the hell are you?"

The man grimaced. "Quincy LaValle. Will you please put the gun away?"

"He's brilliant with numbers, and there's simply no way that your little code would keep him out." Theresa gestured at him to come in. "I had to bring him along to break into Justine and Derek's apartment and then he was getting all protective of me heading off to meet Becca with Satan lurking around, so he came along." She gave him an affectionate smile. "He's turning into quite the manly man, actually."

Quin's cheeks turned a faint pink. "I'll wait outside."

Nick didn't lower his gun as Quincy shut the door. "Anyone else out there?"

"No one I brought. Feel free to shoot anyone who shows up."

He slowly dropped his gun, resting it across Becca's lower back. "Who are Derek and Justine?"

"Justine's the Guardian of...well...something, and Derek is her husband, and they've become even more boring than before now that they're married. Quin is Derek's twin brother, and he's actually become quite cool, for a mortal human." She eyed Becca, who hadn't moved. "Did you guys have a sexual marathon or what?"

"It lasted for days." He lifted his head so his mouth was next to her ear. "Becca. Wake up. Theresa's here." She didn't move, and Nick frowned and gently shook her shoulder. "Becca."

Again, no response.

Theresa's amused smile faded. "What did you do to her?"

"Nothing, I swear." Nick carefully rolled Becca off him, and she landed on her back, limp and silent. Alarm rang inside him and he laid his hands on her cheeks, reaching inside her. He could feel the standard coolness of her void, but there was weird vibrating that felt foreign. And he couldn't find any light within her, not even buried deep. "Come on, Becca, respond." But she didn't, and his heart began to beat faster. "Something's wrong."

"Yeah, all the blood leaking out of her leg." Theresa pulled a vial from around her neck. "Seriously, what have you guys been up to? I'd never believe Becca would partake in a sexual marathon."

"She didn't." Nick frowned as he kept sending his energy into her, not at all certain the problem was her loss of blood, but Theresa already had Becca's sweats rolled up over her thigh and was sawing through the makeshift bandage with a razor-sharp claw.

He looked again. Yes, claw.

Theresa didn't even look up. "I can shift partially. That's my dragon claw. It's sweet, isn't it? I could rip out your innards with this thing."

"Yeah. Try it." He pulled Becca onto his lap, trying to give her more surface area to draw from, sending his life force into her. But he could feel she wasn't drawing on it. Why the hell not?

"Oh, you don't want to push me, big guy." Theresa bent low over Becca's thigh, her hair covering her face. "Shit, girl, what'd you get yourself into?" She uncorked the vial and poured it into Becca's gaping wound, then tipped some into Becca's mouth.

Nick frowned, twitching with the need to rip the vial of unknown origin out of Theresa's hands. But he had to trust Becca's judgment. She'd believed Theresa would help her, and so he would have to, as well. "You're sure about that stuff?"

Theresa sat back and winked at him. "Magic potion. Watch."

Nick stared at Becca's leg, startled when he realized that sparks were starting to fly out of it. Blue, green, red...

"I love this part." Theresa leaned forward and let the sparks bounce off her skin. "Be careful, though. You could get burned."

Nick ignored the warning and leaned down next to Theresa to peer at Becca's leg, ignoring the sparks dancing on his skin. As he watched, her leg began to heal...but he felt no answering response in her body. If anything, she was even darker inside. "This isn't working."

Theresa frowned, concern growing in her yellow eyes. "But her leg is healing. She should be waking up." She patted Becca's face. "Rivka! It's me! I'm going to have sex with your boyfriend if you don't wake up soon." When there was no response, she let out a noise of distress and jumped to her feet. "What did you do to her?"

"Something else is wrong." He scooped her up and rose to his feet, his heart hammering in his chest. "We have to get her to a hospital."

Theresa held out the vial. "I'll give her more drinks of Mona. That'll do it. I know it will." Her voice was getting shrill and she looked like she was starting to panic. "She can't die! She's my friend!"

He stopped, stunned at her words. "Mona? You mean Desdemona's Temptation? The Goblet of Eternal Youth? That's what you gave her?"

"Um..." Theresa grimaced. "No?"

"Don't lie to me." He walked back over to her and grabbed her shoulder with his free hand. "Did you use the Goblet on her? I need to know what I'm dealing with."

She pursed her lips, then nodded. "Yes. One drink heals injuries, two makes the being pretty darn tough to kill, and three makes them immortal, unless they get beheaded."

"But she's already immortal."

"Which is good, because I'm not supposed to make anyone immortal. But she's still got human vulnerabilities, so maybe this will work. Put her down."

Nick set Becca back on the bed, and Theresa knelt beside her. "Hold her still. We'll give her another drink."

He slipped his hands under Becca's head and held her steady while Theresa poured it in, stroking her neck to help her drink. "Drink number two."

She sat back on her heels and waited. "Come on, Becca. You're too bitchy to die on me, I know it."

Nick smiled at the affection in Theresa's voice, while he cradled Becca's head and stroked her hair. "You guys are good friends?"

She nodded. "We have to pretend we aren't so Satan doesn't kill me, but I love her. I'll do anything for her." She chewed her lower lip and patted Becca's cheek. "Girlfriend? Wake up. You're scaring me."

Nick reached inside Becca and found nothing but emptiness. The faint spark of life was fading. He clenched his jaw. "It's not helping."

"Then we go with the third drink." Theresa took a deep breath as she uncorked the vial. "I am so screwed if the Council finds out I'm doing this. It's so illegal." She poured it into Becca's mouth. "But three drinks will totally work. Short of being actually dead, there's nothing that three drinks of Mona can't save."

"Mona won't revive the dead?"

"Nope. Dead is dead." Theresa corked the bottle. "That should do it. Come on back, Becca."

They waited.

Nothing happened.

Theresa's eyes began to fill up with tears. "Don't you dare die on me! Wake up!"

Nick shook his head, his hands getting clammy. "It's not working. Give her more."

"There is no more. Three is the max. There's nothing else to do." Theresa jumped up. "Three always works. Becca! Are you listening? I'm going to kick your ass if you don't wake up right now!"

Nick's mind raced as he tried to figure out what to do. If a full dose of Mona hadn't healed her, what would? There had to be something. His chest tightened, and he scooped her up and crushed her against his chest. He fed his concern into her and felt a faint stirring deep inside. *She was still with him.* Then he thought of his ma. Was there a chance she could do something? "I know someone who might be able to help."

Theresa smacked him in the shoulder. "Then what are

you waiting for! Take her there! Why are you standing there talking?"

"I'm not." He stepped into the circle in the middle of the room, and a faint humming filled him, and then they were back at his ma's house.

Yasmine was sitting in the kitchen drinking hot cocoa and sharing Saturday-morning pancakes and bacon with Paige when Nick appeared next to the kitchen sink, Becca clutched against his chest. "Becca needs help."

Paige let out a cry of distress while Yasmine jumped up and cleared the table with a crash that sent plates and food flying in all directions. "Put her on here."

He set her down, leaning heavily on the table while his ma laid her hands on Becca. Paige hovered behind her, tears filling her eyes. "What's wrong? Is she going to be okay? She's like my mom and my best friend and if something happens to her..."

"She'll be fine," Yasmine snapped. "Go outside and find me some acorns. I need them."

Paige was out the door before Yasmine stopped giving the order, and Yasmine smiled. "That girl is so enthusiastic. I love her energy. I don't even need the acorns, but I could tell she was about to lose it."

"Ma." Nick could barely keep the tension out of his voice. "Becca."

"I'm working on her. Relax, Nicky." Yasmine fell silent and Nick ground his jaw while he waited, tapping his foot restlessly on the antique pine floor.

After a minute, Yasmine shook her head and muttered something under her breath as she continued to work on Becca.

Nick felt like his head was going to explode. "Talk to me, Ma."

"All the rot she took from Jerome is still inside her. She didn't cleanse it." She laid her hands on Becca's chest and chanted something.

Nick dropped his head with relief. "That's it? God, I thought it was something bad. You'll show her how to cleanse it?" But when Yasmine didn't answer, he snapped his head back up. "Ma?"

Then Becca groaned, and Nick spun around to cup her face. "Becca? Can you hear me?"

Her eyes fluttered open, hazy but alert, and she looked at him. "Nick?"

His hands tightened on her cheeks. "Yeah, it's me. You scared the crap out of me."

She wrinkled her nose. "I feel like hell."

"Sit her up," Yasmine ordered.

Becca's gaze flickered past his shoulder. "Your mom's here? Why?"

He supported her back and helped her sit up, keeping his hands on her waist, reaching inside her to reassure himself that her life force was pulsing again. It was. *She was really okay.* He took a deep breath and sat down hard in the chair next to the table, his legs suddenly weak. "We're back at her place. How's your leg?"

Becca frowned and shifted her leg. "It's fine. Where's Theresa? Did she leave already?" She rested her hand on his head, her fingers lacing through his hair, drawing on his light.

Yasmine grabbed Becca's chin and turned her face toward her. "Did you work on Nicky?"

"Yeah."

Yasmine snapped her fingers at Nick and he leaned forward so she could lay her hand on his forehead. Then she looked at Becca. "I'll show you how to finish."

"Finish?" she asked. "What didn't I finish?"

"Replenishing," Yasmine said. "When you take out negative energy, you have to replace it. You do it to yourself at the same time."

"How do you do that?"

"Through your right palm." Yasmine gestured at Nick. "Come around."

He scooted his chair closer while Becca turned to face him, her legs hanging off the edge of the table at the knee. Nick leaned between her knees and rested his forearms on her thighs. God, he wanted to just reach up and haul her against him, breathe in her scent and take a little tour inside her body to see what was going on. Make sure she was really okay.

Becca reached for him, and then her soft touch pressed on his forehead. "Like this?"

He felt his ma's hand rest on top of Becca's. "No, you're not generating any healing energy," Yasmine said. "Find it in your body and give it to Nick."

He waited, but he didn't feel that warmth.

Yasmine muttered something under her breath, and he opened his eyes to see her place a hand on Becca's chest. "Try it again." They all waited a few more minutes, but Nick didn't feel any heat from Becca.

Finally, Yasmine dropped her hands and shook her head. "It's what I was afraid of."

Becca fixed her eyes on Yasmine. "What are you talking about?"

"You don't have a healing resource to draw from. You

have the ability to attract the negative energy, but you have nothing to replace it with. You're just negative energy."

Naked, vulnerable disappointment flashed over Becca's face, and then she shuttered her expression. "Oh."

Nick tightened his grip on her waist and rubbed her lower back.

"You shouldn't heal," Yasmine said. "The replenishing part is important; otherwise you leave empty gaps that can be filled with anything, including energy that is more negative and damaging that what you took out."

Becca pressed her lips together, and Nick felt her withdraw. He stood up and pulled her against him. For an instant, she resisted, then she relaxed into him, and he felt her draw on his energy. He felt her disappointment, hidden under layers of resilient denial.

"The problem is that you took the Chamber Terrors from Nick and Jerome into you, and you can't get rid of them." Yasmine gave Becca a sympathetic pat on her shoulder. "Unless you can find a source of light to draw from, it will stay in your system. I settled it down, but..." She hesitated.

"But what?" Becca's voice was quiet.

She met Becca's gaze. "But it's just temporary. It'll keep coming back until it destroys you. Until I can't pull you back from it like I did today. You have to cleanse yourself."

Becca couldn't believe what she was hearing. "Or I die?"

Yasmine nodded. "Or you die."

Well, damn. *Didn't that just figure? Try to do some good and it kills you.*

Nick tightened his grip on her, and she could feel his concern. "You're sure, ma? But she's immortal."

Yasmine turned to wash up at the sink. "The Chamber rises above the law of immortality. Something always does." She grabbed a paper towel and dried her hands. "She needs to find a positive source of energy to draw from so she can cleanse herself."

"She can draw on me. She already does."

Becca couldn't help but smile at his authoritative tone. Big strong man accustomed to solving all his problems by sheer brute force and willpower.

Yasmine shook her head. "It won't be enough to cleanse them from her system. It has to come from within her. It has to be a part of her."

"Then who?" he demanded. "Or what? Tell me and I'll get it."

Yasmine reached out to touch Becca's cheek, an affectionate gesture that had Becca scrambling off the table and out of reach before she could succumb to the temptation to lean into Yasmine and get the first mom-hug of her life. Like she wanted to open *that* door.

"I don't know, but you two have about a day to find out."

"A day?" Becca repeated. "You can't give me like a few hundred years or something? People live in the Chamber for hundreds of years. That's the point of it. An eternity of suffering and all that fun stuff. Only the really weak ones die, and even that takes a long time." She set her hands on her hips. "And trust me, I'm not weak."

"Well…" Yasmine rubbed her chin. "I guess it could be that long. I don't really know. I figured it was better to err on the short side, though, given the fact that it nearly took you out already."

"It was the blood loss." She flared up a fireball and shot it into the cast-iron sink. "See? I'm fine. All good now." She ignored the concerned looks on both their faces. "So, I'm a little itchy with these buggers running around inside me. It's no different than harvesting some ADHD souls." She dusted off her hands, annoyed that they were still looking at her with worried expressions. "Hello? I'm fine. You need to stop giving me those mopey looks. If Satan sees you looking all upset about me, he'll come down and cut out your eyes. I have too much to do to bother finding a damned light source right now." She looked at Nick. "I need answers. I'm tired of playing games, and I'm running out of time."

Nick's forehead furrowed and he glanced at his mom. "Ma. Maybe you should check on Jerome."

Yasmine flicked an interested look at Nick, then nodded. "I expect you're right. I'll see you guys upstairs." Then she grabbed her hot cocoa from the counter and walked out.

Becca turned away from the speculative look on Nick's face and opened a cabinet. No, she was not going to get bogged down in empty predictions of her death in less than a day. "Where are the mugs? That hot chocolate smells fantastic. I'll drink while you tell me how the hell the Markku figured out how to live without Satan's life force." She opened another and found dry goods, and turned around, only to find Nick right behind her.

Way in her personal space. "Back up, big guy."

He set his hands on either side of the counter by her

hips and moved closer. "You're wrong. You need help to get rid of those Terrors."

He was so close, she could smell his faint scent, clean and fresh, like soap. She took a deep breath, inhaling it into her body. "Don't try to change the subject. I'm fine, trust me. Rivkas are tough, and I'm particularly tenacious. Besides, we need to find Satan Jr., remember? Take him out. Save Satan. Free your sister. All before midnight tomorrow night when the time runs out in the pus blister. Priorities, Nicky."

He didn't back down. "You can't help me with my sister if you're dead, and I can't figure it out on my own. You're my hell expert." He paused. "And it would piss me off if you died."

His concern pulsed at her, and a part of her wanted to let go of her resistance and fall into his aura. Instead, she set a hand on his chest. "I will save myself. Your only job is to give me information I need. That's it."

He narrowed his eyes. "You're not getting any info from me until I know you're going to stay alive, and you need me to do that."

"I need no one."

"Did you need Gabriel?"

She wrenched her gaze off his face and stared over his shoulder at the kitchen. It was so homey. Cute. Normal.

She froze as she felt Nick's lips on her neck. "Don't do that."

He kissed her collarbone, and she felt his heat creeping over her.

"Cut it out." She closed her eyes and tried to steel herself against his emotions. "I don't want this."

"You need me." His breath was hot on her neck, his

lips tender against her throat. "Let me in and we'll get rid of those Terrors. I have enough light for you to draw on so you can cleanse yourself. I'm half Markku, but I'm also half healer. We'll get you taken care of, so we can go after my sister and your freedom. Don't be a fool, Becca. You have to save yourself."

"I'm not a fool. I'm goal oriented, and I know I don't have time for this..." But she tilted her head back as he kissed along her jaw. It wasn't just a kiss. It was Nick's kiss, and all that went with it. His lust, his concern, his love—not for her, she knew, but the man was practically overflowing with love for his family—his arrogance that he could help her. It crept under her skin and permeated her cells, infusing them with heat and warmth and things she couldn't even name. "Nick..."

"I'm not doing this because I love you, so Satan has nothing to worry about. I'm his man-friend, remember? I'd never steal his girl." He kissed the corner of her mouth, his tongue flicking out in a quick touch that sent spirals of heat through her. "I'm doing this for my sister...And for your freedom. That's it."

"I'm not his girl." She clutched the edge of the counter, trying desperately not to fall into Nick's spell.

"You're no good to me dead," he whispered into her mouth. "Or insane." His lips brushed hers as he spoke. "Satan would appreciate my need to keep you alive. He'd probably even support it."

"He'd kill you." She let her lips part under his, then nearly moaned when his mouth descended over hers, his lips so demanding that her whole body swelled up in response. *Oh, God. I can't stop myself.*

His hands left the counter and slipped under her T-shirt,

cupping her shoulder blades and pressing her against him until her breasts were crushed against his chest, her nipples so hard that they felt like they were going to pierce her own body.

It was just lust. She realized suddenly that he wasn't trying to invade her body with his life force and his emotions, turning her into a pile of mush; he was giving her space. She relaxed slightly and released the counter to grab his waist, digging her fingers into the firmness of his muscles.

He made a male noise of satisfaction, and then his tongue was there. Everywhere, and he tasted so good, like man, like *Nick*.

She wriggled against him and slipped her hands under his sweats over the taut butt she'd admired in his safe room, grinning when he smiled into her mouth. "I like a woman who takes charge."

"Good, because I have control issues."

"I noticed." And then she was up on the counter, her legs around his waist while his hands roamed her back, her ribs, her breasts, while he kissed her like he knew he could find her soul if he kissed her deeply enough.

She couldn't stop. Couldn't get enough. Wanted more. "Nick—"

He answered with a flare of emotion that slammed her so hard she lost her breath. It curved around her body, into her soul, seeping through the walls she'd erected. *Oh, God.* He'd waited until defenses were down, and then he'd slammed her. Her soul reached out for him, drinking greedily at everything he had to offer. She was losing herself to him, merging with him, and it felt so right and so wrong...so scary. *I can't do this.* "Nick, stop." She hit his shoulder with her palm, and he froze, his lips still on hers. "Stop," she whispered.

"Don't shut me out." His voice was hoarse. "You need me."

"I can't need you." She was appalled at how breathless she sounded, how desperate. Maybe he wouldn't notice.

He pulled back, far enough that he could look her in the eye. "You really believe Satan will make you kill me if we have sex?"

"Not just for sex. For..."

One eyebrow went up. "For what?"

She concentrated on smoothing out the hair on his chest. "If he thinks I care about you at all. Or you care about me. He'd never stand for it. And when you do that thing with your emotions when you're kissing me...well...it sort of..." She took a deep breath. "...it makes it different."

"Different." His hands were on her hips now, his thumbs making circles.

She looked up at him, still fiddling with his chest hair. "Don't get me wrong. I don't care about you, or Dani, or your mom or Paige or any of you guys, but if I did kill you, I'd feel really bad. Because I'd know that the only reason you had to die was because of me, and after that whole thing with Gabriel...well...I'm not really up for another guilt trip, you know? I don't want that kind of burden." *And I hate how I lose myself in you. How you make me not care if I'm in control anymore. I can't handle that. I need to control myself.*

"I can understand that." He was gazing at her with an inscrutable expression on his face, almost as if he'd heard every word she hadn't spoken aloud.

"So, it's not to protect you. It's to protect me." She took

a deep breath and managed a grin. "It's all about me, of course."

"Mmm…"

She frowned. "Mmm? What does that mean?"

"It means, I'm thinking."

Her frown deepened. "There's nothing to think about. You need to keep your distance from me." She pushed on his chest, not that he moved. "Even if you *could* help me with the Terrors, it's too risky. When I cut my ties to Satan, it'll be enough. I won't be dark anymore, the Terrors will hit the road, and life will be grand." Her voice grew stronger. "Don't you see, Nick? The only way for me to beat the Terrors is to break free of Satan's life force. *That's* how I have to do it." She rubbed her temples, suddenly so tired. "I just have to stay alive until I get it done." She slapped her hand over his mouth when he started to talk. "And don't you dare tell me I'm not going to be able to do it. I don't need to hear that right now. Got it?"

He nodded, but she felt like he wasn't really agreeing.

Paige's face appeared in the window, then she yelled and banged on it, then disappeared from view, and Becca could hear her running around the house to the door.

Nick stepped aside as Paige bounded into the room, then launched herself at Becca, throwing her legs and arms around her in a huge hug. "I'm so glad you're okay! I was totally freaked out! Never pretend to die again! I love you!"

Becca grunted from the impact, and her arms went around Paige to keep them both from losing their balance. "Get off me, apprentice."

Paige hugged her tighter. "Being around Yasmine made me realize how lucky Nick and Dani are to have a mom.

She and I decided that you're as close to a mom as I've got, so you can't die. I need my mom."

Oh, God. She wrenched herself free of Paige's grip, panic whizzing through her body. "I'm not your mom."

Paige beamed at her. "You are now. I've adopted you. Every girl needs a mom. And I pick you. I mean, you're already telling me I can't have sex with guys. That's such a mom thing! Plus, you let me borrow your clothes. I mean, they're slut clothes, but that just means you're cool!"

"Paige..." This couldn't happen. "You have to stop this insanity right now." She heard Nick shift behind her and she glanced at him, surprised to see a soft look on his face as he watched Paige. What was that about?

"*Mom.* That sounds so cool, doesn't it?" Paige said.

Becca focused on her apprentice, grabbing Paige's shoulders. "Don't you get it? *I can't like you.* If you screw up as an apprentice, Satan will order me to kill you. If he realizes I like you, he'll order me to kill you. If he finds out you like me more than him, he'll order me to kill you!" Her knees started to tremble at the thought of killing Paige, and she sat down hard when Nick thrust a chair under her butt.

Paige beamed at her. "Well, too bad for him, right? Never come between a mother and her babies when she's protecting them, and all that."

"Paige—"

"I'm going to go check on Jerome. Bye, Mom!" And Paige darted out of the room, her feet thudding on the stairs as she sprinted up them.

Oigh. She groaned and looked at Nick, who was leaning against the fridge looking thoughtful. "Save me."

"Save yourself. She's just a kid. You should be able

to handle her. Kill her off. Get her out of the way." He levered himself off the fridge. "Or can't you? Feel a little protective of her? Kind of like how I feel about Dani?" He came to a stop in front of her. "Or do you feel like you couldn't live with yourself if she died and you could stop it?"

She stared at him, unable to reply, because that's exactly what she was feeling.

He brushed her wrist with his fingers and then nodded with satisfaction. "The timer goes off on the pus bubble at midnight tomorrow night. If Satan has to die to save Dani, then he has to die."

Becca clenched her jaw, finally beginning to understand how he could make that statement. "Then I guess I'd better be disconnected from him by then."

Nick's eyes flashed, and he nodded. "I'm going to grill Jerome about what he knows about the Dani situation." He hesitated. "Jerome read the files on the Council's experiments with the Rivkas. He might have some ideas that could help you get free of Satan's—"

She was already out the door and halfway up the stairs before he finished talking.

Seventeen

By the time Nick got to Dani's old room, where Jerome was staying, the women had all pulled up chairs around the bed. His ma was working on him while Becca tried to pressure his ma into letting her interrogate him. Becca's leg was jiggling with impatience, and Paige was staring at Becca with a look of total adoration on her face. Something inside him twitched at the sight of all these people he cared about in the same room, working together.

He sat down next to Becca, letting his shoulder brush against hers, and felt a smug sense of satisfaction when she didn't move away.

Yasmine sat back. "He's up for a short interview." She frowned at Becca. "Short."

Nick stood up and loomed over his best friend, who was looking rather pale on Dani's flowered sheets. "Did you sleep with my sister?" He managed to keep his voice even, but he couldn't keep his fingers from digging into the footboard so tightly that it cracked under his grip.

Yasmine jerked upright in the window seat. "What? Jerome and Dani?"

Jerome paled. "I meant to tell you—"

Paige stood up and slammed a pillow down on Jerome's face. "Bastard! You broke her heart, and that's why she had to start dating that jerk who got her entombed in that vesicle of hell pus!"

"What?" Jerome snatched the pillow out of her hand. "Who is she dating? When did that start?"

"Oh, like you get to be jealous!" Paige shouted. "You're a bastard."

Jerome groaned and let his head fall back on the bed. "I didn't mean to hurt Dani," he said, his gaze searching out Nick's. "I was just not prepared for the situation and how it turned out—"

Nick held up his hand. "Skip the details. Dani's in trouble now, and we need to know everything you know."

"Dani's in trouble?" Yasmine's voice was lethally quiet as she rose to her feet from the window seat. "You've been here all day and you didn't tell me my baby girl was in trouble?"

Becca slipped her arm around Paige's shoulders as the girl grabbed a heavy dictionary and headed toward the bed. "Give him a chance to tell us what we want to know before killing him. Works better that way."

"I don't want information. I just want to hurt him. I'm a Rivka. I'm supposed to inflict harm on others."

"Yes, on people who are already in hell who have bargained their souls to Satan." Becca sat Paige back down in a chair. "You don't beat up innocents, even if you don't like them. Sit." She held up a finger as Paige's mouth opened. "No. Just be quiet. And remember, you're a Rivka. You don't have friends. Which means you don't get to avenge Dani's honor."

"But—" Paige snapped her mouth shut as Becca held up her finger for silence again.

"Why don't you go for a run?" Becca suggested. "Rivkas have to stay fit."

"A run? Now?" Paige blinked. "You're just trying to get rid of me."

Becca smiled. "Yes, but I'm also trying to teach you how to calm yourself down when your emotions get out of control. Now go."

Paige muttered under her breath the whole way out the door and they heard the front door slam.

Yasmine hands were clenched tight. "What's going on with Dani?"

Nick explained the situation quickly, watching Jerome's reaction. His friend got more and more agitated and paler the longer Nick spoke. By the time he finished, Jerome was pulling on his boots to head over to Dani's apartment. "I have to go see her." He fumbled with the laces and cursed, and didn't even bother to duck when Yasmine smacked him in the forehead for swearing. "God, I can't believe she's been blistered." He jerked his gaze up, looking at Nick. "You have to kill Satan, you know. We can't let Dani die."

Becca cleared her throat. "I'm right here. If he kills Satan, which I won't let him do, then I die."

Jerome made a "so what" gesture with his hands. "I don't love *you*."

"You love her?" Yasmine asked. "Then how could you leave her?"

Jerome stood up and raked a hand through his hair. "I freaked out. It was *Dani*. I went to find her a couple days later, but she disappeared. I thought she was blowing me off, so I let her. Figured we both needed time to sort it out." He stopped talking suddenly as his gaze landed on the bookshelf, where there was a picture of Dani from her high school semiformal. He stared at it for a long moment, then sank down on the desk chair and groaned, leaning forward and pressing her photo to her forehead. "Dani," he whispered. "I'm so sorry."

No one walked over to give Jerome comfort.

Nick felt the pain emanating from his friend, but he didn't care. Couldn't care. All he could think about was Dani, and the fact that Becca's life was also tied into the mess. "Jerome. We think Dani was dating Satan Jr."

Yasmine squawked with disbelief, and Jerome's head snapped up, his eyes bleary. "You're kidding." Jerome stood up and paced the room, clutching Dani's picture in his left hand, cursing repeatedly to himself.

"How in the world would Dani have met *him?*" Yasmine asked.

Jerome stopped and turned around. "There have been rumors going around that Satan Jr. had been recruiting Markku to help him in his battle to dethrone Satan. I knew Nick was the only one who could fend off any Markku if the rumors *were* true, which is why I hired him."

Nick frowned. "Why didn't you tell me that?"

"Because I wasn't supposed to know." Jerome took a deep breath, obviously trying to pull himself together.

"What does this have to with Junior and Dani?" Yasmine asked.

Jerome looked at Nick. "Dani knows Nick's dad was Markku."

"Impossible." He looked at his ma. "Isn't it?"

"I never told her, and since she has a different dad, I never thought of it. It had no bearing on her."

"She knows, and it pissed her off that you guys didn't trust her with the information," Jerome said. "It also made her mad that Nick was something special, with his hell blood. She wanted to be like him."

"From hell? Why?"

"Because she looked up to you." Jerome looked at Yasmine. "Because she knew you were the favorite. She wanted to be noticed."

"And how do you know all this?" Nick asked. "Why would she tell you?"

Jerome shrugged. "I guess she trusted me."

"And you betrayed her." Nick's fists clenched again. The glass in Dani's picture cracked and the room began to shake from his rage, but he couldn't stop it. "You drove her into the bed of a sociopath."

Jerome was on his feet now. "I'm going to make it up to her, so back off!"

Then Becca was by Nick's side, her hand on his wrist, silently sending him her inner strength. Her self-control. Gratefully, he latched onto it, ratcheting down his rage until he had it back its cage.

"Hey!" Yasmine snapped her fingers. "Settle down. We need to focus. Nick, you can kill Jerome later." She pointed at Jerome. "How did Dani meet Satan Jr.?"

Nick took a deep breath and threw his arm around Becca, pulling her against his side, drinking in her strength. She wrapped her arms around his waist and allowed him to feast, and he felt her satisfaction that she could help him.

"I don't know how Dani met him," Jerome said. "But

after we...ah...well, after our relationship changed, that's when all that shit went down with the Goblet and Satan and Satan Jr. I got busy, and she thought I was using work as an excuse to avoid her." His fingers tightened on the picture. "She got pissed and said that Satan was more important to me than she was." He shrugged, looking beaten. "She was right, in a way."

Becca interrupted them. "Junior's been frozen for three weeks, so who put Dani in the blister two days ago? Who wants Satan dead?"

God, she was right. He was obsessing so much about Dani's virtue he was losing sight of the bigger picture.

Nick sat down and pulled Becca down onto his lap so he could think, relieved when she settled against him without protest, apparently realizing he needed physical contact with her to focus. "Dani wasn't in the bubble the first time she called, which was right after the Markku broke in after Satan Jr. When she called back a couple days later, things had changed. She wasn't in control of the situation anymore." Nick rested his chin on Becca's shoulder and let his mind sort out the information. "So, Dani's call must have been a ruse to get me away from Satan Jr. so someone could get to him. When I didn't go the first time, the stakes were raised so I'd have to go after Satan. Added bonus if I killed Satan." He stood up, pacing the room. "So, they wanted Satan dead and Satan Jr. free, and they used Dani to do it." He turned and face the group. "But who are 'they?'"

A door slammed downstairs. "Becca! Omigod, Becca! You won't believe this!" Paige raced up the stairs and flung the door open. Her face was flushed and she was drenched in sweat. "There's a bus coming up the driveway. It's full of souls Satan released from hell who want to kill you. Apparently, your location got posted on the Internet and they're all coming. I ran back through the woods to beat them here." She paused to bend over and suck in some air. "What do you want me to do?"

Nick smiled when Becca just sighed with annoyance. No panic on her part.

"A busload of assassins?" Becca ambled over to the window and flicked the curtain aside to reveal dust rising from behind a hill, no doubt from the bus. "I really don't have time for this." She glanced at Nick, and he could see the worry in her eyes. Too many threats closing too fast on her. Her time was running out.

"Can I deal with them? Please?" Paige asked, her fists clenched by her side.

Becca hesitated. "Are you sure you're ready? There's lots of not-so-nice people out there."

"Totally! Can I?"

"Sure." She hesitated, then said, "Hold out your hands."

Paige stuck them out, still breathing heavily, and Becca hesitated, then clasped them, palm to palm, as Nick sat up more erectly. Was she doing what he thought she was doing?

After a moment, Paige shrieked and yanked her hands free. "Oh my *God!* What did you do? That *hurt!*" She hopped around the room, her hands clenched in tight fists.

Becca smiled and threw a fireball at her. Paige immediately threw up her hand, and a fireball shot out of her palm and crashed into Becca's. Paige stared at the mini-explosion. "You gave me fireballs?" she whispered.

"I figured you needed it to deal with the bus."

Nick felt a flash of pride for the apprentice. "You earned it, Paige."

"I love you!" Paige threw her arms around Becca, and Becca couldn't help but smile as Paige danced away from her. "This is so awesome." She shot one at Nick, then giggled when he batted it away. "Sturdy elf, my fanny. You're not an elf, are you?"

He couldn't help but chuckle, despite the load in his chest. "Go harvest some souls, will you?"

"You bet." She bolted for the door, then stopped and spun around when Becca called her name. "What?"

"Um..." Becca peeked surreptitiously around the room as if she didn't want to be caught being supportive. "Call me if you get in trouble, okay?"

"You got it!" Then Paige charged out the door, and they could hear fireball explosions as she ran down the stairs.

Becca shot Yasmine an apologetic look. "Bill me for the damage she does, okay?"

Nick cocked his head, recognizing the softness in Becca's body language. It was so striking to see it, so the antithesis of everything she tried to be. "You made her day, *Mom*."

She glared at him. "Shut up." Then she walked over the window and casually flipped the curtain aside to peer out, her brow furrowing in concern as Nick heard the screech of bus brakes.

"That's it." Yasmine smacked her hands down on her thighs. "Watching Becca with Paige makes it so obvious. Who would want a child to succeed more than a mom?" They all turned to look at her, and she nodded. "Find

Satan Jr.'s mama, and I'll bet you find the person who's causing all this trouble."

"His ma?" Nick grimaced. "Given that Satan Jr. is exponentially worse than his dad, the thought of his mother is just plain scary." He looked at Becca. "Who is she?"

"I don't know, but Satan must." Becca peeked outside again, then threw a fireball out the window, nodding with satisfaction when Paige shouted up her appreciation. "Let's ask him."

"How? He ordered you not to bother him again until he said he was ready to see you."

She tossed him her cell phone. "No, but as his new man-friend, you could."

He caught the phone. "Satan's in the middle of making love to his woman." He tossed it back. "There's no way he'll be answering his phone." He stood up. "We'll have to go find him."

She rolled her eyes and dialed. When it went into voicemail, she shoved the phone in her pocket, scowling with frustration. "The clock keeps ticking and things keep getting in the way."

Nick touched her arm, surprised to feel the anger emanating from her. Becca's feelings were simmering a lot closer to the surface than they used to. "Grab some of Dani's clothes. I'll be back in a sec." He spun and walked out the door, and they could hear him jogging down the stairs.

Becca realized she was still wearing Nick's sweats and T-shirt. No bra, no underwear, and entirely not appropriate for taking on Satan. Snuggly and comfy, but not battle worthy.

"I'll find you something." Yasmine headed for Dani's

dresser and pulled out some jeans, undergarments, and a black T-shirt. Yasmine handed Becca a pair of hiking boots, then waved at Jerome, who swung around to face the wall.

Becca peeled off Nick's oversize T-shirt and picked up the sports bra. A little small, but it was better than what she was wearing. She yanked it on, and then the shirt, eyeing Jerome as she tugged the too-snug jeans on. "Did the Council find a way for the Rivkas to survive without Satan's life force?"

His shoulders tensed. "I have no idea what you're talking about."

Becca frowned as she wrenched the zipper up on the jeans that were a couple sizes smaller than she would have liked. "Jerome, give it up. Nick told me about the experiments."

Jerome groaned. "I'll kill him. That's beyond top secret."

Becca snorted as she reached for the socks Yasmine had given her. "I'm about to go interrupt Satan's lovemaking to save the woman you drove into Satan Jr.'s arms. I think you can manage to tell me about a few experiments. And you can turn around now. I'm decent."

Jerome faced her, with a sigh of resignation. "The Rivkas have to be supported by Satan's life force. Nothing else from hell worked, and there was no way to repeat what the Markku did. Satan had changed the constitution of Rivkas to make them more dependent. They can't store his energy, so we couldn't do it." His rubbed his fingers over Dani's photo, which was still clutched in his hands. "Not only did every Rivka die, but everyone the Council tried to link them to died, as well. Everyone died. There's no way to break free. We had the best scientists and historians and experts. There's no way."

She felt a sinking feeling in her belly. "Did you try linking Rivkas to each other? They're both from hell."

He nodded. "They have no life force to generate. It didn't work."

"What about Satan Jr.?" Yasmine suggested. "It wouldn't be a big deal to risk his life, and he's got Satan's life force."

Becca looked at her in disbelief. "There's no way I'm walking away from Satan to put myself into Satan Jr.'s hands."

Yasmine set her hands on her hips, her face tense. "Then what are you going to do? My daughter's life will not be sacrificed for Satan's sake." Her fingers twitched as she took a step toward the dresser, her eyes glancing toward it. "I won't let you take out my daughter."

Becca tensed, suddenly certain Yasmine had a gun in there. "She'll be fine. I owe Nick." She yanked on the boots, ignoring the waistband digging into her stomach. "You know, Yasmine, you're kind of an oxymoron." She stood up. "You heal me, and then you freely admit that you won't mind if I die." She was suddenly glad she hadn't accept Yasmine's comfort earlier. To have it taken away was far worse than never getting it originally.

Yasmine drew her shoulders back. "You would do well not to judge what you do not understand, young lady."

"I'm not young. I'm a hundred years old. You're what, fifty-seven? Old in human terms, sure, but not in my world."

Yasmine's eyes flashed. "Until you have buried a husband and done the unthinkable to protect your children, you are nothing but a baby."

Becca saw the pain in Yasmine's eyes and knew suddenly that there was worse out there than what she was living. She gave a slight incline of her head. "I'm sorry."

Yasmine nodded. "Apology accepted."

Nick appeared in the doorway with a duffel bag over his shoulder. He'd changed to black boots, a pair of black jeans, and a leather jacket that had enough bulges to suggest he was ready to take on an army. His eyes glittered, and he looked ready to fight. He held out his hand. "Ready to go find the leader of hell and kick his ass?"

She wrapped her hand around his, trying to revive her will after the discouraging conversation with Jerome. If he was right, what the hell was she going to do? "I won't let you kill him."

He met her gaze and he frowned. "What's wrong?"

She lifted her chin. "Nothing."

But he tightened his grip on her hand, and she felt him tap into her core and get the answer for himself. He cursed quietly, and she lifted her chin and met his gaze. "I'm not giving up."

He looked down at her as they started to fade. "Fuck giving up," he said, "I hate losing."

And just like that, she had hope again. Barely a flicker, but it was something.

It was what she'd needed.

And she'd gotten it from him. Not from herself.

Unsettling, but at the same time, it made her feel . . . lighter.

Eighteen

Nick frowned as Becca rubbed the back of her wrist over her eyes six hours later. They'd been searching all of Satan's haunts for him, including his two mansions in hell, his flat in London, his Caribbean island getaway, and all the five-star hotels in New York City.

He'd been at none of them.

They'd tried calling Satan, but as Nick had predicted, he wasn't answering his phone.

The last few times they'd shimmered, Nick had noticed that it took Becca a little longer to get them to fade and then re-form. She'd lost some of the sparkle in her eye, and he was starting to get concerned. "How are you feeling?"

"Fine." She scratched her collarbone, and Nick narrowed his eyes.

"You're itchy."

"No, I'm not." She dropped her hand, and then rubbed her fist over her thigh. "I'm fine."

"It's the Terrors, isn't it?"

Her gaze flickered to him. "I can handle it." She held up her hand and stepped back as he reached for her. "Don't touch me. If Satan's nearby, he'll sense it when our life forces mingle. You'll be dead in a heartbeat."

The stubborn set of her jaw told him he wasn't getting anywhere, and the paleness of her face told him time was running out for her. "Becca—"

"So, this is Iris Bennett's house." She turned away and gestured at a quaint red brick house they were standing in front of. White trim, well-manicured bushes, and a bright blue door. "Thanks to her legacy as an ex-Guardian, she lives in one of the nicer neighborhoods in purgatory, while her fate is being decided." She set her hands on her hips and studied the house. "I wouldn't have thought Satan would lower himself to seduce Iris in such plebian surroundings, but I suppose if he had to hang out in purgatory in order to get Iris naked, he'd do it."

Naked. An image of Becca flashed into his mind, and he could feel the softness of her body under his hands again, feel the hum between them as he reached inside her . . . and the void she always threw up to keep him out.

She glanced at him as she headed up the cobblestone walkway, then spun around and grabbed his arms. "Stop looking at me like that! This is serious! Satan will kill you if he thinks you care about me."

Her grip felt cold against his skin, and he flipped his hands over to holds hers. "Exactly how bad do you feel right now?"

For an instant, he felt her greedily draw on his energy, and she slammed up a wall. "I can't." Then she ripped her hands free and spun back to the door.

He could feel her shuddering as she lifted her hand to the doorbell, and he fisted his hands by his side to keep from grabbing her. That brief touch had told him exactly how much she was worried about all of them. Him, Dani, Paige, Theresa, and Yasmine. Worried that Satan was going to think she cared about them. Worried she was going to have to kill all of them. And absolutely determined not to let that happen.

She hadn't wasted any concern on herself, not that he was surprised.

She dropped her hand without ringing the doorbell, her face scrunched in frustration. "I can't interrupt him. You have to do it."

"Hang on." He set the duffel bag on the front step and pulled out the powerwasher he'd snagged from his ma's garage. He left it on the step and jogged around the house, where he found a hose neatly curled up on a hook on the side of the house. He turned on the spigot, then grabbed the end and tugged it back around front, where Becca was standing with a small smile on her face.

"You're going to powerwash him?"

"Yep." Nick kinked the hose to cut off the water flow, then screwed the end of the hose onto the powerwasher. "The water won't kill him since it's not purified, but it should be fast enough to melt him a bit before he can dodge it and kill me." He slung the strap of the powerwasher over his shoulder and aimed the nozzle at the door. "You know, he's going to disown me as his man-friend after this."

"I thought you didn't want to be his man-friend."

"Better than his enemy."

"Sometimes."

He kicked the door with the toe of his boot. "Open up, Satan. It's Nick Rawlings."

"My man-friend!" There was a scuffle from inside and

a yelp from Iris, and then the door was flung open, revealing Satan in all his manly glory. "Today you die!" He lifted a glowing finger, and Nick shot him in the gut, which instantly began to melt.

Satan shrieked and slammed his hands over his crotch. "Do not attack my manly bits!"

Nick kept the flow going, not daring to slow it down. "I just want to talk to you. Can we talk?"

"No!" Satan's voice was laced with pain as he doubled over, protecting his crotch. "I must kill you for interrupting my lovemaking session! As soon as you stop, I shall—"

Nick shot him in the mouth and grinned as Satan's ranting turned into muffled garble. He felt Becca's amusement and glanced at her. "Want to have a go at him?"

She shot him a disbelieving look. "Really?"

He held the gun out to her, keeping his finger on the trigger so the water didn't slow. "It's all yours."

She reached out, then dropped her hands, an envious gleam in her eyes. "I really shouldn't."

He grabbed her hand and set it on top of his. "There. I'm still doing it, but you can enjoy it, too."

Her fingers tightened over his where he was holding the trigger down, both of them ignoring the sputtering howls of outrage from Satan. "Better than roses, for sure."

"You're so low-maintenance."

"I don't know. I think most guys would consider flowers to be a little easier than powerwashing Satan."

"Most guys are pansies."

She smiled, a genuine smile laced with a flicker of true happiness that made him want arrange for her to powerwash Satan forever. "So true."

He put his free arm around her shoulder and held her close while they stood together and watched Satan scream and writhe under the water, her fingers never leaving his on the trigger. "If I ever get married, this is what I'd want to do for my honeymoon," she sighed.

He raised his brow. "I'll keep that in mind."

She glanced at him. "Nick—"

"Stop." They both turned back to Satan to see Iris standing behind him, her arms folded across her chest and her eyes glistening with outrage.

They both lifted their fingers off the trigger, and Iris caught Satan as he oozed to the floor in a misshapen pile of mushy male. She eased him down and then turned to them, her fists clenched and rage vibrating through her body. "Give me one reason why I shouldn't let him kill you when he re-forms."

And he'd thought Satan was the one he was supposed to worry about.

Becca stepped in front of him. "I'm so sorry to interrupt, Iris, but we have serious problems going on. I had no choice but to come—"

"I don't care if hell is breaking loose. I will not permit hell's business to be conducted in my house."

"Actually, hell is breaking loose, now that you mention it—"

Iris held up her hand. "Get away from my house." Then Satan moaned and Iris squatted next to him, propping his head up with her hands. Nick noticed that it was already starting to re-form, and there was a bit of a gleam in Satan's eye as Iris's cleavage dangled in front of him. "Are you all right, darling?"

"I am in much pain," he declared. "A full-body massage will be necessary to revive me."

"We think Satan's ex-lover is out to get him," Becca said.

Iris immediately stood up, and Satan's head thunked back to the carpet. "She can't have him."

Satan sat up, his belly still looking like a bowl of pudding that had been attacked by a vicious five-year-old. "My love is jealous! How delightful!" He pulled himself up using the banister, leaning against it. "Give me one more minute, man-friend, and then I will kill you."

Nick looked at the gleam in Satan's eyes and knew Satan was going to attempt to do exactly that, and then Nick would have to kill him. Sure, it would save his sister, but it would kill Becca, and Nick was just not up for that. So, he needed to give Satan a reason not to come after him and force him into a decision he didn't want to make yet. "I interrupted you because your favorite Rivka is dying, and I thought you could help."

Satan jerked off the railing, his eyes going so wide that Nick could see the whites all the way around his corneas. "What? You lie!" He grabbed Nick by the neck and threw him up against the wall, pressing his face against Nick, oozing fury and deep, unabating terror. "It is not funny joke."

"It's not a joke," he growled, willing himself not to lunge for Satan and take him out. *Keep it together, Nick.* "Look at her."

Satan swung around and looked at Becca, who was feverishly scratching her arms and shifting her weight. Her skin was sallow and her eyes were bleary. He dropped Nick instantly and swept across the room and grabbed

Becca's shoulders and shook her. "How dare you die! That is not permitted! I order you to live! I order you! Do you hear me?"

Becca winced. "Let go of me."

And then Iris was beside him, her hand on his arm. "This isn't helping, darling. Stop shaking her and let's go into the living room and find out what this is all about, okay?"

Satan didn't loosen his grip, staring at Becca as if she would disappear right before his eyes. "You die now?"

"No, not now."

"Not in one minute?"

She sighed. "Satan, trust me, you can survive without me, I promise."

"No!" He started shaking her again. "You do not die!"

Nick stepped up and quietly moved next to Becca. "You're hurting her." He kept his voice as calm as possible, but he knew his anger was building, and he set his hand on Satan's arm, his fingers digging in just enough to get Satan's attention. "Let go of her *now*."

Satan jerked his gaze to Nick, then his eyes narrowed. "You care about my Rivka?"

Becca cursed and Nick shook his head, tapping his foot against Becca's to reassure her. "I'm using her for my own means, and if she dies too soon, she'll be useless to me. Release her. Now."

Satan cocked his head. "What is your reason?"

No way was Nick getting his sister involved with Satan. "It's personal." He tapped his fingers on the back of Satan's hand. "Let go."

Satan's eyes flashed, and he released Becca to face Nick, his index finger beginning to glow red. "You are man-friend, which is why I did not kill you immediately, but there is no reason not to kill you now."

"I can keep Becca alive."

"*I* keep her alive," Satan corrected. "Only me."

"Now you've done it," Becca muttered under her breath. Then she cleared her throat. "Satan, here's the deal. Satan Jr.'s mom is mounting a major assault against hell and you. We need to have a chat with her. Who is she?"

Satan shot a guilty look at Iris. "I do not recall her name."

Iris narrowed her eyes. "What's the look for?"

"Nothing." He put his arm around Becca and hustled her off to the living room, where the couch pillows had been built into a cave on the middle of the floor. There was a pair of handcuffs and some massage oil inside, and Becca made a noise of disgust. "Tell me, Rivka, why do you die? I fix."

She sat on the couch a little too heavily, and Nick wanted to go sit next to her and lean against her, but he couldn't, not with Satan being so protective. Instead, he stood behind her, his hands gripping the back of the couch on either side of her head.

"One of our leads on tracking down Satan Jr. got tossed in the Chamber and I pulled the Terrors out of his body," she explained. "But now I can't get them out of me."

Satan sucked in his breath and sat back on his heels, a muddy gray aura suddenly bursting to light all around him. His pain and horror hit Nick so hard that Nick actually grunted and had to sit down. "Iris! Come hold me! I need you! My Rivka is going to die."

Iris didn't move from the doorway. "Not until you tell me what's going on with your ex-lover."

Satan spun around, a look of utter disbelief on his face. "How do you reject me at a moment of greatest need? I give much for you!"

"You tell me why you got that guilty look on your face when Satan Jr.'s mom was mentioned, and then I'll hug you."

"But—"

Nick couldn't stand it anymore, so he hopped over the back of the couch and landed next to Becca, drawing Satan's attention back to them. He could feel the dark jealousy pouring out of Satan, along with his total devastation. "It's your Chamber," he said. "Surely you must know how to cleanse her."

"Why would I know that? People who go in Chamber are supposed to suffer terrible fate. They do not get healed." Satan stood up and paced the room, his hands clasped behind his back. "This is much worrisome. The Chamber was designed most specifically to torture Rivkas. It is most excellent for that." He came to a stop in front of Becca. "I order you to tell me exactly how you feel right now."

She sighed. "I itch. I'm tired. I feel...crappy."

"Aigh!" Satan grabbed his hair and tugged on it. "This is much bad! Much bad!" He sank down on a recliner and dropped his head between his knees and began to take deep breaths. "Too much to cope with. I cannot deal. Need to destroy world."

Nick shoved himself off the couch and sat on the edge of the coffee table, and leaned his head next to Satan. "I can help her," he said quietly.

"No, you cannot," Satan whispered, his voice broken. "She is doomed. I toy with her much and pretend I kill her, but I never will. I cannot live without her." His bent further toward the floor, his hair almost touching the carpet.

"I have healer blood."

"Do I care? No! I do not care!" Satan sucked in a quaky breath and his shoulders quivered.

"My light can give her the strength to keep the Terrors at bay until we can figure something out. I can keep her alive."

Satan took another breath and turned his head slightly, listening.

"She won't let me do it," Nick continued. "When I merge with her that way, it becomes intimate, and she doesn't want to be disloyal to you."

Satan lifted his head. "She would choose to die rather than be disloyal?"

Nick nodded. "Yes."

Satan turned his head to Becca. "This is true?"

She gave Nick a wry look. "Basically."

Satan sat up. "You challenge me and try to break free, but it is all a farce because you love to tease me, no?"

"Of course."

Satan clapped his hand on Nick's knee. "Man-friend, you offer your services to keep her alive? Is this what you do?"

Nick managed to look unhappy. "There's only one problem."

Satan's face fell. "What is that?"

"To connect enough to help her, we might need to have sex. Intimate sex." He met Satan's gaze. "It wasn't in my plans, but for you, my new man-friend, I would do it. If you want me to." He glanced at Becca and saw the hope in her gaze. He gave her a nod, and she smiled faintly.

Satan nodded empathically. "Yes, I do. I do. Have sex with her. Do what is necessary."

Nick sighed. "You'd owe me."

"Of course. I would expect no less. What do you want?"

"He will decide later," Becca interrupted. "He needs to think about it."

Nick looked at her. "I do?"

"Yes."

He shrugged and turned back to Satan. "I need to think about it."

"Very good. Very good." Satan took a deep breath. "You keep her alive, yes? I will assign my best researchers to determine if there is way to save her. She must not die before I have answer." He leaned back in his chair. "I will wait while you have sex with her. Then we will discuss disruption of hell."

"No." Becca's protest was quick. "Not here."

"Yes, here. I do not want to risk your life."

Nick got up and sat next to Becca, putting his arm around her and pulling her up against him. She immediately started drawing on his energy, and he relaxed slightly as he felt his light begin to restore her. "This will be enough for the moment."

Satan's brow furrowed. "I can feel that. It is most intimate."

Becca tensed against him, and Nick gave Satan an easy grin. "So, now you realize the sacrifice I'm making to help you?"

Satan frowned. "Yes, yes. I understand. Most big favor. I do not like favors. Decide soon what I owe you, or I kill you both."

He felt Becca's wry amusement at that comment and knew that Satan's threats to kill Becca would never scare her anymore. Not after this display. And Satan wouldn't kill Nick, either, not as long as Nick was all that was keeping Becca out of the grips of the Terrors.

She took a breath, and he could feel the void inside her filling, pushing back the Terrors. Somewhat. Not completely. But enough for the moment. "Satan, someone used the blister machine and linked the bubble to your life force. Is there a way to save that person other than killing you?"

"Of course not. What kind of leader of hell would I be if my tortures had easy escape?"

Nick frowned. "Are you sure? Nothing?"

"Of course I am sure. I am Satan. I know all."

Nick closed his eyes for a brief second. *Satan has to be wrong, too arrogant to admit weakness.* There simply had to be a way to save his sister that didn't entail killing Becca incidentally.

"Who had access to the Goody Room?" Becca asked.

"Ah…" He cleared his throat and snuck a glance at Iris, who was still by the door. "My fair Iris does not want hell's business in her house. Perhaps we should take this discussion to my offices—"

"No." Iris walked across the room and sat down in another armchair and crossed her legs, the smooth material of her expensive black pants gliding with the movement. "I find politics fascinating. Please continue, or I'll think you have something to hide."

Satan looked at Nick. "Help?"

"Lies are bad. Be honest. Always better that way."

Satan looked at Iris again, then back at Nick. "Lies are quite good, actually. I find them most useful."

Becca sat forward, her hand gripping Nick's knee. "Okay, so instead of getting all over Satan, I have a question for Iris."

"Oh, most excellent. Question for Iris." Satan beamed at Becca. "Ask away."

"Why did you ask Satan to release the souls in hell?"

Iris stopped swinging her foot. "Because I don't approve of his day job."

"And you thought that sending bad people back into the mortal world to prey on the innocents would be a good idea on what level?"

Iris blinked. "Is that what's happening?"

"Yes. These people are bad, Iris. That's why they're there. He's releasing all the worst souls."

"And they're all trying to kill Becca," Nick added, then tweaked her nose when she glared at him. "Hey, I care if you get assassinated before I'm through with you, even if you don't."

Iris turned to Satan, who was frowning. "Why didn't you release the ones on my list?"

"I did." He nodded. "That is not a lie. I have been going from your list. One soul for each orgasm. I was most admiring of your choices. Very bad people. Some of my favorites. Will be great fun to harvest them again. But I am not happy they are going after my favorite Rivka. Should they not be fearing my wrath if they hurt her? Do they not respect me?"

"No!" Iris frowned. "That list was of people who didn't deserve hell. She told me—"

"Who told you?" They all asked the question at the same time, and Iris jerked back at the joint assault.

"A woman in my purgatory women's support group," she answered. "She works in the admissions office in purgatory, and she'd gotten a list of people in hell who didn't deserve it. We both thought it was would be doing a service to release those people..." She stared at the room. "The list was wrong?"

"The list was wrong." Becca drummed her fingers on Nick's thigh, and he smiled at her unintentional contact. Now that she wasn't worried about Satan killing him, he could feel her drawing on him with every ounce of her body. He was feeding her as best he could, but he could still feel the conflict inside her, the restlessness, the itch. He knew how desperate she was by the fact that she wasn't trying to block him.

She needed more, and soon.

He set his hand over hers. She flipped her hand over and curled her fingers around his, and then started jiggling her lower leg.

"Who is this woman?" Satan asked. "Why do you discuss our relationship with her? Is it not sacred to you?"

"Her name is Rosemarie Galoux." Iris ignored the last two questions. "She's my friend. She's been very supportive about my efforts to merge my life with yours..."

"Rosemarie Galoux?" Satan's mouth dropped open, and then he started to laugh. "Why did you not tell me this? Did she tell you not to tell me?"

"Yes...why?" Iris was frowning now.

"That is Satan Jr.'s mother! She has been manipulating you." He slapped his thigh. "She has not lost her devious ways. Most impressive. Befriending my lover is most ingenious, and convincing you to manipulate me is most cunning. Women's purgatory support group? I am much impressed. Rivka, send her letter of congratulations and invite her to next planning session on hell."

Iris was staring at him. "Rosemarie is your ex-lover?"

"Yes! Most entertaining, no?" Satan sat back. "No wonder my son is so devious. Perhaps I should not have been so quick to discard her. Perhaps she would have made good queen of hell."

"What?" Iris's voice was steely. "You want her instead of me?"

"No, no." Satan was on his knees in front of her in an instant. "She does not fill my soul with love. She is simply sex and cunning. Useful. Handy. You see?"

"I hate to interrupt," Nick interrupted. "But what about the bubble machine?"

Satan gave Nick a look. *"Later,* man-friend."

"No, now." Iris flicked him off her. "Tell me all."

Satan stood up and faced her, puffing out his chest as if he was trying to remind her of his virility. "Very well. I will tell you. After you gave me final rejection a month ago, before we reconciled, Rosemarie texted me to discuss how we could work together to get our son out of freezer. She was much admired of me, and I was much in need of being admired, so we had lots of somewhat hot sex—" At Iris's outraged roar, he hurried on. "And after she left, I realized my Goody Room key was missing, but then you came back to me and I was so enamored of my love for you that I forgot about missing key until my best Rivka ask me about blister machine this very minute. And then I reject Rosemarie and tell her you are my one and only and she was much angry. So you see? You should feel proud she came after you. It means you are much threat to her."

Outrage rolled off Iris as she leapt to her feet. "You slept with another woman last month?"

"To be fair," Becca said, "you'd been rejecting Satan for two hundred years. It wasn't as if you had a claim on him."

"But he was pursuing me! He wasn't supposed to lose interest!"

"I did not lose interest." Satan darted over to Iris, taking her hand in his. "But I am a man. I am Satan. I must maintain my ego at all times, and I had to take emergency action. It is who I am. Being a god among peons is a burden I must accept and live with."

"That's not an acceptable excuse to have sex with your ex-lover." Iris pulled her hands out of his and took a deep breath. "I need some space."

Satan nodded. "I think that is best."

Iris looked stunned. "You do? But you never want space from me."

"My Rivka is dying. My son and ex-lover are making plans behind my back that I do not know about because I am giving you much vaunted orgasms instead of ruling all things with ruthless control. You want to make me into wuss man. I do not like wuss man. I do not like that souls no longer fear my wrath. I am not the man I once was, and I do not like that."

Iris met his gaze. "You could be so much more than what you are."

"I am already magnificent. You do not appreciate me. I accept you how you are, yet you seek to strip me of all that makes me manly man."

Iris stiffened. "That's not true."

"No? You would take me as I am?"

"I..." She glanced at Nick and Becca, and Nick could feel the love pounding from both of them so fiercely that it actually hurt his chest. And the pain. *So much pain.* Iris walked across the living room and picked up her purse. "I'm going for a walk. Alone." She hesitated, but when Satan didn't protest, she turned and walked out the door.

Satan stared after her, then turned back to Nick and Becca. "Well, then, so we must find Rosemarie. I do not know where she lives. She finds me." He frowned. "I do not know what she is, either. I thought she was human, but she would be dead now if she was. But she is quite not dead." He smiled. "She was very feisty in the bedroom last month. Not like Iris, but..." Tears suddenly filled his eyes. "My Iris is gone. There is no hope for us. I cannot go on without her, but I cannot go on with her." He groaned and slumped back in the chair, then stared at the wall behind Becca, blinking hard.

Becca frowned, and Nick felt her concern for Satan. Bad boss or not, she was worried about him, which just added to the complexity of her nature. There was nothing cold and heartless about his Rivka, nothing at all.

"Are you going to be all right?" she asked Satan.

"I am most excellent." Satan took a deep breath, but Nick could feel his anguish cascading off him. "I think maybe I need some time alone." He looked at Nick. "Keep my Rivka alive." His eyes got even more watery. "I tell my researchers to look for cure." His voice cracked slightly, and he looked horrified. "I must go. People to kill." And then he disappeared in an explosion of gold and black bubbles.

"Well, okay then, now we have a name," Becca said briskly just as Nick turned toward her to ask her how she was feeling, waving him off. She pulled out her phone and hit speed dial. "Theresa? It's me. Yes, I'm fine. I need your help..." She looked at Nick. "No, he didn't abduct me. I'll tell you later. Can you please have Zeke find Rosemarie Galoux for me? Thanks. Call my cell, and yes, I'll tell you later." She snapped her phone shut and shifted restlessly. "Theresa's husband can find anyone. He'll be able to tell us where to find her in an hour or so." She wiped the back of her hand over her forehead and stood up, tugging her shirt away from her ribs. "I need to go home and change. These clothes of Dani's are driving me nuts."

"It's the not the clothes. It's the Terrors." He slipped his fingers around her wrist and pulled her toward him, not letting her shut him out anymore. "You need me, Becca." He brushed his lips over hers and almost winced at how cold they were. "Take what I can give you."

She pulled back slightly to look at his face, and he knew before she spoke what she was going to say.

Nineteen

I'm fine." She twisted free, and he let her go, his fingers drifting off her skin, sending shivers up her arm that made her want to fall into his embrace and let him make her feel alive. "Listen, Nick, I appreciate the whole getting permission from Satan to have sex, but I'm not going to sleep with you. I just can't, okay? I'll just go visit your mom and she can take care of things. Keep me going."

"My ma is already drained enough. She can't help you."

Oh, well. Best laid plans and all that crap.

His eyes flickered with determination, and he leaned into her space. "My sister's life is at stake. Hell is breaking loose. You don't have the right to let yourself die just because of your emotional baggage."

"Oh, now, see? That's just a like a man. Ordering me to stay alive. You and Satan both. What right do you have to tell me to stay alive?" She rolled her eyes. "That is my *whole* problem with my life! I have no control over any choice I want to make, and then you come in and think you can order me around, too." She glared at him. "Don't tell me what I can and can't do."

He held up his hands in apology. "Just one question, then."

She eyed him as she shoved her hands in her front pockets to keep from rubbing at the burning sensation creeping over her skin. "Only one? I doubt it."

"Do you want to die when you don't have to?"

"You know I don't."

"So, why won't you take advantage of the fact that I can help you?"

She stared at him, then spun away. "I have to go." She dissolved into the floor but was too slow, and Nick grabbed her arm before she had fully faded.

She came up through the floor of her bedroom, Nick with her, totally in her space. The instant they formed, he grabbed her arms and backed her up until she was against the wall. His eyes were dark and angry. "Why would you choose dying over intimacy with me? Satan gave you permission. You are not going to be responsible for my death." His grip tightened. "Do you hear me? You aren't going to cause my death. No blame. No responsibility. It's *okay.*"

Her throat tightened at the intensity on his face, and she realized he knew, like, really *knew,* how deeply Gabriel had affected her. "Satan lies," she whispered. "He changes his mind. You saw him. He's desperate over me. You won't be safe—"

He bent his head and kissed her.

It wasn't soft.

It wasn't sweet.

And it sure as hell wasn't gentle.

It was heat and emotion and light and passion— everything she wasn't. And everything she craved with every fiber of her being. Everything she'd yearned for since she was first created and walked among humans and saw what she couldn't have. Nick was all that, and so much more.

His mouth assaulted her, and she couldn't stop herself from kissing him back, kisses designed to drain the soul out of another instead of kisses intended merely for physical response. His fingers dug into her upper arms, and she didn't care.

No, she cared.

She wanted more.

His life force pressed at her, and she instinctively resisted its invasion, even as her body arched against him, her fingers found his hair and tugged on it, pulling harder than she intended, Nick groaning in response. "Let your barriers down," he whispered into her mouth as his fingers tugged her shirt out of her jeans. "I can't get in there by myself."

Her head hit the wall as she dropped it back to allow him access to her throat. "If I do, I'll never want you to leave."

"So, I won't." He bit the soft skin on her throat, and she shuddered, still trying desperately to keep him out of her soul.

She smiled at his arrogance. "How are you going to manage that?"

"Same way I'm going to save my sister without killing Satan." He lifted her arm and kissed the inside of her wrist, then licked his way down her arm.

She wriggled against him, trying to fight it. *I don't want to become dependent on him. I can't be dependent on him.* "How are you going to do that?"

"I'm still working on it." He reached her mouth again, and she forgot about what she was going to say.

His life force pushed at her, and he began to leak through her defenses. Not much, but she felt the faintest hint of his passion, of his love or his energy deep within her, and an intense yearning rose inside her with such force that she had to wrench away from him. "Stop."

He stopped, lifting his gaze to her eyes. "It's your choice."

She stared at him, and suddenly, she knew, more than anything, she wasn't ready to give up yet. Not on her dreams to be free of Satan, not on her dreams to have her own life force. Which meant she had to do what it took. And she could feel the Terrors eating away at her, digging in, destroying her. *I can do this.*

Even if it meant that her life as a Rivka would be hell once she let herself be touched by Nick. Once she knew what it was like to really be alive.

But she could handle it. She had to handle it. *My life is worth this.* She met his gaze. "I'm in."

He frowned. "You sound like this is a card game."

"That's all it can be to me. All I want is for you to give enough positive energy for me to get the Terrors reduced enough to keep me going. That's it. Nothing more. With as minimal intrusion as possible."

Something flickered in his eyes, but he shrugged. "As you wish." And then he kissed her again.

Hard. Deep. Penetrating. Crushing her with his life force, heat burning from his touch everywhere their skin touched. She threw her arms around his neck and pressed herself against him, drinking in everything he was giving her.

It swirled inside her, made her feel warm and hot and—

"You're not letting me in," he whispered as his hands slipped under her shirt, his touch searing her skin. "Drop your shields."

"I'm trying." She kissed him back harder, her body stirring with things she hadn't felt in so long. *Come in, Nick.* He was burning inside her, and she could feel his emotions. His lust, his worry for his sister, his desperation, and she grabbed onto it and pulled it into her heart, into her soul, where it circulated and rushed around.

God, he was alive. Throbbing with vitality. *You feel so good.*

"Becca, I can't get past your barriers."

"Yes, you are." She couldn't stop the moan as his hands flicked over her nipples. "I can feel you inside me."

"I'm there, but I'm not a part of you. I have to be part of you to get the Terrors subdued. They have to think my light is you." His hips pressed against hers, and she wiggled against him, against the part of him that was so hard.

She felt his renewed thrust at her senses, and she tried to open herself to him, to bring him inside, but she could feel what he meant. He was inside her, he was light, and he was energy, but they were still two separate beings. "I can't give up myself," she whispered. "I don't know how." *And I'm scared to.*

He growled with frustration, then scooped her up against him, spun around, and tossed her on the bed. She'd barely landed when he was on top of her, tugging her shirt up, his hands covering her body like he couldn't get enough of her. "Stop thinking. Just let go."

"I always think. It keeps me alive." She jerked when his mouth closed over her nipple through the sports bra that Yasmine had given her.

"Not this time. This time, thinking will kill you." He bit gently, and she twisted under him, and then he bit harder, rubbing his teeth over the sensitive tip. "You've got to let your defenses down."

She scrunched her eyes shut and concentrated on the feel of his body against hers. On his skin, on his touch, on the feel of his kisses on her body. She opened her eyes when she heard him groan with aggravation. "What?"

"You." He kissed the tip of her nose. "You've got to relax."

"How? You're asking me to do something I don't do."

He rolled off her and propped his head up on his elbow so he could look down at her. "You have to trust me."

She eyed him. "What are you talking about?"

"You're keeping me out because you don't trust what I'll do when I get in there." He laid his palm over her heart, and she felt the pulse of his energy. "This isn't about sex, Becca. This is about the mating of our spirits and our souls."

She swallowed hard. "I can't."

"Yes, you can."

She shook her head and sat up, tugging her shirt back down over her breasts. "No, I'm not made that way. I've spent my entire life learning how to keep my emotions out, learning how not to care about anyone. Learning not to trust anyone. Doing everything possible to create and maintain my independence." She looked at him, willing him to understand. "I had to find a way to protect myself, and I can't drop it like that."

"You cared about Gabriel. I still feel his presence inside you, so I know you let him in."

She hugged her knees to her chest tightly, protecting herself. "It destroyed me."

"No, it didn't." He trailed his fingers through her hair. "It made you stronger. It made you cautious. But you still have that ability to care inside you." His fingers massaged her scalp, and she closed her eyes to enjoy the sensation. "I felt that spark of life inside you. I know it's there."

She rested her chin on her knees as he continued to touch her. "I don't want to have those kinds of feelings."

"Yes, you do."

She didn't answer. How could she? He was right. And he was wrong. But dammit, she didn't want to die from some stupid Terrors. Why couldn't she let go? She lifted her chin. "Let's try again. I'm sure I can make myself do it."

Nick sat up, pulled his shirt over his head, and the womanly side of her trembled at the sight of his muscular chest. "Give me your hand."

She released her legs and put her hand in his. He cupped it softly, and she felt a tremor of his energy. But he wasn't pushing it at her. It simply *was*. He laid her palm on his chest. "What do you feel?"

She couldn't help but smile. "A hard male body."

He made a noise of disgust, the twinkle in his eyes belying his irritation. "You women. All you can think about is sex."

"When I'm in bed with a gorgeous guy like you, yeah."

She felt a little more relaxed at the exchange. "What can I say? I'm a slut."

"I can tell." He tapped his fingers on the back of her hand, which was still on his chest. "Close your eyes and lie back."

She shivered with anticipation and did as he said. "Now what?"

"Stop talking."

"You're so demanding. How do women put up with you?"

"They don't. They all kick me out of their lives within a week or two." He scooted up against her so his body was pressed against hers along the length of hers, then pulled back, as if he'd changed his mind. Before she could register her disappointment, he said, "Sit up."

"Up, down, you're so indecisive." She sat up, and then she caught her breath when he pulled her shirt over her head and tugged off her sports bra. Then he was straddling her, unzipping her jeans and sliding them down over her legs, with a slow deliberateness that had her wanting to jump up and throw him down. "No foreplay?"

He just gave her a smile that had her belly curl as he stood up and shucked his jeans and boxers. And then he laid back down next to her, pressing his body against hers like he had before, only this time, it was skin to skin from chest to ankle. He draped his leg over hers, entwining them together.

She squirmed against him, drinking in the sensation of a man wrapped around her, of his sex hard against her hip. Everywhere their skin touched, she felt alive. It wasn't just sex, it was life. And he wasn't just a man. *Nick.* The touch of his skin was wild, hot, overwhelming, addicting, and it made her want more. So much more. She reached for him, to pull him down toward her, but he didn't let her.

He didn't kiss her. Didn't caress her. He simply picked up her hand and placed it on his chest. "Now close your eyes."

She did, expecting him to touch her.

But all he did was hold her hand over his heart. "Tell me what you know about me."

She frowned. "What are you talking about?"

"Go inside me and tell me what you see."

"Oh. You mean like you do to me."

"Yeah. I'm open to you. All you have to do is go in. I promise I won't return the favor."

She hesitated, but the curiosity was too great, and she ever so carefully let herself drift into his body. Like he'd promised, she slid right in, and she was awash in the rumbling emotions that were Nick. It was far more intense than what she'd felt when he was pushing himself into her, and the intensity of it almost made her cry out.

"Tell me what you feel." His voice was a soft caress over her skin that made goosebumps pop up, his skin scorching hers along the length of their naked bodies.

"I can't tell. There's...so much." She opened herself more to him, sifting through all the heat and passion inside him. "Love. You're like this big love machine."

She felt his smile. "For who?"

"Dani. Your mom. Jerome." She blinked at the sudden pressure around her own heart. "I can't believe how intense that is. Doesn't that scare you?" God, he was so

intense. His love was so pure, so automatic, so uncon-
ditional. To have someone feel like that about her...she
shook her head. *You will never have that.*

"Loving that intensely is what keeps me alive."

She felt the truth of his answer and suddenly knew,
deep down in her soul, she wanted him to love her like
that. To stand behind her no matter what. Nick would always be there for her. Always. *God, Becca. What are you
thinking?*

"What else?" he asked.

She tried to shake herself from the love pulsing at her,
and she reached further into his essence and found something darker. "Your dad. You miss him. So much." She
wanted to hold on to that pain, and she pulled it into her
own heart. Because it was familiar. Comfortable. Something she knew. She tucked it in her body, comforted by
it. "What happened to him?"

"He died." His voice was gruff, laced with pain. "What
else do you see?"

She caught a hint of anger, and she followed it. "You're
pissed at Jerome."

His body tensed and the air around him grew warmer.
"He slept with my sister. I have to wring his neck."

She smiled. "You saved him."

"So I could wring his neck. What about Paige?"

She frowned, searching deeper for the fainter emotions. His life force was pulsing under her touch, and she
rolled into her side so she could press the front of her body
against his, needing more surface area to reach him. She
opened her senses, searching for Paige. "You like her."
She was surprised, and warmed. "You're worried about
her." She felt a flicker of her own distress for Paige, fight-

ing the busload of assassins, and her trepidation merged with Nick's and they became one.

"She's a sweet kid. No match for being Satan's Rivka." He released her hand and rested his hand on her hip, his thumb circling against the skin.

She felt the press of his lips to her shoulder, and she wriggled against him.

"Keep searching. Find out my secrets. Ignore what I'm doing." He gently pushed her on her back and kissed her on the mouth, his tongue brushing over her lips ever so softly. "Surely I have more to tell."

She arched under him as his chest hair tickled her nipples, as his thigh slid between hers. "You're an angry, bitter man."

He slid his hand along her thigh, trailing kisses down the side of her neck. "Yeah, so?"

She caught her breath as a searing fire flowed over her. "You hate the Council for killing your dad." His rage slammed into her, and she gasped at its intensity, writhing under it, seeking to mingle it with her own anger over her own life. "You hate the life he left you."

"He forbade me to take revenge." His hands moved more restlessly over her body, and his thumb slid over the sensitive part between her legs, sending heat spiraling through her, mingling with the rage and anger boiling inside him. "I have to live every day unable to right the wrong that stole my dad and my life."

She felt his anger at his lack of control over his destiny, and recognition flared deep inside her. "I know," she whispered, as she was vaguely aware of his fingers slipping inside her, of his lips taking possession of her mouth. *You hate not being able to control your life.*

As do you. His response was silent, but she knew what he said. She could feel him deep inside her. *We are the same, Becca.*

His touch was everywhere on her body, awareness vibrating between them.

You're so alive. She clutched at him, kissed him, tried to draw him into her, closer, desperate to have him under her skin in all ways. *I need you.*

I need you, too, gorgeous. And then his body was over hers, his skin sliding along hers, and she could feel his pain, his anger, his love for his family everywhere they touched. His love was so bright, so intense, hurting inside her at the same time, she could feel it trying to fill her up, to dive into every corner of her being.

Tears blinked at the corners of her eyes, and she tried to regain control of herself. *No...I don't want to feel it. I need—*

And then he thrust into her, and her body screamed for him, for the heat, for the pure love he was driving into her body at every level of her being.

His voice whispered through her mind. *Embrace the light, Becca. Be alive.*

His love, his passion for life, the brightness of his spirit was too much and it slammed into her, overwhelming her, and she gave herself into it. Drank it greedily into her soul as she welcomed him into her body. He drove into her, into her being, into her body, and she screamed for more, even as she felt like more would rip her apart. *I don't care.*

She reached for him, felt him answer, and wrapped her soul around his, and he did the same as their bodies reached the crescendo, mixing love and anger and raw, potent sex. And light. It exploded inside her, around her, and she screamed. Nick's hoarse shout echoed hers, and they clung to each other as the tremors racked their bodies and their souls and their energies. Everywhere they connected, on every level they were one.

Twenty

Becca felt the first press of tears as soon as Nick withdrew and rolled off her, even though he pulled her into the curve of his body and wrapped his limbs around her, holding her tight against him. *Dammit.* She missed him already. Missed his life force, missed the intimacy, missed how alive she felt when she was one with him.

"What's with the tears?" He kissed her forehead, and she knew he could feel her grief without having to look at her face or see her expression.

She knew, because she could still feel every emotion rolling around inside him. It was like they were connected in a way they hadn't been before. But at the same time, there was a gaping gulf between them. She could still feel his spirit, but it wasn't a part of her anymore. Inside, she was empty, more empty than she'd ever been before, and she felt so lost it was almost overwhelming.

She pressed her face into his chest and breathed in the scent that was him. "I can't feel the Terrors anymore."

"Good." He stroked her hair. "So then, what's wrong?"

"Can't you tell?"

He was quiet for a moment, and she felt him reach

inside her through wherever their bodies were touching. She was too tired to block him, and besides, what was the point? He'd been to her most intimate places already. There was nowhere left to hide. Nothing left to conceal.

She was raw, exposed and vulnerable.

But she realized it was okay. Nick would never take advantage of her vulnerability. She knew it as surely as she'd felt his grief about his father. He might know her in a way no one else did, but she'd been inside him just as far.

"You're feeling sorry for yourself."

She lifted her head to peer at him. "What?" Why wasn't he giving her all sorts of warm fuzzies and sweet nuzzles of comfort?

He frowned at her. "I can't believe you're feeling sorry for yourself. You just had the greatest sex in the history of the Otherworld, and you're the first Rivka ever to feel what it was like to be truly alive, and you're sitting there feeling sorry for yourself because you can't have it all the time."

She sat up and looked at him. "You're serious."

"Damn right I am." He rolled onto his back and studied her, his green eyes still heavy with the aftermath of their lovemaking. "I thought you were a fighter. Not a whiner."

She glared at him. "I don't whine."

"I didn't think you were the type, but there's some serious whining going on inside you right now."

She stared at him, then broke into a smile when she realized what he was doing. "That's so low."

"What is?" He gave her an innocent look that she didn't buy for a second.

"Taking advantage of your insider knowledge." She poked him in the chest, then rolled off her bed, suddenly feeling better. "Now you know that insulting me pisses me off and goads me into action, and you're taking advantage of that to manipulate me and make me feel better." She walked into the bathroom and flicked on the shower, peeking back at him. "I hate being manipulated." *But I love that you made me feel better.*

His arms were behind his head, his ankles crossed, and he was fully naked and not at all embarrassed. He looked rather like he owned her bed and was enjoying that fact immensely. "It was hell on my ego to have you cry after such a magnificent performance by me. I had no choice but to call you on it."

She laughed as she stepped into the shower. "You sound like Satan."

He snorted. "I do not."

"Sure you do. Makes sense. I felt him inside you while we were making love."

The shower curtain was ripped aside, startling her. His eyes were wide awake now, his body tense. "What did you say?"

She squinted at him through the water dripping off her lashes. "I said I could feel Satan inside you."

"Are you joking, or did you really?"

She thought back to the flare of recognition when she'd found that part of him, well hidden, but definitely there. It was part of what had connected them. "I'm serious, but what would you expect? You were created by him."

"Satan's life force is still in me?"

"So? Trust me, you've got a mild case of it." She turned and wet her hair, letting it cascade over her. Then she froze and turned back to him. "You have Satan's life force in you."

His eyes were tight on hers, and he didn't answer.

There was no need.

They were both thinking the same thing.

After a moment, she found her voice. "Everyone they tried to link the Rivkas to died."

"We don't know that they tried Markku."

"I'm sure they did." She cleared her throat, trying to suppress the surge of hope bubbling inside her. "Nick, let's be realistic. You can't support me, and even if you could, I wouldn't want to do it. It would make me subservient to you. We wouldn't be equals anymore." She met his gaze. "I can't be your slave, Nick. I couldn't live with that."

"I'd never ask you to be."

"But that's the way it would be. We wouldn't be able to help it." But God, to be supported by his life force, to feel his energy inside her all the time...No. His personality was too strong. *I will not trade servitude of one type for another. It's not enough.* She turned away and dumped shampoo on her head, scrubbing furiously. "Besides, even if the linking didn't kill you, Satan would when he found out you'd taken me from him, man-friend or not. I won't use you for my own ends."

She felt his amusement. "You're a Rivka. You should have no trouble using me," he said.

"Yeah, well, I like to break the Rivka rules whenever possible." She turned and let the water wash the soap out of her hair as she heard her phone ring in the other room. "Will you get that? It's probably Theresa with the location of Satan's ex-lover."

He hesitated, and then she heard the shower curtain move and he was gone.

She groaned softly and leaned her forehead against the wall of the shower, letting the water cascade down on her back. *Get yourself together, Becca.* So what if she'd just had her world altered permanently by the best sex ever? So what if she'd never be able to look at Nick or her own life the same way again? What was she thinking, turning down Nick's offer? It would give her everything she'd ever wanted, wouldn't it?

But it might kill Nick. Or make her his slave, changing their relationship forever.

Dammit. Why couldn't she just say yes? Nick had messed her up. Distracted her from her goal. Made her too damned complicated.

Nick tugged open the shower again, his face grim. "That was Theresa with Rosemarie's address, but after I got it from her, Paige beeped in. She's in trouble."

Paige was in trouble? A fear unlike anything she'd ever felt knifed through her, and she had to grab the rail in her shower to keep from collapsing.

"Becca?"

She flung back the curtain, steeling her heart against the visions of all the harm that could be befalling her apprentice. "Let's go get her." Her voice cracked slightly, and she knew Nick noticed, but neither of them mentioned it.

Not that ignoring it would make it go away, but it was all she had.

Becca and Nick made it to Yasmine's cabin in less than three minutes, re-forming on the top of a hill outside.

Bodies were strewn all over the ground outside the cabin, and a big yellow school bus was on fire. No movement other than the billow of black smoke. Becca swallowed hard, her heart slamming in her chest. "Do you see her?"

"No." Nick's hand was on her shoulder, and she didn't shrug it off. "She's not down there."

"So, that's good." At Nick's penetrating glance, she shrugged. "Well, because I can't use her to replace me if she's dead, right?"

"Give it up, Becca," he said. "You love her."

"Shut up."

He simply took her hand and started down the hill, and she followed him, picking her way around the bushes and a still-flaming tire from the bus. They made it to the bottom of the hill and walked around the bodies. She tested a few. "She's taken all their souls already." She stood up. "Paige! Can you hear me?"

There was a squawk from behind the house, and they both broke into a run.

Nick made it around first and skidded to a stop when he saw what was going on.

Paige was lying on her back, writhing on the ground, moaning and sweating and clutching her stomach.

"Paige." Becca dropped to her knees beside the apprentice, blinking back tears. "What's wrong?"

"Get them out," Paige whispered. "Get them out."

"Get what out?" She felt better when Nick kneeled next to her, realizing that she had a partner. Someone who would help her.

He laid his hand on Paige's head, gently stroking her hair. "It's okay, kid, we're both here now. Get what out?"

"The souls I harvested. It burns."

While Nick comforted Paige, Becca ran her hands over Paige, then found a pulsating darkness by her left shin. Tears burned her eyes, and she sat back, her heart tighter than it had ever been. "Sweetie, that's not one of the souls you took."

"What the hell is it, then? It's like acid-eating fire."

Becca laid her hand on Paige's forehead next to Nick's, trying to offer comfort like he was doing. "That's your soul, honey."

"Mine? What are you talking about?" She groaned and rolled onto her side. "It hurts, Mom. Make it stop."

Oh, if only she could. She'd do anything to stop what was happening to Paige. "When you killed all those people out there, did you enjoy it?"

"Well, yeah, of course. I'm supposed to, right?" Paige reached out and gripped Becca's hand. "I mean, they were there to kill you. They deserved to die."

"Yes, but there's a difference between doing what you have to do, and enjoying it." She patted Paige's hand, an empty action, but she didn't know what else to do. "By taking so many lives and enjoying it, your soul is becoming dark. You're embracing your destiny."

Paige opened her eyes, her brows furrowed with uncertainty. "You mean my soul is turning black? I'm officially truly evil?"

"Satan's life force has taken over, yes."

Paige struggled to a sitting position and Nick moved next to her to help her sit up. "Well, it's a sucky feeling. Make it go away."

"I can't." She managed a smile that she didn't feel, crying for Paige's loss. "It's what you wanted, Paige. You've officially crossed the line, and you're well on your way to becoming a real Rivka."

Paige furrowed her brows. "So am I going to feel like this always?"

"Only while you're going through the transition. Right now, your body is fighting the transition to the dark side, but once it...consumes you, you'll be fine." She'd seen it happen with other Rivkas. They were cold, empty, and inhuman. Entirely without remorse or the capacity for any kind of human emotion at all. It made life as a Rivka so much easier, but after what she'd felt with Nick...she wouldn't want to be spared the pain. She wanted every minute of light she could get, no matter how much harder that made it to return to her real life.

Paige pursed her lips together. "Well, that's cool. How do I finish the transition? Because I feel like hell right now."

"It'll just happen as you do more of these types of things and learn to embrace it." She patted Paige's arm. "Congratulations."

Paige beamed at her through the pain. "No wonder you're Satan's best Rivka. Making me turn black already. How long did it take your soul to turn black?"

She sat back on her heels. "Mine isn't. I never let it happen. I never enjoyed my job, not really. So my soul never got black, which is why I'm different than other Rivkas. I'm just tortured and miserable. But you...you enjoyed it, and that changes everything."

Paige's mouth dropped open. "You're serious? Your soul isn't black? You haven't been consumed by evil?"

"Yes." She felt Nick's gaze and looked up at him, hum-bled by the look of respect in his eyes. "It doesn't make me special," she told him. "It made me miserable."

"It made you amazing." He leaned over Paige and kissed her softly, but she could feel his emotions even from the short kiss.

She tightened her lips against the new surge of moisture in her eyes. What was *wrong* with her? So what if he was impressed? Since when did she care what anyone else thought of her? *Stop being so emotional. You're a Rivka, for hell's sake.*

"Well, forget it, then. I don't want a black soul." Paige staggered to her feet. "I'm not doing it if you didn't do it."

"It's too late, and you won't care soon anyway. You won't care about what I think or Dani or anyone else. You'll just care about Satan."

Paige stared at her. "I'll stop caring about you? And Dani? And Nick? And Yasmine?"

"Yes, but that's for the best. It's so much easier that way—"

"No!" Paige stomped her foot. "I refuse to do it. I will not give up my friends and my mom."

"Paige—"

"Why didn't you tell me this before? How could you let me do this to myself? You're supposed to protect me!" Paige glared at Becca and Nick. "I hate all of you." Then her eyes widened. "Omigod. My blackened soul liked that emotion. It twitched! I can't hate, can't I? I have to love! That's how I'll beat this." She threw her arms around Becca, knocking her to the ground. "I love you." Then she leapt up and tackled Nick, who caught her before she could take him out. "I love you, Nick." She twisted off him and started circling them. "I love the trees. I love the blue sky. I love the sun." She held up her arms and lifted her face. "I am love! I am good!"

Becca propped herself up on her elbows and watched her apprentice worship the sun. *Go, Paige.* Yeah, it would make Paige's life tougher to care about others, but it was so much better, too.

Then she frowned. Since when did she believe caring about others was better?

Since she met Nick.

The man in question held out a hand.

She grabbed it and let him pull her to her feet, and something leapt between them at the touch, something more than what used to be there, and she knew why she'd changed.

Nick had changed her.

She frowned, and he lifted her hand and kissed her fingertips. "I want you to consider my offer. Let's try to use me to support you."

"So Satan can kill us both?"

Nick's eyes flashed with anticipation. "I'm not afraid of him. Let him come after us. I'd love to give him payback for all the grief he's given you. This is what you want. Why are you turning it down?"

"I…" She swore, not able to articulate her fear of him dying for her. She couldn't live with his death on her hands. "It's complicated. Just let it go. I'll find another way." She ignored his look of frustration and turned to Paige, not quite able to bring herself to let go of his hand. "Paige, we're going to find Satan Jr.'s mother. Theresa's husband found out where she is, so we're going to check it out. We think she's the one who bubbled Dani. You want to come, or you want to stay here with Jerome and Yasmine?"

Paige stopped spinning and leapt over a pile of leaves to wrap her arms around Becca's waist. "Jerome and Yasmine are at Dani's place. Jerome was freaking out and couldn't deal, so Yasmine took him." Her eyes flashed. "And of course I'm coming. I have to kill that son-of-a-bitch for blistering my best fr—" She stopped suddenly, her eyes widening. "Dammit! I can't kill him. I have to love him?" She scowled and kicked the turf. "This *sucks*."

"Killing is okay if it is done to save those you love, and if there's no other option," Nick said.

"Oh." Paige brightened. "Well, let's go then. I'm sure I can find a reason why I have no other choice."

Becca wrapped her arms around both of them and held them close. "Okay, Nick. Where to?"

"Northern Maine." He said the address, and she closed her eyes and took them just outside their target.

They peered over the grassy knoll at the scene below. There were tents everywhere in the meadow, the sounds of lovemaking coming from many of them. And three copulating couples that hadn't bothered to make it to the tents. Nick grimaced and covered Paige's eyes.

She smacked his hands away. "Oh, come on, Nick. I can handle this."

"You're too young."

"She's a virgin," Becca added.

"I'm Satan's spawn," Paige grumbled. "I think I can handle a little sex." She flared up a fireball and waved it at Nick. "Back off."

He was about to argue with her when he saw Becca's body tense. "What's going on?"

"Those men below...do they seem familiar?"

He dropped next to her to study the scene below, frowning when he noticed the shimmering air rising from the mating couples. "They're Markku." A sense of belonging wrapped around him as he stared down. "This must be where the one who attacked me came from."

"Markku? Really?" Paige wriggled up next to him and looked down the slope. "They're seriously bad news, aren't they? Indestructible and all that?"

Nick recalled what his assailant had said about them vanquishing the post-battle weakness. If that were really true..."Be careful around them."

"I'm always careful." Paige plopped down on her belly next to Becca. "So, what's with all the sex? This place is like a brothel." At Becca's sharp look, she shrugged. "I spent my first three weeks in hell. They're all over the place. But not like this. I can practically feel the sex vibes coming from down there."

"You can? Really?" Becca looked down there again, and then nodded in understanding. "There are Penhas down there."

"Payne-yas?" Paige repeated. "What's that?"

"Penhas?" Nick opened his senses and was hit with a rousing slam of lust that had him growing hard instantly. He growled and slammed up his shields. "Damn."

"Their weapon is sex," Becca said. "They're so alluring that I've heard of mothers sacrificing their children for Penhas sex. They're like a drug. Once they get in your head, you'll do anything they want in order to get them to have sex with you."

Paige looked wary. "Are you going to sacrifice me?"

"No, because I just had—" She looked at Nick. "Their power gets stronger the longer it's been since you've had sex."

Paige pursed her lips. "Well, hell, I'm totally screwed, then. I should stay up here, huh?" She scowled and bunched her fists. "I wanted to help, not hide."

"You can help by keeping watch. You'll be able to see things we won't. Call me if there's something we need to know." Becca turned back to the meadow below, her gaze landing on a deluxe RV in the shade. "I'm thinking the RV is the command center."

Nick threw his arm around her shoulder. "Let's go check it out."

When they re-formed behind the trailer, Nick nearly staggered from the Markku vibes all around him. He reached out for them and felt their lust as they rutted away...and at the same time, he sensed regret. Frustration. A loss of control. Desperation. "The Markku are being controlled by the Penhas," he whispered. "There are female Markku here as well, and they're all at the mercy of the Penhas." He had a burning need to help them, but he willed himself not to be distracted. He was here for Dani, not to save the other Markku. They would have to wait.

"Penhas are nonconfrontational," she whispered back. "They don't control other beings." Then again, they weren't supposed to go after things like the Goblet of Eternal Youth, and she'd already seen that happen...which now made sense. "I think Satan Jr.'s mom has been using the Penhas to advance her son's agenda for a while.

Penhas came after the Goblet a few months ago. Almost worked, too."

Nick eased up next to the trailer and felt for any emotions coming from within. "You think his mom's a Penha?"

"No idea." She scooted next to him, pressing into his body, and he could feel her reaching inside him to try to feel what he was sensing. He opened to her, allowing her inside, and smiled with how right it felt.

"Is anyone in the trailer?" she asked.

"There's anger. Fury." He stopped talking as a crescendo of voices rose from within. A male voice shouting, a woman's yelling back.

Something crashed from inside, and the door slammed open right next to them.

They quickly dove under the trailer as a man stepped outside. He was wearing a gold jumpsuit with sparkly gold boots and had bleached blond hair. He whirled back toward the trailer, and Nick jerked his head underneath so he couldn't be seen.

"I'm tired of you trying to run my life," the man shouted. "You think that just because you got me unfrozen that I should bow to you and let you tell me what to do."

Satan Jr. Fury slammed into Nick, but before he could move, Becca reached out to wrap her fingers around his wrist. "Not now," she whispered. "Wait."

He immediately drew on her strength and self-control to gain control of his anger. She snuggled against him, reaching into him to help him build his shields. "I like that I can help you," she whispered.

"You and me both," he said as he curled his fingers into

the grass, forcing himself not to jump up and punish the man for what he'd done to his sister, feeling Becca's control winding through his being, tamping down his need to retaliate.

"I'm your mother. I have every right to do what I think is best for you," a woman's voice said. There was a soft step above their heads, and then a pair of women's feet came into view, clad in stilettos and black stockings. The faint scent of perfume drifted under the trailer, and Nick felt his groin tighten.

"She's Penha," he whispered. "I can feel it."

"You're fine," Becca whispered. "You had sex twenty minutes ago."

He dropped his head. Beads of sweat trickled down his back, and he latched even tighter onto Becca, drawing her against him, rubbing himself against her to try to use her to block the influence of the Penha, but he suddenly became aware of her breasts pressed against his chest, of the soft curve of her hips under his hands... "This isn't working," he gritted out. "She's powerful."

"So are you." Becca's voice was calm. "Shut her out."

"I'm trying," he muttered.

"You blistered Dani!" Satan Jr. shouted. "How could you do that? You know she was going to be my queen!"

At the mention of Dani, rage flared inside him, and Nick embraced his anger, trying to force the sexual need out of his body. He and Becca could control anger. Lust, not so much, apparently.

"I had to get her brother out of the Council offices!" Rosemarie snapped. "There was no way to get through him. These Markku you found for me are weaklings in comparison to him."

Becca raised her brows at him, and he shrugged.

Satan Jr. growled in frustration. "He still has the post-battle weakness. You could have taken him out when he was down!"

"I wasn't willing to risk your life on that!" She snapped. "You should be thanking me. Besides, Dani was using you. It's Jerome she loves."

There was silence, and Nick felt Satan Jr.'s denial before he even spoke. "Dani loves me. I am the one who will make her queen of hell."

"No, you arrogant fool. Dani was using you, and once you were frozen, I realized it. Putting her in that vesicle of hell pus was the best thing I could do for you. If her brother succeeds in killing Satan, then you'll be the leader of hell and you can manipulate her into anything. If he doesn't, then Dani will die, which is what she deserves anyway."

There was more silence. Then, "It still pisses me off I can't kill Satan myself."

"Yes, well, we have to accept the fact that your shared blood keeps you from killing him and make other arrangements, right?" Her voice turned soothing and sultry, and a fresh blast of lust crashed into Nick.

Shit. "She's extremely powerful. No wonder the Markku have no chance against her." He dropped his head, willing himself to stay still, when all he wanted to do was crawl out from under the trailer and beg her to ride him until he collapsed from exhaustion. He'd have no chance at all if she actually directed her powers at him.

Becca slipped her hand under the front of his jeans, and he nearly exploded right there. "Better?" she asked.

"Sort of," he croaked. Now he wanted Becca so much

that he was in actual physical pain. "You're killing me." He felt her own lust flare, and he groaned. "We can't have Penha-induced sex under here," he whispered. "We'll never be able to be quiet. They'll find us."

Her hand stilled in silent admission that he was correct. "Then we better get out of here soon, because your lust is starting to affect me."

There was the rapid thud of feet fast approaching. "Your highness?" a new male voice said.

"Yes?" Rosemarie said.

Her highness. He looked at Becca. "Queen of the Penhas?" It made sense now.

"No wonder Satan couldn't resist her," Becca whispered. "After two hundred years of celibacy, even he had no chance against her."

"Our cameras are picking up two visitors at the blister," the new person said.

"Who are they?"

"The girl's mother and a guy claiming to be her true love. The mother has a chainsaw and is trying to cut through the bubble."

Nick swore under his breath. "We need to get them out of there."

There was the sound of Junior's fist hitting something. "It has to be Jerome. I'm going to go kill him."

"Don't be a fool. He's the future of the Council now that Otis and Paul were caught throwing him in the Chamber. I heard that he's already been ordered to find two replacements to assist him on the Council. We have to get him under our control and use him."

"I don't care. I'll kill him." Satan Jr. whirled to leave, and then there was a sharp whistle from Rosemarie.

Suddenly, there were three pairs of dainty bare feet with painted toenails around Satan Jr. and the air was so thick with lust that Nick could barely breathe. Satan Jr. groaned, and Nick felt Satan's Jr.'s resistance and anger vanish, replaced by a burning sexual need that had Nick drawing blood on his own lip to keep from groaning.

"Take him to his tent," Rosemarie ordered. "I will deal with him later." She turned suddenly, her toes facing the RV. "Who is here? I smell lust that is not one of my men."

Nick clenched his fists.

"Little man," Rosemarie said, her voice smooth and silky. "Come out now and be my stallion."

Nick began to shake with the effort of keeping still. "Get me out of here, Becca. *Now.*"

Twenty-one

When they re-formed at the top of the hill, Nick dropped to his knees and clutched the ground, trying to get control of the sexual need consuming him. "I can still feel her. She's looking for me. We need to get out of here. Or we need to have sex. Just make it fast or I'm not going to be able to resist her call."

"Trust me, I'm wanting sex right now as much as you are. Let's just get Paige..." Becca frowned as she looked around. This hillside was empty. "Paige?"

There was a giggle, and they turned around to see Paige's tousled head pop up from behind a bush. "Oh, you're back already. What's the rush?" Her shoulder was bare, and her cheeks were flushed. "I'm fine. You can go do your thing and—"

"What are you doing?" Becca nearly shouted with motherly outrage when the bushes moved to reveal a half-naked Markku with his hands around Paige's waist and his lips buried in her navel. "Who the hell are *you*?"

Nick's lust began to fade, chased away by a rising roar of fury, and he staggered to his knees as the Markku grinned up at Becca, his blond hair falling over one eye. "Hi."

Paige wrapped her arms around the man's shoulders. "We're soul mates...umph." She disappeared from sight as the Markku hauled her under him and dropped his body on top of hers. Paige made a noise of delight and wrapped her legs and arms around him, wriggling her body against his.

Nick leapt to his feet and bolted for the bushes. "Get off her!"

"Paige Darlington, get out from under him right this minute!" Becca ordered as Nick grabbed the Markku by the back of the head and yanked him off the kid. The Markku's hand slipped out from under Paige's shirt.

Nick flung him across the clearing, nodding with satisfaction when he crashed into a tree and thudded to the ground.

"Colin!" Paige shrieked, scrambling to her feet.

Becca tackled the apprentice as she tried to sprint after the Markku. "It's the Penhas, Paige. Fight it!"

Nick jumped in front of the Markku, who was already on his feet and starting after Paige again, his eyes glazed with lust. Nick forced himself not to break the kid's head open, reminding himself that he was under the influence of the Penhas. "Markku. Stand down."

The man blinked, then looked at Nick, his eyes suddenly clearing. "What?"

"What's your name?" Nick asked.

"Colin Meissner, sir." Then suddenly, he let out a noise of astonishment and fell to his knees at Nick's feet, his head bowed. "I am your servant."

"What? Why?" Paige stopped struggling against Becca. "Why are you Nick's servant?"

"He is our leader."

A sense of responsibility swelled over Nick. *This is your man.* He cursed. "Get up."

The man scrambled to his feet, his gaze fixed on Nick. "You have come to free us. I knew you would come."

"I'll free you," Paige shouted. "Just finish what you started."

Becca shoved Paige down on the ground and pressed her hands to her shoulders. "Paige, look at me." When Paige's eyes were fixed on her face, she nodded. "We ran into Penhas. You and Colin were both under the influence of them. You need to regroup and get in your own mind again, okay?"

Paige stared at her, and Nick saw her eyes beginning to clear. She nodded slowly and took a deep breath. "This is way intense out here."

Becca cautiously released Paige. "You okay now?"

"Yeah, I think so." Paige sat up and shook her head to clear it.

Nick looked at Colin. "What's going on up here?"

Colin sat down on a nearby rock, his body quivering with relief, making Nick wonder how long the kid had been trapped in the throes of Penha lust. "Satan Jr. has been tracking the Markku for the last two hundred years. When he finds us, his mom shows up to recruit us." Colin winced. "There's not a lot we can do to resist."

Nick nodded, all too aware of the power of Rosemarie Galoux. "What about the lack of post-battle weakness?"

Colin looked bitter. "A lie. We all still have it. But she waves that out as a recruiting carrot, and that, combined with the sex, has snared every Markku so far. And then once we're under her spell, she never lets us break free. She keeps us up at that camp and keeps the Penhas around. Even when we go out on a mission, we have to be back before her influence can wear off." He frowned. "This is the first time I've been myself since I got here." His gaze flicked to Nick. "It's you. You ordered me to get control and I did." There was definitely awe on his face. "I knew you'd come back for us."

"Come back? I was never here."

"Come back to the race. We've been waiting."

Nick frowned. "But the race is extinct... or mostly, anyway?"

"Not at all. There's plenty of us around, but we've been aimless since we don't have a leader. Since we don't have you."

Nick shifted, realizing that Becca was looking at him with great interest, and he was suddenly consumed with the intense conviction that he'd let the Markku down. Like he'd missed something. But what? "What's Rosemarie going to do with the Markku?"

"Use us to rule hell once her kid takes over. Kill all the Rivkas and use us instead." Colin scowled. "That spoiled loser has no significant powers of his own, except harvesting souls and being an ass. His ma is creating his future for him."

"What about the Penhas?" Becca asked. "They're a nonviolent, nonpolitical race. I've never heard of them using their powers this way."

Colin nodded. "She got kicked off the Penha throne after she got knocked up by Satan, and from what I hear, that pretty much pissed her off. Ever since then, she's been plotting to get back at him. She plucks the most powerful Penhas out of society and dumps them in her camp to do her bidding. Junior steals the souls of their families and holds them in limbo. If they don't do what she wants, he tortures them so horribly that the Penhas don't dare resist their queen." Colin flicked a relieved gaze at Nick. "Yeah, well, I'm fine now that our leader is here."

Becca looked at Nick. "You're their leader?"

He shrugged. "I have no idea what he's talking about." But it felt right. If felt like it fit. "We need to take her out. That'll make everything else fall down. We'll just go down there and kill her—"

Becca held up her hand to wait. "What do you know about the blister machine, Colin?"

"I'm the one who set it."

Paige's face fell. "My best friend is in there. You set it?" She grabbed a rock off the ground and hucked it at Colin, who didn't even bother to duck as it bounced off his forehead. Paige instantly yelped and clutched her shin where her black soul was manifesting. "Dammit! I can't even hate him for bubbling Dani?" She took a deep breath. "Fine. I love him, but I'm still going to kick the shit out of him...Aigh!" She dropped to the ground, hugging her shin.

Becca quietly moved to sit next to Paige, stroking her shoulder. "Don't give up, Paige. Fight it."

Colin stared at her. "Is she all right? She's a little..." He made a circle next his temple with his index finger.

"There's nothing wrong with her," Becca snapped, unable to stop her eyes from glowing red. "Did you actually set the blister machine, or were you simply present?"

"I set it." He glanced at Paige. "I couldn't help it."

Paige snorted. "Give me a break. You can always help it if you want to." She sat up and folded her arms over her chest. "You're weak."

His face darkened. "I'm not weak. You try fighting off the Penha power and—"

"Colin!" Becca snapped her fingers to get his attention off Paige. "When you set it—"

A blast of sexual need suddenly filled the air, and both men dropped to their knees with a groan.

"Omigod," Paige whimpered, clutching her stomach. "It's back." She started crawling toward Colin. "Colin?"

She moaned as he wrapped his arms around her waist and tossed her on her back beneath him. He dropped on top of her and began kissing her fervently while Paige made little noises of joy and wrapped herself around him.

Becca scrambled over to Nick. "We have to bail." She reached out to grab his wrist.

"Don't touch me." He jerked out of her reach, the front of his jeans tight and bulging. "We're too connected now. You'll be sucked into my lust and we'll both lose it."

"We have to take the chance, or we'll lose it anyway. Grab me at the last second, okay?"

At his nod, she crawled over to Paige, sweat dripping down her temples. The air was growing thicker with carnal need as Rosemarie got closer, and Becca caught a flicker of male Penha sent her way. She shuddered, even though she should have been fine, given her recent romp with Nick. She had a feeling Rosemarie was amplifying all the sexual need around her. She grabbed Paige's arm. "Don't let go of Colin, Paige. We're taking him with us."

She could only assume Paige's muffled moan was an acknowledgment. She looked at Nick, who was on his hands and knees, head down, taking deep breaths. "I'm going to start the fade, so make sure you grab me before I'm gone."

He nodded once, and she slid her ankle right next to his fingers, so all he'd have to do was move slightly.

Sudden desire seized her, and Becca looked up to see a beautiful woman in a red halter top and a leather mini come sprinting over the crest of the hill, two male Penhas flanking her. The woman was wearing the stilettos Becca had seen while hiding under the trailer, and she knew it was Rosemarie. There was so much lust emanating from her, even Becca wanted to have sex with her. Or the men. Or anyone. Or especially Nick.

"Get us out of here," Nick groaned.

Becca started the fade immediately. Then Nick grabbed Becca's ankle and an orgasm ripped through her so fiercely that she screamed and fell to the ground, and Paige slipped out of her grasp.

"Paige!" She reached for her apprentice as everything turned gray, and saw Paige's head turn toward her, her eyes wide. Becca shouted, and Colin jerked around to look at her. Then Paige and Colin both lunged for her, and then everything was gone.

Becca was still screaming Paige's name when they came up through the floor of Becca's apartment, fighting against Nick. He grabbed her and dragged her against him, holding her tightly against his body. "Becca! Stop! She's gone."

"She can't be." She struggled against him, and he felt her desperation. "We have to go back and get her. Let me go!"

"We can't! Not right now! Rosemarie will have us both at her mercy. We can't fight that. You have to calm down."

"She's a virgin, Nick! I can't let her first time be Penha sex! It'll be like rape." Becca tried to get her hands free to throw a fireball at him, and he clamped his hands around her fists so she couldn't get them open. "Let me go, dammit!"

"No! You'll get roped in just like the Markku." God, he wanted to let her go, and help her go back, but they'd both be lost if they did. "Becca. Look at me."

She ceased her struggling and met his gaze, her green eyes searching his desperately. "They'll use her, Nick."

"They'll try, but she's resourceful."

"She's an apprentice."

"Who took down a busload of assassins from hell."

"She's trying to save her soul." She moaned softly and gave in, collapsing against him. He tightened his arms and held her, drawing on her grief and her worry. "I suck as a mother. I can't keep anyone alive or even a virgin. Why do people keep coming into my life when it's so not a safe place to be?"

"You're too hard on yourself. I'm still alive, right?"

She buried her face in his shirt. "Only until Satan realizes you manipulated him for your own gain."

"He's not going to kill me. I won't let him."

She lifted her face and looked at him. "You're either arrogant or stupid."

"Or I'm right."

She sighed, and he felt her latch on to his confidence, needing to believe that there was hope. "So, how do we get back there without losing ourselves?" She pulled herself back from him and took a deep breath. "Sex twenty minutes before we went wasn't enough to fight off her power."

He sighed. "I don't know. Have sex while we're there?"

"If that's the best we can come up with, we're screwed." She sighed. "I have to find a way to save Paige. I have to." She walked into her kitchen and pulled open the fridge, resting her head against the freezer door for a moment before reaching inside.

"We'll find a way." He walked in behind her, surprised at the homey kitchen with its peach-colored cabinets, floaty curtains, and tiled floor. It was soft and girly, nothing like the image Becca tried to project, which he was beginning to suspect had absolutely nothing to do with who she was inside. He sat down at the table as Becca set a bottle of water in front of him. "How are the Terrors?"

"Having a party." She sat across from him and took a drink of water. "Water helps me resist Satan's orders. He and water just don't get along, you know?" She pressed the bottle to her forehead. "I don't have time to take any orders from him right now." She looked at Nick. "We could go back at night, while the Penhas are sleeping. We were all okay until Rosemarie focused on us specifically."

Nick nodded as he twirled the bottle in his fingers. "If I can get the Markku out from under Rosemarie's influence, they can subdue the Penhas. I seemed to have some sort of link to them."

She studied him. "And why is that, exactly?"

He looked at her. "I was wondering the same thing myself. Maybe we should get an answer?"

Twenty-two

Nick noticed that Becca's fade was slower this time, and the re-formation in Dani's condo took more effort than it should have. He reached out to her before he let go and felt the hum of the Terrors back in her body already, along with the pressure of the void from Dani's room. *Shit.* They were running out of time for her. "Come here."

She looked at him for a moment, then sighed and walked into his arms. He felt her reach out for him, and he met her, wrapping his soul around hers. It wasn't as intimate as it had been while they making love, but she was definitely letting down her barriers. "You're getting better at letting me in."

"Don't tell anyone," she grumbled as she snuggled into his body. "I have an image to protect."

"Not a word." He closed his eyes and they stood there, holding each other, and he felt the warmth of her energy much closer to the surface. Her worry. Her desperation. Her fears. He moved his lips toward her ear and whispered. "What are your Terrors?"

She pressed her face against the bare skin of his neck. "Of being alone and empty. Of having no one care if I die. Of never loving someone, and then, if I do, of killing them. These images keep flashing in front of me, getting stronger and stronger as the Terrors get more powerful." She paused. "What were yours, before I took them out?"

He thought back to the Terrors that had nipped at his soul before Becca had extracted them. "Of not fulfilling my legacy." Not that he understood that one. Or maybe he did. Ever since he felt the Markku at Rosemarie's camp, he'd felt different. Like he knew what his role was. "Of..." he hesitated.

"Of what?"

"I saw you die." He could still feel that anguish he'd felt when he'd had that vision of Becca dying in his arms while he was in the Chamber. He tightened his grip on her and concentrated on merging with her life force to support her, and to comfort himself that she was still alive and still with him.

She lifted her head to look at him. "Why me? Why not Dani?"

He shrugged, and brushed her hair off her forehead. "Those were the Terrors the Chamber selected for me. I don't know why. Maybe Jerome already had dibs on the Terror of Dani dying."

"You think?"

He looked down at her, into her green eyes. "I don't know." And then, because he couldn't stop himself, he kissed her. The swell of emotion between them was instant, and he reveled in the connection between them as she reached for him with her body and her soul and everything that made her alive. He deepened the kiss and slipped his hands down to her butt to pull her against him, needing to get closer. Needing more. Needing *her.*

"Nick?"

They broke the kiss and turned their heads to see Yasmine standing the doorway to the living room, looking concerned. He felt Becca start to pull away, so he tightened his grip against her, until she relaxed back into him with a sigh of resigned contentment. "Hey, Ma. How's Dani?"

"Well, since Jerome got here, the bubble seems to have gotten a little less black. I really wanted to cut off his head with my chainsaw, but I think he actually cares about her." Yasmine eyed them both. "What's going on?"

"We lost Paige," Becca said, resting her head on Nick's chest, her arms tight around his waist. "We need to go retrieve her."

Nick tucked Becca into the curve of his body. "We found Junior's ma. She's leading a team of Penhas and appears to have some hold over the Markku." He didn't miss the flicker of alarm on his ma's face. "Oddly enough, I was able to order one Markku out from under her spell for a moment, and he called me his leader, said they were waiting for to rescue them. What do you make of that?"

Yasmine paled. "I have no idea."

He rubbed his jaw on Becca's head, warm and content with her soul snuggled against his. It made him feel calm. In control. Even though something told him his world was about to come crashing down, she gave him control. "Apparently, there are tons of Markku around. Was there a particular reason you and pa repeatedly told me that the Markku were extinct? That my life would be in danger if anyone ever found out I was Markku?"

"Nick—"

"No lies, Ma. I want the truth."

She glanced at Becca, then looked back at Nick.

"I'm going in there after the Markku," Nick said. "Anything you can tell me to help make sure I don't get killed would be nice," he said dryly.

"No. Don't go after them. They aren't your responsibility."

He studied her, aware that she'd used the exact words that he'd used himself to describe how he felt about the Markku. "Oh, but I feel quite certain they are. What's up, Ma?"

She hesitated, then sighed heavily and sat down on the couch, dropping her head between her hands. When she looked up, she looked old for the first time Nick could remember. "Walk away, Nicky. For me?"

He just looked at her, drawing on Becca's calmness to keep his emotions under control. "No more secrets."

Yasmine pressed her lips together, then finally nodded. "As you know, your great-granddad was the leader of the Markku rebellion when they broke out of hell and he died protecting his people. But what you don't know is that it wasn't simply that he led the rebellion. He was their true leader, a role one can only be born into. Your pa inherited that position, and he was unable to deny it. He died trying to protect the Markku, and he didn't want the burden. He and I decided we would never tell you the truth about who you are, and to hide you from other Markku so you would never have to give your life for something you didn't care about."

He closed his eyes as a feeling of absolute rightness settled over him. *I am their leader.* Now he understood the restlessness that had crawled under his skin his whole life. His need for more, a need that no job for Jerome had been able to lessen.

"You have a purpose," Becca whispered.

He opened his eyes and looked at her and smiled. "Yeah, I do. Got a couple, actually."

She narrowed her gaze at him, and he looked at his watch, not quite ready to go into detail. "It's only seven o'clock. I think we should wait until after midnight to go back. Give Rosemarie time to go to sleep."

She gave him a look that made his groin tighten. "So, what do we do from now until then?"

Before Nick could suggest they do a little work to get rid of the Terrors, the condo vibrated, gold bubbles exploded from the wall, and Satan leaped into the room, wearing a hand-tailored custom suit of Italian descent. His hair was slicked back, he was freshly shaven, and his wingtips were so shiny they looked like they were actually mirrors.

Satan's eyes were glowing, and he was not the same leader of hell they'd last seen curled up Iris's chair in tears. Either Satan had recovered from a broken heart in record time, or he was trying to delude himself.

Nick reached out and caught a faint hint of misery, and he knew what the answer was.

Like it should be a surprise that Satan overcompensated about something.

"Rivka!" Satan danced across the room and grabbed Becca's hand, which was all he could reach since she was still entwined around Nick. "I have answer! I have solution! Is that not wonderful news! You do not have to depend on elf to stay sane and alive! Most excellent news, no?"

Becca tensed against Nick, and hope cascaded off her body. "What is it?"

"Is quite simple!" He beamed at them. "Since my man-friend has proper energy assimilation to help you fight off Terrors, we connect you to his life force long enough for you to cleanse them, and then you come back to me. Is good plan, no?"

"No!"

Satan spun around in surprise as Yasmine leapt to her feet. "Who are you, little mortal woman of perky breasts?"

"Nick can't support a Rivka. They will both die."

Satan frowned. "I do not like people who contradict me. My reputation is dicey already, despite my last three hours of harvesting all the souls I previously released, in a heartless and cruel fashion which they deserve. See? Even you challenge me. I punish you for it, no?"

"Satan," Becca interjected. "Don't."

He spun his head toward her. "Why not?"

"Because she's a healer. I need her to show me how to break free of the Terrors once I have the light in my body."

"You do?" Satan looked at Yasmine, who didn't look at all afraid. "Substantial disappointment for me. I suppose you shall live, but do not tell anyone that I permitted you to challenge me, or I shall cut out your tongue and hang it above my office door. Yes?"

Yasmine's eyes flickered with darkness. "Nick can't support her."

"Yes, he can. My researchers say he can, and they are always correct, because if they are wrong, they die pain-ful death." He turned back to Becca. "You shall repeat the process you did before, and this time I support you and we hook your life line to my man friend. Then, you heal yourself. Then we bring you back to me. Most excellent plan, no?"

Becca stared at him, too many thoughts whirring through her mind. Hope for herself, fear for Nick's life, fear that she would never be able to go back to Satan after being free of him, fear of what Satan would do to Nick if Satan realized she didn't want to go back. She glanced at Nick, who was looking thoughtful. How could she get that close to him and then let it go? She had to.

Nick looked at her. "Let's do it. A brief connection won't risk my life, I'm sure." He touched her cheek. "It will buy us time."

"Yeah, until tomorrow night when Dani's time is up."

Nick's grip tightened. "I'm not giving up—"

"Nick. A word with you," Yasmine interrupted. "Now."

He frowned at her tone. "What now?"

She eyed Satan and shook her head.

"He can't do it," Jerome said from the doorway. "The Council experimented on Markku, using them to support Rivkas. The Markku died after a week, and so did the Rivka, even after they restored the Rivka to Satan. Nick can't do it."

Satan was studying Jerome carefully. "You are Council, no?"

Jerome looked at him. "Yes."

"You were part of the Rivka experiments?"

Jerome looked surprised. "You know about them?"

"Satan knows all. I have most excellent spy network. I was most curious to see whether Rivka could break free of me, so I watched experiments with much interest. I was quite pleased with results. Where do you think the Council got all their Rivka subjects?"

Becca stared at him, and Nick felt her sense of betrayal. "You offered up your Rivkas to be killed?"

Satan spun to her. "Only the inferior ones, of course." He brightened. "Oh, most excellent reminder. Let us try this with your apprentice first to see if she lives. Then if she does, we will know if it works. Where is she? I love expendable Rivkas." He turned around, searching the room. "She is here, no?"

"She's on a mission," Becca said. "Not here."

"Retrieve her. What could be more important than sacrificing herself?'

Becca ground her teeth, offering up the only excuse she knew Satan would accept. "She's losing her virginity." *Please let that be a lie.*

Satan's eyes widened. "Oh. Most sacred time. We must not disturb her." He reached out and set his hand on Becca's arm, then frowned. "The Terrors are strong. How are you not screaming yet?"

She shrugged. "I'm stubborn."

"Stubborn and soon to die," Satan said. "Come, we must do it now. Man-friend, prepare yourself. We do the switch now."

"No!" Yasmine jumped between them. "I won't let you. Nick, Pa believed his destiny as the descendent of the leader of the Markku was to protect all Markku, and he felt that the Rivkas fell under that cloak of protection, since they were the next round of Markku. So he volunteered for the Council's experiments, hoping he could help get the Rivkas out of hell." She lifted her chin. "The Rivka drained him dry, and he died within a week."

Nick stared at his ma in stunned disbelief. "But he said he was poisoned by the Council. That they arranged for him to die because he was a Markku. That's why he made me promise never to tell anyone I was Markku." Becca burrowed against him, and he tightened his grip on her, reaching out for her, for her honesty and integrity. He felt her respond to him, welcoming him, and he clung to it greedily, needing her.

"He didn't want you to have the burdens of being Markku," Yasmine said. "He felt he had no choice but to stand up and protect his people, and he wanted you to be free of that. So he cut you off from your people, and I agreed." Her voice grew hard. "I won't let you make the same choice your father made. If you volunteer, you and Becca would both die. I won't lose my son as well as my husband."

"You are descendent of Treat Fontaine?" Satan asked slowly, his eyes gleaming with interest. "Of Hale Fontaine?"

Nick drew himself up, not liking the calculating look in Satan's gaze, not quite able to dismiss the years of dire warnings from his ma and pa about what Satan would do to him if he found him, the descendent of the man who broke the Markku out of hell. "Hale was my pa. Treat was my great-grandpa. They were good men."

"Ah." Satan did a slow walk around Nick, assessing, while the tension in the room thickened. Nick felt Becca's heart racing against his, but her gaze was steely and calm, and he drew on that control as well.

Satan laid a manicured hand on Nick's shoulder, then

his mouth curved into a delighted smile that revealed gorgeous white teeth. "You still have my life force inside you. Interesting. That must be why my researchers knew you could support my Rivka."

"I have my own life force," Nick said.

"Don't touch him," Yasmine said. "Or I will kill you."

"Kill me? Hah. You cannot kill the leader of hell. You made me laugh with great mirth. I respect good bluff. You amuse me."

Yasmine spun on her heels and marched out of the room.

Satan turned his back on her and faced Nick and Becca. "I am most interested in you, Fontaine offspring. I think my Rivka will learn much having you be her life force. I have grand ideas for your future, so try not to die, but if you must, I see you in hell, I am sure." He leaned in, sniffing Nick. "You do not smell Markku. Must be healer blood why I did not recognize you. Most interesting disguise. Hale Fontaine is smart man, mating with healer to keep offspring hidden." He stepped back and clapped his hands. "Rivka, let us begin. You have only about twenty minutes until you die from Terrors, so we must start."

"Wrong choice." Yasmine stepped into the room, cradling something in her arms that Nick couldn't see clearly. There was some sort of cloth draped over it. "My daughter and my son will not die for you."

Satan sighed and turned to face her. "You are much annoying. What daughter?"

"She's in your death blister."

"Oh, is that your daughter? Is she here?" He lifted his head and sniffed. "She is! I wish to see this blister. How very excellent!" He turned to head down the hall toward the bubble, and then Yasmine whipped the cloth off and settled what looked like a modified machine gun on her shoulder.

"Oh, *shit*!" Becca ripped out of Nick's grasp and lunged for Yasmine. "Satan, down!"

Satan dropped instantly as Yasmine pulled the trigger and a blast of gunfire exploded out of the barrel of the gun. Then Becca's body slammed into Yasmine and the two women went down. The bullets ricocheted all over the condo, exploding the chandelier and shattering the plaster ceiling. The light fixture sizzled as Nick grabbed the gun out of his ma's hands and dust fell on him...dust and...he looked up. Water?

Then he heard a female groan, and he looked down to see Becca sprawled in the ground, clutching her stomach. "Becca?" He threw the gun aside and was on his knees next to her as Yasmine moaned and held her head, lying in a heap next to the wall. "God, woman, didn't I tell you not to scare me like this again?" He rolled Becca over, his hands frantically flying over as he tried to find where she'd been hit, his heart racing. "Where does it hurt?"

"Satan," Becca whispered. "Is Satan hit?"

"Bullets can't hurt him." He tugged up her shirt and pushed her hands out of the way, but her belly was intact. "Where are you hit?"

"Satan..." she moaned. "Check him."

"Fine. I'll check." He jumped up and ran into the hall. "Satan?" He stopped in shock. Satan was down on the ground, motionless. "Satan?" He knelt next to him and his knees squished. "What the...?" He looked down at the puddle of water, colored water. His gut froze, and he pulled up Satan's shirt. The water was leaking out through Satan's skin, taking parts of Satan with it. "Oh, *shit*."

He scrambled back to Becca, who was curled in a ball, a single tear glistening on her left cheek. "He's down. What's going on?"

"Dying," she rasped. "We're both dying."

"How?" He grabbed her shoulders, his fingers digging in. "How can he die from a bullet? How do I stop it? Tell me!"

Yasmine sat up, wobbling slightly. "I shot him with bullets loaded with purified water. The bullets explode once they are inside him, poisoning him."

Nick's heart sank as he pulled Becca onto his lap, feeding her his life force with everything he had, but he could feel her fading. Fast, so fast. "Why would you do that?"

"To save you and Dani."

"But we still had until tomorrow night to figure out how else to save her." He kissed Becca, hugged her limp body tight. "It hadn't come to that yet."

Yasmine struggled to her feet. "Jerome?" she shouted. "How's Dani?"

"The bubble's almost gone," Jerome yelled back, disbelief in his voice. "She's starting to wake up. Dani? Oh, God, *Dani*."

Yasmine slipped in the water and nearly went down before she caught the edge of table. "You'll thank me when this is over, Nicky." Then she turned and wove her way back toward Jerome, calling for her daughter.

Becca moved in his arms. "Theresa..."

"The Goblet won't help." He hugged her against him, felt her spirit not even try to reach for his energy. "Take my life force, Becca. Just take it."

"...to link me to you...call...her...." Her fingers fumbled for her pocket, but she couldn't make them work.

"Dammit!" Nick roared with anger and grief, then yanked the phone out of her pocket and called Theresa. He didn't give her time to speak. "How do I link Becca's life force to mine? She's dying. Dammit! She's dying!"

Theresa wasted no time on trivialities. "Where are you?"

Nick recited his sister's address.

"It's not far from me. I'll be there in five minutes with what you need. While I'm on my way, get as much dirt as you can and spread it over the floor. You need natural things. Pure. Elemental."

"*Hurry.*"

"I'm a dragon. I fly like the wind."

Nick hung up and kissed Becca, then laid her down and bolted for the kitchen to see what he could find.

Twenty-three

Ten minutes later, there was still no dragon.
They were running out of time.

Nick had Becca on a bed of dirt and organic rice and spinach, and had dragged Satan out into the living room next to Becca. He had a hand on each of their chests, driving his life force into both of them, summoning up the dark life force that had lain dormant inside him his whole life. "Feed off me," he ordered them. "Just stay alive." His voice broke. "Becca, stay alive for me."

There was a flicker from Becca, and he knew she couldn't do it on her own. "Satan, you son-of-a-bitch. If you die, I will kick your ass for letting my woman die."

No response from the leader of hell, though Nick was sending him everything he had. He tried again. "If you die, Iris will never have the chance to apologize and tell you how much she loves you."

There was a rumble from deep inside Satan, and Nick felt something latch on to his life force, the grip so fragile Nick dared not move. "That's right, big guy. Hang on for Iris."

Where the hell was that dragon?

"The bubble's down," Yasmine shouted. "Nick, get in here and help us."

Oh, God. The bubble was down. He thrust his life force harder into Satan and felt his soul twitch in response. "You're still with me," he whispered. "Iris won't want you to die. She needs you, man. Stay alive for her."

There was a thrust inside Satan, but it was so weak, and Nick knew they were running out of time.

"Did you hear that? She made a sound. She's coming around," Jerome said, his voice throaty with emotion. "Dani, I love you. Come on, baby, wake up."

Not yet, Dani. Not yet, please.

There was suddenly a loud crash and the living room window shattered as a huge blue-green dragon burst through it, landing with a crash on top of the coffee table. Wood exploded in all directions and three pictures crashed to the floor. She tumbled over her head and crashed into the opposite wall in a tangle of claws and tails. "Sorry I'm late. I had to stop by Becca's to get the stuff."

She shifted back into human form as she shrugged off the dragon-sized backpack she'd been wearing. She was stark naked as a human, and Nick hoped she wasn't going to take precious time to get dressed. She didn't bother, and his respect for her shot up. "We're losing them," he said.

"Not on my watch." Theresa pulled out a bunch of shot glasses and gold balls. "You keep them going. It'll just take a second."

Nick's body began trembling with the effort of keeping Satan and Becca alive as Theresa ran around him, setting up the shot glasses in a circle around them and filling them with water. She yanked Satan's jacket off him and set it in the middle. Then she kneeled at the foot of the circle, glancing down at the floor. "Spinach?"

"You said natural. It's organic. It was all I could find. There were only two plants in the place."

"Hope it works."

"Don't say that," he growled. "It *will* work."

She ignored him. "Okay, so I guess I'm going to say the words, since she can't. That would work, right?" She wiped her palms on her thighs, and there was a sheen of perspiration on her forehead. "Okay, let's do it."

Nick bent down, putting his head next to Becca. "Come on, babe. You can do this."

Theresa closed her eyes and crossed her wrists, chanting words he didn't understand. Then she shouted and flame exploded out of her nose and ignited Satan's jacket.

Then Nick was hit so hard with an unseen force that he flew back and smashed into the wall. He rolled to his feet, then stopped, his lungs aching, his body so heavy he couldn't move. He dropped back to his knees, his hands on the floor as he tried to recover. Heat scorched his soul, and he felt like he was on fire, like he was burning up from the inside. "What happened?"

"Nick?"

He jerked his head up in disbelief, hope flaring deep inside him. "Becca?"

She was sitting up, supported by Theresa, looking wan and weary, but alive.

"Becca!" He dragged himself over the floor and fell into her, wrapping her body up in his. Energy pulsed between them, and he groaned with the intensity of it. He could feel every beat of her heart, every pulse of her thoughts, every hint of emotion. They were one, and it was so intense and overwhelming and right. "God, I thought..." He cupped her face between his and kissed her, nearly melting into the kiss as the swirl of her emotions flooded him...then he paused at the blast of icy fear he took from her. He kissed her again, reaching inside her and realized what was scaring her...*Paige.* Paige was dying with Satan because she was still connected to his life force. He pulled back and looked at Theresa. "Hook Satan up to me, too."

"No." Becca's voice was stronger now, and a pulse of anxiety hit him. "You can't support both of us. I can feel the drain on you already."

"Do it," he ordered Theresa. "I won't let Paige die."

Theresa looked back and forth between them, confusion and indecision on her features. "Um..."

"Becca, tell her to link Satan's life force to mine. Now. Before Satan dies," he ordered, nearly overwhelmed by Becca's grief and her worry over Paige. He felt her concern about him, as well, but he shoved it aside.

Becca stared at him, a look of horror on her face. She didn't take her gaze off his face when she said, in a wooden voice, "Theresa, do what he says."

"Right." Theresa went back to work, refilling the shot glasses.

He frowned at Becca. "What's wrong?"

"You ordered me, and I had to do it."

He felt the blood drain from his face. "No."

She nodded. "You control me now."

Theresa started her chant, and Nick flinched as the pressure began to build on him again. "I'm sorry, Becca. I didn't mean to—"

She held up her hand. "It's how it has to be. I just..."

She closed her mouth, but he knew what she'd been about to say.

I just want to be free to be me.

She'd traded one life of servitude for another, and he was the master. Dammit! "I'll find a way out of this, I promise."

"Jerome?" Dani's voice echoed through the apartment, and he and Becca stared at each other in horror. Dani was awake, which meant Satan was dead. And *Paige.* They were too late.

Then the fire exploded from Theresa's nose, and Nick was flung across the room again, crashing through the guest room door and smashing into a dresser. He landed on the carpet, unable to move as a mirror thudded on his head and crashed on the floor. His muscles were frozen. So heavy. Couldn't breathe.

Then Becca was by his side, touching his face. "Nick? Are you all right?"

He shook his head to clear it. "I just need a sec. I'll be okay."

"Naked-breasted dragon again?" Satan's weary voice drifted into the room. "You like to flaunt your body before me, do you not?" Then he groaned softly and there was a thunk as if he'd let his head drop back down to the floor. "Ow."

Becca nearly dropped to the floor with relief at the sound of her boss's voice. "He made it." She looked at Nick. "Do you think Paige did? Or was it too late?" She couldn't keep the fear out of her voice, didn't bother. He knew how she felt about Paige, and he wouldn't tell anyone.

He touched her face. "I'm sure she's okay."

Becca closed her eyes, then opened them again, searching his face. "You shouldn't have done it."

"Done what?"

She clocked in him the chest, not buying the innocent expression on his face "Risked your life for me. All you did was prolong my own death and add yours into the mix. And now you support Satan, which means you indirectly support all his Rivkas, including Paige."

"And I support you directly."

She felt him reach out for Paige, and felt him fail to reach her but get a hint of Satan's lust and power. He instantly threw up a shield between himself and Satan, keeping their souls separate, but she felt the strain on him already. Felt his life force laboring under the effort. "It's too much for you." But her fingers tightened in his shirt, not quite able to let go. "It was stupid," she whispered. He'd risked his own life for hers, and she felt totally overwhelmed by the act. "I don't understand. How could you do that?"

He shrugged. "Instinct. I just did it."

But with her hand on his chest, she could feel all the emotions running through him, and there was something warmer, soft, curling around her, making her feel safe...and loved...

She pulled her hand back. She wasn't safe, and now he wasn't, either. "How bad do you feel, supporting us?"

He raised his brow. "And how do *you* feel, not being a part of hell anymore?"

She stared at him, suddenly becoming aware of a dancing lightness inside her body. Of the feeling of happiness, of light, of sunshine. She couldn't stop her smile. "Is this what you feel like all the time?"

"It's my healer blood. Very positive and rah-rah." He looked happy, so pleased. "I'm glad you feel it."

"It's..." She pressed her hand to her chest and felt the energy pulsing out of her. "...amazing. I don't know how to explain it. It's like...like I see the world in a different way." She looked at Nick and suddenly felt overwhelmed by her feelings for him. "Even if I die, thank you for this gift, Nick. I..." She spread her hands, wanting to drink the light into her soul. "I'm alive. For the first time ever, I'm alive."

"And that, my dear, makes it all worth it." He cupped the back of her head and drew her against him, and kissed her, and it was like millions of lights exploded in her mind, in her heart, in her soul, igniting every inch of her being. "I just need one kiss..." And his mouth was on her throat, his hands on her breasts, and she moaned softly, tipping her head to give him access as his lips trailed across the edge of her neckline, nipping and searching.

I need it, too, Nick. Despite the fact she reported to him now, they now were equals in the essence of their souls. She was light with darkness, and so was he. They were both, and they were one.

She climbed onto his lap, drinking in all that he was, wanting more, needing more, and for the first time, giving back. *I have light to give him.* Her fingers crept into his hair, and her mouth responded to his kiss as his hands wrapped around her and pulled her against him, diving in deeper and deeper with his kiss and his energy and everything he was.

And she was right there with him. Sharing, not just taking. "This is so incredible," she whispered. "I've never felt this before."

"Me either."

And then she forgot what she was going to say, too overwhelmed by his touch, by his kiss, by the feel of his body shifting against hers, by the pulses of his soft energies that felt so at peace. So content. So right.

His hands slipped around her waist, pulling her against him, and she went willingly. More than willing. She needed him like this. Wanted him. Wanted to share the light that was both of them.

She straddled his lap and settled herself on top of him, nestling herself against his growing hardness as his hands slipped around and cupped her ribs as his teeth nipped at her collarbone. "Cleanse the Terrors," he whispered against her skin, his breath so warm and alive.

"How?"

"Chase them out with the light." He slipped her shirt off over her head and she tugged his off, then they pressed together, skin to skin, and she gasped at the electricity charging between them, wrapping around her spirit and snuggling in deep. She took him in, but realized it was different now.

It wasn't just him. It was her. They were both there, inside her, feeding her light. It should be unequal now that he was her life force, but it was the opposite. He gave her her own strength, her own light, and she didn't have to take it from him anymore.

Oh, but she wanted to. She wanted it all.

His teeth grazed her nipple and she let herself moan as she'd never wanted to before. She felt his smile against her breast as he scooped her up and raised her to her feet, so she was standing over him.

Then he slid his hands up her legs, staring up at her with a gleam in his eyes.

"The door," she whispered.

He glanced past her, then smiled. "You closed it when you came in." His hands went to her waist and unzipped her jeans with a slow deliberateness that had her curling in anticipation.

"Did I?" She sounded breathless and didn't care. "What foresight I have." She set her hands on his shoulders as he tugged her jeans over her hips, sliding her underwear down with it, until she was exposed in front of him.

"That's a Rivka for you. Always on the ball." He wrapped his fingers around her thighs and tugged her closer, until her knees were pressed against his chest, as he was still sitting up, leaning against the dresser, while she stood over him. "Close your eyes and let the light consume you."

Yeah, that sounded like a plan. Screw holding back to save her sanity when she returned to Satan's life force. This was too amazing... She gasped as she felt his mouth between her legs, and a brilliant shaft of light shot through her being, through her soul, chasing away all that she hated about herself, all that she'd been forced to be.

She trembled under his touch, letting him support her as she clutched his shoulders, drinking in all that he was, and that *she* was. *I am who I want to be.* For once, for this moment, she was light, she was life, she was good, and she was *happy*.

Nick shifted under her and she heard the sound of his zipper being undone. She closed her eyes, finding the Terrors in her body and plucking them out, one by one, exploding each one with her lightness. She felt their screeching protests as they left her, and knew that she'd won.

Then Nick's hands were on her hips and he guided her down, his mouth trailing up her belly and over her breasts and sucking on her nipples as she sank onto him, throwing her arms around his neck, holding him as close as she could as he filled her, her body and soul opening to him and drawing him into her, welcoming every part of who he was to the light she had waiting for him.

He groaned softly and whispered her name as his arms went around her, holding her as tight against him as she was holding him. Her breasts were crushed against his chest as they moved. As she took Nick deeper inside her with each stroke, with each thrust, she wanted more.

Gave him more.

Nick caught her face in his hands as the light built within her, illuminating the darkest corners of her soul, bringing his essence into every crevice, every part of who she was. He opened his eyes and kissed her, even as the crescendo built. "We are one," he whispered. "Forever."

She couldn't stop the tear from trickling out of her eye. "We are one," she agreed. *But not forever.* Just until she returned to Satan.

"No." He kissed her hard and his hands went to her hips again, moving her as he drove into her. "You will not regret this moment. You will not be sad. This is light, and this is joy, and this is what you are now." His last words fell into her mouth as the blinding light consumed her. "Live it, Becca."

Her body clenched, her soul reached for his, and he was there, he was inside her, around her, holding her, caring for her, and giving her all that she'd ever wanted, and her body and spirit screamed with all that she was, and all that he was, and he clutched her to him as their bodies and souls exploded together, as one, and she gave herself to his keeping, and he to hers, and then she could think no more, holding on to him as desperately as he held her as they rode the crashing waves they'd created together.

This time she didn't cry when he held her afterward. She snuggled against him, smiling, still feeling just as whole and complete as when they'd been making love. "The light doesn't leave," she whispered against his chest.

He kissed her hair and pulled her closer, as if that was possible. "That's because it's your light now. Not mine."

"But it is yours." She lifted her head to frown at him. "Isn't it?"

He ran his fingers through her tangled hair, his gaze so soft and affectionate that she tried to memorize it so she could recall it when her life was back to normal. When she couldn't feel what she felt now. "My life force supports you, but the light is yours." He laid his hand on her heart. "It's always been in you, but now it's free."

She opened herself to his touch, adoring how he made her feel. "You freed it, then."

"Nope. You did, because you wanted to be alive." His green eyes were serious and intense. "I just gave you the ability to do it, but you did it. It's all you, babe."

She grinned, realizing as he spoke that it was true. She'd felt that light when she'd been healing Jerome, even though she hadn't been able to complete the task, had felt that love when she'd loved Gabriel, before she'd closed herself off. But now . . . now she wasn't afraid to hold back, and she knew that part was because of Nick.

He'd given her the courage, and his life force had given her the ability. She twirled her fingers in the dark curls on his chest. "It's about damned time I freed myself. I've been working on it for a hundred years."

He grinned. "When you're immortal, one century is nothing."

She raised her eyebrow at him. "Only a lowly mortal would think that." She frowned. "You are mortal, right?"

He nodded. "I'm indestructible, but my life span is only a little longer than the average human. We lost our immortality when we broke out of hell."

She cocked her head. "Was it worth it?"

He shrugged and fingered the thin gold chain around her throat. "Having never been immortal or stuck in hell, I wouldn't know. But right now, I feel pretty damn good about where I am."

His voice was just gruff enough to make her heart skip. *Was he serious?*

Before she could decide whether to ask, he was kissing her again, his hands running lightly over her skin, as if he was memorizing her body. Light and heat soared inside her again, and she reached out with everything she had, needing his touch, and needing to feel his skin against hers. *How could she ever walk away from this?* She rolled over on top of him, kissing him back, suddenly consumed by the need to be with him again. To imprint the moment on her soul forever, so she could never forget it.

A light tap sounded on the door. "Guys, I really *really* hate to be the cold shower here," Theresa called out. "But Satan's not exactly doing that well right now. I think he might still be dying."

Nick stopped kissing her, and his hands stilled on her

body. He lifted his head to look at her, his eyes dark with passion and intensity. "I'm not going to let you die."

She nodded, too overcome by the sudden urge to hold him tight to trust herself to speak. *I don't want to let go of you. Ever.*

He cocked his head as if he'd heard her words, then he kissed her again, a farewell kiss that promised more. If only they didn't have a leader of hell to save, a sociopath to kill, and a lifeline to restore before they all died. Life. Such a pain in the butt sometimes.

She took a deep breath, then unwrapped her body from his, climbing unsteadily to her feet, suddenly realizing how tired she felt physically. Nick grabbed the edge of the dresser and pulled himself to his feet with a groan. "God, I feel old."

Her elation faded. "You're already being drained."

"And how do you feel? Like you could run a marathon?"

Her soul did, but her body . . . "I feel like kicking back on the sofa and watching bad television for the rest of the month."

He nodded and put his arm around her. "My pa lasted a week supporting one Rivka. I figure Satan's at least a double drain, so we've got maybe a couple of days. We need to get him liberated and get you hooked back up to him as soon as we can." He kissed her lightly, and pulled away before she could respond, then handed her her clothes. "Let's go save your boss from hell."

"He's not my boss right now. Can I torture him before we save him?" she asked, trying to keep the tone light as she pulled her clothes back on, aware of Nick watching her, heat evident in his gaze.

"Be my guest. Who would I be to stand in the way of a Rivka and her torture?"

"You're such a great guy. No wonder I like having sex with you."

He had started to walk toward the door, but he turned around at her words, his eyes dark. "That, my dear, was making love. Not having sex. Keep it straight." Then he turned back around and pulled the door open, leaving her standing there stunned.

He didn't mean it that way, Becca.

He couldn't have. Could he?

She pressed her lips together as she followed him back out to the living room. How could she go back to that dark existence? She peeked at Nick, saw the tired lines around his mouth, and knew with absolute certainty that she *would* return to Satan. In a heartbeat. As soon as she could. There was no question. To save Nick, she'd do it without hesitation.

Nick stopped, staring at the floor. "Oh, *shit.*"

She looked down, and her heart turned cold. Satan was motionless, ashen, and there was a steady drip of colored water off his left earlobe.

Satan's revival hadn't lasted. He was dying fast, and dying *now.*

Twenty-four

Becca dropped to her knees next to Satan and laid her hands on his face. Cold. Clammy. And a little mushy. "He's still melting." She pulled her hands away, leaving the imprint of her fingers on his cheeks. "That can't be good."

"It's kind of gross, too." Nick handed her a paper towel, and she wiped the Satan film off her hands.

Theresa knelt next to him. "Maybe we should give him a sip of Mona." She held up her vial. "I've still got her. I put a decoy in Justine and Derek's condo, so they have no idea I have her." She grinned. "I do enjoy messing with them. They're way too uptight."

Becca's heart tightened with emotion for her friend that she'd never felt before. "That is so sweet. You know the Council would throw you in the Chamber if you gave Satan a sip of Mona, and you'd offer it anyway?"

Theresa's amber eyes widened. "Why are you looking at me like that?"

"Because you're my friend." She felt the awe of those words when she spoke them and knew they were true. Understood what it meant, finally.

Theresa grinned. "Really?"

"Yeah." She hugged Theresa, and her throat tightened when her friend's arms went around hers. "But when I get linked to Satan again, I'll probably be a cold bitch again, so don't take it personally."

Theresa pulled back, her eyes bright. "Why do you have to be a cold bitch again? Why can't you stay linked to Nick?"

"Because it's killing him. And me."

"Oh. He's not much of a man if he can't support his woman in the style she deserves, then, is he?" Theresa looked at Nick. "And to think I was so impressed ten minutes ago when you were keeping them alive. First impressions can be so deceiving." She made a tsking sound of disappointment that had Nick raising his brows.

"Sorry I'm so inadequate," he said.

"Don't be sorry. Just be more of a man."

Becca grinned at the interaction. She would love to see Nick and Theresa get to know each other better. They'd be quite evenly matched, she had a feeling.

Satan moaned and she bent over him, her heart aching just a little bit for the man who'd basically been her dad since she'd been created. The dad you hate, but the dad that will always be dad. "Satan? Can you hear me?"

His eyes flickered open a crack. "Why do I feel like cow patty?"

"Because Yasmine shot you with purified water bullets."

"In the back like a coward?" At Becca's nod, he closed his eyes. "Cheater," he murmured. "Useful morals. Hire her, Rivka." He sighed, and his chest wobbled a bit with the effort, sort of like a Satan Jell-O mold. "Shot by old woman. Most embarrassing."

Becca frowned at the note of dismay and resignation in his voice. At the lack of ego that sustained him. This wasn't the Satan she knew.

"She's a cunning lady," Nick said. "Nothing to be ashamed of."

She mouthed *thank you* at Nick, and he nodded.

Satan cracked his eyes again to squint at Nick. "Man-friend? Why do you look more handsome than usual?"

Becca shot Nick a worried glance. How would Satan take it to know he was supported by a Markku? He needed to stay alive, not give up.

Nick glanced at Becca. "You want to field this one?"

"Yeah, I guess." She stroked Satan's hair, then frowned when clumps of hair stuck to her hand. She quickly brushed it off on her pants before Satan could see. Who knew what that would do to his psyche if he realized he was losing his physical beauty. No mirrors for him at the moment. "Nick is, um, using his life force to keep you alive..." She stopped at the look of utter defeat on Satan's face. "It's not so bad—"

"I am not a man." Satan's left ear slipped off his head down the side of his neck. "I am servant to half-breed mortal Markku. Kill me, now, Rivka. I order you."

"Don't be ridiculous. You'll be dominating hell in no time."

His eyes opened again. "You do not respond to my order?"

"Um...Nick's supporting me, too."

"I am pathetic lump of cat poo. No wonder fair Iris did not succumb to my efforts." His left ear slid off his neck and landed on the floor with a splat. "I am not man. I am not leader of hell. I am not worthy."

He was giving up. She looked up at Nick, her heart pounding as she felt Satan's face soften under her touch. "We can't let him do this, Nick. We need him to stay alive."

Nick flexed his jaw. "Let me try."

Nick knew how dangerous this moment was. If Satan died, Paige and all the Rivkas would die. And so would he and Becca, in another day or two. He shook his head as Becca scrambled back from Satan and Nick straddled the gooey leader of hell. Who would have thought there'd be a day when he was trying to save the life of the leader of hell? Now that Dani was safe . . . He closed his eyes for a minute, suddenly allowing himself to realize that. Emotion swept over him, and he felt his throat thicken.

"Nick?" Becca frowned at him. "Are you okay?"

He lifted his head. "Fine." He bent down and grabbed the front of Satan's shirt with both fists and hauled him to a sitting position, except that his head flopped backward like his neck was an overcooked noodle. "Get his head."

Becca and Theresa scooted behind him and propped up his head so he was looking at Nick. Nick growled at Satan loud enough that the leader of hell opened his eyes. "Listen, Satan, I'm in charge now, and I order you to get your act together."

"Too vague," Becca said. "You need to be specific."

Satan grinned, his lips drooping unevenly. "Silly boy. Did you learn nothing from my favorite Rivka?"

"I order you to live."

"That doesn't work," Becca said. "He tried that with me and the Terrors, remember? You can't order death away."

He groaned with frustration, then had an idea. He bent

his head close to Satan, closing his eyes against the wave of lightheadedness at the sudden movement. *Keep it together, Nick.* "Rosemarie is the queen of the Penhas. She has arranged to have Iris kidnapped and tossed to the male Penhas to be their sex slave for all eternity."

Becca's eyes widened, and she suddenly turned her head away in a coughing fit, but Nick managed to keep a straight face as Satan's eyes snapped open. "My Iris? Brought to orgasm by other men?"

"Many other men. Good-looking men. Who are great at sex."

"No." Satan's voice grew stronger. "That is wrong. She cannot have sex with other men. It is only me! I kill all those men."

Nick shook his head. "The only way to save her is to kill Rosemarie. She's controlling all the Penhas. If you kill her, they'll leave Iris alone. She'll be safe."

Satan nodded, the folds of his neck making a squishing sound. "It is done. I kill her. Let us go. Bring her to me." He lifted his arm, which drooped sharply at the elbow. "I shoot her with hell fire. Most satisfying."

Nick grinned, relieved to see the spirit in Satan's eyes, even if he was continuing to melt. "By coincidence, we were going to head over to her camp tonight. We'll bring you along."

"Excellent." Satan sagged back down, and Theresa and Becca helped him settle on the floor. Satan gave Nick an annoyed look. "You are bad life support. I still melt. Disconnect me."

Becca stood up and stepped over the pool of water around Satan's head. "He's too weak. He can't support himself yet."

Nick's quads were starting to ache enough that he was beginning to get worried. "I'm not generating enough life force to compensate for the seriousness of his injuries, and he's draining me too quickly. I think he's going to keep getting worse."

Becca's eyebrows knitted in concern. "You have to cut us off, Nick. It's the only way."

"No."

"We're killing you, Nick. Don't be a hero."

He looked at her. "I'm not trying to be a hero. I just can't let you die."

She set her hands on her hips. "Well, find a way to do it! I'm not going to let you die!"

"Kiddos." Theresa stepped between them. "This is all very heartwarming that both of you are professing your love in such subtle ways—"

Becca caught her breath as Nick's eyes widened in shock. *I don't love him.*

"—but our boy here is melting pretty fast and if we have any chance of getting him into the Penha camp without dividing him up into Tupperware containers, we need to go now."

Becca refused to let herself dwell on Theresa's remark about love. What did the dragon know about that subject, anyway? She was a sex addict, not a love therapist. "Let's go, then."

Nick nodded. "I just have to check on my sister and make sure she's okay. Two minutes?"

"It'll give us time to make Satan presentable." Theresa squatted next to him. "You're one lucky man that I'm the reigning beauty queen expert, Satan. If anyone can make you look good, I can."

But Nick didn't leave, his mind still reeling from Theresa's comment. Love? Between them? Impossible. Wasn't it? He watched Becca fuss over Satan, and smiled when the leader of hell preened when she told him that she was still quaking in fear from him and admired him more than any other being.

His cold Rivka had a soft heart... and a very savvy mind.

She looked up at him, as if she'd felt him watching her. "What's wrong?"

"Take off all your clothes now."

She rolled her eyes. "Sex fiend." Then she went back to work, a pleased smile on her face.

He knew why she was smiling. "Found a loophole in my order, huh?"

"There's always a loophole. And I'm smart enough to find it."

As he'd suspected. Despite the fact their life forces were one, he had no control over her, unless she wanted him to, because it wasn't in his heart to control her. "So, if you're so good at dodging my orders, why'd you cave so fast when I told you to tell Theresa to link Satan to me to save Paige?"

She froze and looked up, her face wary. "You caught me off guard."

He shook his head, denying her excuse. "It was because my order spared you from having to choose between saving me or saving Paige."

She stood up. "That's not true. I—"

"Who would you have chosen to sacrifice, Becca?"

She stared at him, and he saw from the expression on her face that she couldn't have made that choice. Even though he knew she loved Paige like her own daughter, she hadn't been able to make the decision to risk his life to save Paige's. A deep warmth began to spread over him, and he knew what she didn't realize.

Becca loved him.

A fact she would never, ever, let herself acknowledge, because of her own past.

Unless he helped her unlock her heart.

"Are you going to talk to your sister or what? We need to go," Theresa interrupted.

He reached out and trailed his fingers through Becca's hair, and she looked up at him. "What?"

"Nothing." He forced himself to turn away and sprinted down the hall toward his sister. As he ran, he whispered three words under his breath. Just to see how they felt when he said them.

They felt right.

He paused in the doorway, his chest constricting at the sight of his little sister sitting up in bed, flanked by Jerome and his ma. Her face was flushed, her eyes bright, as if she'd never been interred in a pus blister. "Dani?"

She looked up. "Nick!"

She jumped off the bed and launched herself at him. He caught her with a thud and held her tight, breathing in the soft scent that was hers. Twenty-two years old, and she still smelled like baby powder. He hugged her fiercely. "God, I was worried about you."

She buried her face in his chest. "I'm so sorry, Nick. I screwed up big time."

He smiled into her hair. "Yeah, you did."

She pulled back and looked up at him, and he saw a

wisdom in her eyes that hadn't seen before. Knew she'd never be the same carefree girl he'd taken care of for so long. Not that he'd expect anything else. Hanging out by a man-eating acid pit would rock anyone's foundation.

"That's it?" she asked. "That's all you're going to say? You aren't going to yell at me or threaten to take away my condo or beat up Jerome?"

He sighed and ruffled her hair, recalling Paige's accusations that he'd controlled Dani's life, and suddenly realized he *had* been overprotective. He'd needed to protect someone, and without his heritage to embrace, he'd put it all on his sister. He smiled, realizing he was suddenly no longer consumed with the need to rule her life. She didn't need him, but the Markku did. And Paige. And maybe, hopefully, if he was lucky, *Becca*. "It's your life. As long as you don't cause any more battles with hell, I'll stay out of it, but I'm always here if you want me for anything."

She hugged him, her eyes brimming. "You're the best, Nick."

He grinned, realizing he couldn't remember the last time she'd told him that. "So, I give you space, and now you like me?"

"Something like that." She glanced back at Jerome, who still looked haggard and pale.

He stood up. "Nick, I asked Dani to marry me."

"Did you?" Nick kept the inflection out his voice. Jerome might be his best friend, but he'd treated Dani badly. "And?"

"I'm waiting for an answer," he said meaningfully. "Dani?"

Dani turned to face Jerome. "I had a lot of time to think while I was stuck in that catatonic state, watching that acid pit eat away at my floor. I realized that I needed to change some things, and the first one is standing up for myself."

Jerome frowned. "But I *love* you."

"I used to love you," she said. "But that ended up really badly for me, so I think I'm going to stay away from love for a while." She smiled. "You're more than welcome to grovel and genuflect and try to win me over again, however."

Nick grinned at his ma, who was smiling. Dani was going to be all right. "I gotta go."

Yasmine looked at him, and her smile faded. "You look like hell."

"Nick, come on," Becca shouted. "We really need to go."

"She's alive?" Yasmine's lips pressed together in sharp disapproval, but Nick could also see the worry in her eyes. The deep, intense fear for his safety.

"I'll be okay, Ma." But they both knew it might not be true.

"Okay?" Dani glanced between them. "Where are you going? It's over, right?"

Yasmine stood up from the bed with a heavy sigh, then walked over in front of him. For a moment, they both stood there, then she reached for him and he hugged her back. Tightly. She kissed his cheek. "Be safe, Nicky."

"I will." He looked at Jerome.

His friend put his arm around Dani and nodded his unspoken agreement to take care of Nick's women if something happened to Nick. "I've been asked to recruit two new Council members now that my two comrades have been exposed. If you survive, the job belongs to you.

And Becca, if she wants it. We need more women on the Council."

Nick grinned at the thought of Becca on the Council. The Otherworld would never recover, and damned if he didn't want to be by her side watching her churn things up. "I'll check with Becca and let you know."

And then Nick turned and walked out, unable to respond to Dani's frantic questions about where he was going.

Twenty-five

They landed on top of the hill next to the Penha camp with an ungraceful crash that had Theresa scrabbling with her claws. Satan shrieked and dove onto the grass, and Nick grabbed Becca and yanked her off Theresa's back just before the dragon did a header into a stand of trees. She popped up immediately, yanking her spiked tail out of a pine tree. "Sorry. Adrenaline rush."

They'd decided to fly on Theresa's back instead of having Becca or Satan transport them, trying to lessen the drain on Nick. Maybe not the best idea. "Everyone okay?"

Satan rose to his knees, his cheek indented in the shape of a pine cone. "I am most excellent, other than the fact I feel like shark entrails. I am ready to kill ex-lover. Come, let us find her." He staggered to his feet and promptly toppled to the side. Theresa grabbed him with her claws and set him on her back. "Why don't you ride the dragon? It'll make you seem very imposing."

"Excellent idea. I like imposing."

Becca's heart melted at the tremor in his voice. Satan was trying to be so tough, but he was seriously hurting. What were they going to do?

"Not now." Nick's voice was deep and reassuring in her ear. "We need to rescue Paige and take out Junior and his ma so they don't kill you or Satan, and then we'll deal with him. Focus. Okay?" He squeezed her hand, and she nodded.

"It's really distracting to have all these emotions," she muttered.

Nick grinned. "You've always had them, but now you're embracing them. Just control them like you used to."

"Yeah, okay. No problem." She shook the cramps out of her shoulders and tried not to think about how weak she felt. At least the Terrors were gone. Looking on the positive side and all that. "So, let's go."

The four of them crept to the edge of the knoll and looked down. The RV was in the same place, and the tents were quiet. The sexual energy was much lower than it had been before.

"Mmm..." Satan moaned. "Do you feel that?" He held out his arms and lifted his face as if he were embracing the sun. "So much sex vibe. I feel it revive me."

"Paige is in the second tent on the right," Nick said. "I can feel her energy now that we're close to her. It's weak." He shifted restlessly. "My men are down there, too. They aren't asleep. They're waiting for me."

Becca smiled at the energy rolling off him. Nick was alive tonight, in a way she hadn't seen him before. This was who he was, out here with the Markku and the Rivka, protecting those who needed him. He was amazing, a warrior, a passionate man. He was everything, all in one. He was dark, he was light, and he—

"I'm like you," he said, as if he'd read her thoughts.

"All that I am, you are too." He caught her wrist and pulled her against him. "We are one, you and I." He kissed her hard and deep, and she opened to him instantly, welcoming him, desperate for him. He held her tight and then released her without another word.

Then they started down the hill.

They were within fifty yards of the encampment when the first wave of lust swept them. Becca gasped as sexual desire slammed into her, falling to her knees beside Nick and Theresa as a battle cry sounded and the tents flew open to reveal Markku and Penhas alike, charging them.

"As really amazing as this feels," Theresa gasped. "I'm guessing this is a bad thing."

"Nonsense!" Satan leapt off Theresa's back, landing with an energetic thump beside her. "This is magnificent! I feel like new man!" He pointed a finger at the oncoming troops and it glowed red.

"Stop!" Nick shouted. "I order you not to injure or hurt anyone but Rosemarie or Satan Jr."

Satan whirled on Nick, his eyes blazing hot red embers of rage. "You scum-sucking pig! I forbid you to order me! Break the link now! Let me go!"

"I think he's feeling better," Becca muttered. "Isn't that good news? You better release him."

Nick staggered to his feet, his voice cold and hard. "Kill Rosemarie and Satan Jr. and I'll release you. Not until then."

Satan roared with rage, and fire erupted from his skin. "I will not be made to be impotent! You shall pay!" Then he disappeared in an explosion of gold bubbles, and an instant later, the windows of the RV lit up with a gold light.

"He's in." Becca ducked at the sound of a gunshot, and the dirt exploded around them. "Nick? Can you deal with these guys already?"

"Trying. Hard to concentrate with my brain in the front of my pants," he muttered. He stood up straight up and faced the men. Dirt exploded around his feet and he turned toward the onslaught of men. "Markku!" His voice boomed across the clearing, and all the Markku stopped dead in their tracks. A bullet bounced off his shoulder. "Markku! Disarm the Penhas without hurting them." He grinned as the Markku turned and started fighting with the Penhas. "I have really been missing out."

Then a fresh wave of lust slammed them, and his smile dropped off his face. "Oh, shit." He spun and started to sprint for the trailer, trying to unbutton his jeans as he ran.

"No!" Becca jumped up. "You don't get to have him!"

She bolted after him, jumping over Theresa, who was writhing around on her back, her eyes closed and her lips curved into an expression of pure dragon bliss.

Becca realized she wasn't going to catch him, so she faded, popping up out of the ground in front of him. She grabbed his feet as he tried to jump her, and he crashed to the ground. She jumped on top of him and slammed her mouth onto his as he bucked under her.

For an instant he fought her, and then suddenly he was all over her. His mouth, his hands, his body. His lips clamped down on her nipple through her shirt, and she nearly came off him in response. "No," she managed. "Not here."

"Yes, here." His voice was raw and hoarse. "It's you or her. I don't want it to be her."

"Well, when you put it that way . . ." She let him rip her shirt off as she faded them into a nearby tent. When they popped up, his hand was down the front of her jeans and she was fighting to get his zipper undone.

And then it was over.

The lust simply vanished from the air.

She sat up, her chest heaving, her hips still straddling Nick. "He killed her." The air was still, silent, except for the shouts of the Markku as the Penhas stopped fighting. It was simply the fresh scents of grass and dirt and pine needles.

Nick dropped his head back on the ground and groaned. "Thank God." He reached up and tucked her left breast back into her shirt. "That wasn't the way I wanted to seduce you before we both died."

"Such a gentleman." She frowned as she looked down at him, noticing red marks on his shoulders from her fingernails. "I thought I couldn't hurt you."

He touched his shoulder where the marks were. "It must be because I'm supporting you guys. I'm getting more vulnerable."

She grimaced. "Well, let's get Paige and get out of here. All the stuff to reset the links is at Dani's place. Satan seems recovered enough to support himself again. Who knew sex would revive him?" She rolled off Nick, smiling to herself when he trailed his fingers over her hips as she left.

"Comes in handy to have a leader of hell who's a sex

addict, apparently." Nick sat up, then caught her arm as she started to crawl out of the tent. "Becca, once I cut Satan off, I might have enough life force to support you. We could try it."

She stared at him, every instinct in her body shouting at her to say yes. To live in his light. To share with him. To be one with him. But she looked at the deep lines around his mouth, at the scratches on his shoulders, and knew she could never accept his offer. "It's not worth it, Nick."

He caught her hand. "Yes, it is. You can't go back to Satan. I felt the darkness in you when we went through the acid pit, and I know who you are now. You can't go back. It'll destroy you."

She forced a smile. "No, it won't. I'll be fine."

"Becca—"

She kissed him, tasting his soft lips, feeing his whiskers scraping her chin. His fingers went to her hair, and she pulled back. "Let's go find Paige."

He didn't move. "I won't let you break the link. I can't let the woman I love go back to hell."

Her heart leapt and she smiled. *He loves me.* Then she took a deep breath and faced him, knowing what she had to say, because she loved him. "If you love me, you won't make my decisions for me. Give me that gift, Nick, the gift to make my own choice."

"What?" He scowled. "I tell you I love you and all you can do is use it against me to force me to let you go back to hell, when I know all you want is to be free of it?"

No, Nick. All I want is for you to live. She managed a flippant grin. "I'm a cold-hearted Rivka, Nick. Get used to it." Then she scurried out of the tent before she could change her mind.

Theresa was standing so close to the tent that Becca tripped on the dragon's front claws and nearly crashed into her chest. "That man just offered you his heart and his life and you spurned it." The dragon's voice was dripping with disbelief. "Do you have any idea how damaging that is to a man's ego? He'll never recover. You have ruined him forever."

She scowled at the dragon and started walking toward Paige's tent, eager to get away before Nick came out of the tent. "It's rude to eavesdrop."

"As if I care." The dragon lumbered along next to her. "It's his call if he wants to risk his life for you. You should let him. It'll make him feel all manly and he'll reward you with great sex."

"He'll die."

"Maybe he will, but if he does, so what? Dying for the one you love is what it's all about. It's the basis of life."

She kept walking, barely able to withstand the ache in her chest. "Why die if you don't have to? I get relinked to Satan. I'm alive, he's alive, everything's good."

Theresa jumped in front of her, blocking Becca's path just as they arrived at Paige's tent. "Were you really alive before, Becca? Were you?"

She stared at the dragon. "No," she whispered. "But I am now. And because of that, I can love, really love for the first time, and I love him too much to let him die for me."

The dragon's scaly face softened. "That is too sweet.

Sucky situation to be in, of course, but totally sweet." She snuffled her nose against Becca's cheek, and Becca had to blink back tears. "Go rescue your apprentice, you badass. I love you."

"Back at you, dragon." Then Becca ducked inside the tent and left the dragon outside.

Paige was on her back groaning, her eyes closed, a fireball clutched in her hand. Apparently, although Satan had revived from the infusion of sex vibes, his link to the ever-weakening Nick was keeping him from gathering enough power to support Paige.

Becca squatted in the entrance. "Paige? Can you hear me?"

Paige flung the fireball at the entrance, a nice shot that caught Becca clean in the chest. "Get out," she rasped. "I will not be taken." Then she moaned and clutched her shin, cursing to herself even as she churned up another fireball in her palm.

Becca smiled softly. "It's me, honey." She hesitated. "It's Mom."

Paige stirred and lifted her head, dark circles under her eyes as she gazed at Becca. "Mom?"

She smiled. "I'm here, sweetie."

"No sex. Kicked Colin's ass." Her eyes fluttered shut. "Made soul blacker." Her voice trailed off, and she wrapped her hand around her shin. "Pisses me off." She moaned. "I want to stop feeling like hell."

Becca pulled Paige against her and kissed her forehead. "Soon, baby, soon."

Nick and the dragon stared at each other, and he was unable to keep the smile off his face.

"I assume you heard that," Theresa said.

He nodded. "She loves me." *She loves me.* The words sounded so right. So magical. So perfect.

The dragon let her amber gaze drift over him. "So, what are you doing to do about it?"

"Try to change her mind about going back to Satan."

She scowled. "Aren't you going to throw her over your shoulder and manhandle her into submission, since she's too stupid to know what's right?"

He shook his head. "I can't take her choice away from her, Theresa. She's right about that."

"So, you're both going to be martyrs?"

"Not a chance." He grinned. "I intend to be very persuasive—"

There was a sudden popping sound, and Nick's back exploded in a burst of fiery pain. He recognized the poisonous burn of gold instantly and spun around, staggering to stay on his feet. Satan Jr. stood there with a gun, his features contorted with rage. "You came here and ruined my plans. Stole my Markku. Got my mom killed, though she kind of deserved it. And now you die a horrible and painful death by gold. Enjoy."

"You son of a bitch!" Nick lunged for Satan Jr. and tackled him, slamming his knee into Junior's gut. The kid screamed and fell on the ground as Nick groaned and tried to pull himself back to his feet. The world began to spin, and the gold seared his body.

Draw on the gold, Nick. He sucked the deadly poison into his body, found strength in its burn, and crushed his hands around Satan Jr.'s throat. "You'll never destroy another innocent girl," he whispered. "Now you die." Satan Jr.'s eyes widened and he coughed and tried to kick Nick in the shin. "Nice try, but no chance." He watched the kid's eyes widen with the realization that he was going to die—

"Nick!" Theresa shouted. "It's Becca! You're killing her."

He realized suddenly where he was drawing his renewed energy to fight Satan Jr. and the gold from. *Becca.*

He dropped Satan Jr. and sprinted for the tent, diving through the flaps. Becca was gasping on the floor and Paige was on her hands and knees moaning. Satan's renewed life force was apparently providing interference from Nick draining Paige, but Becca was dying. "Oh, God. What have I done?" He pulled Becca into his arms, trying to stop his drain of her life force, thrust all he had into her. "Take it, Becca, take it back."

"Becca's dying," Theresa wailed. "Do something!"

"Go get the stuff we need to break the link." The edges of his vision were starting to blacken. Shit. He wasn't going to make it long enough for the dragon to go back to the condo to get the supplies. Too dizzy. The vial around Theresa's neck glinted, and he had to close his eyes against the glare. Paige groaned and collapsed, and he realized he was starting to lose her, too. He was probably starting to drain Satan, as well, taking away Satan's ability to support Paige. "Find Satan! We need to break him off from me so Paige will be okay, and we have to hook Becca back up to him. He's recovered enough that his immortality should pull him through—" He stopped suddenly as he realized what he'd said. "Wait!"

She whirled back around, the vial dangling around her neck, her body halfway out of the tent. "What is it?"

"Give me the vial."

Theresa yanked if off instantly. "It didn't help her last time—"

He grabbed it from her. "No, it's for me. Since Satan and Becca are immortal, they need an immortal life force to support them. *Satan's* immortal life force. A mortal can't support an immortal. It makes sense." He chugged a drink of it and set it down, holding Becca to his chest. *Three drinks.* He was breaking all sorts of Otherworld laws by drinking from Mona, by becoming immortal, but he didn't give a rip. "How long do I have to wait between drinks?"

"Not long. Maybe a minute. You think it'll work? Becoming immortal?"

"It has to." He looked at his watch, then felt Becca convulse against him. He cursed and held her tighter, sending her all the energy he had. "I love you, Becca. You hang on for me." He felt a pulse from deep within her, and he pressed harder with his life force.

His back was screaming, and he closed his eyes as the tent began to spin.

"Take the next one." Theresa's voice was distant, faint. "Nick? Are you still with me?"

"Got it." He fumbled for it, then felt her claw wrap around his hand and guide it to his mouth. He drank hard, then let his hand drop. "Tell me when for the next one." He gave up sitting and let himself fade to the floor, pulling Becca up against him. He could feel her warmth against him and he closed his eyes, let himself drift.

"Stay with me, Nick."

He jumped at the sound of Theresa's voice, as she brought him back from wherever he'd been.

"Nick. Here." He felt the cool crystal against his lips and struggled to remember what he was supposed to do with it. "Drink it, you dumbass! Drink it now!"

He drank it, and then the world went black.

Twenty-six

Becca had a headache from hell.

She groaned and pressed her hand to her forehead, then felt something shift under her. Something warm. "Nick?" She opened her eyes to see Nick smiling down at her, his eyes half-mast and weary. "What happened?"

"Let's just say I'm going to have to use my connections on the Council to keep Theresa and myself out of the Chamber. Want to go work for them with me?"

She raised her brows. "I already have a job at Vic's."

"Mmm..." He thumbed her cheek. "How do you feel?"

She worked herself to a seated position and flexed her arms. "Pretty good, actually." She cocked her head. "Still linked to you, if the raging love consuming me is any indication. What's up?"

"Mom!"

She turned just in time to catch Paige as she flung herself into Becca's arms. They both tumbled backward and landed in a pile on Nick, who chuckled and wrapped his arms around both of them. Becca brushed Paige's hair out of her face and looked at Nick. "What happened?"

"You needed Satan's immortal life force to keep you

alive." He grinned. "Theresa helped me take care of the immortal part. So now, I have Satan's immortal life force in my body, keeping you alive without a problem."

Becca stared at him, hope exploding inside her. "You're serious? We're all set? And fine?"

He nodded. "We're all good."

"My favorite Rivka!" The tent flap opened, and Satan stuck his head inside. "I am much healed. Let us restore our life forces and conquer hell again." He nodded at Nick. "Man-friend, I am much glad you decided to let my son leave unharmed. Excellent decision."

Becca glanced at Nick's face, surprised to see it calm. "You let Satan Jr. go?"

"Easy choice." He kissed her forehead. "Easy choice."

Satan batted Nick away from Becca. "Do not manhandle my Rivka anymore. I am recovered. I take over."

Becca and Nick looked at each other, and she knew she couldn't go back. But it would be a serious damper on their success if Satan decided to kill them off. Then she had an idea, and she turned to Satan. "Satan, you still owe Nick a favor, don't you?"

His eyebrows went up, and he waited.

"He wants you to release Paige and me from Rivka duty and your life force. Nick will support us."

There was total silence in the tent, and then a stream of black smoke began to pour from the top of Satan's head. He lifted a glowing red finger at Nick.

"I order you not to kill or injure me," Nick said quickly.

Satan turned the finger toward Becca, and Paige shouted and tried lunge at Satan, but Nick grabbed her by the ankle and hauled her back. "Or anyone in this tent!" Nick yelled.

Theresa immediately shoved herself the rest of the way into the tent, leaving virtually no room for anyone else to move. "I'm in the tent, too," she announced.

Satan's gaze flickered with rage. "I kill you and your family for trying to steal my Rivkas. I do not owe you that level of a favor. You cannot take them."

Well, so much for that grand idea.

Theresa sneezed, and the vial bumped Satan in the ear. He whacked it aside, then turned to look at it, a gleam of anticipation in his gaze. He reached out to touch it, and Theresa yanked it out of his reach. "Don't even think about it, big guy. I'm not going there again."

"Wait!" Becca leaned forward. "Satan, being killed by an old lady with a gun was pretty pathetic, don't you think?"

"Do not bring up that incident ever again," Satan ordered her. "Never happened. I do not recall it."

She happily ignored his order. "Well, it shows that you're vulnerable, and it's just a matter of time until someone else tries it again, only this time Nick won't be around to save you."

Satan glared at Nick. "Man-friend did not save me. I used him to save myself."

"Anyway," Becca continued. "What if Nick and I were able to persuade Theresa to let you take three sips of Mona and become more indestructible? So that water couldn't take you down? Only beheading?"

Theresa squealed and clamped her hand over the vial. "Oh, no way, girlfriend. The Council would so kill me."

"I can take care of the Council," Nick said. "Trust me on that one."

Theresa shook her head. "No, seriously, that's a really bad idea. Do you have any idea how bad that Chamber is?"

Becca and Nick exchanged glances. "Yes," they said in unison.

"No deal," Satan said. "I will just steal Goblet and take immortality for myself."

Theresa wrapped her fist around it, and Nick gave Satan a long look. "You forget, Satan, I can just order you not to. I'm not giving you back your own freedom unless you agree."

Satan cocked his head. "You blackmail me? Threaten me?"

"Yep."

Satan broke into a huge smile and clapped Nick on the shoulder. "Most impressive negotiating. I admire underhanded tactic. For that, I agree. It is deal. I will release my favorite Rivka and her pathetic apprentice to man-friend in return for three drinks of Goblet. And then I call in my debt that my favorite Rivka owes me." He looked at Becca. "You will continue to be my Rivka, even though man-friend supports you."

She studied him, saw the vulnerability in his eyes, and felt her heart soften. Satan wasn't just bluster. He'd be lost without her, at least until he recovered from his breakup with Iris and developed some self-confidence. "How about I just become your friend?" When his face didn't change, she added, "Best friend. I'll become your best friend. That's better than a Rivka, because I'm doing it because I want to, not because I have to."

Satan cocked his head. "Best friend? What does that mean?"

"It means you can stop by and visit any time. We'll hang out, give each other advice, and help each other out of tough situations. And it means we don't ever use deadly force or torture devices against each other."

Slowly, Satan nodded. "That is excellent idea. I like that. Will you harvest souls for me, too?"

"Nope. You'll have to get one of your other Rivkas to do that."

"Will you train them?"

She grinned. "If you pay me well enough."

He beamed. "Excellent. I am very rich. I pay you for services and I get best friend for free. It is deal?"

She nodded. "Deal. Debt paid?"

"Debt paid."

She grinned and relaxed against Nick, who hugged her tight against him.

"So, we agree?" Nick asked. "Your immortality in exchange for Becca and Paige's freedom?"

"It is deal." Satan held out his hand, and Nick grasped it. "You must come to dinner with your woman on Sunday, man-friend. We have much to discuss."

Nick grinned. "I'll have to check with Becca. She's in charge." Then he winked at Becca, and she smiled back, still not quite able to believe what was happening. Satan had released her? She was free? To be with Nick?

Theresa's tail flicked. "Okay, enough with the sappy stuff. I'm not handing over this vial to Satan until I get a written release form from the Council freeing me of all liability."

"Then let's go," Nick said. "I want this settled." He

grabbed Becca's hand and smiled at her. "Will you take us back to Dani's apartment so we can break Satan's link to me and hook up Paige instead?"

She grinned. "When you ask so nicely, of course."

And then she faded the entire group into the ground.

"Hello? Becca? We brought breakfast!"

Nick opened his eyes at the sound of a door slamming and female laughter coming from the front of Becca's apartment. He recognized the voices of Theresa and Paige as they discussed how to save Paige's soul and debated about who was the Markku who'd actually tried to kill Becca, since he hadn't been at the Penha camp.

He kissed the collarbone of the woman in his arms. "Sweetie, your girlfriends have arrived for some bonding."

She stirred, and the feel of her warm body against his made him grin. Her backside pressed against his groin, and she made a soft noise of contentment. He kissed the nape of her neck and slipped his hand down and flattened it over her bare belly as a cabinet slammed in the kitchen.

"Where do you keep your coffee filters?" Theresa shouted. "Never mind. Paige found them."

Becca shifted and laid her hand over his, entwining her fingers around his. "Where'd they get a key?" she mumbled.

"I gave it to them."

She twisted around so she could face him, her eyes sleepy and content. "Why'd you do that? You know I like my privacy."

He pulled her closer so he could kiss her. "Give it up,

Rivka, I know you love them. You're just one big ball of love these days."

She smiled and kissed him back. "Never. I'm a cold-hearted shell of a woman." Then she opened her eyes and looked at him, her hand pressed to his bare chest, and opened her soul to him.

He slipped inside her with his spirit and wrapped himself around her deep, pulsating warmth that he knew so intimately, and let her feel how much he loved her.

She smiled, her eyes warm and soft. "I love you, too."

Her cell phone rang suddenly, and she leaned past him to check the screen. Then she grinned and shut the phone off and tossed it on the floor.

He smiled at her pleased expression as she settled herself on top of him again. "Who was that?"

"Satan." Her eyes were dancing and her joy sparkled into his being. "I didn't take his call."

He pulled her tighter against him, basking in her happiness. "Good feeling, huh?"

"Been waiting a hundred years for that moment." She kissed him, and he felt her love in the simple touch. "Thank you for giving me my freedom."

"You think you're free?" He grabbed her around the waist and tossed her under him, propping himself up over her. "Ravish me now, woman. I'm going to make you my sex slave for all eternity."

Her eyes widened with amusement as she made no move to ravish him. "Promise?"

He laughed and shook his head. "You're never going to worry about me controlling you, are you? I'm powerless to command the woman I love."

She wrapped her legs around his waist and tugged him

down. "Oh, you've got lots of power, Nick. More power than Satan ever had over me, and it's all voluntary."

He grinned at the happiness in her face. "I love you, you know."

She slid her hands through his hair. "I know. I love you, too. And my friends. And Paige. So much love in my life. Who'd have thought?"

"Oh, I knew it all along."

She rolled her eyes. "Such arrogance. How will I ever humble you?"

He grinned wickedly. "Oh, I beg you to try. Humble me, please."

She raised her brow. "You're begging me already? I knew I wore the pants in this relationship."

"No way, my darling. Neither of us is wearing pants for the rest of the day. Or night. And probably tomorrow."

She grinned as he began showing her exactly why he didn't want her wearing pants. "But my friends are waiting for me..."

He threw her legs over his shoulders. "Your friends love you enough that they'll understand if you make them wait."

"They do, don't they?" She arched up to meet him, clutching the sheets as the light began to build inside her with every move of his hips, and knew that finally she was home.

About the Author

Golden Heart winner Stephanie Rowe wrote her first novel when she was ten and sold her first book twenty-three years later. After a brief stint as an attorney, Stephanie decided wearing suits wasn't her style and opted for a more fulfilling career. Stephanie now spends her days immersed in magical worlds creating quirky stories about smart, scrappy women who find true love while braving the insanity of the modern world and Otherworldly challenges. When she's not glued to the computer or avoiding housework, Stephanie spends her time reading, playing tennis, and hanging out with her own fantasy man and their two Labradors. You can reach Stephanie on the Web at www.stephanierowe.com.

MORE LAUGH-OUT-LOUD
HUMOR AND DELIGHTFUL
PARANORMAL ROMANCE FROM

Stephanie Rowe!

Turn the page for a preview
of her new novel,

Sex & The Immortal Bad Boy

available in November 2007.

Paige jerked awake, clutching her hands to her chest against the pain searing her body. She knew instantly that the blackness in her soul was trying to take over, trying to consume her while she slept.

She threw herself out of the bed, slamming into the wall as she gasped for air.

She dropped to her knees, her hands flat on the floor as her body recoiled, as the air vanished from her lungs.

Trying to take her.

I am good.

I love my friends.

I. Am. Love.

Her fingers dug into the floor as a convulsion of pain knifed through her heart. Her mouth opened, no sound, no air, no anything.

She lunged for the night table, where an orchid sat, a gift to her roommate from her new boyfriend, given with love. Representing all that was pure and alive.

She crushed the blossom in her fist and scrunched her eyes shut, sending everything black into the plant as fast as she could. She felt the orchid scream as she filled it with death and pain and hell, shredding the life from the flower, just how she killed every living thing she touched.

The plant exploded in a billow of black ash, and Paige felt a wave of relief even as her calf convulsed with pain, feeding on the death she'd just caused. The pressure left her lungs and she dropped to the floor with a moan, her cheek pressing against the soft carpet. "God, that sucked."

She closed her eyes and thought about Dani and Theresa. Embraced her love for Becca. Felt the pain recede into her leg, settling back down. Until next time.

Next time.

What innocent thing would she have to kill next time to save herself? And how much farther would that death take her toward her future?

She rolled onto her back with another groan and draped her arm over her forehead. "There has to be a better way—" She froze, suddenly aware she wasn't alone in the room anymore.

There was another presence. A dark one. Not from hell...but deserving of it.

Slowly, she moved her arm so she could peek at the room. She couldn't see anyone or anything. But she could feel it.

Something eased up her bare leg. Something cold. Something evil. Something definitely not human.

She opened her hand, ready to flare up a fireball as she felt it creep its way along her thigh. The touch was so light that she never would have noticed it if she weren't already so freaked out by almost getting sucked into a void of mindless hell.

It inched up her belly, along her ribs, to her throat, until the whole front of her body was covered with a flittering itch—it settled on her like a blanket, pressing against her, like it was trying to get through her skin.

She forced herself to wait, to lie still, certain she had only one chance to take it out. No move until she knew where to hit it. Let it think she hadn't noticed it.

But God, she wanted to twitch, to scratch, to kick the creepy feeling off her. Because that's what it was. Nothing more substantial than a feeling. But a really, really bad one.

Her neck tickled and she felt it creep around her throat, encircling her like a necklace.

Or a garrote.

Oh, lovely thought.

Instantly, the itch turned to heat, then weight and then flesh.

A human body. On top of hers. Fingers crushing her throat.

Her eyes snapped open and she found herself looking at the face of a man, a man with the blackest eyes she'd ever seen.

Anguish flashed over his face; his hands on her neck softened to a caress. She summoned a blue fireball and slammed it into his side.

He cursed and jerked to the right. She shoved him against the wall with a fireball to the chest, and then scrambled to her feet.

He was on his feet just as fast. She hurled another fireball at his face as he whirled to face her. He ducked, and the fireball slammed into the wall behind him, leaving a charred black hole through to the kitchen. Then he was on her again, his body slamming into hers.

She plunged a fireball into his back as he tackled her

onto the bed, and the smell of burned leather drifted up to her nose.

He pinned her to the bed with his knees, slammed her palms together, and crushed them between his hands so she couldn't pull them apart.

So she couldn't shoot a fireball.

Damn. Disarmed just like that.

Then again, he couldn't choke her while his hands were occupied with hers.

Impasse.

For a moment, neither of them moved. They stared at each other, and Paige could make out the lines of his face in the shadowed light. His hair was dark, tousled and thick, and a scar on the left side of his jaw ran down his neck and disappeared under the collar of his black leather jacket. There was the faint twinkle of something next to the edge of his dark T-shirt. A gold chain, maybe? His shoulders were so wide he positively loomed over her, and she could feel darkness vibrating off him, saturating the air around him.

He was dangerous. Deadly. And...she inhaled and caught a whiff of his scent. It was smoky and dark. Like a campfire. Like woods. Like man. She breathed deeper, drinking his essence into her. She'd never smelled anything like him before. He smelled...right. Like bone-deep, soul-shattering *right*.

He leaned closer, his dark eyes searching hers with a desperation that was startling, his grip on her hands still tight. He was straddling her pelvis, and he was such a solid, immovable weight across her hips that she knew she'd never get him off.

If he were going to kill her, he'd have to let go, and then she'd act.

So she didn't fight. She simply waited for him to make the next move.

But then he dropped his head, pressed his face to her throat, and sniffed, his breath a warm tickle on her skin. His hair brushed across her cheek, a fragile caress that coaxed the tiniest sigh from her.

He froze for a split second, then eased himself back ever so slowly past her face, watching her closely as he settled his weight on her hips again. He brought her hands back down to her chest, so that his own hands rested between her breasts, not quite touching them, but close. So close. His jaw worked . . . in frustration? "You're not her."

"Her who?"

"Becca Gibbs."

Paige frowned. "You came here to kill Becca?"

His grip tightened on her hands, the tendons in his neck pulsing. "Where is she?"

"Far, far, away in a place you'll never find. Lucky for you." Paige tested his grip on her hands, tugging slightly.

His fingers squeezed hard, immobilizing her but not hurting her. Then he leaned forward, hovering like a big tower of manliness. "I have to find her. Tonight." He ground the words out, each syllable precise and loaded with threat that wasn't reflected in the bleakness of his eyes, eyes that were now violet. "Tell me where she is."

Paige stared into those eyes, into those depths of pain, and suddenly realized they weren't the eyes of a killer. He wasn't going to kill her. Now now. Not ever. Whatever evil she'd felt before he'd taken his human form was simply gone. No doubt he was dangerous, but not to her. She relaxed instantly, her body melting under his weight. "Didn't anyone ever teach you to say please?"

Surprise flickered over his face. "You want me to say please?"

"You invaded my bedroom, scared the shit out of me, disarmed me, tossed me on the bed, jumped on top of me, and tempted me with your most delicious scent, all without an invite. Not that I minded, of course. I like a man who takes charge and smells good while doing it." She watched a confused expression cross his face. "But I have to object to being bossed around. A little politeness would be nice." She breathed deeply, basking in his scent. Strangely, now that she knew he wasn't going to kill her, she actually felt even more attracted to him. Was she a pathetic Rivka or what? Shouldn't she like a man with death on his mind? "So anyway, I think I deserve a little respect, quite frankly."

She thought maybe she saw the faintest quirk at the corner of his mouth. Finally he said, "Tell me your name."

"Paige Darlington. You want my rank and serial number, too? My phone number? My birthstone? And you forgot to say please. You might have the broadest chest I've ever seen, but you still need to say please."

One eyebrow went up. "Why are you in Becca's bed?" He paused. "Please tell me." His voice was reluctant, as if he'd never said please in his life.

"I think the more important question is why you're here to kill Becca." She shifted her hips slightly, and he sank more deeply onto her, crushing her into the mattress. It felt . . . snuggly.

Yeah, sure, he was a deadly killer guy, but she was a deadly killer kind of girl, so she actually felt like she was home. In familiar territory.

Annoyance sparked in his eyes, and suddenly his eyes

went black again...but more than that, they were cold. Harsh. Empty.

The eyes of a killer, after all.

Well, who knew?

She felt a shiver of excitement. "You're one of those boys that doesn't get brought home to meet the parents, aren't you?"

"Call Becca. Tell her to come home."

Paige snorted. "As if." She wiggled her hips again to see if she could tempt him to press harder against her.

He did. "Stop."

"No." She wiggled again, and he shifted so his legs were twisted around hers, completely immobilizing her. His body covered hers from hip to toe. He let out a barely audible groan as he settled down on her, and he closed his eyes for a second before opening them back up and fastening them on her again. God, it felt good to have him doing the twisted pretzel thing with her. She'd felt so alone and...She froze, staring at their entwined hands. "Holy shit."

He frowned. "What?"

"Your hands. Are they okay?"

He glanced down at his hands, which were still wrapped around hers. "What are you talking about?"

She stared at his face. "You're not in pain? You're not shriveling into a blackened pile of ash? Or exploding into dust?"

He shot her a look of annoyance. "Do I look like I am?"

"No, no you don't. That's the thing." She tried to sit up, and he let her, still keeping her hands in his grip. She leaned forward and he didn't back up, so her face bumped his. Skin to skin.

And nothing happened to him.

"Oh, God. I can touch you." Her throat tightened up and she slumped forward, pressing her face into his neck, breathing in his scent, feeling the heat of his skin.

She felt his alarm, and he jerked back.

"No, no, don't go. Let me do this for a second, please." She was unable to keep the plea out of her voice, and she looked up at him. *"Please."*

He stilled, and for a minute she thought he was going to push her away. But then something changed in his face, something so subtle she wasn't sure what it was, and she knew he was going to let her. Her heart tightened and she moved slowly, so as not to spook him, nuzzling into the crook of his neck. She closed her eyes and drank in his humanity, his touch, his nearness. She could feel his pulse against her skin. It was so slow, so steady, so controlled. *I need this. I need to be touched.* "I thought I'd never feel this again."

He didn't move away, but she could feel his rising tension as she breathed in his scent and his essence, basked in the roughness of his stubble against her forehead, until finally he spoke.

"Enough." His voice was a low growl that made chills run down her spine.

Slowly, she lifted her face and looked up at him. He was staring down at her, the hard lines of his face drifting in shadow. His eyes were black, fathomless. Dark. Damned.

He wasn't a killer.

He was damned.

How interesting.

She knew he'd reached his limit, so she collapsed back on the pillow, concentrating on the feel of his hands still holding hers together, imprinting the nuzzling moment in her memory so she would be able to recall it at will, in case she never got to touch anyone again. *Don't think like that, Paige. It's just temporary.* "So, you're not from hell, because I'd know that." She injected as much cheeriness into her voice as she could. "But you're thoroughly tainted. Nothing redeemable left inside you anywhere. That's why I can touch you without hurting you. How'd you get that dark?"

He let go of her so suddenly that she didn't even see him move. One minute he was on top of her, his body wrapped heavily around hers, and the next he was on his feet at the end of the bed, his hands gripping the footboard so hard that it was creaking. "Where's Becca?"

She propped herself up on an elbow, her body screaming at the loss of human contact. *I can't let go yet. It wasn't enough.* "Touch me again."

His face grew harder. "What?"

"Touch me. Anywhere." She lifted her bare foot and pointed her toe at him, unable to keep the desperation out of her voice. "I'll answer your questions only while you're touching me. *Please?*"

He stared at her for a long moment, then peeled one hand off the bed frame and wrapped it around her foot.

The instant his fingers curved around the arch of her foot, she felt her body relax. "You know, sometimes you just don't appreciate things until you lose them. Have you ever noticed that?"

"Where's Becca?"

"Okay, so you have a one-track mind. Got it." She flexed her foot, felt the roughness of his hand on her skin. "She's out of town. With her new boyfriend. Who's the leader of the Markku." When he didn't respond, she cocked her head at him. "You know, the Markku? The indestructible badasses that used to work for Satan before they broke free? So, really, between the two of them, you're better off that she's not here."

His thumb slid over the ball of her foot. "When's she due back?"

"A couple weeks." Paige reached over to the bedside table and tossed her phone at him. He caught it easily with his free hand, not releasing her foot. Yeah, it was a caress, but she also suspected that she no longer owned her foot. He'd taken control of it . . . was he trying to manipulate her with a little footsie?

She watched him more closely. "She's on speed dial number two. Try it. She's got her phone off. I can't reach her, and trust me, if I could I would. I've got some issues going on."

He tightened his grip on her foot as he examined her phone, using his hand to make sure she didn't go anywhere. As if. She hadn't gotten her fix of human contact yet, and she wasn't letting him bail until she was good and sated.

He scrolled through the numbers, apparently found the one for Becca, hit the send button, and put the phone to his ear. After a moment he frowned and tossed the phone back at her.

She caught it and let it drop on the bed next to her. "So, what's your name?"

He wrapped his other hand around her foot and began to massage it, his fingers kneading softly.

"Oh, wow," she groaned. "Do you have any idea how good that feels?"

His thumb dug into the arch of her foot. "Do you work for Satan, too?" His voice was casual, with a hint of sensual allure that made her belly curl.

She glanced at him, and her lower body clenched at the blatant sexual need on his face... but the calculating look in his eye instantly halted her descent into a languid pool of sexual mush. She yanked her foot out of his grasp and flared up a fireball. "You're not *that* good at foot massage, buddy. It'll take more than that to turn me into a simpering pile of female uselessness."

His jaw flexed with irritation, and she flung the fireball at him and ordered it to stop right in front of his throat. To her surprise, it stopped exactly where she'd wanted it to, hovering like the kiss of death.

He shifted to the right, and it moved with him.

"Wow. That's the first time it's actually worked. Do you have any idea how many things I've burned up while practicing that?" She jumped to her feet and bounded across the bed toward him, where he stood immobile with the fireball at his throat. "Tell me your name."

"Jed Buchanan." There was a grudging respect in his voice that made her grin.

"Jed, huh?" She set her chin on top of the fireball, so the tip of her nose pressed against his. Skin to skin. *Sigh.* "Well, Jed, why do you want to kill her? A little problem with Satan? Pissed off that she's going to harvest you for hell when it's your time? Because that's definitely where you're headed, you know."

And just like that, his hands whipped out again and hauled her against him, trapping her hands between his corded thighs, palm to palm once more. The fireball hovered between them, nearly brushing his throat.

"Damn you're good." And well muscled. And, well ... utterly tempting.

"Thank you." He almost smiled. "Call off the fireball."

"Or?"

He simply raised his brow and tightened his grip on her, trapping her against his solid body.

Her only defenses were rendered completely useless, and they both knew it. She couldn't hurt him even if she wanted to. Which she totally didn't. She would be so happy to be held against the heat of his body for the rest of the millennium, assuming, of course, that she didn't have this little inner wraith to deal with. Oh, idea alert.

He scowled. "What?"

She leaned her head to the side so she could see around the fireball. "How much do you cost?"

His scowl deepened. "What are you talking about?"

"You're a hired assassin, right? That's why you're after Becca." When he didn't answer, she decided that was his big, strong, manly way of agreeing with her. "So, I'll pay you more. Work for me."

He was silent for a long moment.

"Hello. Earth to Jed? You with me?"

"What do you want to hire me for?"

The curiosity was evident in his voice, and she grinned. "Two things. Protect me from myself, and touch me."

His body stiffened. *"What?"*

She felt her cheeks heat up at his tone. "I'm not going to hire you as a male prostitute. Geez. I just meant touching. Casual touching. Arm around the shoulder. Friendly fistfights. Stuff like that. I mean, yeah, you're totally hot and all, but merging with your black soul would send me over the edge for sure. It wouldn't be worth it." Besides, the one thing still pure about her was the fact that she hadn't had time to have sex before she blew up her soul, and she wasn't about to trade in her virginity when it was all she had left. "You can handle that, right? Just some casual friend touching?"

His grip loosened slightly, and she responded by dimming the fireball and moving it to the side a bit, so he could actually lower his chin without singeing his whiskers. "Protect you from yourself? What's that about?"

"Ah, yes." She sank more deeply against the heat that was him. See? Nonsexual touching was enough... yeah, this was so nonsexual. *Give it up, Paige. You so want him.* She made herself pull back slightly, and she cleared her throat. "See, I have these urges that are no good for me, and clearly, you're strong enough to keep me from giving in to them, as evidenced by the fact that you've disarmed me twice tonight already. So, you touch me, and make sure I'm a good girl, and I'll pay you twice what you're getting to kill Becca. Deal?"

"Urges?" There was a light in his eyes that made her lower regions flare up in blatant disregard for her nonsexual-touching plan.

She rolled her eyes, unable to smack him in the chest since her hands were still anchored between his thighs. "Oh, for hell's sake. Urges to kill and maim and stuff like that. Why do you keep taking everything sexually?"

"Because you're barely wearing anything and you're pressing your body up against mine so tightly that I can feel your every curve." His voice sounded a little harsh. "And your hands... have inched up."

"Oh." She suddenly realized her breasts were smashed against his chest, and the T-shirt she'd worn to bed was hiked up over her hips, tangled in his arms where they were wrapped around her. And her thumbs were rubbing against the inseam of his jeans, right where...*oh.* "I...hadn't noticed."

But she was noticing now. Hoo, boy...

He looked down at her, his face so close to hers. "Are you Satan's right hand?"

"No, I am not. I no longer work for Satan in any form, though I am considering hiring myself out as a contractor once I get my personal issues resolved." She cocked her head. "Is that why you want to kill Becca? Because she works for Satan? Because if that's it, then you should know that she quit. She's left the biz entirely and works full-time as vice president of Vic's Pretzels. She's out of town on a business trip, and her new hottie is with her visiting some of his subjects. Combining business with pleasure. A twofer."

He rubbed his hand over his forehead, suddenly looking so weary. So human. So...drained. "You're sure?"

"Of course I am. I know these things."

He sighed with visible frustration. "If I let you go, promise no fireballs?"

"Of course not. Well, if you try to kill me, I'll fireball you. What kind of an idiot do you think I am?"

This time his mouth definitely quirked in a brief smile. "Promise no fireballs unless I give you a reason to use them?"

She contemplated for a moment, then nodded. "I'm in."

He slowly loosened his grip and relaxed his thighs, and she slipped her hands out from between his legs, settling back on her heels as he released her. Two steps to the right and his hand was on the bedroom door.

"You're leaving?"

"Yeah."

She jumped to her feet, feeling slightly panicky about the thought of losing the only living thing she could actually touch. "I'm serious about the offer to work for me."

His eyes were unreadable. "I know."

"So? Will you do it?" She held her breath as she waited for his answer.

She thought she saw a flash of regret in his eyes, and he shook his head. "No."

"But—"

Then he disappeared.

What? She vaulted off the bed and ran to the door, and felt a swirling prickle on her legs, and she looked down. Darkness surrounded her legs, and then it shot away from her and down the hall, disappearing under her front door. She stared after it, awareness dawning as she realized what he was.

And what he could offer her.

So much more than she'd thought.

So, so, so much more.

She didn't even bother getting dressed. She simply sprinted out the door.

THE DISH

Where authors give you the inside scoop!

From the desk of Stephanie Rowe

Becca Gibbs from HE LOVES ME, HE LOVES ME HOT (on sale now) has been Satan's right hand for three hundred years, and she's getting a little tired of catering to his every whim. It might *sound* exciting to work for the most powerful badass in the Otherworld, but in actuality life as Satan's best Rivka isn't really all it's cracked up to be. Here are her top five complaints:

1. **No will of your own.** Since Satan created you and you're kept alive by his life force, you have to obey all his orders, theoretically, at least. Lucky for Satan he's not so good at filling in all the loopholes, so if you're really smart and willing to take the heat, you can subvert his wishes pretty regularly. It's not enough to get free from his influence, but it can annoy the hell out of him. A girl has to take what she can get.

2. **Getting assigned a pesky apprentice.** Like you're not already busy enough trying to stroke Satan's ego, finding a way to break his hold on

you, and keeping hell from breaking loose, you also have to find the time to train an over-enthusiastic newbie who is more likely to get herself killed than harvest any souls. Not to mention the fact that she's trying to steal your job, rendering you obsolete. You ought to just kill her and send her back to hell, except she does make you laugh, and damn, it's been a long time since you laughed about anything.

3. **Having assassins after you.** Doesn't anyone realize you're just doing your job? It's not like you *like* having to harvest souls and bind them to hell . . . well, okay, it *is* kind of fun to take down the black souls who deserve to be tortured for all eternity. But still, it's not personal. So why do they all feel the need to come after you when they sneak out of hell? So annoying!

4. **Being Satan's therapist.** He's the leader of the Otherworld. You'd think he'd have self-esteem and total dominance over his women. Alas, not so much. So what if you have souls to harvest and hot men to appease? If Satan needs to cry on your shoulder, you better make time for him—seriously, you better.

5. **Getting stalked by gorgeous men who think you can solve all their problems.** Well, okay, one gorgeous man who only needs help with one hell-related problem. A man who makes

you feel alive in a way you haven't felt in two hundred years. A man who just might hold the key to everything you've ever wanted, or he might destroy you instead.

Stephanie

www.stephanierowe.com

♥ ♥ ♥ ♥ ♥ ♥ ♥ ♥ ♥ ♥ ♥ ♥ ♥ ♥ ♥ ♥

From the desk of Julie Anne Long

I have a confession to make. Whenever I set out to write a novel, my primary objective isn't necessarily to entertain a reader—it's to entertain *myself*. I mean, if I'm going to spend 100,000 words on a finite set of characters, I want to feel invested in their joys, triumphs, and tragedies; I want to laugh with, be intrigued and moved by, and dare I say it, aroused by them (which means, my hero had *better* be hot). In fact, I'll go so far as to say it's my *responsibility* to my readers to keep myself entertained, because if I do my job right—create a vivid world and populate it with vivid people—I think *my* pleasure in creating becomes the reader's pleasure. (Do I have a great job, or what?)

Take THE SECRET TO SEDUCTION (on sale now), for instance. It wraps up my trilogy about the Holt sisters, Susannah, Sylvie, and Sabrina, separated when they were very young when their mother, the mistress of a much-loved English politician, is framed for his murder and forced to flee, leaving them behind. In the first two books Susannah (BEAUTY AND THE SPY) and Sylvie (WAYS TO BE WICKED) begin to unravel the decades-old mystery of their birth—a journey involving attempted murder, complicated villains, naked swimming viscounts, and surly dwarf choreographers, among other notable. And along the way they find each other as well as love, of course, with men as passionate, challenging, and unique as they are. As you might have guessed by this cast of characters, I've managed to keep myself entertained.

But my challenge for the third book was: how on earth do I follow surly dwarf choreographers and naked viscounts? The answer: with something completely different. Sabrina, the third Holt sister, raised to be a good girl by a vicar, is an excessively clever and dutiful girl, an even-tempered girl, or so she thinks. But she is a Holt, after all. I knew it would take a dark, deliciously wicked, sinfully clever, and subtle man to bring the Holt out in her—the pride, the passion, the temper, the will, so I invented The Libertine, a.k.a. the Earl of Rawden, the scandalous poet of THE SECRET TO SEDUCTION. He does the job rather nicely. Of course, Sabrina has a thing or two to teach him, too. I had a wonderful time bringing the two of them together.

I've spent three books' worth of time with the Holt sisters and the men who love them, and bidding farewell to them is poignant and satisfying and in many ways an enormous relief. Sort of, I imagine, like sending rambunctious kids off to college. Of course, somewhere in the recesses of my imagination, they all live on, having more adventures, arguing, loving, and growing old. And if I've lived up to my responsibility as a writer, they'll live on in your imaginations, too.

www.julieannelong.com

Want to know more about romances at Warner Books and Warner Forever? Get the scoop online!

WARNER'S ROMANCE HOMEPAGE

Visit us at www.warnerforever.com for all the latest news, reviews, and chapter excerpts!

NEW AND UPCOMING TITLES

Each month we feature our new titles and reader favorites.

CONTESTS AND GIVEAWAYS

We give away galleys, autographed copies, and all kinds of fun stuff.

AUTHOR INFO

You'll find bios, articles, and links to personal Web sites for all your favorite authors—and so much more!

THE BUZZ

Sign up for our monthly romance newsletter, and be the first to read all about it!